Ma... *USA Today* bestselling author **Sara Orwig** has three children and six grandchildren. Sara has published 100... C...

V... ...n of Fame, Sara... ...vice won Okla... Novel of the Year. Sara loves family, friends, dogs, books, beaches and Dallas, Texas.

Karen Booth is a Midwestern girl transplanted in the South, raised on '80s music and repeated readings of *Forever* by Judy Blume. When she takes a break from the art of romance, she's listening to music with her college-aged kids or sweet-talking her husband into making her a cocktail. Learn more about Karen at karenbooth.net

Also by Sara Orwig

Callahan's Clan
Expecting the Rancher's Child
The Rancher's Baby Bargain
The Rancher's Cinderella Bride
The Texan's Baby Proposal

Texas Promises
Expecting a Lone Star Heir
The Forbidden Texan
The Rancher's Heir

Return of the Texas Heïrs
In Bed with the Rancher

Also by Karen Booth

A Christmas Temptation
A Cinderella Seduction
A Bet with Benefits
A Christmas Rendezvous
Forbidden Lust

Discover more at millsandboon.co.uk

ONE WILD TEXAS NIGHT

SARA ORWIG

ONCE FORBIDDEN, TWICE TEMPTED

KAREN BOOTH

MIX
Paper from
responsible sources
FSC
FSC® C007454

This book is produced from independently certified FSC™
paper to ensure responsible forest management.

For more information visit www.harpercollins.co.uk/green

Printed and bound in Spain
by CPI, Barcelona

MILLS & BOON

First Published in Great Britain 2020
by Mills & Boon, an imprint of HarperCollinsPublishers,
1 London Bridge Street, London, SE1 9GF

One Wild Texas Night © 2020 Sara Orwig
Once Forbidden, Twice Tempted © 2020 Karen Booth

ISBN: 978-0-263-28002-9

ONE WILD
TEXAS NIGHT

SARA ORWIG

With love to David.

One

Jake Reed's pickup bounced as he sped across an open field on his Texas ranch. Nearby, cowboys on horseback herded his cattle toward the east side of his ranch while a huge wildfire swept the area to the west. None of the noise of cowboys yelling, frightened cattle on the move and Jake's and other cowboys' pickups could drown out the crackle of burning branches, the snap of tree limbs and the occasional crash of a falling tree.

As fire consumed the dry February grass, billowing gray smoke spread overhead, obliterating sunshine. Mesquite vanished in the swift-moving fire. A plane circled above, and Jake glanced at the screen he had set up in his pickup. Hap Green, one of his hands, was flying around overhead with a camera, relaying pictures of the fire to Jake's screen. The pictures confirmed that his house was safe right now—a huge relief. They had radio communication also, so Jake could ask questions.

As long as the wind held in the west, Jake knew his house wouldn't be in danger. Even now, as the wind began to shift from the north, his ranch house would remain out of the fire's path. His house was far to the east, but he knew how fast fires spread and how easily a tiny spark from a burning cedar could blow, land on a roof and ignite a house, so he remained vigilant. He and some of his men had plowed a large area on two sides of his house, as well as around the outbuildings and other homes. They had dug what was, hopefully, too big an area for the fire to jump, but if the wind kept shifting, nothing would be safe.

He saw the barbed wire fence separating his land from that of his feuding neighbor—a Blake. Both families had fought since they had settled in Texas after the Civil War more than a century and a half ago. He felt a jolt of surprise when he glanced across the fence and saw someone kneeling on the ground by an animal.

He turned his pickup to drive closer, and in seconds he saw it was his neighbor Claire Blake. The solitary Blake living in the area, she owned the family ranch now. Even though he saw her at cattle auctions, rodeos, the bank and grocery in Persimmon, Texas, their nearest small town, they hadn't really spoken in years—except when they had gone to court to fight each other.

He motioned to one of his men to keep going forward, and then he continued to the fence. Her pickup was parked too far away for her to get to it quickly, and she had her back to the fire—unwise with a fast-moving blaze in high wind.

Her grandfather had brought in Texas red cedars as a windbreak. Big mistake in Jake's view. They turned out to be nuisance trees, gobbling up groundwater, spreading rapidly and defying control, and he fought constantly to keep them off his land. Now the fire was sweeping through them on her ranch, each cedar exploding in flames when mere sparks touched it, the blaze spreading faster than a man could run.

If she didn't get out in the next few minutes, she wasn't going to get out alive. Even though the Reeds had a long history of fighting the Blakes, he couldn't leave her to burn. He remembered that Sunday when he had been driving past her church and he'd seen her laughing with a companion. She'd looked so attractive that if she had been anybody else except a Blake, he would have approached her. She was never with her brothers, Clyde and Les, who had caused a lot of trouble for his dad when they were growing up with mischief that they called harmless pranks. Claire lived alone out on the family ranch, and none of her family ever came to see her. Maybe she couldn't get along with her brothers any more than most of the other people in the area. Still, she was a Blake, and probably as annoying as the rest of her family. He didn't speak to her and she didn't speak to him. Despite all that, he increased his speed, bouncing over the rough ground toward her and the raging fire.

She was kneeling over an animal—a dog, he saw now—with her pickup a hundred yards behind her, too near a stand of cedars and native oaks, too near the fire. The minute he stepped out of his truck, he looked up, turning to face the wind.

The wind was changing directions—no surprise—

but it was what he had been praying wouldn't happen, and it was going to be deadly. More of his land would burn now. He knew from flying over their ranches that if the wind came fully out of the north, her home would be engulfed. And right now, they, as well as the dog, were in the fire's path. Still bending over the dog, she seemed totally oblivious. He was surprised, because the general consensus in the area was that she seemed to be a good rancher. He yelled, but the fire and wind drowned out his call.

He leaned down, pulling the barbed wire strands wide enough to step between them, avoiding the barbs while going through the fence quickly, then ran toward her.

"Hey!" he yelled again, and when she looked up, she jumped to her feet and stepped back as if he was a threat. Damn. He was risking his life for her, and she'd better not fight him about going with him.

Claire Blake looked up from the birthing dog before her, glanced over her shoulder and was startled to see her neighbor waving his arms and running toward her. Even though he was handsome as the devil, he was from a family that might as well have been related to Satan himself. Whatever he wanted, he'd better leave her alone, which he always had in the past. For a moment, she wondered if this was his dog and she had wandered onto her land to have her pups. No matter. She didn't have to do one thing Jake Reed said. All she had to do was take care of the dog and the five newborn pups in front of her, because they were in danger from the fire. She turned back to look at the dog spread on a blanket in front of her and the tiny newest pup in her hands as she cleaned the little wrinkled brown Lab puppy, its eyes still tightly closed. Thankfully, for her and the exhausted new mom in front of her, this was the last.

She knew the fire raged behind her and they had to get out. Would Jake help her with the pups? No, she had never counted on anything from him, and she wouldn't start now. If the situation had been reversed, her brothers wouldn't have helped him. She had to get the dogs out on her own.

"Queenie, you picked a lousy time to have your babies." She didn't know the dog's real name, so she gave her a temporary one. "We've got to get out of here. I wouldn't blame you, but please don't bite my neighbor." She ran her hand over the dog's head, and Queenie's tail thumped.

"You've got to go," Jake Reed yelled as he ran toward her.

"Duh," she mumbled. "I know we need to get out," she said, still working over the dog and pups.

"The wind's changing. You and the dogs will burn," he yelled. As he drew closer, she stood and faced him. Even under the circumstances, the thought crossed her mind when she saw her neighbor that he really was the best-looking guy in the next six counties.

She dragged her eyes from him, and for the first time in a while, she glanced at the fire. Shock chilled her, driving all other thoughts from her mind. The fire had changed direction and was nearly upon them. It seemed just minutes ago she had looked at it and deemed them out of immediate danger. Then she turned to Jake.

So, what was he doing here? Coming to save her? She couldn't believe that. No, the dog must be his. "I didn't notice how fast the fire is moving. I need to get the dogs into my pickup. If I take—" She gasped as her eyes lit on her vehicle. "Oh no."

"I'd forget that one," he remarked, stopping near her as flames engulfed her pickup. "I'll get mama dog. Grab the pups and let's go."

"My pickup…it was fine a moment ago," she said, not sure what shocked her more—her destroyed truck or the fact that he was offering to get her out of the area.

"Is this your dog?" she asked him.

"Hell, no. Let's go," he ordered, picking up the dog. "Grab the pups and get into my truck. Move it," he snapped. "Your pickup is toast. We're next. Go, dammit."

"I had no idea—" She realized she had been too focused on the dogs and had made what could have been a fatal error in ignoring the fire for a few minutes. That sent shivers all over her.

"Put some pups on her so she doesn't think we're taking them away from her," he said. Claire quickly placed three pups on the mother.

"C'mon, move," he shouted over his shoulder. "We've got to get out of here while we can."

His brisk order cut through her shock, and she grabbed up the remaining pups and rushed after him as he ran for his pickup. She glanced back once, and even in the heat of the raging inferno, sweat running down her face and body, she was chilled.

As he ran ahead of her, his long legs covering the ground easily, she realized she owed her life to him.

Her worst enemy. He had rescued her and the dogs from dying in the inferno. How would she ever repay him when she didn't even like to speak to him and rarely ever had? She had made a terrible error in turning her back on the fire, but she'd made just as big a mistake in getting into a predicament where her rescuer was Jake Reed. A lifelong enemy of her and every member of her family. How was she going to cope with the fact that he had just saved her life? Just as bad—how was she going to cope with the nagging awareness of how appealing and sexy he was?

Two

Jake could feel the heat and hear the roar of the fire and the constant snap and crackle behind them as cedars exploded, consumed by flames.

Sweat ran down his face and back from the fire's heat. It was the middle of February with warm Texas winds blowing, spreading the fire and fanning the flames. Trees ignited and burned instantly while the dry winter grass fueled the intense fire.

At the fence, he held the dogs closer against his chest and then he jumped the wire. Carrying the pups in a bandanna, Claire slipped between fence strands and caught up with him.

In minutes he had the mother dog and pups in the back of his pickup on a blanket.

"I'll ride with them," Claire said, turning to climb

into the back. He took her arm, and the minute he touched her, she looked up at him. For an instant he was lost in big, thickly lashed green eyes that made him forget danger, fire, circumstances, everything except his neighbor and worst enemy only inches away with her wide eyes focused on him. A tree crashed and shook him into awareness of his surroundings again.

"She's fine. Get inside," he ordered. "Hurry." He dashed around to get in, starting the engine as she climbed in beside him. He turned his pickup away from the fire that was only yards behind them now. When the wind changed direction, the fire had begun to fan out. The blaze picked up force, and more cedars burst into flames behind them.

She twisted to look back and shivered. "You saved us. If you hadn't yelled, I wouldn't have made it out. The dogs wouldn't have, either."

Jake glanced in his rearview mirror. Thank heavens he had almost every cedar on his place dug up. Some had gone to businesses and places in town that wanted them. Others had just been cut up for posts or firewood.

He glanced at her; she wrapped her arms around herself as if she trembled. It shocked him that she had been so oblivious to the fire, because she ran her ranch by herself and he'd always thought of her as competent. It also shocked him that he had just saved her life—his biggest enemy. Actually, her family and her no-good brothers were the really bad ones. But she was blood kin to them and had grown up with them, so she was bound to be just like them. Even if it had been her rotten brothers in danger, he couldn't have gone off and let them burn. He was glad they'd saved the dog and pups, too. He couldn't have left them, either.

While he drove swiftly away from her property, the pickup bounced roughly. He didn't care. All he wanted to do was get more distance between them and the fire that was traveling with lightning speed now. He knew how easily they could get trapped in a ring of flames.

"Are you okay?" he asked after a few more minutes when he finally felt he could slow down.

"No. I'm not okay," she snapped. "I know what I'm losing," she answered, but he was relieved that her voice was firm, and she didn't sound on the verge of losing her composure. "I really let down my guard. I made a major mistake by not watching the fire and getting out of there sooner. It really shakes me up when I pull some bonehead stunt running this ranch. This time, if not for you, my mistake would have been my last."

She looked back over her shoulder. "I'm still worried about the dogs bouncing around back there. They don't know they're being rescued."

"Don't worry about the dogs. They'll be fine, and we're getting them to safety with us. And you did cut it too close, but we all make mistakes. Don't ever turn your back on a wildfire except to get away from it."

Her phone buzzed, and she answered. At the same time, he received a call. It took only seconds for his call. When he finished, he saw her call had ended.

"That was the sheriff," he said. "They're telling everyone to evacuate this area. I need to get all my hands out," he said, calling his foreman.

"Just before you appeared, I had the same call from one of the deputies. My place is in the fire's path. I've already told all my people to get out, but I'm checking anyway." She made a call.

When the fire had started, Jake had had the foresight to get his livestock moved. Now that the wind had shifted out of the north, driving the fire across her ranch and more of his, he was glad he'd done that and relieved his house was far to the east and out of the fire's path, though some of his acreage was sure to burn.

"I'm sorry you're taking a direct hit. That fire's going right across your place."

She twisted in the seat to look behind her. "I'm going to lose my house and everything in it," she said so softly he barely heard her, and this time he noticed the waver in her voice. He glanced in his rearview mirror to determine they were leaving the fire behind. Then he slowed and stopped, letting the motor run. She was turned away from him, her shoulders slightly hunched.

"Well, this is a first for more than a century—a Reed and a Blake together without fighting," he said, more to himself than her. "I'm sorry about your ranch. That's a tough one," he said, meaning it. He didn't like her or her family. He didn't know her, but he knew her rotten brothers and had fought the older two in schoolyard fights, played against them in football and witnessed their hijinks enough to know he really didn't like them or their dad.

She turned to look at him and he gazed into those big emerald-green eyes again, with long, dark brown lashes that needed no makeup to be beautiful. That thought shocked him. Her skin was flawless. She was tan from being outside. Her dark red hair was in a thick braid that hung down her back. Her lips were full, red and appealing. Her mouth looked soft, kissable. With a jolt, he realized where his thoughts were going. Of all the women on the earth, this was the one he did not want to find highly appealing or start fantasizing about. Then he remembered the fire and how she was going to lose her home and her belongings.

"I know we've been enemies all our lives and have never even said a civil word to each other before, but I'm sorry you're going to lose your house," he said, surprised at himself, because he had had some bitter courtroom fights with her over ranch disagreements. "That's tough."

"Thank you," she whispered, looking down and turning her head slightly. "It hurts." She was silent a moment, and so was he.

"You may not really know much about me," she said in a low voice and then hesitated. He thought she wasn't going to say anything else, but then she started again. "Long ago, I lost everything important to me except the ranch," she said softly. "My maternal grandfather owned the ranch, as you know. My dad and my brothers never liked it, and my grandfather gave it to me. Now I'm going to lose my home, and then all I'll have is the land and my livestock. Sometimes a person needs more than land and livestock," she whispered. "I'm sorry, but this has been tough, and I don't see any improvement looming."

She ran her fingers lightly across her eyes. He felt sorry for her because her father and brothers never came back to the area, and her mother had died years earlier. She had a sister, but she and Jake's brother had been a closed chapter since the year they had married and run away. For a moment he thought of the secrets he knew about her family, the ones she didn't know. And never would know. He wondered if she had friends or anybody who cared about her.

Impulsively he put his arm around her shoulders, the gesture shocking him that he could feel sorry for someone he had disliked for a lifetime. An even bigger shock—she was soft, appealing. He put that out of his mind quickly.

"Sorry. Right now, there's no easy way to stop that damn fire," he said. "That's part of the hazard we face in living out here," he added. The moment he slipped his arm around her and drew her closer, letting her lean against him, awareness of her shook him. She was soft and smelled sweet in spite of being outside and caring for the dogs. She placed one hand against his chest as if to push him away. Only she didn't push in the slightest.

She looked up at him, and he felt enveloped in those big green eyes that stopped his breathing and made his heart pound. A silent protest flitted through his thoughts that he couldn't possibly feel this response to her. He absolutely didn't want to discover that this was the one woman who could make his heart race just by looking at him. All the common sense, caution, generations of fighting between their families, having little more than a dozen civil words spoken between them in their entire lifetimes and those words they'd said in the past few minutes—it all dissipated when he looked into her eyes. He did not want to feel one iota of attraction to her. But he did. And he was absolutely sure that feeling was mutual.

There was no woman in his life right now, but he

needed to get one fast if he was having this kind of reaction to a Blake. They both came from families that hadn't spoken for generations, over a century of animosity, bitter battles from the tales of early-day relatives. At least his relatives had told him plenty. He knew things she didn't. From stories handed down, they each had a legacy of feuding families, with hangings, stabbings, shootings, cattle rustling—all kinds of robberies and torn fences. And now, in his own lifetime, there were still secrets. He wondered about her and her life. She was a neighbor who lived a solitary life. He didn't think she ever went out with anyone or partied or had any social life.

Thoughts of what he should do ran through his mind. Even as those thoughts struck him, he struggled to look away from her big green eyes until his gaze lowered to her mouth. Her full, rosy lips looked incredibly kissable. Oh damn, what a thought. He almost groaned aloud. His gaze flew back to meet hers. When something flickered in the depths of her eyes, he realized he was right. She felt something, too.

Instantly, that knowledge had a double effect—first, he didn't want her to feel anything. Second, the realization that she did feel something made his heart race faster and gave him a more intense awareness of her.

He had seen her, passed her in town, gone to the same school—although at three years older, he had been in a different grade. In the past they had either fought or ignored each other. Until now.

Until today, he'd let his foreman or one of the cowboys handle any problems that had occurred due to their adjoining ranches. They rarely had to talk to one another and that worked for them. Often, she did the same and the two foremen worked things out.

As he glanced again at her and she looked at him, he realized it was the first time he had really noticed her.

How long had he looked at her? A couple of seconds? Ten, fifteen? Whatever time frame, he felt as if his whole life had changed in a subtle but irreversible way. He would never again see her the same way he always had. Worse, right now, he wanted to tighten his arm around her, pull her closer and kiss her. That shocking thought galvanized him to move away, and he released her. Instantly she scooted away, and her cheeks became pink—adding to her beauty. How could she suddenly be appealing? She was a lifelong enemy, as well as an enemy of every relative he had ever had. Generations of relatives over the last century. And now he was caught in a hot attraction? Oh wow, did he need to call someone and go out with a good-looking, fun woman.

When Claire Blake moved away, she looked back at her ranch. "Oh my heavens. My whole ranch is on fire, and now the flames are headed right for my house. From the first moment I heard about this fire, I hoped this wouldn't happen."

He reached in front of her to get two clean bandannas out of the glove compartment. He held one out to her. "Put this on and maybe it'll help filter out the smoke. I'll get us and the dogs away from this."

"Thanks," she said, taking the bandanna to tie it behind her head and over her nose and mouth. It just made him even more aware of her big green eyes. He drew a deep breath, coughed slightly and wished he didn't have any kind of response to her. He never had before today. Now, he knew that no matter what happened between them, he would never again see her in the same impersonal way he always had.

"The sheriff said to evacuate, so that's what we'll do," he said, turning to drive and trying to focus on getting away quickly.

She didn't answer, and he glanced at her. She was looking back, and she ran her hand across her face. He was certain she wiped away tears.

His screen crackled, and his pilot's voice came in. She twisted to look at his screens. "What are those?"

"I can get pictures sent from one of my planes. I have someone flying around, getting those pictures of the fire so I know what's happening. He's flown out of this area now because of the smoke. Even if he could get a picture, I don't think you'd want to see your house."

"No, I really don't."

"Don't worry, he's just taking pictures of my place unless I tell him differently."

She nodded and looked out the window over her shoulder.

Rain was predicted in late afternoon, and he prayed for her sake it arrived sooner. He looked up at the sky, but it was hidden by the smoke spreading in all directions overhead. He knew from flying over their land before that she lived in the original big farm home that was said to be over a century old. It would hurt to lose your house no matter what, but an old one like that would be really tough. It had lasted all these years, but there was no way it would survive this raging, out-of-control wildfire that was consuming everything in its path. He suspected her house was filled with hand-medowns from generations of her family—heirlooms that she treasured. They wouldn't make it through the fire. He felt sorry for her, which surprised him.

"Claire," he said, her name rolling off his tongue for the first time in his life. He had never called her by her first name, and saying it made him think again of the moment when he had looked into her big eyes and then at her mouth that looked made for kisses. He almost groaned aloud at that one. She was Claire Blake, he reminded himself. A Blake—the despised and hated enemy, including all her rotten relatives, for generations as far back as his family history went.

He didn't think she ever went out with anyone. She was a loner, staying on her ranch. On Friday or Saturday nights when he was out, he never saw her. He rarely even thought about her and never had wondered why he didn't see her. Now he wondered. And the minute he realized that, he knew he shouldn't. He should go right back to ignoring her and seeing her the way he always had—a neighbor whose entire family had a feud with his family. But he knew he couldn't see her just that way anymore.

Without doing anything except looking at him, she had turned his life topsy-turvy.

She was going to need a place to stay tonight. Within the hour she would be homeless. None of her family lived close now. Her father and brothers had all moved away, but she needed to be out here. She couldn't walk away from her ranch and all the people who worked for her.

He dreaded asking her to stay at his cabin. He liked his privacy, and they were bitter, lifelong enemies. So why was he about to offer her shelter? To get shut up in his cabin with her for an indefinite period of time?

What worried him the most was the unwanted, unreasonable attraction she had stirred. He didn't want to be attracted to a Blake, much less one who was a loner, almost a recluse. He wished he could stop thinking about her appeal, but that was impossible with her sitting close. He didn't want to think about spending the night with her in his cabin or, even worse, maybe a couple of days together. He was sure after a few minutes that unwanted and unreasonable attraction would disappear as swiftly as it had come. But even as that thought ran through his mind, he remembered how soft her lips had looked.

"Claire, I have a cabin on the river about thirty miles from here. It's far enough away to be okay. You can come stay there. It's big. There's plenty of room." Even as he said the words, he hoped she would refuse, but he suspected she had no other choice. Where else could she go?

She glanced up, her eyes widening in surprise, and from the crinkled line around them he knew she was smiling. Just the thought made his insides clench again, causing another worry. If she stayed with him, would he keep having these physical reactions to her?

As a kid, he'd thought she was plain-looking, and he paid little attention to her. She was three years younger, so they were never involved in anything together.

He responded to women, to being with a good-looking woman or a fun woman, but this was a totally unwanted, unpredictable, shocking response to a woman he had spent a lifetime avoiding. Not to mention the hostility between their families and sometimes between them. Something she seemed to have put on hold as much as he had.

"Stay with me," he surprised himself by repeating. "It's a big cabin, and we ought to be able to get through a night or two under the same roof."

A faint smile lit her eyes again and was gone in an instant, but that tiny smile made his heart clench again. What could it mean if he was continually having this intense reaction to his deepest and maybe only enemy? Well, only enemy in the area. Her brothers, who'd moved away, would fall into that category. Just the two older ones, he amended. Her younger brother, Laird, had always stayed out of the fights.

Jake knew that her two older brothers hated him, and the feeling was mutual. Ironically, their reasons were probably as good as his. He didn't want any part of them. They had secrets they tried to hide from everyone. They would be shocked if they ever discovered he knew what they knew.

Years ago, when his brother had eloped with her sister, they'd mostly severed ties with their families so they weren't around, either, though Jake kept in touch with his brother.

If he stopped to think about it, Jake knew a lot about her family, while he suspected she knew almost nothing about his. And he would never tell her what he knew or how he knew it. There were secrets he had promised to keep, and he definitely needed to keep them from her.

"I'm sorry for the circumstances," he said, "but other than my brother and your sister, this is the first time in generations that I know about when a Reed and a Blake have been civil to each other."

"Well, under the circumstances…" She shrugged, and he knew what she meant. Then she looked away. "You saved me and the dogs, and now you're offering me a place to stay… I don't know what to say." He was about to utter *Say yes* when she turned back to him and told him, "Except I'm grateful. I'll go to your cabin. Actually, *we'll* go to your cabin," she added, nodding to the dogs in the back of the truck. "Thank you."

"You're welcome," he said, smiling at her, thinking that was another first in his life in dealing with her. He'd spent too many years fighting with her family to want to become friends with her, and that feeling was mutual, he was sure. So he shifted his gaze to the road ahead of him and dragged his thoughts back to the business at hand. "We're close enough that I can keep tabs on the location of the fire until it's out. It's too close for comfort, that's for sure, and the wind isn't predictable."

"I'm glad I got my animals out and everyone who works for me, and their families are safe and accounted for."

"Amen to that one," he said. "We had good advance notice on this fire." A few minutes of driving later, he said, "I keep the cabin stocked with food because I stay there often to fish, so we'll have plenty to eat."

"At the moment I don't feel like eating. All I can do is think about my house. I have houses on the ranch for several of my employees, too, and when those homes burn, my folks will lose their possessions." He heard her take a deep but shaky breath, and out of the corner of his eye, he saw her brush her fingers over her eyes again.

"I'm sorry, but this hurts. It's just another loss in what seems like a series of them."

He shot her a curious glance, and she went on to explain. "My mom died when I was seven. My big sis took her place and was a second mother until four years later, when she eloped with your brother. They cut all ties, and my sister was another big loss in my life. She left me a letter telling me why she felt they had to cut those ties. Regina was eighteen when she eloped. Now I'm thirty and she's thirty-seven."

Jake recalled that time. His brother had only been twenty-one.

"After they eloped, my dad and brothers weren't exactly sympathetic about my losses." She shook her head and turned to the window, and he figured she was done telling him about her life. But she continued.

"My mother had money of her own from her family. She left that money to Regina as long as she took care of me until I was eighteen. If for any reason she stopped caring for me before I was eighteen, the money went to me, and that's what happened when she married your brother—a sizable amount of money went to me. Somehow that money was a buffer between my dad and my sister and later between my dad, my brothers and me. I think they hoped I would take care of their bills if they couldn't. Thank goodness I never did have to."

As she talked, his gaze kept flitting to her. Her story was sad, but his thoughts were more on her appearance, those big green eyes that he had never noticed before. Also her thick red hair, a dark red. It took an effort to keep his focus on his driving, but he couldn't stop thinking about her. Idly, he wondered how she would look if she ever let her hair out of that braid. Startled when he realized his train of thought, he tried to get his attention back on what she was saying.

"My dad remarried and moved to south Texas. Then, when I went to college, I got away from my brothers and they moved on, too, getting jobs in Dallas and Houston. None of them like ranching, so they don't come here often. I'm trying to reconnect with them, but we live far apart, so that makes it difficult."

He was thankful her family didn't come back, but he didn't say so.

"I wonder if any of my family may see my house in flames, because this fire is big news, I'm sure."

At the mention of the fire, Jake glanced back at the screen, at the information and pictures from his pilot. He was sorry her home was burning, but it wouldn't change the bitter feud they'd both grown up observing. That wasn't something that would ever change. Every member of his family had fought or had trouble with or just disliked her family, and vice versa. It was the way they were all raised, and it wouldn't ever change. It hadn't changed in the last century and a half, and he saw no earthshaking event, even this fire, that would end the feud. That was impossible. He suspected after today, she would go right back to refusing to speak to him, and he would do the same with her.

Even though he was increasing the distance between them and the fire as he drove, he watched for any new hot spots. So far, so good.

"I've made a life for myself," she continued, "and I love ranching. I love my horses."

"I've seen your horses—you have some fine ones,"

he said. Yeah, her horses might be great, but her family was lousy. She probably thought the same about his family.

They rode in silence for a few minutes until she started talking again. "I had the house remodeled and have made a home I love, something stable in my life. It's going up in smoke right now, or maybe it's already just ashes," she said in little more than a whisper.

"Claire, you'll rebuild. You've already been through a bunch of disasters and survived. You'll survive this one," he said quietly, amazed he was trying to console a woman who had been an enemy all his life. It still gave him a peculiar feeling to address her by her first name. Up to now, she'd simply been "my enemy neighbor" any time in the past when he had thought about her.

Out of the corner of his eye, he could see that she looked at him intently, and his pulse jumped. Once again, he felt that urge to put his arm around her to console her. And he knew what he wanted was more than consoling her. Glancing at her, he had a sudden urge to reach out and pull the bandanna away so he could let his gaze sweep over her features, and he felt his pulse rev up another notch. When they didn't get along and she was his enemy, how could a mere thought cause this?

When he went out on weekends, he saw gorgeous women, sexy, fun women who flirted with him, and his reaction wasn't as intense as right now with a woman who didn't even like him. They had a truce at the moment, and even if it lasted for a few days or a few weeks, which he seriously doubted, an attraction was impossible. Only it was happening, knotting his insides, making him hot and causing him to want to reach for her to taste those fabulous lips.

It would seem she'd worked some magic spell on him, except she looked as dazed as he felt, and he suspected she definitely didn't want to feel any attraction to him.

His phone buzzed. "Here's my foreman," he said to her and took the call. When he ended the call, he glanced at her.

"All my people are accounted for and out of here. When we first heard about the fire, we started moving livestock and getting families and their pets off the ranch. I left one bunch of cowboys moving my cattle and was headed to join another when I saw you and the dogs."

At the mention of the animals, she looked over her shoulder at them. Satisfied they were okay, she turned back. "I was the only protection the dogs had. I had to do what I did. But if you hadn't come—" She shook her head. "Well, thanks again for the rescue. You went against all you've been taught, but you saved my life and the dogs. I owe you big-time for that one. In fact, I'll have to be nice to you now," she said, but she sounded as if that was a major calamity.

"I wouldn't leave you or the animals to burn," he answered.

"Frankly, I'm not sure my brothers would have come to your rescue," she admitted. "The feud is still strong in our generation. It isn't ever going away. They always said your great-granddad shot and killed my great-grandfather."

Feeling a little flare of annoyance, Jake shook his

head. "My family always said your great-grandfather shot and tried to kill my great-grandfather. And the feud goes further back than those guys. However it went, I couldn't leave anyone behind to burn. Not even your brothers or your dad, in spite of our history. At least I've never shot at your family, and I hope none of you have at us. Just our great-grandparents exchanged gunfire."

"I've been told that, but I didn't know if it was the truth. I figured it was," she said, and he glanced at her to see her studying him. Her bandanna accidently slipped down, and he notice a deep pink in her cheeks, and he wondered what she had been thinking. And he knew he shouldn't speculate on why her cheeks had flushed.

He tried to shift his thoughts to something neutral and impersonal. It was an impossible task with her sitting so close. His reaction to her stunned him. He had seen her off and on all his life, but because she was a Blake, he'd paid little attention to her.

"By the way," she said, turning to him again, "since we are speaking to one another now, I saw in the local paper and in one of the ranch magazines that you're one of four ranchers who have donated large sums to rebuild the old arena that burned in Fort Worth. For years, that was a bitter subject with my family."

"So I've heard. I heard that your family planned to buy the land decades ago when it first came on the market and were going to build something there, but my family slipped in and donated the money to the city for an arena before your family could buy the property."

"That's close to the version I've heard. Maybe a little more cheating by your family to get the city to build

an arena. We'll never know," she said, a smile wrin-
kling her eyes.

"That was all before our time, so we'll never know,"
he said, but his thoughts were really on her smile that
made him want to smile in return. Her eyes seemed to
twinkle when she smiled, and it made her even more
appealing. *More appealing.* That was staggering. He
didn't want to be aware of her at all. Once again, he
told himself he needed to get out more. He'd stayed on
the ranch the past few weekends. He wasn't going to
in the future. Not with this kind of reaction to a Blake.

"I'm glad the arena is being rebuilt. I love rodeos. I
loved that arena. Thanks so much to you and your cousins for contributing to build a new one."

"You're welcome. I liked that arena, and so did my
cousins and my friends. We all competed there. We
wanted to see it rebuilt and continued."

"I don't know your cousins."

"One of them, Cal, contributed to the arena. He
worked out of the country, although he owned a Texas
ranch. He worked for the government and was killed
in an accident. We've asked that they name the arena
after him—the Cal Brand Arena."

"I'm so sorry you lost your cousin," she said, sounding as if she meant what she said.

"Thanks. He was a great guy, and we miss him, even
though we didn't see a lot of him these last years."

He appreciated her sympathy and was pleased that
she was interested in the arena. "What do you know,
we can get along for a few minutes."

She looked startled and nodded. "I hope so," she
said quietly, and he wondered if she was thinking about

fights they'd had in the past and how cold they had been when they had gone to court with boundary disputes, arguments over water rights and other complaints. They'd never conversed with each other on those occasions. This was a first. He didn't expect this sudden friendliness to last, though. Too much history in their families.

"You've put a good distance between us and the fire now," she noticed. "For a minute there I was worried about us getting away. The fire has to have reached my house by now," she added. She got out her phone and in minutes had news and pictures. "I don't think I'll get a picture of my house because of the smoke. Every once in a while, the wind clears the smoke enough for a picture, but it's just ranch land. I'm not sure I even want to see a picture of my house."

"They're probably getting the pictures from a drone," he stated. "Don't look. It won't help you. We got out with our lives. That's the main thing. Focus on that."

She nodded and turned to look out the back window and watch the fire. "When my sister ran away to marry your brother, she left that letter for me, like I told you. She explained they had to leave because of my father and brothers. I've always kept her letter because that's all I have of her. Now even that has burned and is gone."

He sat quietly, remembering how his brother had told him he would have to disappear because her dad and older brothers would come after them. His brother had shared secrets with him, but her sister hadn't shared any with her, judging from her few remarks. Probably because Claire was only eleven at the time. He had vowed to keep his brother's secrets, and he always had.

His thoughts shifted to the present. He was still shocked he was taking her home with him. They would be under the same roof—his worst enemy in the entire world living in his house, eating with him, talking and getting to know each other. They were acting civil to each other right now, but he knew that was because of the fire and danger and her loss. It was temporary and superficial. They had generations of hatred ingrained into them, and it wasn't going away. He would help her, but he still didn't like her. She had no clothes—nothing, he realized. When he could, he should drive her into Persimmon. She could pick up a few essentials there.

He glanced at her, and at the same time she turned to look at him, and he felt a clutch to his insides. His truck bounced over a couple of big stones, and he jerked his attention back to the road. He focused on his driving, but surprise over her features stayed with him. He'd always thought her incredibly plain, but he knew it was because of the way she dressed, either in overalls or jeans, with no makeup, her hair in the thick braid that hung down her back. So why was she looking so attractive to him now?

He wished she had refused to stay at his cabin, but she'd probably figured the same as he had—that the only motels anywhere in the vicinity would be totally booked with people driven out by the fires. He had invited her to stay at his place, so he was stuck with her. Too bad it was only a getaway fishing cabin and didn't have all the guesthouses his ranch home did. With them both beneath the same roof, was he even going to be able to tolerate her?

That thought made him grit his teeth. She had grown

quiet, and he wondered if she was having the same thoughts about him. He knew she didn't like him and considered him her worst enemy, because she had told him so more than once.

In a short time, they were on a highway heading east. Would thirty miles to the east be safe from the fire? He would just have to keep up with the reports and be aware of the fire and wind conditions. But, for now, they were safe, and he motioned to her that they could finally remove their bandannas.

"We both need to pray for rain," he said, breaking the silence in the truck. "We're supposed to have rain later today, but there's no seeing the sky for all the smoke."

"The rain will be too late for my place," she said in a monotone.

"Sorry. You're right. What about your livestock, cattle and horses? Where'd they go?"

"Do you know Dan Sloan?"

"Sure."

"Yesterday when we got the first warning, Dan contacted me. He sent some men to help and moved my cattle to his place for now. He's down the road to the east—farther east than your ranch, as you know."

"You had to move your livestock around my ranch, then, to get to him. When you move them back, let me know and you can cross my ranch."

With the bandanna now around her neck, she smiled, a big smile that warmed him like sunshine and made his pulse jump.

"Thank you. It will be a lot quicker and easier to cross your land. The Sloans are very nice people," she continued, and he tried to focus on what she was saying.

"They invited me to stay with them, but they already have his brother and his brother's family, which includes five more kids. I didn't want to impose on him, and I don't want to impose on you."

"No need. It'll just be the two of us," he said, and the minute the words were spoken, he felt his breath catch. He had answered matter-of-factly and impersonally, but it didn't come out that way.

"...the two of us..."

The words echoed in his mind and sounded far more personal. What kind of chemistry did they have between them? He wouldn't have thought any kind would be possible, but she stirred some responses in him as if she were sitting there flirting with him, which she wasn't at all. Besides, she was as plain as a mud hen. The moment that thought came, he had a vivid memory of her face. He glanced at her again and looked into big, gorgeous green eyes with thick brown lashes and dark red hair. She wasn't as plain as a mud hen at all—she just projected that image until he got up close. That realization shocked him, and he wanted to stop driving and turn and really look at her. He realized how ridiculous that would be. She was a Blake, and he'd better not forget that.

"Damn," he said without realizing he had even spoken aloud until she turned abruptly to stare at him.

"Is something wrong?" she asked, sounding worried.

"Sorry. I was just thinking about the fire and your loss," he lied.

"That's nice of you," she said. "I figured you might not really care, but it's nice to know you do."

He glanced at her again and was caught once more

by those gorgeous green eyes. Quickly he turned back to his driving. "Damn," he said again, this time under his breath.

They rode in silence for a while, and then he heard a slight sound from her. He glanced at her and saw that her hands were on her face and she was shaking. He checked the rearview mirror. They had put a big distance between themselves and the fire, so he slowed and cut the engine, turning to put his arm around her lightly.

"Claire, I'm sorry you lost your home," he said, really meaning it, because that would be a devastating loss.

She turned to him, placing her head against his chest as she cried. For an instant she sobbed, but then she got control. With no tissues for her to wipe her face, he held out a clean bandanna. "Here, take this."

She took it and just held it. "You just have an endless supply of bandannas?" she asked, trying to smile. But her smile vanished as she wiped her eyes. "I'm sorry. I feel stupid crying again. It's just that I've lost everything. All my life I've been losing what I love," she said so softly he could barely hear her. "I don't ever want to fall in love, because I'd lose the person I love. I don't even want to get real close to friends any longer. I'm glad I still have my ranch, but it's going to be burned to a crisp." She shook her head.

"Cry all you want," he whispered. "You've lost your home. That's big." He tightened his arm around her, turning her to him and slipping his other arm around her for now, concentrating on consoling her.

But no matter how hard he tried to focus on those things, he couldn't fight the awareness of her in his arms. She was soft, sweet-smelling, with lush curves.

He liked holding her far too much. He didn't want to look into her big, green eyes or at those rosy, full lips that were visible now. Again, he almost groaned aloud thinking about her.

He was taking her home with him. He'd already had her in his arms twice. That stunned him, because until today, they'd rarely acknowledged the other one's existence. He didn't know what she did or what she liked— he had never given two seconds worth of thoughts about her and he rarely had even seen her. This was all a first in his life—and not a welcome first.

He didn't want to like holding her in his arms. He didn't like wanting to kiss her, and he didn't want to find her desirable.

Claire Blake was as off-limits as if she was poison to his system. So why was he holding her close? Why was he so aware of her?

He should let her go. He should get her out of his arms, out of his pickup and out of his life as fast as he could.

How could he do that now when he had invited her to come stay at his place? What was he going to do with her as his houseguest for the next few days?

Worse, how could he get through the night when all he wanted to do was kiss her?

Three

Her ranch burned. Her family home destroyed. Heirlooms passed down from generations gone. Treasured family pictures reduced to ashes.

Claire thought of all that loss and cried quietly. No matter how she tried to get her mind off her losses and get control of her emotions, she couldn't. And then she became aware of Jake's arms around her, strong and reassuring. She was being held closely against his rock-hard chest, something solid in her suddenly battered life. She tightened her arms around him, for just a moment yielding to the heady feeling that all was not lost and there was hope, however imaginary, that she was held tightly in the secure arms of a friend.

From the hour he was born, Jake Reed had been an enemy, just as she and all her family were his enemies.

That feud had been drilled into her from the time she could toddle. As far back as she could remember in her childhood, she had heard how his family had rustled her family's cattle, stolen their horses, tried to claim water rights in the area where the ranch boundaries met. She'd heard how early relatives had fought duels with his family members, waylaid them and attacked them, robbing them, how they had set fire to their land and their houses.

She had no idea how much was truth and how much was exaggeration fueled by anger and hatred, but she had been taught to dislike all Reeds—and that included him.

For this moment, though, she could overlook the feud and the animosity to rely on the friendship and comfort he was giving her. He had saved her life and the dog's and the pups' lives, as well. For that, she would be eternally grateful to him. For the moment, she couldn't think of Jake as the enemy. Actually, far from it. Jake's arms felt wonderful around her, and when she had looked into his eyes, she had wanted him to hold her. In truth, she had wanted him to kiss her. That thought shocked her because kisses could only mean all kinds of complications in both their lives. There was another reason she didn't want to be attracted to him. Jake had a reputation of loving and leaving the ladies. He'd had more than his share of female friends in his life, and he always was the one to break things off as far as she knew.

Between the feud and his reputation, she didn't want to risk her heart with him at all.

Besides, they could never date. One date would bring

out the animosity in both families. No, they had to remain adversaries.

She thought of their relationship thus far. The court
battles they'd had. She recalled fighting him when he
tried to divert two of the biggest creeks that provided
them both with water. She had won in both cases, but
then he had won a court battle over old boundary lines
that gave him access to another creek that crossed her
ranch.

Unfortunately, at present, his arms around her were
the best feeling in the world. She knew she shouldn't
enjoy being held so much, yet at a time when she felt
incredibly alone in the world, his embrace and reassur-
ances were solace for her broken heart over the loss of
her home. She'd never get that kindness from her brothers or her father, and her friends were scattered in Dallas and she didn't keep up with them closely. She was
close to some of the people who worked for her, but not
close enough, since she was still their boss.

Right now, she relished Jake's arms around her. He
was sexy, handsome, broad-shouldered, exciting. He
had saved her and the dogs—a man of action, able to
get the job done quickly and efficiently—something
her father and brothers had never done. She admired a
man who could.

"Better?" he asked in a deep voice, and she looked
into his dark brown, thickly lashed eyes that took her
breath and held her immobile. She couldn't look away
and her heart drummed, and she wanted his kiss—
which was total insanity, because it would only muddle
their lives. Up until the past moments, she would have

been certain he would never want to kiss her, but she couldn't think that now. Not when she met his gaze.

The moment she looked into his sexy dark eyes, she knew he wanted to kiss her as much as she wanted him to do so.

She groaned. "We shouldn't ever," she whispered, and curiosity filled his eyes.

"We shouldn't ever what?" he asked in a husky voice. "Kiss? We both want to. We're adults, both single. Why not?" he added, and she was lost. The slight dark stubble on his jaw and chin added to his ruggedly handsome appearance. She felt as if his dark eyes could look right through her and that he knew every thought in her head.

She knew better, but his gaze was riveting and hot, stirring desire, something she didn't feel for any of the local cowboys or ranchers or any other man she knew. Until now.

She felt caught and held by Jake's gaze, and she also felt he could see the longing that was consuming her. Her desire was unwanted and unreasonable because they were deepest enemies, but she was ensnared and could barely get her breath. How long had it been since she had kissed a man or been kissed? How long since she had even been out with one?

Too long, she answered herself.

And right now, wanting to kiss him was all she could feel or think.

As his arm around her tightened, he leaned down the last few inches until his mouth covered hers. Excitement streaked through her, stirred by his mouth on hers, his tongue over hers. Feelings bombarded her, hunger for so much more of him, for his hands on her. She tightened her arms around him and kissed him in return, her tongue stroking his, hot, wet, so sexy. Desire shook her, and she held him tightly.

His kiss rocked her, building a raging response deep in her and making her want him more than she would have dreamed possible. She knew for certain that she had never been consumed by kisses that fanned the flames of longing the way his were. Even as her need intensified, she reminded herself that this was not the man to get deeply involved with. She shouldn't be melting in his arms.

He shifted slightly so he held her pressed closer against him with his arms still tightly around her. When she leaned away a fraction, his dark-eyed gaze consumed her. Yearning for more of him swept over her, as they kissed again.

Time ceased to exist for her, and she didn't know how long they kissed, but she finally realized that she had to stop kissing him as if they were the last two people on earth with only hours to survive.

With an effort, she shifted slightly and leaned away. Gasping for breath, she scooted out of his embrace, and he let her go. She couldn't tell from his expression what was going through his thoughts. She fought a battle with herself to avoid reaching for him again. How could she feel as if his kisses were the kisses of a lifetime when he was the one man on earth who was a total enemy? Only he wasn't an enemy at the moment. Right now, she just wanted to hold tightly to him and be kissed by him again and forget what she was losing.

Instead, she moved back, staring at him as if she had never seen him before in her life. She almost felt that way. She shook her head. "How do we—I mean, do we go back to the way we were and have always been—feuding neighbors?"

"Think what you will," he said in a husky voice. "You can go right back to the same feelings about me, but there is absolutely no way I'm ever going to forget or regret kissing you."

Her heart thudded again. "Maybe there's no going back to the way it was, but we have to move on from this."

"Yeah. I agree there's no going back to the way things were. We've crossed that line. Our relationship just changed forever," he added.

She shook her head. "I don't think our relationship really can change. That old feud is too much a part of each of our lives. We've lived with it since we were toddlers."

He raised an eyebrow and looked slightly amused. "I will never again see you the same way as I did before we kissed," he repeated quietly in a voice that was as intimate as a caress. All the time he talked, he stared intently at her as if he had never seen her before in his life.

She felt her cheeks flush with heat. "You can't turn off a century-old feud like tap water."

"We just made a good start on it." He slipped his forefinger beneath her chin to tilt her face up so she would look at him. "I'm willing to try. Are you?"

Her pulse jumped again as she gazed into his dark eyes and thought about their kiss. "Oh yes. I'll try," she answered, and it came out a whisper. She felt she had to move away from him, or she would be in his embrace and they would kiss again. While half of her wanted that, the other half warned she would regret kissing him. There was no way they could shake their past, their mistrust—actually, their dislike for each other. You couldn't turn off a lifetime of feelings in a morning. You couldn't really ever turn it off. Not when it had been part of their lives always. Deepest enemies.

This little flare of attraction wouldn't last. She had taken Jake to court before and won against him. She had lost to him, too. But the battle was always there, and she didn't think kisses would change everything between them. As fast as she thought that came another thought—his kisses were like no others she'd ever had in her life.

He wasn't going to be easy to get over. His kisses might be impossible to forget.

She looked up into dark brown eyes that hid what he was thinking. How little she actually knew about him. Could she really trust him?

Her gaze lowered to his mouth, and her pulse jumped. At this moment she didn't care about their future relationship. She just wanted his mouth on hers again and his hands on her to make her forget her losses and the fire.

She caught her breath, blinking, trying to gather her wits. She scooted away, and he shifted back, more into the driver's seat. He turned and started the pickup and then glanced at her again. "Ready to move on?"

"Yes, thanks," she said, meaning it. He had salved some of her heartbreak of permanent loss. She was more composed. At the same time, she realized she had some new problems. Jake Reed had given her the best kiss of her life, but he was also a lifelong enemy of her and her family. How badly had she just complicated her life?

Jake concentrated on his driving. Claire was as quiet as he was, and he suspected she might be in just about as much shock. She had the fire, the loss of her house, her scorched and burned land to worry about. She also had their kisses to think about.

She had just turned his life topsy-turvy. It was an understatement to tell her that he would never forget their kisses. He couldn't stop thinking about them.

They were fleeing a raging inferno behind them, and he was fighting a raging internal fire that made him want to pull off the road, take her into his arms and kiss her for hours.

He had never reacted this intensely to a woman he barely knew and hadn't even been attracted to in the past. He turned the pickup and finally got back on one of his ranch roads, a dirt track that was little more than two ruts with weeds growing up the center, but he knew where he was—it would lead back to a better road and eventually to his cabin.

And she was coming home to live with him for the next few days. Or weeks. He almost groaned over that thought. He hadn't been able to resist kissing her today. How was he going to resist kissing her when he took her home with him? Common sense said he should resist. They had been enemies all their lives, and now was not the time to get deeply and intimately involved with her. Because of her losses, she was emotionally vulnerable, and he didn't want to hurt her.

She could tangle up his life in a huge way. Right now,

he was already tied in knots, confused by the hunger for her, hot, intense and constant—and by his need to get a grip on himself and get back to the way he had always viewed her.

Too late for that. The barn door had been opened, and the horses had already left. A few kisses and she had already complicated the hell out of his life.

So why couldn't he stop thinking about kissing her again?

He could think of too many reasons why he shouldn't—they were lifelong enemies. For years they had fought each other over ranch problems. They didn't even like each other. No, he had to amend that one. They didn't know each other, really. All he had were preconceived notions about her. And she definitely didn't know him. The last reason was a doozy: their families would be enraged if they even became friends.

"You're very quiet," she said softly, and he glanced briefly at her to see her looking intently at him. His gaze lowered as he looked at her lips, and he thought about their kisses.

"Just driving," he answered, focusing on the road and taking a deep breath.

"If you're having second thoughts about taking me home with you, I'll try to keep out of your way, and tomorrow maybe you can take me to town, and I can find a place to stay."

He glanced at her again and felt a twinge of guilt for thinking she would be a problem houseguest. He smiled at her before turning his attention back to his driving.

"I'm fine about taking you home with me. You need a place to stay, and my cabin is roomy enough that we won't be in each other's way. Stop worrying. I wouldn't have asked you if I hadn't meant it," he said, thinking the real problem was keeping his hands off her.

Her kisses had set him on fire, and he wasn't going to forget them for a long time. He took a deep breath and tried to think about the fire, his cabin, his employees and his livestock—everything and anything besides Claire. How could she possibly be that sexy?

He forced himself to stare at the dry ruts and weeds until he got hold of himself. Then he allowed himself a glance at her, just a quick look. She was staring ahead, her emotions evidently under control.

She turned to look at him, and for an instant their gazes met. He felt the jolt all the way to his toes, and that's when he began to worry if he'd ever get hold of himself again. The urge to pull over, take her into his arms and kiss her again was as strong as ever.

He had to get out and spend some time with one of his sexiest, best-looking, most fun women friends. He had some who would fit that description. And not one of them had ever set him on fire with her kisses the way his feuding neighbor had today. Thinking about it, he shook his head.

"Is something wrong?" she asked in a soft voice.

"I was just thinking about my livestock and the fire," he lied. He wasn't about to tell her what he was really thinking. "The guys saved the animals, and that's an enormous relief. I guess you feel the same about yours."

"Oh my, yes. Thank heavens they got mine moved. That's something I can think about that's very, very good."

He smiled at her again, glad she sounded in control

of her emotions and positive about her livestock. She didn't sound bothered or in a dither, but then, he hoped, neither did he sound that way. He just *felt* that way. If he could forget her kisses, his life and his thoughts would calm and settle into his usual routines.

Unfortunately, he had a suspicion he wouldn't forget them in a lifetime.

He drove in silence, and she was quiet, seeming to be lost in her thoughts, so maybe she was adjusting to the situation.

In a short time, he turned up the cleared drive to his cabin. "There it is," he said. What he called his cabin anyone else would call a mansion, even if it was in the woods. The sprawling two-story river home was big and roomy, made of logs with an enclosed wraparound porch. Behind it ran a wide, rippling creek with cottonwoods scattered along the banks. To one side in the front was a man-made waterfall and a pond with exotic plants along one bank and tubs of blooming multicolored water lilies. There were beds of exotic plants and flowers next to the porch of his cabin. There were lifelike statues of wildlife—a mountain lion in a tree, a couple of grazing goats, a collie. He followed a wide drive around the cabin to a six-car garage. The drive was bordered by more green plants and flowers. A statue of a man fishing was at the creek's edge.

She laughed. "So, this is your fishing cabin in the woods, huh? I don't believe we're going to exactly rough it out here."

He smiled at her, his heart jumping as her eyes sparkled with laughter.

"I figured I might as well have something I like," he said.

"It's a fine place, and so pretty on the creek," she exclaimed. "A wonderful home."

"Thanks. I enjoy it out here."

As he parked on the drive near his back door, he turned to her. "I'll put the dog and her pups on the enclosed back porch. What's her name?"

"I don't know, actually. I called her Queenie. I've never seen her before. I just happened on to her having her pups today."

"No kidding?" he exclaimed, glad she'd stopped to help the dog and pups, because if she hadn't, most likely they would have perished in the fire. "That's great," he said and was rewarded with another smile that made his pulse jump and made him think about kissing her again.

"The fire may have driven her from her home. I don't recall seeing her before. She doesn't have a tag. For a while there, I thought she was yours."

"If she doesn't have a tag, then I have the right people here for her—my neighbors the Andersons."

"I know the Andersons."

"Charley Anderson has three teenage daughters. The girls love dogs and cats. Any time we have animals wander onto the ranch, I call them. They come get them and they either reunite them with their owner or give them a home—with them or with friends. Are you willing for me to turn Queenie and her pups over to them?"

"Yes. It sounds like a good deal for all concerned, especially Queenie."

He took out of his phone and began typing. "I'll text

them right now, and Queenie and her pups will soon be on their way back to their owner or to a good home."

"Great," she said. "That's a big relief." When he was done, he walked around the truck to climb into the back. She followed him to the side of the bed, and he picked up two puppies to hand to her.

"You take these, and I'll carry her and the other pups to the porch for now until the girls come," Jake said.

They had just settled the dogs and the pups when his phone buzzed with an incoming text. He looked at it. "The girls will be over soon to get Queenie and her pups." He sent an answer and looked up, smiling at Claire. "They'll be good to these pups, don't you worry."

"Thanks again. I'm sure it'll all work out."

As they walked to the door, he wanted to take her arm, to touch her again. But if he touched her again, there was a chance he might kiss her again, and that was something he had to resist. Something he had to stop thinking about.

What was it about her that had him constantly wanting her, constantly aware of her? She wasn't doing one deliberate thing to cause his response. He needed to remember who she was. Remember that Reeds and Blakes didn't mix and keep his distance.

He didn't like her family, and she was part of them. Even if she wasn't one degree like her bully brothers, she was still related to them. They had the same bloodlines, same parents, same home life, and somewhere that had to come out.

And her family wouldn't like her going out with him at all. If he did go out with her, he knew he'd have to watch his back, because those two older brothers would jump him some night if he let his guard down.

Jake couldn't figure out why he was so attracted to her. He knew a lot of good-looking, fun women who didn't come with problems and dreadful relatives who hated him. Definitely no one else whose family had fought with his well into a second century.

Why did she take his breath away, make his heart pound and stir all sorts of longings? Even now he wanted to stop, take her into his arms and carry her into his bedroom and spend the rest of the day and night there with her.

That acknowledgment shocked him, and he stopped and turned to look at her. She noticed and paused, her brows arching as she got a quizzical look. "What? Food in my teeth? Ink on my face? You're staring at me as if there's something."

"There's something, all right." His voice was thick with desire.

She blinked and held her hand up, palm out as if motioning him to stop. "Never mind that I asked. I don't want to know."

"No, you don't, but I'll tell you anyway, because I'm puzzled. I don't understand why our kisses are so—" he paused and narrowed his eyes as he thought "—so intense, unforgettable...so damn sexy. We've barely spoken until today, and we don't even know each other."

"Oh, we know a lot of things we don't like about each other, but we know very little we do like—that's the part where we're strangers," she answered. A second passed before she added the dagger. "But all we need to know is that I'm a Blake and you're a Reed. So, I think we should forget our kisses and get on safe subjects and keep a little distance between us."

"You're right. Kiss forgotten," he lied. "We'll talk about safe subjects. Ahh, here come the girls," he said as a large pickup pulled up. A man and three teenage girls stepped out.

"This time I hear you have a mama and pups," a tall blond-haired man said, pushing back his hat and smiling at Jake. "Are the dogs fire victims?"

"We're glad to see you, Charley, and yes, we do have a mama and pups. The fire probably is why she wandered away from her home." He said hello to the girls. "I think all of you know my neighbor Claire Blake."

Claire spoke to them as they greeted her.

"We'll get the dogs and be on our way. The girls can't wait to have the little pups."

Claire stood back out of the way as the Andersons gathered the animals and the bedding. Jake followed them to the car, and she went with him.

In minutes they waved goodbye to the Andersons, and she turned to smile at Jake. "Thank you. I'm sure the Andersons will do right by the dogs. And Charley told me to notify him if I have strays on my ranch and he'd come get the dog and find it a home. That's just wonderful."

"They're really good about it, and they don't seem to get overloaded or want to stop," he answered. Jake turned to face her. "Right now, I want to volunteer to help fight the fire," he said, knowing he needed to get away from her and try to forget their kiss. "I'm sure they can use extra hands. That fire is a record breaker."

"I think I should volunteer to help, too. I can't get

out there and fight the fire the way you can, but I'll bet there are some things I can do."

He studied her a moment as he nodded. "You're probably right. We'll head down to the firemen's temporary headquarters. Meanwhile, c'mon, I'll show you where you can stay," he said, and she turned to walk with him into the cabin. They went through a wide hall with a polished hardwood floor and paintings of Western landscapes in gold frames hung on the walls.

They entered a spacious room with another highly polished hardwood floor. The room held an enormous wide-screen television, a game table and groupings of chairs and sofas. Down another hall, she glimpsed a movie room and a large dining room with a fruitwood table that would easily seat over twenty people. She noticed the surroundings, but she couldn't stop her eyes from wandering to her host. He walked close beside her, and she was aware of his height, of their shoulders and arms brushing lightly with each step.

And then she thought about her loss, about not even owning a house any longer, of not having a home, and she hurt again.

"I'm sorry," she said, taking a deep breath. "Everything I see makes me think about my house. I'll get accustomed to dealing with the loss, but right now, it's too recent."

"I'm sorry about your house, but your reaction is understandable, and you don't need to apologize. You don't need to explain it to me, either." He stopped in front of open double doors. "I'm across and down the hall where that door is open. This suite will be yours. Let's go look. I'm sure the bed has clean linens."

She barely heard what he said, because she was still thinking about him being "across and down the hall," which was oh so incredibly close. He looked the type to sleep in the buff—and then she tried to drop that thought as if it were a burning cinder. She looked up at him while he talked, but all she could think about was how handsome he was, and then she was lost in memories of his kiss.

She forced herself to focus on what he was saying. "…and I have someone who cleans every two weeks when I'm away and then comes once a week when I'm here. I have a cook when I'm here for very long, and I have a garden crew."

"Do they all drive out from town?" she asked, barely aware of what she said to him, because she was too conscious of his broad shoulders, how close he stood and his riveting dark gaze that kept her pulse racing. Now they were under the same roof, just down the hall from each other for how many nights? How was she going to be able to resist him? They obviously had something between them, or they wouldn't have shared a kiss that she didn't think she would ever forget.

"Most everyone who works for me lives around here," he continued, and she tried to focus on what he was saying. "There are houses scattered nearby—actually in walking distance. You just don't see them because of trees and bushes."

"Don't go to any trouble because I'm here. I can get along rather easily. A roof and a bed will be sufficient."

He smiled and nodded. "I'll get us some sandwiches. We may be working all night. You know where the kitchen is. You can meet me there." He left her to go to his suite, and she stood a moment to watch him walk away. He had long legs encased in tight jeans that were faded with wear. When he passed out of her sight, she turned to enter her suite and get ready to go.

The moment she stepped into her suite, she shook her head. It was furnished with antiques, which she loved, recognizing some very old and very fine pieces, or else excellent reproductions. Her bed was larger than king-size with a frilly white canopy and a white bedspread.

"Some cabin," she said, shaking her head. There was no way his two-story mansion in the woods could be called a cabin, except that was what he called it. It was too big and too elegant. And now she would be spending the night with him here…alone.

Jake let out his breath when he entered his suite. If he kept busy the whole time Claire was with him, he probably could get by without kissing her again. He knew he had to try. He thought about his brother who had married her sister and how their lives had never been the same since. They were cut off from their families, living far, far away and keeping their whereabouts secret.

He couldn't stop the response he had to Claire, but he knew he needed to resist her. "Yeah, right," he whispered as he passed through his big sitting room into the bedroom. The suite held a custom-made bed, a large desk across the room and beyond the desk a big TV screen. He stopped by a table and picked up a remote control, pushed a button and in minutes he began to get pictures of burned acres, of parts of his ranch, pictures still being taken by Hap Green and sent back to him showing the fire and the damage already done. Hap didn't fly into the smoky parts, but the fire had already destroyed large areas, and they could get some shots of it in the distance. Jake shook his head and put down the remote, leaving the pictures on.

He got ready to go. He was certain the firefighters could use his help some way, and probably the workers would be glad to have Claire's help.

He went into the bathroom to use the facilities, and when he came out, his eyes lit on the huge bed. Unbidden, images of Claire sprawled out on the sheets assailed him. His breath grew ragged as he imagined him joining here there, making love to her. The thought nearly sent him up in flames.

He groaned and raked his fingers through his hair. "Damn," he whispered. Claire in his bed. He shook his head. "With her family and yours," he said aloud to himself, "that's the way straight to trouble."

So why was it exactly what he wanted?

Four

In less than half an hour, Claire joined Jake in the kitchen to eat a sandwich before they left. To take her mind off the fire and her loss, he tried to talk about something else.

"Is there a guy in your life?" he asked once they were seated at the table. He was suddenly aware he knew nothing about her except the family feud.

She looked startled, then amused as she shook her head. "No, there isn't. I don't go out often. I think I may intimidate some men. And I think some just don't like me because I'm a rancher and run the place. That tends to make me a little set in my ways and bossy, maybe."

He shook his head. "I've spent time with you now, and you weren't either. You're adapting to a huge change in your life," he said. "And bossy? You'd be a lousy rancher if you weren't. Someone has to be in charge."

"I know, but some guys don't want to take out a bossy woman who can run a ranch."

He shrugged. "Wouldn't bother me, I'll bet. Go out with me next Saturday night and we can see how I deal with going out with a bossy woman," he said, shocked again at himself and his reactions to her, even more shocked that he'd asked her out without giving any thought to the consequences of his invitation. And he knew he wanted her to accept. After lecturing himself to keep his distance from her, he was trying to get more entangled than ever.

He barely knew her, but he wanted an evening with her. As fast as that thought came, common sense said he shouldn't want to spend one single evening with her. She was a Blake. The family feud was as strong as ever. She wasn't the woman to get involved with. But he wasn't listening to his own advice.

Her eyes widened in surprise, and then she laughed, a sound of mirth that made him smile and want his arms around her more than ever.

"You're joking, of course. We'd set the town on edge, and our relatives would explode with everything from dismay to anger to rage. I don't think there would be one happy person in my whole clan who would approve of us going out together. You might find yourself in the middle of a fight with my brothers. For that matter, I doubt if there is anyone in your family who would approve of us going out together. In fact, I know they wouldn't, and I don't even know them." She leaned in toward him. "Tell the truth now—they wouldn't approve, would they?"

He looked down into her big green eyes, looked at

her rosebud mouth, remembered their kisses and forgot what she'd asked him. He wanted her.

"I've never met anyone like you," he whispered. She blinked, and then her eyes widened. She drew a deep breath, straightened up and stared wide-eyed at him a moment before her gaze lowered to his mouth.

His heart thudded, and he wondered whether she was going to kiss him.

She shook her head as if coming out of sleep and stood, picking up her plate with her half-eaten sandwich. She stepped away from him, leaving more space between them. She stared intently at him. "I don't know why the attraction, or whatever it is, happens between us," she whispered as if to herself, but he heard her. He had finished his sandwich and a glass of water, and he stood to face her.

"I don't know, either, but we might be really missing something if we let what we feel go by without acknowledging it and acting on it. My reaction to you is unique in my life. I'd wager my ranch that your reaction to me is unique in yours, too."

The words were there between them, and she nodded. "That doesn't make it good."

"I'm sure it's something that shouldn't be ignored," he said with amusement in his voice, and she smiled in return as she shook her head.

"Let's not rush into something. I suggest you rethink that invitation to go out Saturday night. Your brother and my sister married and vanished. They haven't been home since they married because my sister knows my dad and brothers. My brothers' feelings about that feud are really strong. You take me out, and you're a marked man. I'm not about to do something that would get you hurt badly."

"I can't believe that would happen, and I'm not scared of your brothers," he replied. "But I don't want to cause you trouble with your family, so at this point in our lives, we can resist a night out together." He was disappointed, yet he had a feeling she was right. "There's no need to stir up a hornets' nest of trouble with families. We don't have any strong emotional ties, and we can still walk away from each other without it hurting. We better leave well enough alone."

"That's common sense, and I agree."

"I'm not sure I agree with myself," he said, glancing at her mesmerizing green eyes and wanting to kiss her right now.

"Hang on to your decision, Jake. We don't need to go looking for trouble."

"Might be the most fun ever," he said, lowering his voice and drawling his words. She drew another deep breath and gave a shake of her head.

"Jake, we better go and stick to helping out and forget any future together unless it's just waving at each other across the fence." She rinsed her dish and placed it in the dishwasher.

"You're right. Meet you on the porch shortly."

She went outside and sat in one of the rockers to wait. When he stepped out to join her, she came to her feet.

"C'mon. I've called the volunteer center, and they need us. And yes, they'll be glad to have your help."

"I'm willing to do what I can," she said.

"Good," he said, looking up at the sky. "Because we never got the rain they predicted, and now they don't think we will."

When he turned on the highway and headed toward the fire, she groaned. "It looks as if all of this part of Texas is on fire," she said, looking across the horizon. "This fire will get a lot of homes, barns and outbuildings. I just hope ranchers got their livestock and themselves out," she said, stunned by the smoke that totally hid every bit of sky and the dancing flames in the distance that spread as far along the horizon as she could see.

"They're going to need all the help they can get," he said.

"This has to be the worst fire in this area ever," she said softly, realizing a lot of people would lose everything. She fought back tears again, not only for herself, but for everyone who was being affected.

"Just try to focus on what you've saved. You have your animals. They didn't burn."

"Thanks to you, I didn't lose my life in this fire. It's just awful."

"Be careful tonight. Things happen, and everything can change in seconds."

"I'll be careful. I know what a close call I had today." She looked at his profile, her pulse beating faster as it did each time that she got on a personal level with him.

"We've always been enemies, but now…" She left the thought unspoken.

"Yeah," he said. "A kiss sort of changes things."

Unable to smile about it, she nodded. He was right.

But his remark reminded her how temporary this truce was. It wouldn't last—it couldn't, with over 150 years of hatred in their backgrounds. They shouldn't kiss. The minute she reminded herself of that, her pulse jumped and beat at a faster pace. Jake's kisses were the sexiest she had ever experienced, and she had a feeling she was going to feel that way for a long time. She needed to try to forget kissing him, try to stop thinking about it, and above all, resist him from now on. Given their family history, kissing Jake was asking for pure trouble.

Her attention shifted as he drove to where temporary headquarters were set up for firemen. The area was filled with people. There were tents with hastily drawn signs for medical help, for tools, and a desk beneath a tree where volunteers could register to help. Another desk listed emergency help along with a posted list of missing people and other sources of information. She saw another tent with a hastily scribbled, crooked sign that stated Food.

"They almost have another town right here," she said as he parked his pickup in a row of vehicles.

"Well, I see where I need to go. I'll just look for you back here when I'm through." He turned to her. "You're in it now. If you want to quit, you'll have to wait until I'm back to take you to my place."

"Don't worry about me. I'm glad to help, and it looks as if they need it desperately. Let's go." She opened her door to step out.

"See you later," he called and was gone. She could see him moving through the crowd of people because he was taller than most. His broad shoulders made him look capable and reliable. She watched him until she lost sight of him, then lined up at the desk for volunteers. In minutes they had some people she was to drive to the hospital in Persimmon. To her surprise, Jake reappeared. He had a hard hat, a fire-retardant suit, goggles, gloves and a shovel.

"I'm digging ditches. They have some experienced firefighters flying in here, so they're getting more experienced help, which is good. When they let us go, I'll meet you back here. Take care," he said.

She worried about Jake, because the fire was formidable. Then she had to laugh at herself. Since when did she worry about a Reed? Instantly, an unwanted answer popped into her thoughts—since his first kiss. A kiss like no other in her life. A kiss that might be unforgettable. Also, since he saved her life.

Her family would be wild with anger if they knew she was with him. It wouldn't matter to them that he had saved her life. She hoped they didn't even find out about Jake. At least not for a long time. Her two older brothers would plot to beat him up and try to scare him into staying away from her forever. She knew their way of thinking. She hated their interference in her life, and she wanted them to back off. She would be furious if they did anything to Jake, but that would make them think she was really serious about Jake and they had something big between them. Caught between the proverbial rock and a hard place, she just hoped they didn't find out she had even talked to Jake.

Her dad would just be angry, but he wouldn't get involved now. He was getting feeble and wrapped up in his own world, plus he lived far away. To her relief, none of her brothers were in the area any longer, so hopefully they would never even know about Jake.

If she went out with him even just a few times, they would cut her out of the family and never speak to her again—they had been that way about her sister, although Regina didn't know their reactions, because she hadn't ever stayed around for them to snub her.

Her paternal grandparents and her dad had taken Regina out of their wills, ceased trying to communicate with her and told the family to never mention her name in their presence again, that she was no longer a relative as far as they were concerned. She had married a Reed, and to them, she had become a Reed.

Claire felt that the biggest loss was theirs, not Regina's. Sometimes she still hurt when she thought about her sister. Claire had looked up to her and loved her, and she had had so much fun with her when they were young.

She had despised the Reeds for taking her sister from her, blaming all Reeds for the calamity, but over the years she'd gradually begun to process it. Until today. Being with Jake had brought that resentment back. She wondered how bitter he was toward Regina for taking his older brother away from him. She thought about the pain and bitterness she'd felt when her sister had left, and now with Jake, memories were pouring back. They still hurt.

Suddenly she was too busy with the problems at hand and helping people to think about the family feud. She spent the next hours working furiously to help people with whatever they needed.

She worked with other volunteers, finding rides for

people displaced from their homes and lining up places for them to stay. With a furnished car, she took several people back to Persimmon to the hospital.

Time passed swiftly, and then as they moved through the night and into the early morning hours, the stream of people thinned to almost none. Someone thanked her for her help and told her to go home; they would call her if they needed her again.

She turned to find somewhere to wait for Jake when she saw him striding toward her.

He had a purposeful walk that drew her attention. The stubble on his jaw was thick, his black hair was tousled and he had streaks of dirt on his clothes. At the sight of him, her pulse jumped—she was glad to see him. He stopped in front of her.

"Good morning. They're sending some of the volunteers home," he said, his voice firm despite how quietly he spoke. "How about you?"

"The same," she replied. "I was told to go, and they would call if I'm needed again."

"Good. Let's go. Last night more trained firefighters flew in here, and they finally have the fire under control and are beginning to douse it." He jerked his head slightly. "C'mon, we'll go back to my cabin."

"I won't argue with that one," she said, falling into step beside him and keenly aware of his height as he walked beside her.

"Are you tired?" he asked.

She nodded. "Exhausted, really. But I was ready to stay if they needed me."

At his pickup, he held open her door. She slid into the

passenger seat and watched him as he walked around to the driver's side.

"I may sleep all day," Jake said. "If you're hungry, I know an all-night diner if you want to stop and get something."

"I need sleep more than I need food."

"So do I. We'll just drive straight to my cabin and crash then," he said. "Thanks for helping."

"I was glad to do something to help," she answered, too aware of him so close beside her. His disheveled appearance just added to his appeal, and his broad shoulders gave him a look of strength and being capable of getting things done.

Lost in thoughts about Jake, she was silent as he drove back to his cabin. Everything about him amazed her. They had barely spoken in all the years they had been neighbors. Barely spoken until yesterday. Now she responded as if they were longtime friends, which they definitely were not. She figured their time to be civil to each other was definitely limited and that he was being courteous because she had lost her home in the fire. And maybe because of their kiss. That thought stirred another sizzle in her, and she drew a deep breath.

At his house he walked down the hall with her, his boot heels scraping on his hardwood floor. At the door to her suite, he turned to her. "Let's go look, make sure you have everything you need."

She gazed up into his brown eyes. He still had tangled locks of black hair falling on his wide forehead. "I'm fine. I was here yesterday afternoon and I checked. I don't need anything. I'll sleep in one of your T-shirts you loaned me." She looked down at her sooty jeans. "I just want out of these clothes."

"Can I help you there?" he asked, startling her until she saw the twinkle in his eyes, and she laughed as she shook her head.

"I think I can manage all by myself this time," she couldn't resist adding, flirting a little. He was smiling, but when she said, "this time," something flickered in the depth of his eyes.

"I'll remember to ask again," he said, his voice changing and getting deeper with a slight rasp.

"I should resist," she said solemnly and meant it. She shouldn't even flirt with him. She definitely shouldn't kiss him.

"We're entitled to a little fun after the day we've had." He reached out to touch her shoulder, his fingers light as a feather. "Thanks again for helping today," he repeated. "A little help can make a big difference."

She drew a deep breath as she looked into his brown eyes that held unmistakable desire, and her heart drummed. Her pulse jumped because there was no mistaking the hunger in his gaze. He wanted to kiss her. Common sense reminded her that she should turn away right now, ignore the need she felt, resist the intense awareness of his hand on her shoulder, of how close he stood, as well as the consuming look in those midnight eyes holding her in his spell. He smelled like smoke and had smudges on his cheek and shirt, but she didn't care. She wanted his kiss with all her being. She stopped worrying about consequences or the ancient feud.

"Jake," she whispered without even thinking about what she was doing. His arm slipped around her waist and she placed her hand so lightly on his chest, barely touching him, yet conscious of the contact. He was warm, hard and muscular. Her heart raced. "You know we shouldn't," she whispered, yet she leaned slightly toward him. Her lips tingled as her gaze lowered to his mouth.

"Yeah, I know," he answered in a husky voice while at the same time his arm tightened around her and he drew her closer.

"I can't resist you," she whispered again. She tilted her face up, looking at his mouth and then back to his dark gaze. She was hot, tingly, wanting him with all her being.

"Come here," he said in a voice that was the same as a caress. He tightened his arm again to hold her closer as his other hand went behind her head. She had her palm spread on his chest and felt the rhythm of his heart. He was looking at her as if he wanted to devour her.

While her own heart pounded, her lips parted as she stood on tiptoe to turn her mouth up to his. Slipping her arm across his shoulders, she drew his head down to kiss him. The stubble on his jaw was rough and prickly, but she barely noticed. Her heart raced as his lips moved so lightly on hers, and she moaned softly.

She wrapped her arms around his strong body and clung tightly to him. His waist was narrow, his belly flat and hard.

Moaning softly, she thrust her tongue over his. She felt on fire with wanting his hands and mouth all over her. Right now, she was lost in another fabulous, stormy kiss that made her want to be in his arms for hours.

He shifted, running his hand down her back, pulling her tightly against him. She felt his thick erection press against her, and she shivered as he deepened the kiss, fueling her own blaze.

She clung to him, aware of his hand sliding down her back so slowly, slipping down over her bottom.

She tried to hang on to common sense, knowing that if she didn't stop him, they would be in his bed making love soon.

She moved slightly and pushed against him just a bit, but he raised his head to look at her.

Gasping for breath, she stepped back to put space between them. "We can't," she whispered. "We have way too much bad history between us."

Her heart pounded because his dark eyes were filled with desire, his lips slightly red from kissing her. She longed for him, wanting his hands and mouth all over her, but she was still able to pull her wits together enough to know that if she wasn't careful, she would upset her solitary life and get hurt badly, maybe a hurt that would last a lifetime. Jake was unique, desirable. At the same time, there was no way to ignore the fact that he was at the center of the feud she had grown up living in daily.

"We better say good-night," she whispered, turning away from him before they kissed again.

Standing behind her, he leaned close, whispering in her ear, "Claire."

She stopped as his arm circled her waist and he drew her back against him, his hard erection pressing against her bottom while he showered wet kisses on her nape and moved to her ear to let his tongue follow its curve.

She longed to turn into his arms and kiss him again.

At the same time, she knew she should move away and stop before she was naked in his arms in his bed.

His warm breath blew on her ear, lightly tickling her, so sensual and heightening her desire.

"Claire, I want you," he whispered, and she trembled, fighting an inner battle, wanting to turn to kiss him, knowing she should step into her suite and stop risking her heart.

"I can't," she whispered, finally slipping out of his arms. He let her go, and she didn't look back.

She closed the door to her suite, leaned against it and closed her eyes, remembering his kiss, his strong arms around her, his consideration and care for her. She was drawn to him, and she shouldn't be. Not in the slightest. Her entire family despised him and all his kin. She would get hurt, because if she fell in love with him, they could never have even a sliver of a future—not even casual dating. He, too, had plenty of relatives here who would give him a bad time and be dreadful to her. "We can't," she whispered, knowing he couldn't hear her. She stood there against the door until she heard his boots as he walked away down the hall.

She still felt warm all over, recalling his hands and mouth on her, his body against her and his erection clearly ready for love.

Would she get through the next few days without losing her heart to him? She couldn't answer her question.

She needed to go to town, get some clothes, find another place to live and tell Jake goodbye before it hurt too much to walk away from him.

Even though they were neighbors she had never really known him, barely had any kind of dealings with him except when they had taken each other to court to fight over a ranch problem.

All that had changed, and if they kept kissing, she would be deeply in love with him. He had been kind, considerate and incredibly sexy.

She knew, if she wanted, she could go to bed with Jake now. They could make love, and it might be the best sex of her life. She didn't attract men, didn't date, didn't party except on rare occasions with friends in Dallas. So why not have a fling with Jake? Have sex with him? She might not ever have that choice again.

Because the risk would be falling in love with him—a deep, forever kind of love that he would never return. Love was doomed between them unless they did what her sister and his brother had done. If they both fell in love and married, would she want the kind of life her sister had—being forever in exile from her family?

Did she really want to run that risk?

She shook her head and whispered, "No."

Both choices were not what she wanted. She didn't want Jake to break her heart. She wouldn't want to marry him and get cut off from the grandparents, whom she loved. There were some in her family she really hoped to reconnect with—her dad and her brothers. There were others she deeply loved. Claire shook her head. She didn't want that kind of outcast life. Also, she knew Jake wasn't a marrying man. He'd had plenty of women in his life, and they just passed on through and were gone.

She had to keep her distance from Jake because he could be a heartbreaker, but right now she needed his help and a place to stay near her property.

Showering, she felt relieved to wash away the smoke smell and get it out of her hair. She washed her undergarments, hanging them in the bathroom to dry. Her jeans and shirt were saturated with smoke, so she washed them, too. Then, she put on one of Jake's T-shirts that she would sleep in.

Too late she realized that was a mistake. Inhaling his scent, she imagined the white cotton was the gentle touch of his hands on her skin. Right then she knew that despite being exhausted, she'd never sleep tonight.

Surprisingly, the next time she opened her eyes, sunshine spilled through the window. Momentarily, she was disoriented, and then she remembered she was at Jake Reed's cabin. As she thought about her home that had burned, a familiar emptiness filled her over her loss. Memories of the past twenty-four hours swept over her, but memories of Jake's kisses were more vivid than all others except her burned home.

She couldn't keep him out of her thoughts. She recalled being in his arms, held against his chest with his mouth on hers. Just remembering his kiss made her warm and tingly. She had to stop thinking about him. With a rustle of covers, she sat up and swung her legs over the side of the bed.

All her clothes were dry except her jeans. She stared at them in consternation, because she had to wear them, and she didn't want to wear wet jeans.

She dressed in her bra and panties and Jake's biggest T-shirt, which came down to midthigh level and covered her more than a swimsuit would have. She slipped her feet into her sneakers and grabbed the damp jeans.

Hopefully, Jake would be occupied with breakfast, out doing chores already or something away from this part of the house and she could get her jeans into the dryer without encountering him. It wouldn't take more than twenty minutes to finish drying them in a machine.

She opened her door quietly and looked up and down the hall. To her relief, it was empty, and she hurried to his laundry room, flung her jeans into the dryer and in minutes was back in her suite with the door closed. She let out her breath, glad she hadn't seen him. Now if she could just get her dry jeans back, she would be in good shape for the day.

Twenty minutes later, she had her hair in a fresh braid, and she looked down the hall. Again, the hall was clear, so she raced to the laundry room, grabbed her warm jeans from the dryer—and almost ran into Jake as he came out of his kitchen.

Five

"Hey," Jake said, catching her shoulder when they bumped. "Sorry, I didn't see—" He stopped talking as his gaze traveled to her feet and back to her face and she saw the change in him.

"I had to dry my jeans," she said, in a breathless voice. "I washed all my clothes last night, and my jeans didn't dry. This was all I had to wear."

"Oh my," he said. The way he said it and the way he looked at her made her forget her clothes. All she could think about were his hands on her, his warm body against hers and the fact that she wasn't fully dressed. Stepping back slightly, he looked at her. His gaze went over her again, slowly, making her think about his hands and mouth going where he looked now.

"With legs like you have, you shouldn't ever hide

them," he said, his gaze lifting to meet hers. "I have never seen you in shorts on your ranch. I've never seen your legs before. Not like this."

"Well, no, you haven't," she said, barely aware what she was saying to him. "You haven't because neither one of us ever gets close to our mutual boundary if we can avoid it, and I don't wear shorts to work on the ranch. Rattlesnakes, for one thing. Cockleburs, weeds, sunburn, thorny bushes for others."

"You have the best-looking legs in Texas."

She had to laugh at that one, and it helped put her more at ease. "Thank you, kind sir. But you need to get your eyes checked. I have scars from my barrel-racing days. I don't think my legs are quite that spectacular, but right now I need to cover them with my jeans, so if you'll excuse me," she said, hoping to hurry past him. She took a step closer to pass him.

When he didn't move, she looked up and met his dark, hot gaze. She couldn't get her breath, and her heart pounded. Desire filled his brown eyes. She had never before in her life felt as wanted by a man as she did right now with Jake.

When his gaze lowered to her mouth, her pulse jumped.

"Claire," he said softly, his voice coaxing and filled with so much obvious longing that the tension she felt heightened.

"I need to go," she whispered, more to herself than him. "Jake, we've got to stop this. We don't have a future. We can't even have a lunch date. We can't go out together, and kisses just add to the problem."

"I don't think so," he said, sounding as if he meant it.

She shook her head. "Don't look at me like that."

She took a couple of steps to the side, and he placed his fingers lightly on her arm, barely touching her. "Wait a minute," he whispered.

As she paused, she drew a deep breath. She was only inches from him, starting to pass him, and he had barely touched her, but she stopped in her tracks and his voice played over her like a caress.

"Jake, don't hold me," she whispered. "You know I can't resist you."

"I'm not holding you," he answered, slipping his arm around her waist lightly. "You're free to walk away and you know it. Admit it, Claire. You want to kiss as much as I do."

"I might want to, but I know we shouldn't. I can't stop thinking about my brothers. I don't want you hurt by them." She didn't add that she didn't want a broken heart. He had left some of those behind. She knew that much about his past, and she didn't want that pain in her life.

"I'm definitely not afraid of your brothers, and they won't hurt me, I promise you. They're not in town anyway and don't know what the hell is going on here."

"We can't kiss. I'm not even dressed."

"You think I don't know that? And I've never heard that for a reason to avoid kissing," he said with amusement in his voice as he leaned in to place light kisses on her throat. "You're gorgeous, Claire," he whispered, and all the amusement was gone from his voice. His earnest compliment drew her closer, and his wet kisses on her neck made her tremble. She ran her fingers into his hair, and when he looked up at her, she found his eyes hooded with an undeniable desire. A desire she knew was reflected in her own gaze.

"This is so foolish. I'm vulnerable and you'll break my heart," she whispered as his head dipped down and his lips continued their foray on her throat. She didn't know to whom she was saying those words—him or herself. "You're the real danger. Not my brothers. My heart is at risk."

He ran one hand so lightly on her nape, caressing her and arousing her, making her long for more. She moaned as an inner battle raged between what she wanted to do and what she knew she should do.

She should walk away from him. She was going to get hurt emotionally because if they kept touching and kissing, she would be in his arms, in his bed, and, worse, she would fall in love with him.

She couldn't afford that. He would never love her in return, and even if he did, they could never, ever have a future.

She didn't want an affair with Jake, and it would never be more than an affair, because he was not a marrying man. He'd never even kept his series of women in his life for long. They were seen with him for months, and then they were gone.

Even as she argued with herself, she thought about his kisses, to-die-for kisses that set her heart pounding, that made her want hours of sex and his hands and his mouth all over her.

Could she stand being one of the many women whose hearts he had broken in this little corner of Texas?

She knew the answer and knew she should walk

away right now, but then he slipped his hand so lightly beneath the too-big T-shirt, his hand caressing her bare back and leaving a trail of fire that nearly consumed her.

His hand slipped around her waist, drifting up beneath the big T-shirt, pushing away her bra and then cupping her breast. She sighed with pleasure as his thumb stroked her nipple, and for a moment she gave herself over to his loving. She was vulnerable, lonely, hurt by the loss of her house, and Jake was stirring all the longings she tried to suppress, the craving for a strong man to hold her, to make love to her. And she could never find one better than Jake.

"You're gorgeous," he whispered. He cupped both breasts in his hands, toying with her, making her want more of him.

That nagging inner voice wouldn't be denied, however. Its warning echoed in her head until she wriggled away and stepped back, looking up at him and shaking her head. "We can't do this. I'll get hurt."

"I don't ever want to hurt you, Claire. And believe me, you're not going to fall in love with me because we kissed a few times," he whispered, his tongue tracing the curve of her ear.

"Ah, Jake, you know I want you," she whispered. They looked into each other's eyes, and she could no longer refuse him. She wanted his kiss. And he was right—surely she could kiss him once, twice more without falling in love and breaking her heart. She stood on tiptoe, pulled his head down and placed her mouth on his. Her tongue touched his, and then she was lost in his kiss as he wrapped his arm tightly around her, holding her pressed against him with one arm.

His other hand slipped down her back and then inside her lacy panties, over her bare bottom. She heard him inhale deeply, and then he slipped the panties off her hips, letting them fall to the floor around her ankles. While he kissed her, his tongue stroking her, building desire, he caught the hem of the T-shirt and drew it over her head to toss it aside. He stepped back to cup her breasts again and to look at her.

"You're absolutely beautiful," he said in a gravelly, raspy voice. His thumbs played so lightly over her nipples.

Lost in waves that rocked her, she clung to him with her eyes closed as need built from his hands so lightly on her breasts. She realized soon there would be no going back.

You'll get hurt.

That inner warning wouldn't be silenced, no matter how much she wanted to ignore it. Finally, she pushed against him and opened her eyes. The hungry look in his eyes made her tremble, but she kept her resolve. "Jake, I'm sorry, but I'm not ready for this."

Yanking up her clothes, she stepped out of his embrace, trying to avoid looking into his dark eyes that enticed her and melted her resistance.

She realized he wasn't arguing with her or trying to stop her, and she was glad because she knew she couldn't stand one more minute of his seduction. Gathering her things as fast as she could, she wrapped the big T-shirt around her and walked away from him without looking back.

* * *

Dressed and ready for the day, she still couldn't get him out of her mind. Jake—a Reed.

There was no denying she wanted his loving, his kisses, his hands all over her, his male body against hers. With him, she knew she'd have the best sex of her life. But how could she make love to him, fall for him and forget him, when she'd never be able to really get away from him?

He had a big ranch next door to hers—they were both permanently tied to the sprawling Texas land they owned. One day she would have to live next door to him and watch him marry someone else.

She went over it all again in her mind and knew what she had to do. She had to fight the temptation. She had to get out of his cabin and off his property.

"Jake, there's no place for you in my life," she whispered as she walked out of her borrowed room to find him for a ride to Persimmon. She had to go to town and get some clothes.

She found him in the kitchen. The second she walked in, he turned around to her. His gaze swept over her, and she felt her pulse jump.

Jake crossed the room, approaching her, and with every step nearer, her heartbeat quickened. He had the sleeves rolled up on his blue denim shirt that was tucked into tight faded jeans—working jeans. He had on boots, and it took her breath away to look at him.

And then he was only a few feet away, standing close, smiling at her, his hungry gaze on her, and all the determination she'd felt when she'd made the trek from her suite seemed to buckle. In its place came one question: People survived broken hearts, didn't they?

Jake's gaze slid over her, and he drew a deep breath. In tight jeans, a red T-shirt and boots, she looked fantastic. "You look great in those clothes, but I can understand wanting a change. I'll take you to town," he said. His voice deepened and became huskier in reaction to looking at her. Since when did he find his neighbor sexy, appealing and absolutely fascinating? He knew exactly when—since that fabulous, to-die-for kiss that he didn't think he would ever forget. And each one after that first kiss had been just as overwhelming and stunning.

"Jake, on the way into Persimmon to get clothes, I'd like to go look at my house. There might be some things in fireproof boxes that made it through the fire. I'd like to go see. There are a couple of boxes I had money in."

"I hope not a lot of money."

"No."

"Ever hear of a bank?"

She gave him a look, and he noticed the moment when she realized he was teasing her.

"Ever hear of minding your own business?" she replied, and he laughed.

"Let's get breakfast and then we'll go," he said. "I've got sliced strawberries and blueberries. I can scramble eggs and we can have toast," he said, but his thoughts weren't on breakfast as she walked closer. He couldn't stop thinking about how much he wanted to make love to Claire. How could her kiss totally change his feelings for her?

It took all his willpower to concentrate on getting breakfast on the table and keep his hands to himself.

She helped him, putting plates on the table, filling cups of coffee and orange juice. When they were ready, he held out her chair, his hands brushing her so slightly, yet he was aware of the contact.

As they ate, she was quiet, but he couldn't miss the glances she'd flick in his direction when she no doubt thought he wasn't looking. The look in her eyes was not that of someone who viewed him as an enemy. The look in her eyes made him want to drop everything, take her into his arms and kiss her. He ate his breakfast, noticed that she didn't eat much of hers, and then he stopped her from trying to clean the kitchen.

"Betsy comes today to clean, so leave the dishes. Let's head out to your ranch and then go to Persimmon so you can buy some duds."

"That will be a welcome relief," she said. "I dread seeing my house, but there were some metal containers that had important things, so I want to see how they fared and maybe pick them up."

"They could be too hot to move yet. I can get some guys to go get them if I can't get them into the pickup. We'll see," he said, doubtful she had anything that made it through the fire. "It may still be smoldering, and we need to be careful because some areas are probably still burning and can just flare right back up."

"I'll make it quick. I don't think it'll take long to look."

He nodded, looking at her thick braid and wondering how she would look with her hair loose. He realized he was lost in thoughts about running his hands through the thick red hair, seeing it splayed against his pillow, and he turned away, shooing her out of the kitchen. He had a feeling if he didn't, they might not get to town this morning.

They drove across land that still smoldered, and occasionally they passed a small fire, flames still flaring where there was something left to burn. Some structures were either completely gone or were partially burned and still standing but looking ready to collapse.

"Damn, it looks like a war zone. Are you sure you want to keep going?"

"Yes, please. I had two boxes I used for safes. I want to get those. There's money and papers I need."

"Okay. Make this fast. Fires are unpredictable."

"I'll hurry," she answered and lapsed back into silence. He knew she was hurting and this drive to her ranch wasn't going to do her any good that he could see, but if she could salvage something, he would help. He glanced at his watch, because they weren't going to stay long. He'd bring her back if necessary, but he didn't like being here and felt certain they shouldn't be breathing the fumes.

When they entered her ranch, the damage was extensive. Her barn, outbuildings, employees' houses—all were in smoldering ruins. And then her house came into view, and he heard her groan and he hurt for her. There was nothing left of her house except mounds of ashes, burned wood that looked as if a breeze would crumble it. He knew how he would feel if it was his home.

He pulled close and got out of his pickup as she went ahead, handing her a bandanna that she put over her mouth. He had given her gloves and had a pair for himself, because he could glimpse little flares of flickering flames under the rubbish. They both wore boots. He hoped she would hurry, because it wasn't a good place to be.

"Do you want me to put the containers I find into my pickup?"

"If possible, yes. If it takes two to move something, just let me know."

He walked through the rubble. There were metal containers, some too big for her to handle, one that took both of them. She called him to another one.

"I need this one. This is the main one. It's got money and papers," she said, and he looked down at a large metal box with handles on both ends and a dent in the lid. Recognizing the box, he stared at it. "I'll be damned," he said without realizing he had spoken out loud.

"Turn this over," he told her, taking hold of one of the handles, because he knew it was heavy and would take both of them to turn and get it into his pickup. Anger washed over him as he bent to roll it over.

Jake looked at dents and scrapes across one part of the bottom. It was covered in ashes and burned black bits of wood. He swept his arm across it and brushed it off, peering at letters that someone had tried to scratch over while his heartbeat quickened, and his anger increased.

Just as he suspected. This big metal box had belonged to his dad.

Six

"What are you doing?" she asked. "This has money in it and some of my important papers. This is the main container. My dad kept papers in it and guns. He left it for me. I want to take it with us."

Anger made Jake hot, and he looked up at her. "This metal box used to belong to us. My dad's name is scratched in the bottom side. He kept money in it until it was stolen," he said, feeling a deep flash of anger, because her dad and brothers must have been the thieves who robbed his dad. Suddenly he was caught up once again in the feud with her family, remembering that his dad always claimed Claire's father and brothers had been behind the theft.

"This can't be yours," she said, a note of impatience in her voice. "This belonged to my dad. He had it before I went to college. He said it was my grandfather's."

"I think not," Jake said, trying to brush off more debris. "Someone has tried to scratch over a name. We'll take this and clean it up, but I know this box. The corner was dented like that when we had it because a couple of guys who worked for my dad dropped an anvil on it."

As Jake's anger intensified, he remembered times he'd fought with her brothers. He remembered the things her dad had done when her family owned the ranch. Fences cut, livestock stolen—her family was smart enough to never keep the livestock, but his father always thought her dad and brothers rustled cattle and sold them, moving them quickly so they wouldn't get caught.

He thought they did it to be ornery, not for the money at all.

"This is my family's box. Underneath all those scratches, I'll bet I find the name Reed," he said. "Help me lift it." She glared at him as she grabbed a handle and they hoisted it into his pickup.

"Let's get the rest of these metal containers," he said, hurrying through the debris and coughing from the fumes. Anger rocked him, and he could remember other incidents of vandalism that had happened years earlier to their ranch, things his dad had blamed on the Blakes. Jake needed to get himself away from Claire and remember the feud, because he might not be able to trust her any more than he trusted her dad or her brothers. She was a Blake just as much as the rest of her family. She might be far more like them than she admitted. He didn't want to get tangled up emotionally with some woman who had the same blood in her veins as her dad and those thugs that were her two older brothers.

Angry and grim, he worked in silence, gathering up three more containers. "Let's go. We'll come back for more, if need be. No one else is going to come get this stuff. Not out here. Let's get out of here and go where we can breathe fresh air. I promised to take you to Persimmon, but we're going back to the ranch first to wash this stuff off."

"I agree," she said, coughing and climbing into his pickup.

With both of them coughing, they rode without conversation, and once they were away from her place and all the smoke and debris, he took off the bandanna and tossed it into the back. She did the same. They remained silent all the way to his place. When he parked, he turned to her.

"Let's get that box out on the ground. I'm going to shower first, and then I'll clean it up and see if we can read the name that someone has tried to scrape away."

"All right," she said, glaring at him. He felt certain the box had belonged to his family, and he hoped he could prove it. He wondered why she was insisting they hadn't stolen the box, unless she thought her family would never break the law and steal something.

He knew better, but he didn't want to tell her, because she might not know some of the nasty things they had done. She acted like she didn't know. If he learned she had ever helped them steal and do things to his family... His anger rose as he thought about that. He wondered just where she fit in and how much like them she was. Even if she didn't know all they had done, he didn't want to find her appealing. They had too much history between them. And he had a feeling the vandalism and the thefts had been directed only at his family because of the old feud. He had never heard anyone else complaining of vandalism or theft by any Blakes. The old anger that her dad and her older brothers could stir came back full force, and he remembered why he would get so angry at them. Far too often, they wiggled out of blame for anything they had done.

"We have to get out of these smelly clothes. I want to throw mine in your washing machine," she said. "I can't wear these to town or even in your house. I'm getting the hose to wash some of this off out here before I go inside. You may want to do the same."

"Good idea," he said. "I'll get the hose." He wanted to get washed up and then wash that box. He was absolutely certain it would have the name Reed carved into it, and he couldn't wait to show her.

He turned on the hose, walking back to hand it to her first. "Go ahead. I'm taking off my shirt."

"I'm sure you won't mind if I do the same. I'll have as much on as I would if I were in my swimsuit, and I can't stand this smell any longer," she said, placing the hose in the flower bed. With her back turned, she yanked off her boots and socks and then pulled off her red T-shirt.

The moment she did, his mouth went dry, and he forgot the fire, the smoke, the smell, the metal box and everything else except looking at her. Her waist was tiny, her skin looked smooth and she looked soft and irresistible. She kept on the jeans and ran the hose over herself and then turned to hold the hose out to him. When she turned around, she still wore her jeans, but above her waist, she wore only her lacy white bra, which was wet and clinging. Her skimpy bra revealed lush curves that made him instantly aroused, wanting to reach for her.

She was breathtaking and incredibly sexy. She splashed water from the hose over her full breasts and he fought to keep from walking closer, taking her into his arms and kissing her senseless while he caressed those gorgeous breasts. As she ran the hose over herself, she had her eyes closed. "Oh, that is such a relief," she said softly to herself.

An intense urge swept him to close the slight distance between them and take her in his arms. He wanted to step close and remove her bra. He wanted to fill his hands with her full breasts that looked so soft.

"I'm sorry to go first," she said with her eyes still squeezed tightly closed while she held the hose above her head and let water shower over her.

He yanked off his shirt, tossing it aside as he walked to her, wrapped one arm around her narrow waist while he took the hose from her hand and ran it swiftly over himself and tossed it aside.

Startled, her eyes flew open. "Jake?" She looked up at him, and he saw her expression change.

"You're absolutely gorgeous," he said. He was already breathless. Eagerness made him shake, and he was rock hard.

She blinked. "I thought you were angry with me," she said.

He didn't answer but gazed into her big green eyes and saw the transformation in her expression as her lips parted and her gaze shifted to his mouth. Her hands rested on his chest, and she slipped one arm across his shoulders while she ran her other hand over him, tangling her fingers in his chest hair.

His heart pounded, and he could barely get his breath. He unfastened her bra and pushed it down so he could cup her breast in his hand. She gasped and closed her eyes while she leaned closer and tightened her arm around him.

She was so incredibly soft. Her full breast filled his hand. Her eyes fluttered open, and she looked at his mouth as she drew his head down. He placed his lips on hers, his tongue slowly stroking hers as he caressed her breast.

She moaned softly, moving her hips against him.

For minutes, eons, seconds—first it seemed long and then it seemed short—he kissed her and caressed her. She was wet, warm and bare. He wanted her with all his being. He was aroused, wanting her more than he could remember desiring any woman ever.

He wanted to be inside her, to make love to her and forget the consequences.

Suddenly she wiggled slightly, leaning away, and then she stepped out of his embrace and shook her head. "Jake, stop. We were at each other's throats only a few minutes ago, the family feud still alive and strong. I can't do this. You're a Reed. We're not going to tangle our lives and emotions," she said, stepping back, grabbing up her shirt and holding it in front of her as she raced away from him, unlocking the door with the key he had given her and disappearing inside the house.

"Dammit," he said quietly as he let her go. He ached with wanting her. He wanted to bury himself in her soft body, to have her fiery, bone-melting, unforgettable kisses.

He groaned as if he had a terrible wound. She was right. They had over a century of feuding between their families, and he suspected there would be plenty more fussing between Claire and him when he cleaned up that metal box, because he was absolutely certain it would have the Reed name cut into it.

Even as he made the decision to let her go and thought about the feud, their differences and the anger between them with more to come, he wanted her. He craved her, wanted her in his arms. He was ready to make love to her and couldn't keep images of her gorgeous body out of his thoughts. At the moment he didn't give a damn about the feud, the metal box, their differences or the future. He just wanted to make love with her.

He ached to caress her lush, soft, fantastic breasts. She was breathtaking, beautiful, the sexiest woman he had ever kissed. And she wasn't trying to be sexy. What if she wanted to be? That thought could send him up in flames, and he tried to shift his thinking.

"Damn," he muttered under his breath, clenching his fists. He had to ignore her, forget kissing her. "Impossible," he whispered to himself. He would never forget kissing her. He couldn't possibly forget the feel of her breasts in his hands.

She had him tied in knots. They had spent their lives disliking each other, fighting each other or ignoring each other until their first kiss—that sexy kiss like no other he had ever experienced.

He groaned, grabbed the hose and let it shower cold

water over him, wishing he could wash away memories of her body, her mouth, her soft breasts, her kisses, but he knew that he would never forget them.

How he wished some woman would come along who could wipe her out of his memory.

Claire Blake. A Blake with a family of relatives who had fought his for over a century. He had to forget her.

He knew he never would. Not in this lifetime. Worse, he wondered if he would ever stop longing to kiss her.

Swearing quietly, he tossed down the hose, which hadn't really cooled him. He turned off the water, gathered his shirt and boots, and headed for the house. She had hooked the screen door, and he couldn't get in. He rang the bell and waited.

Finally, she came to the door, and he wanted to groan, to gnash his teeth, to ask her if this was a new form of torture that she was using because of the feud.

She had a towel wrapped around her head, hiding her hair, and another wrapped around her gorgeous body—a body that had to be very naked beneath that green towel that matched her eyes.

"Sorry, I didn't intend to lock you out of your house," she said, her cheeks turning pink as she gave him a long, intense stare and he wondered what she was thinking.

She was looking so gorgeous, so appealing, that he couldn't find his voice. What was wrong with him?

She must have picked up on his discomfort, because she suddenly looked self-conscious. "This wasn't such a good idea," she said. "I'll see you later. I need to get dressed." Then she turned to walk away, and he watched her go, that towel clinging damply to her bottom, her long, bare legs revealing that the lower part of her was as gorgeous and sexy as the upper part. Her legs were marvelous. Long, long legs that he would like to feel wrapped around him.

He groaned and closed his eyes to try to stop thinking about having sex with her. He opened his eyes quickly. He wanted to look at her as long as he had a chance. She would come back all covered in something that would completely hide her fabulous body.

He went to his suite, closing the door. From today on, he would never see Claire the way he had before. Every inch of his being wanted her in his cabin and in his arms again. In his bed.

He swore as he got ready to shower and walked into his big bathroom. It was an architectural gem, with a curved shower, huge sunken tub and a glass wall that afforded him an unobstructed view of the outside, though no one could see in. One wall held a built-in floor-to-ceiling tank of exotic tropical fish, while a floor-to-ceiling mirror comprised another wall. Right now, he saw only the shower. He walked into it and turned on the cold water. "Do your stuff," he said to the cold-water faucet. "I have to forget her. A Blake. I don't want to entangle my life with her. As if she would let me. Oh damn. How long will it take me to forget her when she lives on the neighboring ranch? And that is my family's box out there, and it was her thieving dad and brothers that stole it from my family."

Jake shook his head. He could never be friends with her, never trust her. He shouldn't ever kiss her again, not even touch her. He'd be polite, let her stay at his cabin because he had already issued the invitation, but she would soon move on, and when she did, he needed to go back to the way it always had been—not speaking to each other, never socializing, absolutely never kissing.

He groaned. Why was the woman whose family had spent lifetimes feuding with his the one with the hottest kisses he had ever known?

He shook his head. He had to avoid her. She might make that easy for him to do, because she'd be angry as a bear when he took that metal box away from her.

He felt another hot flash of anger over the stolen box. Her brothers had probably stolen it and given it to their dad, who'd kept it and everything in it. He thought about calling his father and telling him, but his dad was probably happily fishing and enjoying his retirement—there was no point in bringing up a bad subject that still didn't have a good solution.

Meanwhile, he needed to get himself away from Claire. They had no future together. So why couldn't he stop thinking of how she looked in that green towel? Damn. The cold water had done nothing to help him.

Claire dried her hair and stared at herself in the mirror, but she didn't see her reflection. She saw Jake's dark eyes on her, remembered his hands moving lightly over her, remembered his mouth on hers as he kissed her.

Her heartbeat raced. She shouldn't be staying at his cabin, shouldn't have undressed in front of him. But the fumes from the fires had permeated her clothing and took her breath. She thought if she still wore her bra, she would be as covered as she always was in a swimsuit.

It must have been a psychological thing, because he had changed the instant she had revealed her bra. For a moment there outside, she'd been caught up in memories of his hands caressing her and the hungry look in his eyes.

With a shake of her head, she tried to stop thinking about Jake. They didn't have a future. Their families had fought since before Texas was a state. And he had accused her family of stealing that big metal box that belonged to her dad. It was her family's box. It had survived the fire, and she wanted it. It was rightfully hers. Her brothers had done some bad things, she knew, but they wouldn't steal.

She felt anger, but it wasn't as strong as other feelings: hunger for his kisses, yearning for his arms around her, for his hands caressing her. Despite everything, she wanted to be in his arms again. She moaned softly, desiring him, knowing she shouldn't, that she had to forget him and banish these taunting memories once and for all. And she needed to move out of his cabin as soon as she could and put distance between them. She looked at her palatial surroundings, the big bedroom with an elegant canopied four-poster bed that she suspected was an antique, the antique mirror with an elegant carved frame. *Cabin* was not the right description for his home in the woods. It was a castle. But it was Jake's, and as much as she reveled in its beauty, she had to leave it.

She didn't think her brothers had stolen that box from him or his family. That would be breaking the law, and they didn't do that. It was just a big metal box, and there were probably millions that looked just like it. There were scratches on it, but no readable names. It would have been obvious if her brothers had stolen it. They would have bragged about it eventually.

She was angry that Jake had insisted from the first second he saw the box that it had belonged to his family.

She shouldn't have gotten so chummy with him. She shouldn't even be staying with him, but she'd never made friends with neighboring ranchers and had nowhere else to go. Her friends were in Dallas, friends she had made growing up, friends of her family, neighbors she'd had in town.

She considered her employees friends, but with this fire, they had terrible problems, too. They needed her help probably more than she needed theirs.

She and Jake were part of feuding families, and that wasn't going to change. The metal box was just one issue. There would constantly be other issues, because they saw life in different ways, and they didn't like each other's relatives.

She knew she was vulnerable because of her isolated lifestyle. She didn't often go to Dallas, where she had friends and at least some social life, but on the ranch, she was alone, in charge, and that made a difference in her relations with everyone who worked for her. Particularly the guys.

And then came Jake. Never had kisses excited her the way his had…

But he definitely wasn't the man for her—a Reed, like the other Reeds.

She should get out of his house, go into Dallas to her condo and never look back. But how could she do that when she was needed at the ranch? Her home had been totally destroyed. She had called her insurance agent briefly, but he couldn't do anything while the area was still burning and off-limits. She'd called the sheriff, her

employees, her builder—the list was long. She had to
stay and, once the fire was totally out, work with people
to get her land cleared and, eventually, her house rebuilt.

There were so many things to do, but dominating
her thoughts were memories of being in Jake's arms,
holding him and kissing him as if they shared the last
kisses of their lives.

"No," she whispered, shaking her head. She wanted
to shut off the memories, stop thinking about him and
his kisses and his hands on her, incredibly gentle, sexy
and breathtaking. She needed to move on with her life
and get back to her routine, where Jake had no part in
her day.

But right now, that wasn't going to happen.

At least not as long as she was living in his house,
kissing him, spending time with him and getting to
know him and getting more obligated to him. She was
wearing one of his shirts right now. How was she going
to get free of him when she needed to stay in the area,
take care of her business and live at his house because
she had none?

She shook her head again and raked her fingers
through her hair. She had to get Jake out of her thoughts.
She was sure when she was out of his house and away
from him, she would be able to bank these memories
of him. She had to, because he was consuming all her
thoughts now.

She groaned, tossed her head to get her long red
braid away from her face and tried to think about what
she needed to do, getting out a list she had made and
retrieving her phone. She went to a desk in her room,
got a notebook and her phone, and called her insurance

agent to talk to him again about her ranch house. As she waited, she glanced down at a picture on the desk. It was in an old-fashioned wooden frame with flowers and held an old black-and-white picture of a little boy. She picked it up and looked at it and recognized the tousled black hair—this must be one of Jake's childhood pictures. He'd been a cute little kid. She stared at it. "You're messing up my life," she said. "Don't kiss me again."

"I can't make that promise," came a familiar deep voice behind her.

Seven

"Good grief, don't sneak up on me," Claire exclaimed, feeling her cheeks flush with embarrassment at him overhearing what she'd said about his kisses.

He looked amused with a faint smile as he came into the room. "I don't think I was too sneaky in my boots. They make a bit of noise on the wood floors," he said, and she could hear the laughter in his voice. She knew he was teasing, but he was annoying her again, and her embarrassment deepened.

"Well, I didn't hear you, and I wish you hadn't heard me."

He kept walking toward her, and her pulse beat faster as he came within inches and tilted her chin up with his finger. She felt opposing reactions—she was annoyed that he was laughing, but she was turned on by his nearness. He was inches away, and that made her heart race and made her want him to lean close and kiss her even though she shouldn't. She was accustomed to controlling a lot of things and the people in her life. She couldn't do anything about the weather and fires, but people she could usually manage. But she couldn't manage Jake. He didn't work for her. He was independent, doing what he wanted to do, and he was a wild card in her life. She didn't know what he would do next. And she was far too drawn to him physically when she should avoid him, because they were still and forever would be feuding neighbors. How had she thought they could be friends? They were steeped in their family feud that would never change.

"You know, if looks could kill, I'd be stretched out on the floor," he said, and she heard the laughter in his voice that just made her more embarrassed and more angry.

"I think we need a lot more distance between us," she said, but the words came out breathlessly and she was lost gazing into his dark eyes that made her heart beat even faster and her desire more obvious. She couldn't get her breath because she knew he was going to kiss her, and she knew she was going to kiss him in return when she shouldn't. She should resist and get a wall between them.

She couldn't stop the anger she felt toward him, but desire was there just as strong. She couldn't understand her own reactions to him. She had never felt this way about any other man before. And then she didn't care. She just wanted his kiss, and her gaze went to his mouth as his arm slipped around her waist and he drew her to her feet.

His lips brushed hers lightly. She moaned softly, winding her arm around his neck and leaning into him, feeling his strong body against her. His fantastic body. Her heart pounded as she kissed him in return. "I wasn't going to do this ever again," she whispered.

"Yeah, I know," he said as he brushed another light kiss on her lips and then her ear. "I wasn't going to do this again, either," he whispered in her ear, his warm breath tickling her, making her want his mouth on hers more than ever. "You want to kiss me as badly as I want to kiss you."

"You and I are bitter enemies, Jake," she said, knowing she meant those words as a reminder to herself as much as to him. Even as she declared them enemies, she ran her fingers into his thick hair and brushed a kiss on his mouth. She should step away, stop him now, but she wanted him with all her being. From the moment he touched her to slip his arm around her, it didn't matter that he was a Reed. It didn't matter that she was angry with him. Her decision to avoid kissing him had vanished like smoke in the wind.

What was important was that she was in his arms and he was showering her with light kisses, and in a minute, they would really kiss, another one of his heart-shattering kisses that she wondered if she would ever get over. At this moment that's all she wanted, more than anything else.

"We've always been enemies, but there's one place where we're in sync, compatible, consumed with mutual desire and intent. Right here. In each other's arms,"

he whispered, showering kisses on her face and throat.
"You want me. I know you do. I can feel it, Claire."
As he talked and kissed her lightly, he caught the red
T-shirt in his hands and pulled it off to toss it away.

"Oh, Jake," she whispered, and he covered her
mouth, stopping her protest that was only a whisper.
Her arm was tight around his waist, and her other hand
was tangled in his hair.

She moaned softly, longing raging for all of him.
Common sense was a dim whisper, warning her that
she was going to regret every minute of kissing and
caressing him and letting him kiss and fondle her. She
knew she should stop him now before she was hope-
lessly lost and in love with him and needing his hands
and mouth and body as part of her life.

"Jake, I'm not going to do this."

"You want to kiss as much as I do," he whispered,
still showering kisses over her breasts as he unfastened
her bra and tossed it away. He straightened to cup her
breasts in his large, warm hands, and he was incredibly
gentle, stroking her nipples so lightly with his thumbs,
slow, light circles around the pink tips, stirring sizzles
that she felt to her very core while he gazed at her with
obvious desire.

"You're gorgeous, Claire. Absolutely beautiful, so
perfect and soft," he said in a gravelly voice, his words
just a whisper, but she heard him.

"You can't imagine what you do to me. I want you
in my arms, in my bed," he said, still caressing her
breasts while he leaned down to trail kisses down her
throat.

Her heart pounded. Desire swamped her, heating

her until she felt as if she stood in a blaze of fire. His hands, his mouth, his words, his kisses—all of them were seduction.

She longed to touch him, to kiss him, to have his hands and mouth on her. She wished he would keep kissing her and never stop.

She closed her eyes for an instant, ignoring the warnings that were clamoring in her thoughts, just yielding to his loving, letting her hands roam over his hard body. Only for a moment, she promised herself, and then she would stop him. She had to if she was going to survive. He would break her heart into a million pieces if she fell in love with him. If she let him make love to her, she knew she would be *in love* with him.

He was too sexy, had too much finesse. She would be swept away, lose her heart to him, a big, handsome, sexy cowboy neighbor, a man who understood her life, who respected her, a man who dazzled her, a man she might fall in love with forever. And that would be pain, heartbreak and hurt that could last a lifetime.

They were enemies, she reminded herself as she clung to his strong body and kissed him, surrendering herself to the most erotic kiss she had ever experienced. And ever would.

His mouth on hers swept her away, dazzled her, set her ablaze with longing for so much more. She didn't know how long they stood there in each other's arms, kissing and caressing each other, tension and need building.

"Jake," she whispered, catching his wrists in her hands and stepping back. "I have to stop. I'll be so in love with you, I will never get over it," she cried. "We not only have no future—your family will be furious."

He was looking at her as if he could devour her, and that made her heart pound more. His desire was obvious and intense. She wanted to step back into his embrace, kiss and caress him and forget every sensible warning.

She fought the urge to toss aside caution and put her arms around him. Jake was fabulous, sexy, kind, intelligent, and his were the best kisses ever. But he was too appealing, a risk to her heart.

She thought about the hurt she would feel if she let herself fall in love with him. She wouldn't be able to walk away without leaving her heart behind. She had never been kissed the way Jake had kissed her. Fantastic, bone-melting, seductive kisses that just made her want more and more.

"Claire, let me do the worrying about my family," he whispered. "I know what I'm doing and what I want. You've been independent long enough to know what you want. And you're making what you want damn evident."

His words were seductive, too. They inflamed her, challenged her, and she felt caught and held by her own desires.

Desires that she knew could be her undoing.

It was the hardest thing she'd ever had to do, but she pulled back from his arms, immediately mourning the lack of his touch, and shook her head. "I can't do this."

He lowered his arms, and his eyes speared hers. The desire she saw in his expression made her feel that she was the most important woman on earth to him. He looked as if he wanted her with all his being and as if he was in love, but she knew better than that. He wasn't in love with her and never would be. She turned quickly, grabbing up her clothes. "This is what has to be," she said, holding her clothes against her. "You have to go, Jake."

He stood there without moving for seconds, his gaze piercing hers, and then, without saying one word, he turned and left her suite.

The urge to call him back was a powerful force, and she mustered all her self-control to fight it.

As she closed the door behind him, she leaned against the cool wood, but she wasn't aware of it. Drifting through memories of Jake, all she remembered were his hands, his mouth, his body, their kisses. Fantastic, sexiest-ever kisses that she would never forget. And her body felt as if it were on fire.

Her emotions held her captive as her thoughts battled each other. Did she really want him to stop? Or should she make love with Jake? He was the sexiest man she had ever known.

He had become incredibly desirable. She wanted him to make love to her. She wanted to make love to him, to discover his fascinating male body, to have his hands and mouth all over her.

She groaned and held her hands over her face. "No, no, no," she said aloud. She knew she shouldn't give in to those desires. Jake partied a lot on weekends. He had women in his life always, and he had never been serious about any of them.

He would not fall in love with her. Claire knew that absolutely. She thought their attraction was a fluke because she was staying with him and they had been caught up in the emotional struggle of the fires. And she thought he had been feeling sorry for her because of her loss and paid more attention to her than he ever would have otherwise.

Men like Jake did not fall in love with women like her. She was solitary, plain, led a life that a lot of men didn't like, although having her own ranch wouldn't bother Jake. But she wasn't his type of woman at all. Claire had seen him out enough in her life to know he liked gorgeous, outgoing women who were fun and sexy and would guarantee him a good time.

Jake was not a marrying man, so at some point, she risked a very broken heart.

Even if they were compatible, could she have a happy relationship with Jake with the family feud hanging over them and influencing everything they did?

Common sense said no, she could not have a good relationship with Jake. Not now, not later, not ever. Definitely, he was not the man for her. She should not get involved with him.

But did she really want to toss aside the chance of making love with him, of having the sexiest night—or nights—of her life with him? Would she look back with big regrets? If only she knew she could make love and then say goodbye to him, not get hurt, just move on, but she suspected if she yielded her body, her heart would be part of the deal.

"I may already be falling for you," she whispered, her eyes still closed while she thought about him. "You're going to break my heart if I don't stop you."

She opened her eyes and mentally told herself she had to stop talking out loud to herself about him, because he had already overheard her once and she didn't want him to overhear her again.

She would probably already have lost her heart to him except for that streak of Reed in him where he could turn right around and annoy her. Like he had over that metal box.

"Dang, Jake," she whispered. She needed to get her mind on business, take care of the calls she had to make about her destroyed house and forget about him.

And she needed to find another place to stay and get out of his house before she surrendered to his seduction.

She got ready to go into town and left to find him.

When she stepped out onto the porch, she heard sounds of metal scraping metal, so she walked down the steps into the yard. Jake was hosing off the big metal box that he had said had belonged to his family. She felt annoyed that he was back on that again. At the same time, her heart beat faster as she looked at his broad-brimmed cowboy hat pushed back on his head, his locks of black hair falling in a tangle on his wide forehead. His jeans were tight on his long legs, his flat stomach and his narrow waist. He had shed his jacket, rolled up his blue denim sleeves and unbuttoned the first three buttons of his shirt.

She saw the tangle of black chest curls, his broad shoulders that made the sleeves of his shirt pull tightly when he leaned over the metal container and tried to clean it off. It was a dull silver, covered with dents and scratches, far cleaner now than an hour before.

She walked close, and he glanced at her and then went back to his task of cleaning the box. She looked down at it and saw the scratches and letters where he had cleaned the dirt and ash.

A few letters stood out clearly: a large straight line with a half circle that looked like the top of a capital *R*. She couldn't read the next letter because there were scratches, maybe an *X*. Then what looked like the lower part of an *E*, and she drew a deep breath. "I don't remember seeing these letters carved in this box before."

"Well, I damn sure haven't been out here carving my initials into the tin," he retorted. "But I sanded down some of the scratches that sort of hid what we have here. I drove back to my ranch house this morning. I needed to look things over anyway, but while I was there, I found my key to this box. I've been waiting to let you open it with my key."

"You haven't tried to open it?" she asked, more aware of the sunshine on his wide-brimmed tan hat that shaded his face, his muscled arms straining the fabric of his shirt and reminding her how it felt to be held in them. Also, she thought about Jake's kisses and for a few seconds forgot the metal box. She was annoyed, but at the same time her pulse raced, and she couldn't stop looking at his strong body, his very kissable mouth.

She wanted his arms around her. She wanted his kisses even while she was angry with him for still insisting her brothers had stolen the box from his family. She could try the key and put an end to his argument.

What if he was right? What if it was a box that had belonged to his family? She glanced again at the *R* that she could clearly read now.

She didn't want to worry needlessly until she knew it without question. She walked closer to him, holding out her hand while she looked into his thickly lashed dark eyes and thought he had bedroom eyes, dark eyes made for seduction. "I had a key at my house for this box, but that key is probably buried by ashes now."

"When we had this, there were three antique weapons we kept in it," he told her. "A Winchester rifle and two antique Colt revolvers."

Her eyes widened slightly, and she was startled, because those guns should still be in the box. That's what had been in there all the years her dad had had the box. He always said his dad had given it to him and his dad had owned it for years. She figured it had been her grandfather's until he gave it to her dad.

But how would Jake know the weapons that had been in their box? Could he be telling the truth? Would her brothers and her dad stoop to stealing something from Jake and then lie about it?

For the first time, she realized they might have done exactly that.

She looked up and met Jake's dark gaze, unfathomable eyes that hid his feelings.

"You know those guns are or were in that box," he said, and she could hear a tight note of anger in his voice. "Also, along with the old weapons was a Glock that belonged to me. I have my initials scratched on it."

Shocked, she realized he had been telling the truth. She raised her chin and nodded. "I still find it very difficult to believe that my family stole this box from your family. They didn't do things like that."

He gave her a look. "Are you going to open it? You have my key."

He was angry and she had been, too, but her anger

had fizzled when he listed those old weapons. Had her brothers stooped to stealing this box? All those weapons except the Glock had been in the box. One of her brothers or her dad could have taken that gun.

There was only one way she was going to find out now. She took a deep breath and stepped closer to put the key in the lock and turn it. She was aware of Jake standing so close beside her. She was even more aware of the anger in his dark eyes.

Anger that might be justified.

Eight

The box was stirring up memories of Claire's ornery brothers and the things they had done. Jake couldn't keep from experiencing a low-burning anger. She had been so absolutely certain her brothers and her dad wouldn't stoop to taking that box from his family, but that's just what they had done.

As she knelt to unlock the box, he watched her jeans pull tautly over her trim butt. Her long legs were folded under her and that thick red braid hung to her waist, once again making him wonder what she would look like if all that red hair was combed out.

Even in his anger, desire still burned hot and strong. He didn't want to feel desire. This morning, dealing with that box, he didn't want to be tied in knots wanting her, but he was. She had always been his enemy, her clan the cause of the feud. She was stubborn and with an annoying family of a rotten dad and two rotten brothers. The younger brother, Laird, wasn't that bad. Even so, Claire still could melt Jake with a look or set him on fire with a touch.

He wanted her in his arms right now. He wanted to peel her out of those tight jeans that covered what might be the sexiest legs in Texas. Then he wanted to caress and shower kisses on them. He wanted them wrapped around him while he made love with her.

"Well, here goes," she said, giving him one more fleeting glance.

He was so lost in thoughts of making love with her while she had her long, long legs wrapped around him that he had almost forgotten the metal box.

And then she opened the lid and let it fall back away from her with a clang while they looked at a box filled with papers. To his disappointment, he didn't see any weapons of any sort. He didn't see any money. Just a mess of papers. He stepped closer and leaned down to look at old bank statements, old tax returns, faded letters and lists of horses that had been bought and sold.

"Well, there," she said, turning to look at him as she stood and placed her hands on her hips.

Annoyed, he took a step forward, reached down and scooped up an armload of papers. Beneath all the mess of papers, in the area he had uncovered, was a long Winchester rifle.

Claire stared down at the weapon. "Oh my word," she exclaimed, her cheeks flushing suddenly. "Jake, I apologize. This must have belonged to your dad, and my brothers…they took it. My dad had to have known where they got it."

It didn't make sense. He should be angry, but he didn't care about the box now or the old weapons. He had proved his point. Now he just wanted his arms around her, to pull her close and kiss her endlessly.

He took out some more papers and revealed the two Colt revolvers. "Well, you can have this metal box, but I want the old guns. The Glock is gone—probably one of your brothers has it. I don't care about the box, either. You keep it to store your papers. I just wanted you to know that it was my dad's."

"Well, you've got your antique weapons and I've got my old records. Actually, you can have the box. I'll buy a new one."

"You keep it. I'll take the weapons because they're collector's items," he said.

She looked down as she bit her lip. "Jake, I really am sorry for what my brothers did. It wasn't right to take these guns. I had no idea."

He draped his arm casually across her shoulders. "I believe you. And I don't want what our families did to keep following us."

She took a deep breath. "Yes, but we're still living with that feud. It'll never go away."

"We can do a whole lot to make it go away," he said softly, tightening his arm around her shoulders slightly to turn her toward him as he placed his other hand on her hip. His big smile was gone as he gazed at her with a solemn expression. Desire filled his dark eyes and made her pulse race faster. "It doesn't exist between us," he said in a husky voice. "We've already kissed it away." His hand on her shoulder moved to caress her nape, light strokes that made her want to kiss again.

She was highly aware of him touching her, of how close he stood and of how intently he looked at her. She wanted his kiss, longed for his arms around her. She forgot about the world, her resolutions to be more cautious about him. The old feud? She didn't think he was correct in saying they had gotten rid of it because of a few kisses. It could come storming back with more fury than ever if their relatives discovered them together, but right now, momentarily, where Jake was concerned, that feud didn't exist. She wanted to be held in his arms to kiss and be kissed.

When he leaned closer, her heart beat faster. "You can't imagine how much I want to kiss you right now," he whispered, brushing her lips with his, making her long for more of him. She wrapped her arms around him as his arm slipped around her waist and he held her against him. His other hand tangled in her hair while his mouth covered hers. Leaning over her to hold her tightly, he kissed her, his tongue going deep, slipping over hers, sending waves of desire through her that made her yearn for more of him, for his hands and mouth all over her.

She had never known a man as sexy as Jake. Warnings and caution disappeared, overruled by desire. She clung to him, kissing him in return while he held her in his tight embrace.

She ran her other hand over him, tossing back his hat to run her hand through his thick hair, down across his arm, down his back. She felt his fingers moving over her, and then he leaned away, and she opened her eyes to look up at him as he pulled her red T-shirt off to toss it away.

"Jake, we're outside. There isn't any privacy."

"There isn't anyone for the next five miles in any direction, but it won't matter," he said, picking her up easily and turning, taking the steps two at a time to the porch and then carrying her inside as he kissed her.

When his mouth covered hers, she closed her eyes and returned his kiss, forgetting her surroundings, lost in his kiss that made her long for more from head to toe. Giddy with his kiss and being carried in his arms, she held him tightly.

His kisses fanned desire until she wanted him desperately, immediately. As he stood her on her feet, she glanced around. They were in his big bedroom, standing near his bed. It gave her pause, and for a moment she felt that warning of caution set in. Did she want to stop him now before they went far beyond kisses?

She placed her hands on his face, looking up and gazing into his dark brown eyes that blazed with such intense desire that she lost some of her hesitation.

"Jake, I—" But she didn't get a chance to finish what she was about to say. Her words were stifled by his kiss. As he ravaged her mouth, he unfastened her bra and pushed it away. His big, callused hands cupped her breasts, and his thumbs lightly drew slow circles on her nipples until his lips trailed down and took over. His mouth captured one nipple, his tongue laving it to a hard pebble.

Sensations rippled through her, building her hungry need for his loving.

She knew if she intended to stop him, now was the moment. Did she want to take the risks to her heart that she knew Jake would cause?

She tunneled her hands through his hair. "Jake—" she whispered.

He looked up into her eyes and then leaned down, coming closer to put his mouth against her ear. "You want this," he whispered, his breath light, tickling her ear. "You want me inside you, hard and fast. I want to make love to you, and you want me to." As he talked, he shed his clothes, kicking off his boots and socks, peeling out of his jeans and briefs. He'd already shed his shirt.

When he stood before her, naked, she placed her hand against his chest. "Jake, I do want this. I want you. All of you." She reached down and captured his erection.

Wrapping his arms around her waist, he smiled at her. "Good, because you already feel how much I want you."

"I think you're the sexiest man alive. I shouldn't admit that to you because it can just go to your head… or other parts that might have a bigger reaction," she said as a smile flickered across her face.

"Come here, beautiful. I want to kiss you until we're both eager to move to the next stage." He reached out again to catch her wrist and draw her flush against him.

"I thought you'd never ask," she said as she went eagerly.

He kissed her neck lightly, arousing her more, driving her mad with need.

"You want my hands on you, don't you?" he asked her softly, his breath falling lightly on her ear. As he whispered, he cupped her breasts in his warm hands and ran his thumbs slowly over her nipples again, making her moan. She thrust her hips against him, wanting more, wanting him totally and completely. He met her need and made quick work of taking off her pants. His tender caresses made her tremble and shake as her need escalated.

"You didn't answer me. Do you want my hands on you? Touching you here?" he asked, caressing her breast. Bliss enveloped her while she clung to his hips and her gaze ran over his broad shoulders and chiseled chest. She wanted his hands on her, and he knew it.

"Yes, yes," she whispered, shoving aside the thought that she might have huge regrets later. "Right now, I want you all over me." She ran her fingers over his engorged manhood, stroking him, hearing his breath catch.

His body was male perfection, his manhood thick and ready. He rubbed slowly against her, just slightly, a sensual brush of their bare bodies. If he did that to make her more aware of both of them naked and holding each other, he succeeded. That contact was sexy, a body and legs caress that made her intensely aware of their nude bodies.

"Ahh, my darlin'," he whispered. "You have no idea what you do to me," he added as he kissed her throat. "You're beautiful, darlin'. Absolutely breathtaking," he whispered, his breath tickling her ear again. His words thrilled her while his caresses fanned desire into a fiery need for all of him, his tongue, his magic hands, his thick manhood that she could feel pressed against her now.

Still caressing her, he stepped back to take a long,

slow look at her. His gaze on her was incredibly erotic, even more so than his touch. He was the lover she thought he would be—deliberate, taking his time to arouse her slowly, looking at her as if she were the most gorgeous woman on earth.

He stepped close again, trailing kisses on her breasts while he slipped his hands lightly down to unfasten her jeans and push them off. When her jeans fell around her ankles, she stepped out of them. She wore her lacy pink panties. Watching her, he hooked his fingers in her panties and slipped them down slowly and then let them drift to her feet. As she looked into his eyes, she stepped out of them while he placed his hands on her hips.

"You're fabulous," he whispered. He wrapped his arms around her and kissed her, one of his sizzling kisses that made her shake.

He picked her up to place her on his bed and then he knelt on the bed beside her, starting at her ankles, running his fingers so lightly over her legs, drifting up to her inner thighs while he trailed kisses where his fingers had been.

He knelt between her legs and leaned down, running his hands lightly on her legs, his tongue trailing along her inner thigh. His tongue swept slowly along her other thigh while his fingers rubbed between her legs. She arched to meet him as he stroked her, erotic strokes that built her need. And then his warm breath spilled over her as he ran his tongue over her intimately.

"Jake, I want you inside me," she gasped.

"Just wait," he whispered, sliding his fingers between her legs to stroke and rub her more, building tension.

"Jake, make love to me," she whispered, moving her hips as he continued to arouse her. "I need you."

"Oh, Claire, we're just getting started," he whispered, his breath hot on the place that yearned for him.

"Ahh, I want you," she cried, clinging to his strong arms, lost in sensations that increased her desire.

"You like that, don't you?" he whispered. "You want my tongue where my fingers have been, don't you?" She didn't answer him; she couldn't form the words. She could only feel her body come alive as he gave her what she wanted.

As his tongue continued to fondle her, building pressure and making her want him more by the minute, she gripped the sheets. Desire and need enveloped her. She gasped with pleasure, closing her eyes, moving her hips. As his hands and mouth played over her, she throbbed with the need to have him inside her right now.

She ran her fingers through his black curls, holding him against her, a sizzling tension building in her. When she thought she couldn't withstand the onslaught any longer, he pulled back from her, and her breath stalled. She watched him step off the bed to get a packet out of his jeans pocket and place it on the table beside the bed. He paused, and his gaze went slowly over her from head to toe as he got back on the bed and knelt between her legs.

She ran her fingers down his thighs as her gaze drifted over him. He was perfection. Broad shoulders, strong arms, chiseled abs, slim hips and a powerful erection. She wanted him with all her being. He had built the need inside her, and now she ached for him.

She sat up and caressed him, showering light kisses

over his body just as he had kissed and teased her. Her hands ran over his fascinating strong body while his drifted so lightly over her. Then she lay back down and held out her arms to him.

"Come love me," she whispered.

As his arms wrapped around her, her heart beat faster. He leaned down, cupping one breast and stroking her nipple with his tongue. His wet tongue moved slowly, drawing circles, exciting her.

"Jake," she whispered, tingling, closing her eyes and shutting out everything except his hands on her and the feelings sweeping over her from his slow caresses that made her tremble with desire.

Suddenly, she wanted to hold him tightly and kiss him, one of those earth-shattering, unforgettable kisses that left her trembling and aching for more. Kisses to remember, if she wanted to, the rest of her life.

"Jake," she said again, this time holding his arms till he looked up at her and met her gaze. She slipped her arm around his neck to bring him down for a kiss. The second her tongue touched his, his arm tightened around her. He leaned over her, kissing her, his tongue stroking hers, his kiss passionate, building desire into a flaming need for both of them. Moaning softly, deep in her throat, she knew she had never been kissed like this. She wanted all of him for hours, his hands and mouth all over her. And at the same time, she thought she'd die if she didn't have him right then.

For a fleeting moment she had a strong feeling that this man would break her heart, but she also didn't want to stop kissing him. Jake's kisses and his loving were worth a risk to her heart.

As he kissed her and held her with his arm around her waist, his other hand slipped down her back to her bottom, lightly stroking her, caressing her and then leaning away to slide his hand down her belly and between her legs, his fingers toying with her, arousing her more.

She thrust her hips toward him to give him easier access, spreading her legs farther apart while they kissed, and his hand drifted so lightly over her. His intimate strokes built her need for all of him.

She had made her commitment and now savored his kiss. He took her breath away with his handsome looks, and now his touch made her desperate for so much more of him.

"You're gorgeous. So incredibly sexy to me. I want you, darlin'. I want you with all my being," he said in a gruff whisper. "I want to know every beautiful inch of you," he said, his voice growing huskier as he sheathed himself.

Even though she didn't believe that she was that fascinating to him, his words thrilled her. "Jake, I want you, too," she said, her gaze raking over his powerful body, his stiff erection. "I want you inside me now."

She reached up to lock her hands behind his neck and pull him down for a kiss. He moved over her and lowered himself carefully, a weight she welcomed while she ran her hands over his back, down across his trim, firm butt.

His body was muscular, powerful and so totally masculine that she became oblivious to everything except his kisses, their tongues touching. Desire built, filling her, making her want him with a desperation she hadn't known before. He must have sensed how close she was, because he moved between her thighs and slid his broad hands beneath her to raise her hips to give him more access.

"Jake."

As she clung to him, she arched her back, raising up to meet him as he entered her. Finally. She nearly cried out with pleasure and need.

His strokes were slow, light, meant to build tension, not offer release. As he moved over her, his gaze raked her.

"You don't know what you do to me," he said, his voice a hoarse whisper.

Her heart pounded with excitement, with a blinding need to achieve climax. His manhood was thick, filling her, and she spread her legs wider.

"Claire," he whispered. "I want to make it last."

She moaned as he thrust inside her again, slow and deep. She didn't know how much longer she could take what his body was doing to hers.

"Put your legs around me," he whispered in her ear, and she did, running her hand over his smooth back as he withdrew slowly and entered her again.

"Jake," she cried, arching her hips, holding him tightly, wanting him deep inside, moving with her.

He took his time now, withdrawing, then filling her until she was arching against him, crying out for him. Then he finally began to pump faster, and she moved with him. They rocked together, hard and fast, while he tried to keep control, to pleasure her as long as he could.

She thrust beneath him, matching his rhythm, clinging to him and arching against him as desire overwhelmed her.

"Jake!" she cried, holding him tightly as he gave one final thrust that carried her to a peak and gave her sweet release.

Clutching him, moving her hips against him, she cried out in ecstasy while he pumped wildly, reaching his climax.

They both sank onto the bed. He held her tightly in his embrace while they gasped for breath. He turned his head to shower light kisses on her face.

"That," he whispered, "was the best. The absolute best."

She barely heard his words as she held him and tried to catch her breath. He had been everything she thought he would be. Her orgasm had been longer, hotter, better than ever before. But Jake had surprised her. As they lay together, he stayed hard, and before her heartbeat could slow down, he started pumping again and she reached the second climax, crying out with passion. She collapsed in his arms, held tightly while they both gulped for breath. As they began breathing quietly, she turned her head to kiss his cheek lightly, his stubby whiskers tickling her lips.

"I can't move," she whispered.

"I think that's my line," he said. He turned to look at her, kissing her forehead, the corner of her mouth, her ear. "You're fantastic." He moved to pull out of her, but she stopped him.

"Ahh, Jake. Just hold me close. I can hear your heart beating. I want you to stay with me."

"I'm with you. Ah, darlin'. I can't move. My bones melted."

She smiled. "I hope so. I wanted it to be good for you, because it was fantastic for me. Now, just hold me close. I don't want to move."

"I don't want you to move. This is perfect," he said, sounding content. She felt cherished, important to him, held against his warm body that was damp with sweat.

No matter what lay ahead, she would never regret making love with him, because he was the best possible lover. And how much had she fallen in love with him because of that? She couldn't answer her own question.

She was held tightly in his arms, their heartbeats and breathing returning to normal while she still tingled all over. She had been right in every way in thinking about what it would be like to have Jake make love to her. He was the consummate lover, fabulous, carrying her out of this world. Each climax had been earth-shattering.

She'd had lovers before in her life—only two, because she had met few men that really tempted her. Jake's kisses had been the sexiest ever, melting her resistance, and her climax had been paradise. She couldn't answer her own question, but she suspected when she shared her body, she'd given him part of her heart. She might be a little bit in love with him, and she would just have to live with that and hope she could get over it, because she had no illusions about his feelings.

He held her close their breath mingled. He was warm, his body solid, so fascinating to her.

He rolled over to prop his head on his hand, looked down at her and smiled. He ran his index finger slowly along her jaw and up to her ear. "I want to keep you here in my bed the rest of the month."

"Well, you can't do that, but I can stay awhile. Later, I need to get back to getting my ranch back in order and everything rebuilt. Sometimes that overwhelms me—everything that needs to be rebuilt. Barns, corrals, fences, my house, other houses, an office. So much to build from just ashes. I really appreciate getting to stay here."

He smiled. "Believe me, you can't appreciate being here as much as I'm happy to have you here. You take your time. There's no rush for you to rebuild and get out."

"Thank you," she said, smiling at him.

"I want you with me. This is a fabulous time," he said, showering light kisses on her throat and then turning her to kiss her again, another deep kiss that stirred desire far sooner than she expected.

An hour later, they were still in bed, and she was in his arms, her naked body pressed against his as he held her close.

"Jake, I was going to town to get some clothes. Also, I need to call all sorts of people about my house and property and get work started on rebuilding. First, I have an appointment with my insurance agent."

"It'll all be there when you do call, and right now they're swamped anyway. Relax and let's enjoy the most fabulous lovemaking ever," he said, his voice growing husky as it did when he thought about making love. "I want you here in my arms, against my body for just a bit longer. What time we wasted. I should have had you as a guest long, long ago and gotten to know you."

She smiled. "After this we should be able to settle our differences out of court, huh?"

"Let's not talk about ranches and differences and problems today," he said while he ran his fingers over her bare shoulder and then down to her breast. "This is a special time." He leaned closer to kiss her lightly on her throat, trailing more kisses over her jaw. "You're beautiful. I can never get enough of looking at you naked."

She wondered if she was already in love with him. She couldn't think about it rationally when she was in his arms with his hands drifting over her.

He held her close now, still running his fingers over her.

"Claire, I want you to stay while you get your house rebuilt. You don't have a home on your ranch or any outbuildings, and you can't throw up a tent until that land is cleared of debris. Stay here with me. That will give us some time together, because when you go back, when we step back into our regular lives, you know our lives won't be the same as they are now."

She shook her head. "No, they won't be the same. And I don't think you've thought through your invitation to me," she said, smiling at him. "I can't get a new house thrown up in a few weeks. That project will take months."

"I know what I'm asking," he said solemnly, and her heart thumped. Stunned by the unexpected invitation to stay a long time with him, she gazed into his dark eyes while her heart beat faster at the thought of weeks in his arms, in his bed, making love often.

"I'll have to think about that one," she answered quietly. "If I stay a long time with you, it will become known in these parts. That could cause an uproar with all my relatives. It could cut me out of my family. I don't want that to happen. I'm trying to reconnect with them. I have to think about that. It's not going to go over well with your family, either. I know you have relatives in Texas, although not close to here, and you know that I do also."

"We run a risk, but I don't think my family will cut me out."

"I don't want to lose my family, but they probably saw my house burn on television. They might yield a little because of my losses. I can't guess. I'll have to think about the risk I take. Also, my brothers may try to catch you alone where they can beat you up for letting me stay here."

"Let me worry about that one. I'll be careful, and I'm not scared of your brothers."

"On the other hand, I need to be near my property to rebuild. I don't have another place to stay. This is perfect for me to work with the contractors on building a new house."

Her breath stilled as she thought of another reason to rethink staying at Jake's cabin.

"Then there's another risk if I stay. I want to say yes right now, while at the same time, common sense tells me if I stay with you and we keep making love, I'll never want to leave you. I'll fall so deeply in love with you, my heart will break when we part. I don't know. I have to give your offer thought before I answer."

"Think about it. I don't think you'll fall in love. You're incredibly independent, accustomed to running your own ranch. You'll just go back to your regular routine."

She suspected he was describing himself and his reactions to staying with someone he had had sex with and then said goodbye.

"I'm not sure you know what you're asking. It's none of my business, so if you don't want to answer, don't. My guess is that you've never invited someone to stay with you that long."

He shook his head. "No, I haven't, but it's different this time. You don't even have a house. You'll be gone a lot on your ranch, supervising and working and just here at night—the best time and when I'm home. You're damn independent or you wouldn't be living over there alone and running that ranch. I think we can work it out, and if we can't, we'll change the arrangements."

She smiled. "You promise to ask me to leave if you get tired of me?"

He gazed back solemnly. "I can't imagine asking you to leave for a long time. I'm not a marrying man, Claire, but I want you here with me. And for the record, I don't think you're a marrying woman, either."

She shook her head as she smiled. "Not to a Reed. You're safe there, Jake. I've told you my feelings on that, and I know you wouldn't ever want to marry a Blake. You lost a brother because of his marriage to a Blake. I lost a sister. So you're right. I won't want to marry you. But that doesn't mean I won't fall in love with you and end up with a broken heart."

"I think you're safe on that one after what you just told me. So you'll stay?" he asked, staring intently at her and sounding as if he really wanted her at his house on his ranch. She was shocked and stared at him while she thought about it.

"I don't have anywhere to go except Dallas, and I need to be out here right now to get things back into a routine. I'll stay here if you will promise—absolutely be honest about it—that you will tell me to leave if you want me out of here."

"I promise," he said instantly, smiling at her and sounding happy, as if she had just given him a wonderful gift. She gazed at him and wondered about what she was getting into. If they fit together as well the rest of the time as they had the past twenty-four hours, she wouldn't want to leave. At the same time, she wouldn't ever want to marry him, because that would be a disaster.

Another thought hit her. Could Jake fall in love with her? Was he so certain his heart was safe, and he couldn't be hurt, or were they both going to end up heartbroken?

Nine

A few hours later, Claire faced Jake and knew she would never view him the same way she had before they made love too many times to count. Her feelings about him had made a monumental change. Could they stay on a friendly basis? How much would their lovemaking improve their neighborly relationship? How much did she care about him now?

She glanced over at the clock and gasped. "Jake, do you know that it's after three in the afternoon?" she said, turning to him as he rolled over to face her and prop his head on his hand. As he smiled at her, she brushed locks of black hair off his forehead.

"I don't really care what time it is. I don't want to leave this bedroom yet. This has been fabulous," he said.

"It's time, Jake. We've been here all night and all

morning, going into the afternoon. It's been fabulous, but it's time to go back into our real world, back to the problems, because I really want to go into town and get some clothes."

"I know you're right." He placed his hand on her arm lightly. "Before we go, I have a question—actually an invitation. We're having a celebration. It's a thank-you dinner Saturday night in Dallas for people who contributed to rebuilding the arena. My cousins and I made a generous donation, and I want you to go with me."

A cold chill suddenly ran down her spine as the world intruded on their idyll.

"We're naked in bed together—I don't think you thought that invitation through. I would love to go with you, but how can we go out in public in Dallas? We could easily run into Reeds or Blakes and all hell would break loose. Besides, it will stir things up for some locals to see a Reed out with a Blake, and you know it. We can ignore some things, but there's no reason to go asking for trouble and for you to take me to an event. I think that's looking for trouble. Worse, disaster."

He shook his head. "This dinner should be okay. They've had several of these thank-you get-togethers, where they report on the progress of the construction, and my cousins have never once come. It's a small group going to a private club, and we'll be in our own room. There's a chance to run into relatives, but it isn't likely. Like I said, I don't remember any Blakes or Reeds that will be at this shindig. We'll just go in my limo, be shut away in a private room and then get back into the limo to go to my apartment in Dallas. The chances are slim."

"And you're willing to take that risk?" she asked.

"I want to take you, so yes, I'm willing to take the risk. I don't think it's likely I'll see any relatives. Frankly, I don't see many of my relatives in Dallas. They're more in Amarillo and scattered in smaller towns, and they don't go to Dallas a lot. There's always that chance we'll see someone, but I think we can deal with it. I'm willing to take the risk and live the way I want to live. It should be a fun evening, and you seemed interested in the arena." As he talked, his fingers ran over her arm and the back of her hand. Then he moved his hand to caress the nape of her neck. Each light caress kept her thoughts on him more than thinking about going out with him and the problems that could mean.

"You know I want to go with you," she admitted honestly.

"Good. So, you'll do it. I'll try to see to it that you have a fun evening," he drawled, and she smiled, shaking her head.

"It didn't take you long to talk me into it. Before we go to the party, though, I really should spend a day in Dallas. I need something to wear, I need my hair done—you know, girl stuff. I'm going to have to get a new pickup and a new car sometime, but I want to go to Dallas for that, too, and I can't go today."

"We can go to Dallas Thursday or Friday and stay in my apartment. I'll get my pilot to fly us to Dallas. You can get ready and do what you want to do during the day. Just leave the nights for me."

"Let's go on Thursday, and I can get some business done," she said, amazed to be planning her life and including him in it. "I'll make appointments, because I have to see about the insurance and a lot of things on clearing my land and rebuilding my ranch house and replacing my vehicles. We moved a lot of things before the fire, so it shouldn't be too much. We've got a routine for emergencies and it worked to save a lot of equipment. Trouble is, you can't move everything. I can get my pickup, and then you won't have to drive me around."

"Come here," he said in a husky voice, reaching out to lift her closer against him as he wrapped his arms around her. Held against his nude body, looking into his sexy, long-lashed dark eyes, she forgot about the weekend, the problems, the things she needed to do. She just wanted his kisses, his loving, their bodies joined. The more they kissed and made love, the more she wanted him. Would she fall in love with him?

If she did, he would break her heart, because she was certain Jake wasn't falling in love. He wanted hot sex, endless hours of loving, but she suspected part of him was locked away, not to be shared, and he wasn't ever going to be in love. And if the impossible happened and he fell in love with her, that would disrupt both their lives and tear them away from their families. She didn't want that, either. There was no good solution to a relationship with him. And she knew she better face that fact and keep a realistic outlook with realistic expectations. Getting involved with Jake Reed meant disaster whatever way she went.

No matter how fabulous and exciting sex was between them, how compatible they had become, at some point, they would have to say goodbye.

* * *

"I think it's time for me to dress—in my same old jeans and in one of your T-shirts. Then let's go into Persimmon and get me some other clothes."

"Whenever you're ready," Jake replied, though if he had his choice, he'd keep Claire naked and in bed for the rest of the day and into the night. "I will say, those jeans you've been wearing still look mighty good on you," he added with a wink.

"Thank you. But I'm ready for new ones. Now, what are we going to do about riding into town together—a Blake and a Reed in the same car? That will turn everyone upside down."

"I'll drop you off at my uncle Bernard's hardware store. The family avoids it unless they desperately need some hardware because he's such a grump."

"He is that, I'll agree, but I figured it was just with my family. That's kind of funny that he is with his own family. Well, he'll still see us and spread the word."

"He might, but it's unlikely. He doesn't pay attention until someone corners him and says they want to buy something."

She smiled and nodded. "Okay. We'll see what happens. I suppose you'll pick me up there, too."

"Might as well. I'll be parked and waiting if you can give me an approximate time."

"Sure. Give me an hour."

"That's not a lot of time."

"Persimmon isn't a big place, and they're limited on what they have. It won't take long because I'm not particular and I'm a fast shopper. Just in case, an hour and fifteen minutes."

"Sounds good to me. Like Scotty's Burgers? If you do, I'll have two when I come get you."

"That would be nice. Now I need to get dressed."

"Can I help?"

She smiled as she shook her head. "I think not. We might not get to town at all if you help."

"Might not, but I'll bet you'd have more fun."

"I can't argue that one," she said as she wiggled away.

He put his hands behind his head to watch her as she got out of bed. She was nude, gorgeous, and he wanted her again. She yanked the top sheet off the bed, wrapped herself in it quickly and started out of the room as he reached for her, but she did a quick step and dodged his hand.

"Claire, come here," he coaxed in a husky voice.

She shook her head. "No, no. We're sticking to our plan. You promised to take me to Persimmon for clothes, and we're not putting that off any longer. We've already made love for hours. See you on the porch." She rushed out of his room and closed the door behind her.

Smiling, he got up to take a cold shower. He needed it. They had made love for hours, but he couldn't get enough of her, and the sight of her nude made him want her just as much as if they hadn't loved at all.

That was a new one for him. In fact, he thought, several things about her were different from his experiences with other women. Not being able to get enough of her was one. He wanted her even more now than he had before their first kiss. And, he didn't want her to go home—in this case, she didn't have her ranch home to go back to, so he might get that wish. Claire wasn't like any other woman he had ever known—independent, a rancher and a damn good one. On top of that, she just might be the sexiest woman he had ever known—that was the real shocker.

Just thinking about her made him want to go find her and peel her out of her clothes and make love again before they left for town. He knew she wouldn't go for it, but that's what he would like to do, and he was shocked by his own feelings. How much was she going to tie him up in knots and change his life?

After an hour in Persimmon, Claire went back to where they agreed to meet. She had new jeans, new socks and sneakers, new underwear and T-shirts in bags and boxes. She saw Jake sitting in the driver's seat of his pickup, his feet on the dash, his head back on the seat.

She put her head in the open window and leaned close to his ear. "Hey, Sleeping Beauty, I'm back," she whispered.

As his eyes opened, his arm slipped around her shoulders. He pulled her closer.

"Jake—" she started to protest. He drew her head down, covered her mouth with his and ended whatever she had been about to say.

His tongue stroked hers, and she forgot everything else, forgetting where she was, what she had been doing, everything except Jake, his mouth on hers in a kiss that made her want to keep on kissing. Finally, she wiggled away slightly, but he kept his arm around her.

"Jake, wait—we're on Main Street. Do you want all our relatives to know we have a truce? And they will hear about it."

"I think you started this," he said in a lazy drawl. "Get in this pickup with me and I'll finish it," he added, making her want him more than ever, even though she laughed.

"I should have known better than to walk up and whisper in your ear like that," she told him. He opened his arms, and she slipped away, walking around to get into the passenger side.

"My brothers will hear about us," she said as she buckled her seat belt, "so watch your back."

"I promise you—I'm not scared of your brothers. I'll take one of my cowboys as a bodyguard," he smiled.

"I'm serious! Please be careful. I'm sure someone saw us."

"You didn't buy anything?" he asked, sitting up.

She motioned to the back seat, and he glanced over his shoulder. "Ahh, that should do it for a couple of days." His gaze went over her. "Nice duds. You look great."

She laughed. "Thank you, but I'm wearing the same clothes I wore when we came to town. Those new ones get washed first. Anyway, for now, I'm finished shopping."

"You were speedy. I brought the burgers about ten minutes before you arrived. Do you want to go to the park and eat them or just sit here in the car?"

"The park. Unless there are lots of people there. Let's go see. It's a pretty day, and we can sit under a tree and I can enjoy my burger."

"I can think of some more fun things to do, but for that I suspect you would want more privacy than the park would provide."

"Yes, I think so," she said, smiling at him.

"And then back to my ranch," he said, starting his pickup.

"Yes, you'll still have a houseguest." Even as she said the words, she couldn't help thinking that she should just go to Dallas, get out of his ranch house, away from him. But once again, she thought how much easier it would be if she stayed at his place to meet people when they came out to keep all the appointments she had set up for the construction of her new ranch house and buildings. She already had four appointments.

"It's easier for you to get things done on your ranch if you're staying on mine, right there next to yours instead of driving out from Dallas every time," he said as if he knew what she was thinking.

"Oh yes. It's a lot more convenient," she answered. But she couldn't deny the truth she felt deep inside. There was another reason she wanted to stay with him: she wanted to be with Jake, in his arms again. Because she knew that's what would happen when they got back home.

On Thursday they flew to Dallas and Jake took Claire to her house, a large two-story in an old part of town. The area was full of multimillion-dollar mansions that had increased in value through the years and still boasted choice properties with large tree-shaded lawns, carefully tended flowerbeds and quiet streets. "Want to come inside and see my home?" she asked when the limo he'd hired pulled into her drive.

"I will when I pick you up. I know you have appointments. I'll be back Saturday night to get you for dinner at six. Sunday we go back to the ranch."

"Thanks, Jake. It'll help get started on my house if I can stay at your place and be right there when the contractors have questions. Once they begin to get it framed in, I can go home."

"I'm in no hurry to get you out of my house," he said.

"Oh my," she said in a breathless voice. "That sounds as if you want me in your bed a long time."

"Do I ever," he said. He slipped his arm around her waist. "You're teasing. I'm not. I want you and I want you in my bed." He kissed away her reply, and when he released her, she was breathless, all her teasing remarks forgotten. She fanned herself.

"Wow, you're one sexy man," she whispered. "I need to go inside and climb into the freezer to cool down."

"Instead, get your shopping done so I can take you to dinner and then to bed."

True. He reminded her she still had to find a dress for the arena celebration. "That's a deal, my handsome friend."

She watched him walk to the waiting limo, get in and disappear down the street. With a sigh she closed the door. "I still think you'll break my heart, but for now I am thoroughly enjoying the sexiest kisses ever," she whispered. "And the best possible sex."

She tingled at the thought of getting dressed up and going out for a night with him, something where they weren't in jeans, she wasn't in his giant T-shirts and wearing singed boots. Instead, she'd look more like the women he usually took out.

"Just wait, Jake. I'm about to give you a night to remember."

* * *

Saturday evening Jake stood at Claire's door after ringing the bell and waiting. He wore a charcoal suit, a red tie, gold links in his French cuffs and his best black boots.

When the door opened, he turned. "Are you—" He stopped as he stared in surprise. If he had been in public, somewhere besides her front door, and simply run into her, he wouldn't have known her.

He could only stare, and for a rare moment in his life he was speechless. He didn't even realize he wasn't speaking and hadn't greeted her. She was stunning, and he couldn't get his breath. Her red hair, parted in the center, framed her face as it fell over her shoulders. He thought about the long, thick braid she'd always had. Now her hair was only shoulder length, a beautiful dark red with streaks of blond highlights near her face.

Her sleeveless dress was a red silk that had a high, round collar, a belted midsection that showed her tiny waist and a straight skirt that went to midcalf that showed off every curve. She wore red platform sandals with high, thick heels, and he could only stare because his normally plainly dressed rancher neighbor took his breath away. She was so gorgeous. The red dress had a seam in front from chin to the hem. It wasn't very noticeable, but he saw it and realized it might be a zipper. He promised himself that before the night was over, he would know if it was a zipper. That thought made him wonder what she wore under the red dress.

"You look fantastic," he said.

"Thank you. You clean up rather well yourself," she

said, smiling at him. "What a handsome devil you are, dear neighbor. My, oh my."

"That's what I say. Damn, you're gorgeous. I think I'd rather cancel the evening and take you to bed. Too bad I can't cancel. But I can't stop staring at you, either. You're stunning."

As she turned to get her purse, she glanced over her shoulder and smiled. "Thank you. That's nice to hear. And you look good enough to kiss, except we won't now because I don't want to get the least bit messed. I have spent the entire day working for this look, and I want a few minutes to enjoy it intact."

"Yes, ma'am," he said politely with laughter in his eyes. "I'm curious, though. Your hair isn't the same length. Did you get a haircut? Or were you wearing a fake long braid?" he teased.

"I got a haircut. I didn't need that much hair, but it was definitely mine."

"I can't stop looking at you."

She smiled at him. "I hope not. That's one goal I hoped to achieve. I wanted to get your attention," she said and meant it. She wanted him to see her in a dress, some way other than as he usually did on the ranch, and especially this last week after all they'd gone through. She wanted this night out, and she had already gotten a reaction from him that made the effort worthwhile. She felt the same way looking at him. He looked so incredibly handsome. He took her breath away. She looked forward to the night out with him, and it was a good cause. Even though her family was angry with his family that they had bought the property first, she loved that old arena and was glad they had rebuilt.

"You've got my attention, all right. You've got my brain's attention and you've got another area's attention, too. If we have an earthquake or typhoon, get me moving, because I won't notice it for looking at you."

"No typhoons, no earthquakes in the forecast, but I'll let you know if one happens."

"Let's go. As soon as I feel we can politely leave tonight, we will. I want to take you home with me."

"You don't have to do that here in Dallas. My Dallas home hasn't burned."

"I want you with me all night, in my arms, in my bed, where I can kiss every gorgeous inch of you. Okay?"

"More than okay," she replied in a sultry voice, wanting to be with him, in his arms, in his bed. "I can't wait to be with you later," she said softly, her voice getting that breathy quality that she couldn't avoid.

"To be truthful, I want you to show me what's under that gorgeous red dress."

"I'll do my best to oblige," she said, smiling at him.

"Maybe we should skip this party," he said, studying her and sounding as if he meant it.

"No, we won't. Stop trying. And we're not leaving early. Not after what I paid for this dress, these shoes and my hair. Not to mention my new undergarments that you get to remove later."

"Dang. That isn't the way to ensure you'll get to stay there long. That just makes me want to carry you off to bed now."

"I just wanted you to know that I'm looking forward to later, but I want to go to the party now. Besides showing off my new clothes, this is for a really good cause.

And I will have an evening with the most handsome man in Texas, and that is saying a lot."

He smiled. "Thank you, my darling. Okay, let's hit the road."

Smiling, she picked up her envelope purse that matched her dress, closed the door and put the key into her purse.

"You'll come home with me tonight, won't you?" he asked.

"If you want, or you can come back here with me."

"Come home with me. I'll get you home when you're ready." He couldn't wait for the evening to be over. He'd seen women he'd taken out who had new dresses, new hairstyles, gorgeous women who looked like they'd stepped off the pages of a glossy fashion magazine, but Claire had undergone the biggest change and the most beautiful one.

He can't believe he didn't realize how beautiful she was before. She was a good-looking woman, and now she was drop-dead gorgeous, and he was stunned how good she looked. He knew she worked on her ranch. Her clothes were practical for that. Her long braid had been practical for being out in the dust and the wind with horses or cattle. But this transformation was astonishing. And he knew what a gorgeous body was under that red silk dress.

He realized she was staring at him. "I'm sorry. Did you say something to me?"

She laughed. "A penny for your thoughts. That isn't what I said, but I'm wondering what carried you away."

"You did. I can't get over how you look. I know you usually are dressed the best way to work on your ranch, but there is a vast difference between how you look on the ranch and how you look tonight."

She smiled. "I must be scary on the ranch."

"You're not a damn bit scary. You look good on the ranch. Haven't I conveyed that I thought you looked great?"

"As a matter of fact, yes, you have. I'm glad you think so tonight, too. I would hate to have gotten my hair cut and you not notice."

"Oh, lady. Every guy in the place is going to notice. I may hang on to you, so they know you're with me and don't come over to flirt with you."

She laughed. "That's not going to happen."

"I would win placing a bet on that one. Let's go so we can get through the evening and go home," he said, taking her arm lightly, looking intently at her and turning to walk to the limo with her.

The ride was quick, and before he knew it the driver held the limo door for them and Jake took her arm as they walked into the tall building, where the club was on the twentieth floor. As they entered the room, a man played the piano softly in a far corner. Tables were set, but no one was seated yet. A cocktail party was going on, and people were on the balcony as well as inside.

They moved around the room to greet guests, and Jake saw that, like the last dinner, the room was filled with guys he'd ridden with and competed against in rodeos, which didn't surprise him, because they were the ones who were the most interested in the new arena. He also noticed the attention Claire was getting from every male in the room.

"My friend Stefanie Grant just arrived," Claire said, calling Jake's attention.

He looked around and saw the woman.

"I'll tell you, Stefanie does know how to make an entrance. She looks damn good, too, tonight."

"She told me who to call to get my hair done. It's the same group she goes to."

"Ahh. I'm glad you took her advice. Damn good advice. Stefanie always looks good. She could fall in the pigpen and look good."

Claire smiled. "I'll tell her you said that."

Jake grinned as he looked beyond her. "Her brother may be here someplace. There are a bunch of donors now, and this party is for all of us. My cousins—there were four of us who donated money. Since Cal died, there are just three of us involved actively now. Wade Sterling is one and he's supposed to be here tonight, although I don't see him now. One of the cousins lives in Colorado, and he hasn't been to any of these dinners till tonight. It's Luke Grayson. His wife and child were killed in a car wreck, and he hasn't been able to come."

"That's awful. I'm so sorry."

"Luke grew up here. He was a backyard neighbor of the Grants."

"I'm sorry to hear about his loss. Speaking of—here comes Stef. She called when she heard about the fire and wanted to know if I was all right. When she found out my home burned, she offered to let me stay in one of her empty houses in Dallas, which was nice of her. She owns Grant Realty, in case you didn't know."

"I know the Grants, and everybody knows Stefanie. Her brother, Noah, and I are friends."

He paused as a slender black-haired woman in a sleeveless black cocktail dress walked up and greeted them. She turned to Claire. "I'm so sorry about your ranch, your house and the other buildings."

"Thanks, Stefanie. The fire was dreadful."

"What about your ranch, Jake?" Stefanie asked, turning to him.

He shook his head. "I was enough to the east that the fire didn't get there. The wind drove it west and then north. If you ladies will excuse me, I see some friends I want to greet." As he walked away, Stefanie turned back to Claire.

"My, oh my, does he clean up good."

Claire gave Jake a lingering look. "I think I said the same thing to him. Yes, he does."

"So do you. Wow. You look absolutely gorgeous.'"

"You look gorgeous yourself. You always turn heads," Claire said. "Thank you so much for recommending the salon and who to book with. I'm really pleased with the outcome. So is Jake."

"I think they're great."

"I need to see you more often. I needed a lift after losing my home and all my things."

"Aww, Claire, I'm so sorry. I couldn't imagine," Stefanie said. Then she brightened. "You said you're staying at a neighbor's house. You didn't say which neighbor. But you didn't have to," Stefanie said, her eyes twinkling. "A Reed and a Blake? I hope those brothers of yours don't show."

"You couldn't drag them into any event honoring ranchers and cowmen and the like. No danger there, and Jake didn't seem to think we would run into his family, so here we are."

Stefanie smiled. "Jake's a nice guy."

"We're doing better than when we've gone to court to fight each other," Claire said, smiling at her friend. "I hope it lasts." Then she remembered what Jake had said. "Oh, by the way, Jake wanted me to pass on a compliment. He said you could fall into a pigpen and still look good."

Stefanie laughed. "Oh my. Tell him thank you for that lovely thought."

"Are you here with someone? May I ask who?"

"Sure, you can always ask. I came with Billy, and I think it will be the last time. I don't know why, but I just don't have the knack for finding the right guy. We argued all the way here…" She waved her hand. "But enough about that."

"I'm sorry, Stef."

"Not to worry, girlfriend. I'm not giving up hope." In an obvious attempt to deflect the conversation from her love life—or lack thereof—she said, "Well, like I said on the phone, I can always find a place for you to stay, Claire, with me or in a vacant house, so let me know if you need a place. Although if I were staying with Jake, I think I'd just settle in until the last inch of your ranch is fixed and ready."

Claire laughed. "I'll remember your advice. If the two of us fell wildly in love, though, there wouldn't be a future with that old feud. If it were like Regina, I wouldn't want that, either."

Stefanie frowned. "I think you're right. Like Romeo and Juliet."

Claire laughed. "That's a first. Later, I'll tell Jake that you called us Romeo and Juliet." She hoped their story wouldn't be as tragic, but she was sure Jake would find the humor in it. "By the way, how's your family?"

"Everyone's good. I'm an aunt again, and that's so much fun."

Claire smiled at a story her friend related, then when they were about to part, she said, "I hope you have a good time tonight."

"I hope you have a good time, too. Jake seems nice. I hope your brothers know nothing about him."

"When they see me with him, I think they'll know better than to interfere. They may be rotten to some people, guys mostly, but they've never been rotten to me."

"Oh, here Billy comes, looking for me. I'll go so you don't have to talk to him and have him ask you why you're here with a Reed. He might not have noticed yet, but he's friends with some of the Reeds. Let's do lunch when you can," she said over her shoulder, and Claire nodded, watching Stefanie's black hair swing as she walked away.

"Claire?"

She turned to see one of the men involved with the arena and smiled at him. "Brink. This is a nice party, and I'm so glad a new arena will be built."

"I am, too. I almost didn't recognize you. You look great," he said. "Was that your house I saw on the news?"

"There were several houses on the news, but yes, the fire went across my ranch and my home is gone," she said, turning as another rancher joined them. She glanced across the room as she talked and saw Jake looking at her as he stood in a group of people, laughing at something someone said, but his eyes were on her, and she felt a tingle just from their exchanged glances. It was another twenty minutes of conversation before a hand touched her elbow and she looked up at Jake.

"Sorry to interrupt," he said, greeting the men standing around her. After he had shaken hands with each one, he looked down at Claire. "It's about time for this to start. If you gentlemen will excuse us, they're asking everyone to find their places."

He held her arm lightly as they moved away from the group. "I know where our places are. We're at the head table. I see Stefanie found you. So have half the guys in the room. You drew a crowd."

She smiled. "Friendly people. Ranchers. I'm a rancher."

"That isn't why you had eight guys standing around talking to you," he said, and she smiled.

"They've asked some of us to find our places because then everyone will," he told her. "So let's find our seats so we will get to eat dinner and get this shindig over with so I can take you home with me and see what's under your red dress."

"Sounds like a deal to me," she said, smiling at him and anxious for the time when she could return to his place and be alone with him.

As they reached the head table, two tall men and a woman were waiting. Jake greeted them and turned to her. "I want all of you to meet my ranch neighbor Claire Blake. Claire, these are my cousins, who have also helped with the building of the new arena in Fort

Worth after the old one burned. This is Wade Sterling and his new wife, Ava Sterling."

Smiling, Claire greeted the Sterlings.

"I've heard a lot about you. I'm glad you two have a truce," Wade said.

"I'm glad, too," she said, smiling in return.

"And this is another cousin, Luke Grayson."

"I'm glad to meet you, Luke."

"I agree with everyone else—a truce is good between neighbors. It's nice to meet you. I have heard about you, too."

"I'm sure you have," she said, smiling at him. "Maybe it'll be better from now on."

They saw pictures of the new arena, the box seats on the ground floor where spectators could be close to the action, the plush suites with walls of glass at the top, plus a cantina with a seating capacity of two hundred that had food service, bars and elegant, comfortable seats with wide screens to also view the action. She saw pictures of the horse stalls and then more shots of another large area outside with seats around an adjoining outdoor arena.

The arena board chairman, John Smith, was master of ceremonies and stood to talk about the arena. He was obviously proud of the strides they'd already made. They were booked solid with horse shows, rodeo events and bull riding.

Finally, in closing, the speaker thanked all the people attending the dinner who had contributed to building the arena and in particular thanked the three of the largest monetary contributors: Wade, Jake and Luke.

As they read more names, Jake became antsy, thinking of how badly he wanted to get Claire out of here and into his arms.

It seemed like hours but was actually only half past ten when they arrived at Jake's Dallas condo. Claire's heart drummed with eagerness, because all evening she had been looking at Jake and imagining herself here with him, away from prying eyes. But she knew what this was. Jake always had moved on from the previous women he'd dated, and she didn't expect him to change. But she wanted this night with him.

"Jake, this is marvelous," she said, stepping into his entryway and seeing the big living room with two walls of glass that offered a spectacular view of the lights of Dallas at night. "Oh my word, what a view."

"I heartily agree," he said. His voice was deep with that rasp he got when he was aroused, and she turned to see him watching her as he unbuttoned his shirt. He had already shed his coat and tie, and her pulse jumped, her heartbeat racing because it was clear what he wanted.

Watching her, he crossed the room to her, tossing his shirt and then undershirt on a chair.

"My, that was fast," she said, thinking about his handsome looks. Then she sighed under her breath and whispered only to herself, "Ahh, Jake. You're going to have my heart." She slipped her arm around his waist as he reached out to slide his hand to her collar.

"I knew this would zip down the front. I do like your dress," he said, watching her as he pulled the zipper down slowly.

"Oh, darlin', are you gorgeous," he said, his gaze going to her breasts in a bra that was only a bit of white lace. "So incredibly beautiful," he added, letting her dress come open. She wore white lace panties that were as skimpy as her bra.

In seconds the silk dress fell around her ankles, and she stepped out of it, removing her bra and panties as he watched. He shed the rest of his clothes while he watched her.

He slipped his arms around her and drew her against his warm, naked body as he leaned down to kiss her. "You're fantastic," he whispered, and then his mouth was on hers and she clung tightly to him.

"I can't wait this time. Next time will be for you," he said after a moment and picked her up. "Put your legs around me."

When she did, he lowered her on his hard manhood and she closed her eyes, gasping with pleasure as he eased into her slowly.

"Ahh, Jake," she whispered, clinging to him and moving with him, each thrust sending waves of intense pleasure that rocked her.

As she clung tightly to him, he began to pump faster. Sensations spread in her, desire hot and intense as she rode him and tension built. She felt her first climax burst with a fantastic surge, ecstasy enveloping her. He continued pumping faster, and in minutes she clutched him, clinging with her arms and legs tight around him as her second climax washed over her while he climaxed at the same time. She cried out while spasms racked her, and then she fell on him, kissing him and holding him tightly until she finally slid down to stand on the floor again while they still kissed.

He picked her up to carry her to bed, stretching out

on his side and holding her close as she faced him. "Jake, I can't move now. You're fantastic."

"I guarantee you, that's my line. You looked beautiful tonight, in your clothes and out of them. Absolutely stunning."

She smiled at him, running her fingers over his whiskers, along his ear, up into his hair. "I think when I move out of your house, my heart may just be left behind with you. Probably another trophy for you."

"I don't have trophies like that or women like that in my life," he said as he looked deeply into her eyes. "I don't know about the future, but I know that right now, I'm in paradise because of you."

"I could say the same thing."

He held her close against him. "This is good."

She clung tightly to him, happy, refusing to think beyond the current moment. She'd had a fabulous evening, and Jake's response to her new clothes, her new haircut and style, had been more than she had hoped for. She knew some rough times lay ahead, because it was inevitable that she would move out of his house and into her new one, but right now, tonight, she wasn't going to think again about anything beyond the moment. And at the moment, she was euphoric. They'd shared hot lovemaking. She was being held tightly against his naked body and in due time he would kiss her again and they would make love again. It was paradise now while she was naked in his arms. She wouldn't look beyond the immediate moment.

With a sigh, she hugged him tightly and put her head on his chest to listen to his heartbeat.

"This is the perfect end to a perfect day," he said, his

voice a deep rumble. She could feel vibrations in his chest when he talked. She ran her fingers over his flat, hard stomach, sliding them up over his chest. "You're incredible, so sexy, so handsome, so exciting," she whispered, wondering if she was already deeply in love with him and if he was going to break her heart when they said goodbye. She had a feeling she would never again know a man who was as sexy and exciting as he.

Claire spent the next week making arrangements with all sorts of people, and by the beginning of March, her land had been cleared and a foundation laid for her new home. She went back and forth from Jake's cabin each day in one of his pickups and then usually stayed at Jake's in the afternoon. She spent every night and some days and afternoons in his bed in his arms, and she refused to think about the future unless she had to, and then only regarding her property.

Late in the day on a Thursday, she knew Jake was working on something in his office. She had been on the phone with her insurance agent and had an appointment set. She had spent the morning selecting tile and wallpaper and flooring for her new kitchen on the ranch.

After three in the afternoon, she was ready for a break and went to Jake's library. Wearing new jeans, new sneakers and a new blue T-shirt her own size, she was thankful to have some new clothes. Idly, she roamed around the room, looking at a large collection of books of all genres.

She glanced down on a lower shelf and saw a small scrapbook. She pulled it off the shelf and saw it was Jake's baby book. Smiling, she sat on the floor to look at it. When she finished, she replaced it and looked at the other books.

On the bottom shelf, she noticed what looked like another scrapbook pushed back where it was almost hidden by books. She pulled it out to look at pictures of Jake when he was in high school. As she closed it to put it back where she found it, a couple of pictures fell out.

She picked them up and looked at a picture of a family—a tall, slender, balding man, a woman who had short, straight brown hair and a big smile. There were four kids, two girls and two boys. The tallest boy looked anywhere from sixteen to eighteen. The others ranged in ages from that to the youngest girl, who looked five or six. Claire wondered who they were. Probably relatives of Jake's, she assumed. More Reeds who didn't live in this area.

She put the picture back and started to move on to the next thing, but she stopped. Something had looked vaguely familiar about the woman. She picked up the picture again to stare at it intently while her heart beat faster. She placed her finger over the woman's hair to just look at her face only.

Claire suddenly felt frozen, as if she was in ice water.

Ten

She stared at the picture, and the chill she felt deepened, making her shake. And then her icy feelings began to change, her temperature climbing as shock changed to fury.

She was certain she was looking at a picture of her sister. Her hair was different, and she was heavier and older, but it had to be Regina. Regina and Jake's brother, Sam, and their family.

As she held the picture and stood, Claire shook with anger. The scrapbook fell from her lap, hitting the floor with a clatter, but she didn't even notice.

She stared at the picture in her hand again. It couldn't have been more than a year or two old for Regina to have a son taller than she was and looking at least sixteen or older. Jake had contact with Regina and his brother. He had a picture of them and their family, so he had to have been in contact. And not that long ago.

She thought of the intimacy she had shared with Jake, sharing her feelings, her body, her hopes, her fears, even her heart. And all the time he had known where his brother and her sister were. He had known about their family. He had to have known and had to have been in touch with them to get this picture.

Regina and Sam had four kids and Jake had known this—how long?

Had he known about them since they left Texas?

In her memory, Claire always thought of Regina just as she had been the night she left. The woman in the picture bore little resemblance to the sister Claire remembered, but everyone changed with time.

Regina had dyed her blond hair brown, or maybe it had just turned brown, because there were a lot of gray streaks now. Her naturally curly hair had been straightened and cut very short—a style she'd never worn before she left home. That was the biggest change, plus the glasses, but those could easily be fake. Or by this time, they might be real. It was difficult to recognize her but not impossible, and Claire hurt again. She had loved Regina, always missed her and thought about her and hoped she was happy.

Claire looked at the picture again. "Regina," she said, running her finger over her sister's picture.

Sam had his arm across her shoulders. He had changed as much as Regina. The hair loss was why she just glanced at him. Sam had had thick brown hair and wore it long. Now it was thinning, leaving a bald spot on the top of his head. His hair was short, with streaks of gray. How old was the picture? It couldn't be very old.

"I've missed you so," she whispered, looking again at Regina's picture. For Regina and Sam to stay away all these years, they must have felt terribly threatened by her brothers and her dad. At the time they disappeared, they probably were right about the reaction of the men in the Blake family. She didn't want to think about what they might have done to Sam. But she knew they would have just barged in and brought Regina home.

And Jake knew where they were, had contact with them and hadn't said one word to her. Anger shook her and was as strong as the hurt she felt that he would do such a thing. He hadn't trusted her at all.

Clenching her fists, Claire trembled with rage, feeling betrayed. She had made clear to Jake how much Regina had meant to her. And he had just listened and never said a word, keeping quiet when she talked about how much she had loved her sister, how much she longed to know Regina was happy and well.

How could he have been so deceitful? How could he have held back and not shared that he knew Regina had a family?

At that moment she was so angry that she was glad he wasn't present so that she had time to pull herself together and think before she told him how she felt. It was probably something like this—some huge deceitful thing—that snowballed into the old feud they were all locked into.

She wanted to get away from Jake, away from his cabin. She couldn't go home to her ranch, because there was still no place to stay on it. She found the website for the hotel in Persimmon and booked a room.

She looked at the picture again. At the four children. Then she realized she was an aunt. Aunt Claire. She turned the picture and saw Regina's neat cursive writing: Sam Jr., Claire Lynn, Becky and Charles. Their grandfather's middle name.

"Claire Lynn," she read aloud, looking at a picture of a teenage girl with curly brown hair. "Claire Lynn," Claire repeated, certain Regina had named their first girl for her. "Aunt Claire," she said aloud, still stunned to discover the picture.

How could Jake have kept this from her? The question tore at her repeatedly as she thought about how she had poured out her heart to him about her pain and overwhelming sense of loss when Regina and Sam eloped.

She shook with anger and pain. She yanked up her phone again to make arrangements to be picked up and driven to Persimmon, where she already had a suite. She didn't want to spend one more minute with Jake than she had to.

She heard boots in the hall and looked up to see Jake standing in the doorway.

Eleven

Jake had walked down the hall looking for Claire. She could slip away from him and she was quiet, even in boots. As he'd reached the open door to the study, he'd almost walked past it, but he'd seen her seated and turned back, smiling as he'd stepped into the doorway. Now he looked at her and at an open book on her lap and a picture in her hand, and his heart sank. He had forgotten about the damn picture of her sister and her family.

"Claire—"

She shook her head. "Don't start, Jake. There isn't an explanation of any sort that will make up for you not telling me that you know where my sister is. And you've known all along." Her voice was low, tight with anger, and he felt his hurt deepen.

"I promised them I wouldn't tell anyone," he said as

he entered the room and started to approach her. When she held up her hand, he paused.

"Stop. Don't you come near me," she said.

"I promised I wouldn't tell anyone," he repeated with an emphasis on the last word. "If I had told you, I would have broken my promise to my brother and to her. I couldn't. I had to keep my promise to them."

A tear spilled down Claire's cheek, and she hastily wiped it away with the back of her hand, and he felt worse. He could see the anger blazing in her green eyes.

"There's nothing you can ever say to make keeping this from me right. I've given you my body. Unfortunately, I probably gave you part of my heart, too, but I will get over that if I haven't already. Your promise is no excuse at all. We're intimate. If you had told me, don't you think I could have kept quiet about it?"

"I don't know. Would you have kept quiet? Or would you want to contact Regina? I think you'd want to talk to her and maybe go see her. I don't see them. They severed relations with everyone here except me. My brother has kept in touch. He makes the contact—I don't. He's never come to see me."

"Have you gone to see him?"

"Yes, four times, after the birth of each of their kids. They invited me to come, so I went. He doesn't come back here. It's your family that drove them away. Mine is bad, but your dad and your brothers are worse. I know Regina wanted to contact you, but your two older brothers and your dad kept her away. She was afraid they would find out. She was afraid of what they might do."

"Jake, there's nothing you'll ever be able to say to make it right or for me to forgive you," she said.

"This is tearing me up. I don't want to hurt you even the tiniest bit."

"Oh, please. Stop, Jake. You kept Regina's whereabouts, information about her and her family, secret from me while we were intimate. When I leave here, I never want to see you again."

"Look, give me a chance here—"

"When I gave you my body, I also gave you my trust. And I expected it to be mutual. Well, it quite obviously was not." She shook her straight red hair back from her face.

"Look, I'm sorry. I did what I thought was best for them."

"Just stop. I've already called for a driver to come here and pick me up. I said I would be by the gate because I know you value your privacy."

"Cancel that and let me take you to Dallas or wherever you want to go," he said, hurting, wishing he could undo what had happened. "I forgot that damn picture—"

"How long ago was it taken?"

"A year ago. They're all a year older now. Claire, they're not coming back. They don't communicate except my brother has let me know when a baby is born."

"How close were you with your brother?"

"Close enough," he answered. "They're scared of your dad and your brothers. And probably rightfully so at first. By now, your dad is older, your brothers are scattered and have other interests. All of them are accustomed to Regina's disappearance, and if she returned, none of you would live under the same roof again, so it's all different now. When Sam and Regina left, they had justification for secrecy."

"I know they did, but it's years later now, as you just said. You could have told me without any repercussions to them. I wouldn't have jumped on a plane and gone to see her or even called her. It just hurts to know that you have no trust in me. It hurts that you kept something so important from me. At least you made it quite clear where I stand with you and how deep your feelings go for me and how much you trust me. I'm leaving, and I don't want to see you again ever."

"I know you have appointments about your house, and you'll need to be out here where you can meet with people and look at the damage, so just stay here and I'll keep out of your way."

"Thank you, but no. I got a suite at the hotel in Persimmon. They had one available, and I can drive back and forth from there, so I don't need to stay here. And I don't want to stay with you one minute longer than I have to. I do not want to see you again," she said slowly and firmly.

With each word, his hurt deepened, and finally he felt a twinge of anger because she wouldn't listen, wouldn't accept his apology, wouldn't give him a chance. If she was so hell-bent on being let in on the secret about her sister, maybe he should just throw the other family secret at her.

"I'll get my things," she said and turned to start out of the room.

"All right, Claire," he said. "You want me to share family secrets with you that concern you," he said, anger and hurt overcoming his judgment. She stopped walking, turned and frowned, staring at him.

"Do you want me to share another big family secret

with you? One you can't tell anyone else and I've never told anyone. I'll be happy to trust you with it."

She crossed her arms over her chest and continued to stare at him. "Okay, Jake, what is it?"

"Here's another one about your family and mine. That third brother of yours. His mother is your mother... but his dad is my father."

"Laird?" Her eyes widened, and she looked stunned.

"Yes, Laird. And he might not know this—he didn't when I was told. His mother is your mother, as everybody thinks, but his dad is my dad, not yours. My dad thought I should know that we're related and both of us are his sons. He didn't tell me until I was older. That's why there was such bitterness and active fighting between our dads and our grandfathers, because all four of them knew the truth."

"Laird is only my half brother?"

"Yes, Laird is half brother to both of us."

She barely heard his answer. Her mind reeled with all the shocks—Regina, Laird—and the pain of Jake's betrayal. That hurt overwhelmed her, and she realized she had fallen in love with Jake or she wouldn't be feeling so hurt by him. She was hurt by what he did, and she was hurt because she would never go out with him again. That was incredible pain, and it meant she was deeply in love with him. She tried to push away the thought and listen, because he was still talking to her.

"...and Laird and I are friends. Now are you happier that you know that secret?"

"That's different from knowing about Regina. That secret about Laird does explain why there was such animosity with our dads. And maybe why Laird is different from my other brothers. Otherwise, that information has little to do with me."

He stared at her and knew there wasn't any fixing their broken relationship, and that hurt. He had never hurt over losing a woman before, but now he felt physical pain. He hadn't intended to hurt her, and he regretted keeping the picture. He wished he could go back and live some moments over to undo the pain he had caused her.

As Claire walked away, she dropped the picture, letting it fall to the floor. She passed him without looking at him and hurried down the hall to get her things. The driver would be at the gate before she could possibly get there.

She had only a few things to pack. When she was ready to go, Jake stood in the doorway.

"I told you to leave me alone."

"Let me drive you to the gate. That's a damn long walk."

"Very well," she said, nodding and knowing he was right. She should have told the driver to pick her up at his cabin. "I don't have much to carry."

She walked to the door, and he followed her into the hall. They walked in silence to his pickup, and he held the door for her. Hurting, fighting tears and still steeped in anger, she climbed in and didn't look at him. As she thought how badly she hurt, she realized this might be the last time she saw Jake.

Maybe her anger with him would help her get over him.

Jake got in, and as he drove, they were both silent.

She'd said all she wanted to say to him, and truthfully, she couldn't wait to get away from him. She hurt all over. She felt angry, betrayed and in pain. Her heart ached. She didn't want to admit that she had fallen in love with him, but she knew she had. How could she have avoided it after their first kiss? It was going to hurt terribly at first to leave him and not see him anymore, but she couldn't stay. Besides, she told herself, she'd always known this day would come sometime anyway.

Trying to get her thoughts off Jake, she thought about what he had told her about Laird. She rarely saw Laird now that they were grown, and they weren't close at all when they were together. Even so, it was still a shock, but it was a possible explanation for why Laird wasn't like her other two brothers. Her mother had had an affair with Jake's dad in spite of the strong feud. She was surprised there hadn't been bigger battles between the dads and between the families, but her mother had her own money, was very independent and had kept a reasonable amount of peace in the family when she was alive.

Then she thought about her sister. Regina had four kids. The oldest one looked almost eighteen. A girl named for her. Claire. She was Aunt Claire. She felt another stabbing pain of longing to meet these children who were related to her. She longed to talk to Regina, just briefly. If Jake had told her about Sam and Regina, would she have been able to promise not to contact Regina?

She didn't want to answer her own question because it didn't matter now. She still didn't know where Regina was, and Jake wasn't going to tell her.

She could understand why Regina had severed ties. Clyde, Les and her dad had been capable of doing real damage to someone if they were angry enough. But as worried she was that they might have even done something to Jake, too, that wouldn't be true now. They were all older. Her dad had probably stopped his fighting long ago because of being older and not well. He wouldn't fight over Laird now at all. The last time she saw her dad, he'd had a cane and an eye patch, and he looked frail.

As rotten as they could be, her brothers had jobs and businesses they started, and she couldn't imagine them fighting now, because now they had too much to lose. They were successful businessmen, Clyde in real estate and Les in construction but she suspected they didn't worry much about ethics.

She stared out the window. Every mile took her away from Jake. She wouldn't see him again, wouldn't talk to him or be with him again. They wouldn't kiss again. That hurt, but she couldn't stay with him after learning that he knew about Regina. He would have shared the truth if he had really trusted her. She wondered how long she would live with the hurt.

They reached Jake's gate, which stood open. "I'll get out here, Jake. You don't need to wait with me," she said, determined not to give in to tears. She hurt, but her anger overrode her pain. "Thank you for taking me in and for everything you did for me."

"I don't want you to go like this, Claire, but you know what you want."

She was still angry with him, shocked over his knowledge of her sister's whereabouts. At the same time, she was in love with him, and telling him goodbye was already the most painful thing she'd ever had to endure.

It had been inevitable from the outset because she'd always known they had no future together. Jake wasn't a marrying man, and she couldn't marry a Reed. She gave a sarcastic laugh to herself. That would bring her brothers and her dad back to town, for sure. But she wanted peace and harmony with her family and keeping Jake close would not be good. And now, she felt she couldn't trust him.

She wondered if the next time Jake talked to his brother if he would even tell Sam that she had found their picture and knew he was in contact with them. If he did tell Sam, would it make a difference?

She wondered, too, if Regina had missed her half as much as she missed Regina. Probably not because when Regina left, she was no doubt wrapped up in being in love with Sam and getting married. Her eleven-year-old sister wouldn't have been that big a part of her life after she left home and married. Especially if she got pregnant right away. Now she had Sam and four kids to love. Regina had probably severed ties and never looked back and figured Claire had gone on with her life, too.

Claire remembered her friend Stefanie's joy over being an aunt and what fun Stefanie had with her nieces and nephews. Stefanie got to see her nieces and nephews. Claire never had and never would. There wasn't any joy in discovering she was an aunt when she couldn't possibly see or talk to her nieces and nephews. Even if they met her now, they would have no interest in her, because they had never known her.

Pain filled her for so much that had happened in the

past, but it was Jake causing the deep hurt. Regina had been gone a long time, and that hurt had dulled through the years—Claire had learned to live with it. What hurt now was telling Jake goodbye, because she had fallen in love with him. She hurt because she loved him, but if she had it to do over, she would react the same way. Jake should have told her about Regina and Sam and trusted her, which he would have if he loved her. Obviously he was not in love with her.

She had known from the start that she was going to get hurt by Jake. She'd known he wouldn't fall in love, and she had guessed that she would. Well, she had, and it hurt terribly to tell him goodbye.

She finally gave in to tears, crying, missing him already, knowing he was gone from her life. Would she ever really get over him? Could she ever forget him?

She heard a car and saw the one coming that had been described to her as her ride. Wiping her eyes, she shouldered her bag and glanced back one time in the direction of Jake's cabin. All she could see were mesquite trees scattered across the fenced fields. Jake had driven away and out of her life.

She turned as the car stopped and a driver got out to greet her and open a back door for her.

Jake drove home and sat in his car after he had parked. He stared into space, seeing Claire and thinking about her. It hurt to have her go and have her angry with him. He had never parted that way with anyone else.

He hated to part that way, and he hated that Claire had been hurt. Honestly, he hadn't thought once about that picture. He hadn't even looked at it since it came last year.

But she wouldn't listen to him now. She was in shock, and maybe when the shock wore off, he could talk to her.

He had always kept his brother's secret, and he was still staying true to his promise. Sam and Regina had never contacted any of their relatives here, including Claire, so he'd just stayed true to his vow of secrecy. After all these years, he didn't give enough thought to Claire still wanting to connect with her sister—and he should have started thinking about that when they became closer and intimate. He'd made a mistake, and he wished he could fix it. But it was too late now. He suspected Claire had said goodbye to him forever.

With a sigh, he got out of his pickup and went inside. He needed to go work—tough physical work that would take his mind off Claire and enable him to get over her. He wished he could talk her out of her decision to leave, but he knew he couldn't. Her relationship with her sister had been tight, and he had a feeling Claire's feelings would never change. She'd never understand why he hadn't shared that info with her—but he had given a promise, and he kept his promises.

He swore softly. He needed to find some work that would take his mind off Claire. He needed to work straight through the night. His nights had been spent with Claire in his arms and their fabulous lovemaking. He was going to have to work himself close to passing out tonight if he hoped to get one second's sleep.

He already missed her, and that surprised and worried him. He had never missed any woman before. He hadn't been ready to say goodbye to Claire. He couldn't recall any time a woman had walked away when he wasn't ready to see her go. But he wasn't ready with Claire.

"Damn," he said quietly. He already missed her, and she had just gotten out of his sight. He went to get some tools. He had some jobs he had put off doing, and now was a good time because they were demanding, physical jobs that would tire him out and take his mind off Claire.

He told himself he'd get over her soon, because he hadn't known her long enough to be deeply serious. What he needed was time and to keep busy and to go out with someone really fun who could occupy his mind.

She wasn't that important to him.

But he couldn't ignore that nagging voice inside his head that repeated the same question over and over again. *If she isn't, why do you hurt so badly?*

He changed clothes, got tools and drove out to an area where cedars had taken root. Even a little cedar was a chore to dig up and get rid of, but hard work was exactly what he needed.

Jake began to dig, working furiously, determined to get Claire out of his thoughts.

It was dark when he returned to his dim, empty house. He went to his gym to work out and run on a treadmill. He hoped to work off some of his worries and also to try to reach a point where he might sleep a little tonight.

He finally showered, dressed in jeans and a T-shirt and went to the kitchen to get dinner, but nothing sounded good—he wasn't hungry, and he missed Claire more than he would have thought possible.

Instead of dinner, he reached for a beer. As he sat at the table with it, he took out his small directory of phone numbers and addresses and looked for his brother's. He sat there for twenty minutes debating whether to make the call. Then finally he picked up his phone and called Sam.

Claire sat in the empty hotel room. She had cried until she thought she couldn't possibly have any more tears left. And then she cried again. She cried over Jake, over her sister, over the whole dang feud.

Her phone rang, and her pulse jumped. It beat even faster when she saw that the call was from Jake.

Her heartbeat raced faster when she answered and heard his deep voice. "Claire, it's Jake. I've talked to Sam," he said, talking fast. "I called to tell him about you and that you found their picture, so I had to tell you a few things."

Shocked, she listened. She hadn't thought about what Jake might do because she was too busy sobbing, missing him and wishing she was with him. How deeply in love with him was she?

"Claire? Are you still there?"

"I'm here," she replied.

"Regina wants you to call them. They were going to call you, but they thought they might have trouble getting through and you would have a better chance. You can FaceTime them or you can just phone. Your choice. That's straight from Regina. When you're ready, I'll tell you the number."

She was amazed. When she could finally formulate the words, she said, "Jake, thank you. Go ahead. What's her number?"

She listened and wrote down the number on the hotel

pad. Her heart raced over getting to call Regina, over Regina wanting her to call and over Jake doing this for her.

"Jake, thank you," she said again. She missed him, wished she had handled things a little differently, but she was still too deeply hurt that he hadn't confided in her. "I'll call Regina now."

"Good luck. It's good to hear your voice. I miss you." His voice grew thick with emotion and then he cleared his throat. "Go on and give her a call."

"I will right now. Thanks," she said, reluctant to break the connection with him, yet knowing it was over between them. She just didn't think she'd ever be able to get past his lack of trust in her. His deception. Besides, she told herself, they wouldn't have had a future together anyway because of the old feud. There was no way she would lose her connections with her family.

Regina had lived all these years cut off from the family members she loved. Jake's brother had lived cut off from his family and from Jake. She didn't want that. Even if Jake got down on his knee and proposed and offered her a ring, she would have to say no.

She didn't want to live cut off from the relatives she loved the way Regina had.

She ended the call with him and punched in the telephone number Jake had given her. In seconds, she couldn't believe it—she was talking to her sister and looking at her. "Regina, I've missed you so much. I'm going to cry, and I can't help it. You look wonderful, and you have a family. I want to see them."

"Jake told us about the fire. I've missed you so, but it seemed best just to sever the ties. I didn't want to take a chance on Dad or our brothers discovering you knew where we are. They would have ruined your life until you told them. I love you too much to allow that to happen."

Her sister wiped at the tears in her eyes. Regina might look different, but the minute they started talking, Claire recognized the sister that she loved. "I'm sorry if that was wrong, Claire. Actually, part of it is still thinking of you as my little sis and so young, which is silly. You grew up just like I did. I'll send you a ticket if you can fly out here and visit us before you start getting all involved in building a new ranch house. Can you come visit?"

"Oh yes," she said, crying with joy and excitement. "I'd love to see all of you. I can come as soon as I can make flight arrangements. But you don't need to get my ticket. I'll get it."

"I should have contacted you, but when I left, you were a little girl, and I didn't think it would be a good idea to call you. If our dad had discovered we were talking, he might have used you to force me to come home. He would have wrung out of you how to get in touch with me if you had known. I was afraid you'd get hurt trying to protect me. Then as the years went by, I just let it go." Regina ran a hand through her short hair. "I still love you, Claire, and I still miss you. Don't think I ever stopped loving you or missing you."

"Oh, Regina, I understand. You were probably right to protect me at that age."

They talked for an hour, and after that Claire spoke to each of the children, getting to know them a little. She couldn't believe the oldest was almost out of high school. When they finally said goodbye, Claire smiled and threw her arms in the air. She wanted to celebrate—with Jake. Then, her smile faded.

Jake wasn't part of her life anymore. And she'd better get used to it.

But ironically, if it weren't for Jake, she wouldn't be back in touch with her sister, nor would she be going to see Regina. She had to at least call and thank him for that.

For right now she pushed aside thoughts about him. She had something more pressing to do: she needed to get her plane ticket and make arrangements to go visit Regina. After all these years, she couldn't wait.

It had been so long since he saw her last. Jake knew Claire had gone to see her sister. She had called him before she left, sounding incredibly happy about the trip. He had called Sam and Regina and talked to Claire several times since she'd gone to visit them. Now she was coming home tomorrow and he ached to see her, to hear about her trip.

He had missed her more than he had ever missed any woman. He thought about her all through his waking hours, and he was making mistakes because his thoughts would drift to Claire and he would forget what he was doing.

He got up on the weekend and cooked breakfast for himself, putting strips of bacon in his big iron skillet. He turned the fire low on his gas range and then turned to get orange juice. He glanced out the window and saw his back gate was open. His big Lab knew how to open the gate and frequently did. Then the dog would go join the cowboys and spend the day around them. The dog had figured out how to open the gate, but he never tried to learn how to close it, despite the countless times Jake had tried to teach him. Jake went out to close it, because the dog could open it and get back in if he wanted to.

Jake gazed at the horizon and thought about the past month. He still missed Claire and wanted to see her as soon as she returned from visiting her sister. Maybe she was over being mad at him. She had sounded happy the last time they talked and actually she told him she missed him. Feeling hopeful for the first time in a long time, he turned to go back to the kitchen and glanced at the window.

Orange flames flickered, and he remembered his bacon in the big skillet. He ran back inside, grabbing a fire extinguisher as he ran through the back entryway.

When he raced into the kitchen, a fire burned in the skillet and had caught a curtain at the window. That's what he had seen burning.

He turned off the gas burner and then raised the extinguisher, aiming it at the curtain, squirting it and putting out the fire in seconds. Next, he grabbed a lid for the iron skillet, covered it and smothered that fire. Taking a deep breath, he pulled out a chair and sat down at the table. That all had happened because he couldn't keep from thinking about Claire.

There was no more denying it. He was in love with her. For the first time in his life, he was in love. He wanted her back in his life. He wanted her in his life all the time.

Would she ever get over her anger with him? She had said she missed him. How strong were her feelings for him? Could he ever get her back?

He thought about the feud and her feelings about that. She had repeatedly told him they could never have a permanent relationship even if they ever wanted one because of the feud. She had said she never wanted to marry and be cut off from her family the way Regina had been. That damned old feud! It was time to end it. He stared into space, racking his brain for any way possible to bring it to a conclusion. Would anyone be willing to join him and let the feud die?

Then he thought about Claire again. When he saw her again, would he be able to persuade her to take a chance on marriage? Did he really want to marry at this point in his life? It was years sooner than he had ever expected to settle down.

He had always thought he would marry when he was in his forties. He hadn't ever wanted to be tied down before that.

He remembered that night they'd lain in bed when he'd told her that his time with her had been paradise. Such true words. He leaned over the table and thought about his life and about Claire. No matter what age he was now, he wanted her back. He missed her. He loved her and he wanted—needed—her in his life. He was ready to settle down with her...but could he ever talk her into marriage? She was a strong person, accustomed to running her life and making her decisions alone. Could he convince her to take a chance on marrying him?

He didn't even know for certain if she was over her anger with him about Regina.

There was a way to get answers to all his questions if he really wanted to. He took a deep breath and began to make plans. The problem that loomed first might be the next to the biggest one—could he get her to see him?

Twelve

It had been a week since Claire arrived back in Dallas and then drove out to Persimmon to move back into the hotel suite. She'd had a wonderful time with Regina and her family, and for a couple of days she was in euphoria from her trip and being with her sister, but that had worn off. She was home now, and she missed Jake. She had gotten along at her sister's because she was so busy with Regina and her family, but since the first solitary night in Dallas and then the next night in Persimmon by herself, she'd missed Jake badly. It surprised her how much she missed him.

She was the one who'd told him goodbye, who'd told him to get out of her life, but now it was a void she didn't like. She missed him in too many ways—his sexy kisses and lovemaking, his upbeat outlook, his companionship, his flirting and constant light touches that built desire but also made her aware that he liked being with her.

How many times a day did she reach for her phone to call him, then stop? He would walk out of her life at some point anyway. The more he was in her life before he said goodbye, the more she would hurt when he left.

At least that was what she told herself, but it wasn't working out well. No matter what argument she used, she still missed him and wanted to be with him.

Could she really take him back in her life when it might just mean more heartache later? She may have changed, but it didn't necessarily mean Jake had. He wasn't a marrying man—he'd told her that upfront—so even if they made up, Jake wouldn't propose. Did she want to live a life of just being with him for a time without marriage?

Even though she didn't know what was in store for their future, she knew she had already forgiven him. And, she needed to think before she called to thank him for telling his brother about her. If Jake hadn't told them, she never would have seen Regina again, and for that she was grateful.

But she needed to figure out what exactly she wanted from Jake.

She paced the suite from door to window, but she couldn't stop the questions that echoed in her head. Could she accept life on Jake's terms? Was she better off just trying to get over him?

Twenty minutes later she was still pacing. She still had no answers. All she knew was that she was wildly in love with him and she had sent him packing. How could she get him back?

Her cell phone rang, and her heart skipped a beat when she saw the call was from Jake. Smiling, she answered.

"Claire, I want to take you to dinner tomorrow night," he said.

"That's getting right to the point," she said. "I'd love to go to dinner with you tomorrow night."

"That's good. Does this mean I'm a little bit forgiven?" She could hear the tentativeness in his speech even though he tried to put it a light tone.

"Yes, you are," she answered, suddenly serious and wishing he was with her right now. "We can talk about it tomorrow night."

"Good. How about seven? And plan on a long evening. We need to talk."

"Now I'm curious," she said, wishing he had asked her for dinner tonight, because she wanted to be with him.

"Any chance we could move this dinner up to tonight?" he asked.

"You're a mind reader—even over the phone. I'd love to move it up to tonight."

"See you at seven."

"See you at seven," she answered, echoing him. She disconnected the call and felt her entire body pulsate. She was too excited to sit still and began pacing again, this time with a smile on her face instead of a frown. She needed something to wear—her sexiest dress. "Jake Reed, I'm about to make you sit up and take notice."

She couldn't wait for the day to pass. She wanted to be with him with all her being. She wanted to kiss him and be kissed, to love and be loved by him. She wanted tonight with him and to make up with him, and if he broke her heart later, she would just deal with it when it happened. She screeched and jumped in the air, throwing her arms up and twirling around. "Jake, I'm going to love you tonight until you never want to let me go."

That might be a pipe dream because he always moved on, but she was going out with him tonight, and maybe, just maybe, he'd stick around awhile.

At exactly 6:59 p.m., when Claire opened the door to face Jake, she wanted to throw her arms around his neck and hug him. He wore navy slacks and a pale blue long-sleeved shirt that was unbuttoned at the collar, and he looked incredibly handsome. She smiled and greeted him.

"Come in. I'm ready. I wanted to say a few things to you before we go out."

"You look gorgeous," he said, his voice lowering a notch.

"It's a dress I don't wear often—not much need for it on the ranch, and it isn't exactly a church dress," she said, glancing down at her black sleeveless dress that had a straight skirt and a plunging neckline. She looked up at him.

"Jake, I had a long talk with Regina, and she made me see how important it was to them that you didn't tell anyone about them. She was grateful for your secrecy and made me understand. I told you I never wanted to see you again, but that's not true at all. Even when I was angry at you, I missed you so much. The thought of us not being together…" she trailed off.

Jake grabbed her hands. "The important thing is

we're here now, and I'm glad. I missed you. And, I promise I won't keep something like that from you again. We're in this together now."

"I've missed you so much," she said.

He pulled her to him, his arm going around her waist as he leaned down to kiss her. She wrapped her arms around his neck, stood on tiptoe and kissed him in return, her heart racing as she lost herself in his fabulous sexy kiss.

Suddenly, he stepped away slightly, taking her hand in his. He gazed at her intently. "Claire, I know you don't think I'm the marrying type, but I think I was just waiting for the right woman. I love you, and I want to marry you. Will you marry me?"

Stunned, she stared at him. "Oh, Jake. I love you. I've loved you despite our families." She stared at him and couldn't get words. Tears stung her eyes. "I want to say yes, but I can't. We can't marry. I can't live the way Regina and Sam live."

She hurt badly. She loved him and suspected she always would, but she couldn't see any way they could marry. "We have that feud, and you know what that means."

He framed her face with his hands. "Listen to me. I've talked this over with Sam. We both think it's time to end that old feud. What I think we should do is have a big church wedding and invite both families."

"Oh, Jake," she said, shaking her head and wiping her eyes before the tears could fall. "My brothers—I can't imagine what they would do."

"I'll tell you what they'll do," he said. He placed his hands on her shoulders. "I've already had a talk with

Clyde with Les. I took the Persimmon sheriff with me, but he stayed in the waiting rooms of their respective offices until I finished talking to them first, and then I called him in, and he talked to them. We're not going to have any trouble from Clyde or Les. I didn't bother talking to Laird, because I don't think he ever was the cause of trouble."

"I don't think so, either," she responded. But she couldn't get her mind around everything he'd said. "You talked to my brothers?"

"I did. They're businessmen now, and they don't want to get in trouble with the law or with their customers. They don't scare me, and they never have. They may have given us trouble in the past, but they won't now. Clyde has his own real estate company, and Les is a builder, and they're both doing well. They are definitely interested in keeping things that way. They won't give anybody any trouble. We have an understanding."

"Jake, they can be so sneaky—"

"So can I. They don't want trouble, believe me. Don't worry about your brothers. You'll see."

"They're not the only ones who live by that feud. A lot of the older people have strong feelings about it."

"Sam and I talked about that. That's why he and Regina and their family will come. They will be present with their four kids. Those four kids are Reeds and they are Blakes—they have both families' blood in their veins. They have relatives in both clans, and Regina is going to contact some of the Blakes and let them meet her kids, and Sam is going to contact some of the Reeds and let them meet the kids. Maybe then everyone will see how ridiculous this old feud is."

"I hadn't thought about the kids. And I never even considered that Regina and Sam would come here."

"Now back to what's important. In case you forgot, I asked you if you'd marry me, and I've told you we can work things out and stay right here in Dallas and on our ranches. So, Claire Blake, will you marry me and become Mrs. Jake Reed?"

She stared at him. "Oh yes! Yes, I will. I love you, Jake, with all my heart," she said, smiling and standing on tiptoe to throw her arms around his neck and kiss him while joy bubbled in her.

Instantly, his arm banded her waist, and he pulled her tightly against him as he leaned down to kiss her.

"Ahh, darlin', how I've missed you."

"I missed you, Jake," she whispered, and then he kissed her again. She didn't know how long they stood there in each other's embrace, bodies pressed against each other, lips together. Her heart raced with happiness. She was going to accept his offer—all of it. She would marry him, and she would stop worrying about the feud. Jake would have to work miracles to make the feud go away, but this would be a start. It might be a very big start.

Sam and Regina's kids might make a giant difference in how people felt about the feud.

When she finally could think clearly about more than the feud, she pulled back and looked up at him. "Are we still going to run two separate ranches?"

"We'll do whatever you want to do," he answered. "I'm open for anything as long as you're in my bed at night."

She laughed and put her arms around his neck again. "We'll have fun, Jake," she said.

"Hey, wait. I forgot—I didn't do this right. I brought you a present." He reached into his hip pocket and brought out a box tied with a pink ribbon. "I got this for you."

She took it from him and unfastened the bow. Her heart raced because she was filled with happiness. She was going to marry Jake, the man she loved, and she would get to keep her ranch. And maybe the sister she loved would be back in her life now.

She removed the wrapping paper and held a small box in her hand. She opened it and gasped. "Oh, Jake," she said, looking at a dazzling emerald-cut diamond.

"I did it backward. I was going to give you that, and when you opened it, then I intended to ask you if you'd marry me."

"Yes, Jake Reed, I will marry you and love you all the rest of my life," she said, looking at the dazzling big diamond and then up at the man who dazzled her far more. "I love you, Jake," she said, meaning it. Then a thought struck her. "We haven't even talked about kids. Do you want kids?"

"Yes, I do. Do you?"

"Yes, I want your kids. I don't care how many. We can decide that as we go."

He laughed and took the ring from her and held her hand. "I'll do this right. I love you, Claire. Will you marry me?"

"Yes, Jake. I love you, and I'll marry you."

He slipped the ring on her finger and drew her to

him to kiss her again. When he released her, he picked up her hand to look at the ring.

Her gaze followed his. "It's gorgeous and it fits."

"Ah, darlin', how I love you," he said, wrapping his arms around her and drawing her to him to kiss her. She kissed him in return while her heart beat fast with joy and love. She opened her eyes, waved her fingers and looked at the dazzling diamond that would always be a symbol of Jake's love. "I'm marrying the sexiest, best-looking guy in all of Texas," she said, smiling at him and hugging him.

"I want to spend a lifetime making you happy," he whispered, showering light kisses on her. "It'll be good. I promise I'll do everything I can to try to make you happy. And you know how well I keep my promises." He looked at her, and they both smiled. "I love you, darlin'."

"I love you, Jake," she said. Joy filled her, and she held him tightly, this rancher who loved the same things she did—and what was most wonderful, he had fallen in love with her. Life was wonderful.

* * * * *

ONCE FORBIDDEN,
TWICE TEMPTED

KAREN BOOTH

For my agent, Melissa Jeglinski, who never fails
to come up with the craziest good ideas.

One

The greatest joy of Tara Sterling's professional life was watching happy clients sign on the dotted line for a multimillion-dollar home.

"The family is over the moon about the house." That might have been the case, but today, this particular family wasn't on hand to complete the purchase. The Bakers were spring skiing in Aspen and had sent a woman from their escrow company as proxy. "They're so thankful you got it for them at such a good price."

"I'm happy to help." Tara waved off the compliment as her assistant gathered and reviewed the paperwork. "It's my job."

"Very well done. There were an awful lot of bidders on this property."

Tara smiled and nodded, thankful for this blip of appreciation. Even if it wasn't directly from the buyer, she'd always accept some gratitude. Tara worked incredibly hard for it—her reputation in San Diego real estate was that of miracle worker. She had a knack for hunting down dream homes, and the negotiation skills to get them at the right price. Reportedly, other agents hated having to face her. They whispered words like *ruthless.* Tara felt that was an unfair characterization. She saw herself as simply unwilling to lose. She'd already lost so much—her mother when she was only nine, her marriage seven years ago, and last year, her beloved father.

The death of her dad had been an especially crushing blow. He'd been her guiding light through childhood and adolescence, a presence so solid that it had been devastating to lose him. It had been fourteen months and she couldn't forget one of the last things he'd said to her— *Don't wait to be happy.* She hadn't realized it until that moment. She *wasn't* happy. Despite meeting new people every day, her world had somehow become smaller— more acquaintances, fewer true friends, and zero love life. Most men were intimidated by her success, and she was disappointed by their lack of vision. If she was ever going to find love again, she needed a trailblazer. A maverick, like her ex-husband, Johnathon Sterling. He had vision. He was passionate and exciting. Unfortunately, he also had a wandering eye and was easily bored. Their marriage had only lasted three years. Half of it had been thrilling; the other half made her feel as though she'd never measure up. At least not as a woman.

So she'd turned to her career for fulfillment, and for a while, it worked like gangbusters. She made piles of money. She took the beautiful home she and Johnathon had shared, and she'd given it a complete redo. She'd bought closets of designer clothes and leased a brand new Mercedes every year. She'd done her best to show the world that her divorce had not slowed her down. One man falling out of love with her did not define her. The only problem was very little of that was making her truly happy. And it hadn't dawned on her until her father passed away.

"If that's everything you need from me, I'll get out of your hair." The woman from the escrow company stood and extended her hand across the meeting-room table.

Tara rose to return the gesture when her sights were drawn to her phone, which lit up with a call from Grant Singleton. Luckily, she had her ringer on Mute. She'd let it go to voice mail. "I believe we're all set."

"Perfect. The Bakers will be so happy to hear that. So will their contractor. He's eager to get to work. He has an awful lot of it ahead of him."

Tara showed the woman to the door. "Getting started on the kitchen right away? I know they weren't happy with the size of the center island and were thinking of adding a pizza oven."

"Oh, no. They're leveling the whole thing."

"The entire kitchen?"

"The whole thing."

Oh.

"New construction," the woman continued. "They didn't see any point in trying to salvage what was there. Once you opened up the kitchen, you might as well tackle the dining room, and it only snowballs from there. I realize the seller did a lot of work on the property, but it's not quite to the Bakers' taste."

This was a common occurrence in the more expensive areas of San Diego County. The land was often worth more than the structure standing on it. But it still didn't strike Tara as any less wasteful to tear down a gorgeous home. "They told me they loved the house. We negotiated based on their personal plea that they wanted to raise their children there."

The woman shrugged. "They will raise their kids there. Just not in that exact house. Gotta get a good deal somehow, right?"

Tara dug her fingernails into the heels of her hands. This was the exact kind of frustration that made her question what she was doing. Money wasn't enough. How much satisfaction could she take in a job well done when clients turned around and bulldozed everything she'd found for them?

"I hope they're very happy," Tara said and bid her farewell. She had to let this go. Just like she'd done dozens of times.

As she turned back into the meeting room to grab her phone, the screen lit up again. Another call from Grant. Grant was an old friend, and business partners with Tara's ex-husband, Johnathon. She and Grant spoke every now and then, but it was odd for him to call her twice in such a short span of time. She should answer.

"Grant, what's up? Is this a butt dial?" Tara could admit that the vision of Grant's butt crossed her mind. She'd never seen it in the flesh, but the man looked amazing in a pair of dress pants, or jeans when he wore them.

"Thank God you answered." Grant's normally deep voice was breathless and desperate. He was usually calm and always in control. But those few words hinted at trouble.

"What's wrong?"

"Johnathon had an accident. I'm at the hospital downtown. How fast can you get here?"

Tara's stomach sank nearly as fast as her pulse began racing. Adrenaline kicked in. She beelined for her office, cradling the phone between her ear and shoulder and grabbed her handbag. "I'm on my way. Twenty minutes if I don't hit any traffic."

"Hurry, Tara. It's serious."

She came to a halt. "This isn't a joke you two cooked up, is it?"

"No. Of course not. Just get over here. We might lose him."

Tara was back to running. "Lose him? What happened?"

"There's no time to explain. I have to go. Just get here." Grant hung up.

Tara raced down four flights of stairs in heels and sprinted across the parking lot to her Mercedes. The midday, early July sun was fierce as she fumbled for her sunglasses. She tried to ignore her heart's thunderous performance in the center of her chest. She fought back waves of nausea. She and Johnathon had been divorced for seven years, but she still loved him and cared about him deeply. Even though losing him had left her hollowed out in the end, they'd had a magnificent ride. She couldn't stand the thought of not having him in her life anymore. And if she was going to allow herself a purely selfish thought in a weak moment, she couldn't live through another personal loss.

But Johnathon was impossibly strong. If ever there was a fighter, it was him. "He'll be okay," she muttered to herself as she zigged and zagged her way through traffic. "He has to be."

Luckily, the hospital had a valet, and she zipped right up to the stand. Tara practically threw her keys at the attendant as she ran in through the sliding doors and up to the information desk to find out where Johnathon was. She rushed down the hall, breathing hard, which only made the antiseptic smell fill her nose more readily. These were not pleasant aromas. They made her think of losing her dad. And her mom. *No more hospitals.* She couldn't stand them.

There was a wait for the elevator, so she hiked up to the fifth floor, emerging from the stairwell, huffing and puffing. And duly disoriented. Where was she? This did not look like a surgical floor and it was miles from the ER. The nurses' station was off to the right, but she only got a few steps closer to it before a hand was on her elbow, pulling her back. She turned to see Grant. All color had drained from his handsome face, making the contrast between his skin and dark stubble so much starker. He opened his mouth to speak, but in that split second, Tara knew, deep down, what he was about to say.

"I'm so sorry. They couldn't save him."

No no no. This wasn't possible. Johnathon was larger than life. He couldn't simply die on a Tuesday with no warning. This made no sense. "What in the world happened? Was he driving too fast on the Pacific Coast Highway again? I told him a million times it was dangerous."

Grant shook his head and pinched the bridge of his nose. "It was a total freak accident. Line drive to the temple on the golf course. I guess he was still conscious in the ambulance, but he hemorrhaged."

Tara clasped her hand over her mouth, struggling to keep her balance. Johnathon was dead. It didn't seem fathomable. He was not only so young—only forty-one—but he despised golf. None of this was fair.

"Where is he?"

Grant gestured with a backward nod of his head. "I had them bring him up to a private room. Miranda's with him right now. I didn't want her having to say her goodbye in the ER or even worse, down in the morgue."

"Who called you?"

"Miranda. She was at the country club, in the middle of a tennis lesson when it happened. She was able to ride with him to the hospital."

Miranda was Johnathon's third wife. She and Tara enjoyed a pleasant enough rapport. Miranda was a highly successful interior designer and had done some work for Tara, staging homes for sale. "This is awful. They've hardly been married a year."

Grant took Tara's hand and led her over to a small waiting room so they could sit. "That's the least of it." His face adopted an even more somber look, something that Tara would not have thought possible. "Miranda's pregnant and Johnathon didn't know. She had to tell him in the ambulance while he was dying. She'd been planning to surprise him with the news. Tonight."

A profound wave of sadness hit her. Johnathon had wanted a family for a very long time. Children had been one of the bigger issues that came between Tara and him. She'd wanted to wait, but she'd assumed they were going to have a lifetime together. "Oh, my God. A baby. And now he's gone."

"I know. I can't even believe the timing. It doesn't seem fair."

Tara felt as though they were all taking a master class in unfair. "Her only family is her brother."

"She's really going to need a lot of support. Help with the baby."

Tara's heart felt impossibly heavy. She and Miranda weren't close, but Tara knew what it was like to be on her own. Adrift. With no one to lean on but herself. "I'm happy to help. Whatever she needs."

"Even as Johnathon's ex-wife?"

Tara nodded emphatically, even as memories of her short and tumultuous marriage to Johnathon flashed before her. Happy days. Sad days. Crazy, inexplicable days. "We were never right for each other. He wanted kids right away. I wanted to get more established in my career. He was always trying to squeeze everything he could out of life and I was too busy being methodical."

"For two people who weren't right for each other, you certainly fell fast." Grant cleared his throat. It wasn't the first time he'd voiced his displeasure with the way Tara and Johnathon got together.

Tara had met Grant and Johnathon on the same night, at a mutual friend's birthday party, eleven years ago. It had been Grant who'd flirted with her all night, and Grant who'd asked her out. But it was also Grant who got called out of town for a family emergency the next day, and it was Johnathon who swooped in like a bird of prey, sweeping Tara off her feet. She'd always chalked it up to fate. And Grant never seemed to suffer. He'd had plenty of women in his life.

"I know. That was just the way he was. Everything moved like lightning. It was stupid, and we were young, but I don't regret it." She heard her own voice wobble. Reality was finally starting to settle in. Johnathon was gone. Her first love.

Grant pulled her into a tight embrace. "Of course

you don't. He was an incredible man. An unbelievable best friend."

Tara settled her head on Grant's shoulder and allowed herself a few quiet tears. She didn't like to cry in front of other people. There'd been too many times in her life when doing that had made her feel weak and vulnerable. But this was different. This was Grant. One of her oldest and dearest friends. A man she'd had a crush on for a day or two before his best friend took center stage. "He was also a human tornado."

"He was indeed."

"What's going to happen to Sterling Enterprises?" Tara asked. Johnathon and Grant had built their real-estate-development firm into a true empire, but Tara had been there in the beginning. She'd thought she was a part of the team, but Johnathon eventually decided it was a bad idea for a husband and wife to work together. He'd pushed her to focus on selling real estate, rather than building. And so she had, because she loved him and he'd had a vision.

"Sterling will be fine."

"You're sure?" She was still holding on to Grant. She didn't want to leave the cocoon of his smell or the comfort of his embrace. Being in his arms right now was like a soft wool blanket on a cold fall day. Nothing like the rest of the hospital.

"There's a plan in place for me to step in as CEO. I just never thought we'd have to use it." Grant gently rubbed Tara's back. "I'll have to coordinate some things with Miranda, since she'll be majority owner now, but I'm guessing that between her own business and the baby on the way, she'll gladly let me steer the ship. I don't see any reason for her to do anything different."

Tara sat back and Grant took her hand again. "You're the one who's going to have to break it to the staff. And fast. Before the media finds out," he said.

He nodded, keeping his fingers wrapped around hers. "And there's a funeral to plan."

It was all so overwhelming. "That's going to be a lot for Miranda to deal with. I'm happy to help. Is there anything else I can do?"

"Someone's going to have to call Astrid. I supposed I'd better start making a list."

"Of course." Astrid was Johnathon's second wife, the Norwegian supermodel, the one Tara didn't like quite as well. Johnathon had married her mere months after his split from Tara, and Tara had always wondered if there had been some overlap between them. Still, Tara had managed to build some affinity with Astrid. It was part and parcel of being a real estate agent. She found a way to get along with everyone. "I'll do it. You have enough on your plate. I'm sure she'll be nothing but distraught."

"Thank you, Tara. I really appreciate that. Are you sure you're going to be okay?" He gazed at her with his deep brown eyes. They were filled with sincerity and compassion, just as they'd always been. He had a big heart.

A totally irrational part of Tara's brain wanted to escape into those eyes—surely nothing could hurt her there. "I will. I'll be okay. How about you?"

"I'm always okay. You know me. We'll get through this. I promise." He leaned closer and kissed her temple, stirring up an echo of the attraction that had been there between them the night they met.

Tara's eyes drifted shut as she soaked up his touch. It had been so long since a man had expressed something so tender toward her. But she could only enjoy it for an instant before the world around her intruded again.

"Max," Grant said.

Tara's eyes popped back open, confronted with Johnathon's longtime lawyer, Maxwell Hughes, who'd walked into the waiting area. He was an imposing man, towering and skinny with dark slicked-back hair, like the evil genius in a spy movie.

"We need to talk," Max stated coldly. "Is there a private meeting room?" He unsubtly slid Tara the side-eye, as if she was somehow in the way.

"I should go." Tara got up from her seat. She was upset enough. She didn't need time in Max's presence. He'd been unbelievably cruel to her during her divorce from Johnathon. "I doubt Miranda wants to see me or talk to me right now anyway."

"Max, give me one minute." Grant ushered Tara out of the waiting room and over to the elevator. He pressed the button for the ground floor. "I'm so sorry about that. The guy clearly has no bedside manner."

"Tell me about it. What do you think he wants? Is this really the right time for a meeting?"

Grant frowned, seeming just as perplexed. "If he wants to talk to me, it must have to do with Sterling Enterprises. Hopefully just a formality with putting me in as CEO."

"Oh. Sure. That makes sense."

"I know. The timing stinks. But let's be honest, everything about this is horrible."

Two

The last time Grant had been in the church in sunny Point Loma, California, with its breathtaking view of the rocky coast and deep blue Pacific, it had been to stand up as best man for Johnathon. That day, Johnathon married his third wife, Miranda. Now, little more than a year later, Grant was here to bid farewell to his old friend.

Grant shifted in his front-row seat and patted Miranda's hand, although she didn't seem to warm to it. He'd been doing his best to comfort her for three days, ever since she called to tell him that Johnathon had taken a line drive to the head. Even then, Grant had been so sure that Johnathon would be fine. If Johnathon was anything, he was a survivor. He'd come from nothing and clawed his way to billions. Johnathon always came out on top.

But that hadn't been the case this time. Instead, Grant

arrived at San Diego Memorial with only seconds to say goodbye. Meanwhile, a frantic Miranda wept at Johnathon's bedside, begging him to hold on. *You can't leave. I'm pregnant.* There was a baby on the way, a child who would never know their father. And a series of events had been triggered, but it wasn't quite what Grant had banked on. After his meeting with Max, Johnathon's personal attorney, Grant had learned that running Sterling Enterprises as its new CEO would require him dealing with all three Sterling wives. They still didn't know it, and Max had suggested they wait until a few days after the funeral to drop the bombshell. Grant was still formulating a plan for managing the aftermath, but for now, all he could do was nod at the poignant things the minister was saying.

"Johnathon was larger than life, instantly memorable and completely unforgettable. He had a heart as big as the Pacific Ocean he so loved to surf in. He was blessed in his life with three beautiful wives, all of whom are with us today. Our condolences to them as they come to terms with Johnathon's untimely death."

A deep sob came from the pew across the aisle. Grant didn't need to look to know that it was Astrid, wife number two, who'd arrived from Oslo, Norway, with absolutely no idea who Miranda was or that Johnathon had ever remarried. Grant had been left to smooth that over, just as he'd done on countless occasions during his friendship with Johnathon. He could only guess what was going to happen when Astrid discovered that Miranda was pregnant with Johnathon's baby.

Grant felt a pang of guilt, realizing how much it angered him that Johnathon had never told Astrid the truth. Johnathon may have loved all three of his wives deeply, but he'd created plenty of trouble for them, too. Grant had witnessed both the good and the bad. He hated the things that Miranda and Astrid had gone through, but in Grant's eyes, the wife who'd been truly unappreciated was the first—Tara. Beautiful, stunning, tough-as-nails Tara.

She was seated only two people away from him. It was impossible to not steal the occasional glance at her, just like he'd been unable to keep his eyes off her the other day at the hospital. She was a singular beauty, with glossy blond hair, flawless and glowing skin, deep blue eyes and full lips colored a soft pink. He'd wanted to kiss them countless times, but Johnathon had always been clear, even after their divorce: Tara was off-limits.

Still, Grant would need to pull her into his orbit now. She was highly skilled at persuasion, which meant she could be a strong ally in helping him deal with Miranda and Astrid. But would she stay on his side? That was a big question. Certainly Tara had loved Johnathon immensely and would want Sterling Enterprises to continue on in his name. But no one could have guessed that the succession plan Johnathon had put in place came with a caveat—one that stripped Grant of control. And now he had to get it back.

The congregants stood as the service came to an end, and Grant excused himself to step out into the aisle as one of six pallbearers. The other five were all employees of Sterling Enterprises, including Clay, Miranda's brother. Separating Johnathon and the business was impossible. They were coiled tightly around each other. Noticeable in his absence was Johnathon's only living family, his younger brother Andrew. Grant had hoped that Johnathon's death would be enough to make Andrew show up. But some rifts ran too deep.

As Grant lifted the casket with the other men, it was impossible to ignore the great weight that now sat on his shoulders. He had to be there for Miranda and the child who would never know their father. He had to care for Sterling Enterprises and keep the company flourishing. He must also be certain that Astrid had the support she needed to get through this difficult time. And he would have been lying if he said he didn't want the chance to be Tara's shoulder to cry on.

The other day at the hospital had only served as a strong reminder that his attraction to her had never gone away. Anything romantic between himself and Tara never would have happened when Johnathon was still walking the earth, but things were different now. Everything had changed. And it was time for Grant to be one of the rare few to move beyond the specter of Johnathon Sterling. Certainly in business. And quite possibly in the personal realm, as well.

Tara dutifully filed behind the other wives as Johnathon was carried from the church. Miranda was first to follow the casket, trailed by Astrid. Each was racked with sorrow, Miranda quietly weeping and Astrid so overcome she struggled to walk. The four-inch heels certainly weren't helping. Tara's place in the processional was last, the farthest removed from her ex. In that moment, she felt it was her job to keep it together. She would speak for all three wives by offering polite nods for the throng of guests wishing to share their condolences. The sea of acquaintances, close friends and perfect strangers said over and over again that they were sorry for her loss. It didn't make it any more real. Tara could hardly believe that Johnathon was dead. She kept expecting him to step out from behind a pillar and declare that it was all a joke.

Tara knew that coming to terms with this loss would not be easy. She must finally face the mix of good and bad feelings about Johnathon, everything she'd avoided reckoning with when they'd divorced. She was deeply saddened by this realization; it left a hole in her psyche, but she couldn't bring herself to shed more than a few tears right now. It didn't matter that this was the time to let it all out. She'd first learned it wasn't in her best interest to show her emotions when kids at school teased her for still crying months after her mother had died. Johnathon had taught her to be tough, as well. Not in words, so much as his actions. He could be sweet when she was down, but he adored strong, upbeat Tara, showering her with affection. Being strong got her what she wanted.

A ribbon of relief zipped through her when she finally stepped out into the blazing sun of the July day. It was a gorgeous summer day, in the midseventies with a light breeze. She was dying to get back to her house across the bay in Coronado, take off her heels and maybe go for a walk on the beach. Clear her head. Begin the process of moving on. But she couldn't leave without speaking to the other two wives.

"Miranda," Tara said, catching up with Johnathon's widow. "How are you doing? Is there anything I can help you with? Anything I can do?"

Miranda turned, hiding behind a dark pair of Jackie O sunglasses. Her ebony hair was back in an elegant twist, but the streaks of mascara on her cheeks showed the evidence of her grief. "How am I doing? My husband is dead." She hugged her Louis Vuitton handbag to her side like a life preserver.

Tara was a little taken aback by the response. She and Miranda had a friendship outside the fact that they'd fallen for the same man. "No. I know. Today is incredibly hard. I shouldn't have asked. It was stupid of me. I'm sorry."

Miranda's shoulders slumped in defeat. "No. I'm sorry. I'm a mess." She shot a quick glance over each shoulder, then pulled Tara closer. "I'm a big ball of hormones. I can't even begin to process the idea of raising this child on my own," she whispered.

"I take it you haven't told anyone."

"My brother Clay knows. You. Grant. A few of my close girlfriends. That's it. I don't want anyone else to know. Not yet. It's too much to deal with. And I really don't want Astrid to find out before she's back in Norway. Johnathon told me how hard they tried to have a baby. Plus, apparently, Johnathon didn't have the guts to tell her that I even existed, so there's that to deal with. I'm sure she hates me."

"Don't say that." It was the polite thing to say, but Tara could only imagine what Astrid might be feeling. She was the sort of woman who put her emotions front and center.

Miranda shook her head in dismay. "Right now, I just want to curl into a ball in my bed, go to sleep and wake up to a different reality."

Tara pulled her into a hug. Normally full of life, Miranda was frail right now. Her pain and emptiness radiated off her. "I'm sorry, Miranda. I'm so sorry."

She stiffened in Tara's arms. "Oh, crap. Astrid is coming this way. I can't deal with her. Nobody wants to see a cat fight at a funeral. Sorry." Miranda tore herself from Tara's embrace, turned on her heel and disappeared into the crowd.

Before Tara had a moment to prepare, Astrid was tugging on her arm.

"I don't know what he saw in her." Astrid's Norwegian accent was thicker now than the last time she and Tara had spoken. Astrid had moved back to Norway right after her divorce from Johnathon two years ago. Perhaps the time in her home country speaking her native language had erased the Southern California edge her voice had once had.

"Miranda's lovely," Tara said. "But you're the most beautiful woman at this funeral, so I don't see any reason to be jealous."

Indeed, Astrid was a true beauty, the sort of woman who wore no makeup and always looked like she was ready for the cover of a magazine. She had lustrous honey gold hair, and was tall and willowy; all clothes looked good on her. It would be easy to envy Astrid, but Tara didn't have it in her. She knew that Astrid had suffered great emotional scars from her marriage to Johnathon.

"I can't believe he married again. He never told me." Astrid's perfect lower lip was quivering.

Tara didn't have an explanation for that. She couldn't begin to imagine why Johnathon wouldn't have told her. Tara had been duly notified each time Johnathon remarried. He'd always framed it as the polite thing to do, although the perpetually-single Tara had felt as if he was only rubbing it in. Unsure of what she could say that would possibly make Astrid feel better, Tara pulled her into a hug. Apparently her role at this funeral was comforting the other wives. "What's done is done. He's gone and we all have to find a way to move on."

"I can't imagine letting it go. Ever."

Tara tried to not roll her eyes, releasing Astrid from the hug. "How long are you staying in San Diego?"

Astrid sniffled. "I still have my penthouse downtown. I plan to stay for a little while. We had a dreary spring at home. Plus, being here reminds me of Johnny. I feel closer to him."

A corner of Tara's mouth quirked up. Astrid was the only person who'd ever referred to Johnathon as Johnny. It did not suit the Johnathon she'd known, but perhaps he'd been different with Astrid. Johnathon was certainly a puzzle of a man. Looking for an exit from her conversation with Astrid, Tara took a quick survey of the crowd, and spotted Grant, his easy smile impossible to miss. She wanted at least a few words with him before she left.

"Astrid, do you have my cell number?"

She nodded. "I do."

"Good. Call me if you need anything. I'll check in with you later, okay?"

Astrid took Tara's hand. "I want to make sure you know that I understand why he loved you. You're wonderful. It's Miranda who makes me question his sanity."

Tara was not about to wade into these waters. "Take care of yourself, Astrid." She pecked her on the cheek then beelined over to Grant, and gripped his arm. "Can I steal you for a minute?"

"You can have me for a whole hour, if you want." The hint of flirtation in his voice was impossible to miss.

She led him to the shade of a large island oak tree.

"You don't want to know what I could do to you in an hour."

Grant smiled and removed his sunglasses, a few tiny crinkles gathering at the corners of his warm brown eyes. He ran his hand through his thick chestnut hair, and pushed it back from his face. He'd neatly groomed his five-o'clock shadow for the service, but it didn't hide the sexy hints of salt and pepper along his jaw. Grant was the hunky boy next door, twenty years later, the sort of man who was comfortable with his good looks, but didn't feel the need to flaunt it. He didn't walk into a room thinking about the way the lines of his suit accented his broad shoulders. But every woman certainly took notice.

"You know, you threaten me with statements like that, but you never follow through. Why is that?" He punctuated his question with a sexy narrowing of his eyes.

"Johnathon would be horrified to know we're flirting at his funeral."

Grant shrugged. "He would've done the same thing if the roles had been reversed."

"That's absolutely true."

He reached for her hand, gathering her fingers and holding them tight. "How are you holding up?"

"I'm fine."

"Don't give me the Tara Sterling, real estate agent to the stars answer, okay? I want the Tara Sterling, woman I've known since before she married my best friend answer."

"I really am fine, but I think I'm still in shock. Ask me again in a week."

He drew a deep breath in through his nose, but didn't

let go of her hand. "I hear you. I think I'm in the same boat."

"I think Astrid jumped straight to full-blown grief."

"I hate that Johnathon never told her that he'd remarried."

"It sucks, but had they been in close communication? She was in Norway, after all. It makes sense that Johnathon and I would talk. We were always running into each other at parties or restaurants."

"They were talking. For sure. He had his chance." He gently let go of his grip on her hand and Tara couldn't escape the tone of his voice. Grant knew all of Johnathon's secrets.

"You should probably keep that to yourself. Astrid's plenty mad as it is. She had some ugly things to say about Miranda." Tara planned to keep mum on the topic, too. She enjoyed having plausible deniability.

"Just like we need to keep the pregnancy under wraps."

"I need to write all of this down. I can't keep up."

Grant's eyes went wide. "I have one more for you."

"You do? Something bad?"

"I need you to keep this between us, okay? Just for a few more days."

"Yes. Of course." A shiver went down Tara's spine. She didn't like the sound of that at all.

"Johnathon split his shares of Sterling Enterprises between the three wives."

If it wasn't for the swift breeze that blew Tara's hair to the side, she would have thought the earth had stopped spinning on its axis. "What? Why?" This made no sense. Miranda was the obvious heir to that stake in the company. She was going to be so upset when she found out.

"He knew that you didn't quite get your fair share when you two split up. Sterling never would've taken off the way it did if you hadn't been there at the beginning."

That much was true, and she'd never really gotten over the way Johnathon had pushed her out. "Wow. So he actually acknowledged that."

"And Astrid was there for him when the company was growing so fast that he was hardly ever home. I think he always felt guilty about that. As for Miranda, that's fairly self-explanatory."

The wheels were starting to turn in Tara's head. She'd been so eager for a chance to pivot to something new and more exciting. To build something, not merely sell it and cash in. Her father had told her to stop waiting to be happy. Was this her chance to do exactly that? "It's going to take me some time to sort out why he would do this." A new wave of sadness hit Tara, washing over her. There was a part of her that would always love Johnathon, faults and all. "Did you two talk about it?"

"We talked about everything. You know that."

"So you knew all along?"

"Not about this." Grant looked off in the distance, unknowingly flaunting his strong profile. "No. This, he kept from me."

"I'm sorry. That's not right."

He turned back to face her. "You don't need to apologize for him. I hope you know that by now."

"What happens next?"

"Max will call a meeting with all three wives. Which is why I'm telling you ahead of time. I need to know if you're going to be on my side."

Tara raised both eyebrows at him. What was he saying? "Your side?"

"You know how hard I've worked. Sterling Enterprises should be mine to run."

Now she was starting to see where this was going. Grant was going to make a play for her shares, and possibly those of the other wives. She wasn't about to commit to anything now. She needed time to think. "You know I adore you." It was good to butter up a man.

"I don't actually know that."

"Well, I do. But I'm sorry. The only side I can promise to be on is my own."

Three

Grant had spent days trying to figure out how this meeting with the three wives would play out, and he couldn't imagine a best-case scenario, one in which they agreed to sell their shares of Sterling to him. His position was admittedly weakened by the fact that he would have to buy them out over time. A substantial chunk of money now, but he'd need time to raise the rest of the capital. He simply didn't have that much cash lying around. His considerable assets were tied up in investments. He'd had no way of knowing that Johnathon would die. There'd been zero time to plan.

Money aside, the personalities of the three wives were a huge X factor. Miranda was normally level-headed, but understandably distraught. With the pregnancy complicating things, there was no telling where her loyalties would lie. Astrid was vengeful and angry over the secrets Johnathon had kept from her, and those feelings would likely only become more intense once she found out about Miranda and Johnathon's baby on the way. Tara was her own wild card, even when she could certainly be counted on for smart and reasonable decisions.

Tara was his most likely ally, but he had a real weakness for her. If anyone was capable of persuading him to do something foolish, it was Tara. Many times over the years, Grant would run into her and find himself searching for reasons to forget about loyalty, if only for one night. Yes, he'd promised Johnathon that he'd never go there. He'd kept his word. But his best friend was no longer here.

Then there was the fact that Johnathon had essentially screwed him out of a chance at reasonable company control by dividing the Sterling shares between the wives. So how far did the promises they'd made to each other go, now that Johnathon was gone?

"Are we ready for this?" Grant paced back and forth in Max's sprawling office, lined with mahogany shelves stocked with law books. His hands were clammy. The back of his neck felt damp. There was no telling how this would go. *Badly* came to mind.

"I was ready days ago. You're the one who asked for a delay. And I only obliged you in that request because we've known each other for so long. The wives should have been notified about this right away. I should have told Miranda at the hospital that her husband pulled the rug out from under her."

"Her husband had just died, for God's sake. Is that really the lasting memory you wanted to plant in her head? That in this instance he shorted her on what was rightly hers?"

A knock came at the door. Max's personal assistant stepped inside. "Mr. Hughes, the Sterling wives have arrived."

"Thank you." Max rose from his seat and buttoned his suit jacket. "Show them in."

Grant stood back, not wanting to appear as the orchestrator of this meeting. This was Max's show, and as far as he was concerned, Max could take some of the heat for what the wives were about to be told. He was certainly paid well enough for it. Still, it was impossible to stay put when Tara was the first through the door. He reflexively propelled himself toward her. Perhaps it was the promise of her embrace, the chance to distract himself with her perfume.

"Tara. Looking gorgeous, as always," Grant said. It wasn't merely a requisite compliment. She looked so beautiful he could hardly think straight—exactly why he needed to keep her at arm's length.

"Thank you." Delivering a skeptical smile, she steered him into a corner. "I'm guessing you didn't tell Astrid and Miranda?" she muttered under her breath.

"I never intended to. That's Max's job. Not mine."

Her sights narrowed on him, seeming suspicious. "So why tell me at all? Why not make me wait?"

He didn't have a good explanation, other than the fact that he'd needed to unburden himself from the secret. The funeral had been overwhelming. "We've known each other for a long time. I couldn't keep it from you."

"What do you have up your sleeve, Grant?" she asked in a whisper. "Are you planning on disputing this part of Johnathon's will?"

"No. Of course not. I'll explain it all as soon as Max has said his piece. I promise you it's nothing bad. This is a windfall for you, right?"

"I certainly never expected anything from my ex-husband. Max made sure of that in the divorce." She cast a look over her shoulder.

"You're on my side, right?"

"Yeah. Sure." She surveyed the room. Astrid and Miranda were noticeably not speaking to each other. "In addition to being on my own side, of course."

That wasn't exactly the answer Grant had wanted. Now he had to hope that money would speak the loudest, and he could get what he wanted—primary control of Sterling Enterprises.

"Ladies, let's go ahead and get down to business," Max said. "Please. Have a seat."

Miranda and Astrid were already occupying two of the chairs in front of Max's desk. Tara took the third, which was in the middle. It was a fitting spot for her. Grant saw her as the bridge between everyone here. Astrid still wasn't speaking to him, as she had rightly figured out that he'd known all along that Johnathon had kept his new marriage a secret from her. But Astrid needed to fall in line at some point. Grant knew things about her relationship with Johnathon that he was certain she wanted kept private.

Grant didn't bother taking a chair, instead leaning against one of the bookcases near Max's desk. He stuffed his hands into his pockets, his pulse picking up again.

"So, as you three likely know, all of Johnathon's personal assets have been left to his wife, Miranda," Max began.

Astrid noticeably shifted in her seat. "Then why are we even here? Did you bring us here to insult us?"

Max peered at Miranda over the top of his reading glasses. "You're here because Johnathon's ownership of Sterling Enterprises was shifted into a separate trust after he and Miranda got engaged. He wanted his fifty-one percent stake of the company to be equally divided between the three of you."

Astrid gasped. Tara pressed her lips together tightly, but didn't say a word.

"Excuse me?" Miranda blurted. "How did I not know about this? How am I just finding out about this now?"

Grant had worried about this sort of reaction, but he kept his thoughts and emotions to himself.

Max held up both hands in an attempt to calm the situation. "The business was already a separate entity when you married. It's in your prenuptial agreement that Johnathon's disbursement of his shares of the company were at his sole discretion."

"And he told me I was getting everything."

"Unless it's on paper, I know nothing about that. But I can tell you that he left a note, which he asked me to read."

Now it was Grant's turn to object. "Hold on. I didn't know about a letter."

Miranda pointed at him accusatorially. "But you knew about the rest of it?"

"Not until the day we lost Johnathon. I assumed it would all go to you, I would become CEO, and that we would simply move forward in a partnership between the two of us." He turned to Max. "You never told me there was a letter."

"I'm following Johnathon's wishes. He wanted this

read to the wives. I didn't really see how it was your concern. Honestly, I'm not sure you should be in the room right now."

"Grant should stay," Tara said. "He was Johnathon's right hand. And he's still going to be CEO. Nothing will change that."

"This had better be good. That's my money. That percentage of the company is rightly mine." Miranda crossed her legs, and then her arms, in a huff.

Max pulled the letter from an envelope, unfolded it and began reading. "Dear Miranda, Astrid and Tara, I've asked Max to read this in order to explain my decision to leave my shares of Sterling Enterprises to the three of you. For Miranda, I realize this might come as a disappointment, but I believe that the fortune I have left behind will last far beyond your lifetime. I know I have provided well. As for Astrid and Tara, the truth is that Sterling never would have become what it is today without their help and support. They shared in some of my success during our marriages, but the company has really taken off since Astrid and I divorced. It only felt fair that everyone share in it. Miranda, you have my undying love and devotion, but I have never stopped caring for Astrid and Tara. They will be a part of me forever, as will you. I hope you can all understand that my heart led me to this decision. It might seem unusual, but it makes perfect sense to me. All my love, Johnathon."

Grant was doing his best to gauge the reaction of the wives, but it was a tough read. The room was eerily quiet. None of them was moving or uttering a peep.

"Leave it to Johnathon to make a big show of things from beyond the grave," Tara said, breaking the silence.

Miranda shook her head. "I can't believe he did this to me."

"It's not like you need the money," Astrid mumbled.

"It's not like it's any of your business," Miranda answered.

Grant had to intervene before this became even more contentious. He pushed back from the bookcase and approached the wives. "Astrid. Miranda. Tara. Please. Let me just try to help you all with this." He took a seat on the corner of Max's desk. "I think the reality here is that what's done is done. I don't like this any more than Miranda does, but none of that matters. It was Johnathon's decision to show his appreciation to Tara and Astrid, just as it was also his decision to put me in charge as CEO of the company."

He drew in a deep breath, knowing that years of hard work and his entire future were on the line here. Any one of these women could make a choice that could hamper his ability to seize control of Sterling. He had to forge ahead with his plea, even when it might not work. "My twenty percent stake of the company does not comprise a majority interest, nor do any of your individual stakes, which I believe, if my math is correct, work out to be approximately seventeen percent of the company for each of you. Since I am already slated to take over as CEO, I would like to propose a buyout of your shares. Enough to give me the same fifty-one percent that Johnathon owned. That will put me in a position to run the company exactly as he did."

"What makes you think I want to do that?" Miranda asked.

"Shush. I want to hear Grant's offer," Astrid interjected.

"Don't you dare shush me," Miranda shot back, delivering a harsh stare to Astrid, then turning her attention to Grant. "Maybe I want to run Sterling. It doesn't matter that Johnathon named you CEO. Maybe I want to buy out the other wives. It's about who owns the biggest piece of the pie."

Grant's heart was racing. Were his years of hard work about to go down the tubes? "Nothing has to be decided tonight."

"Grant's right." Tara slid him a look that suggested she might still be on his side. He clung to the idea. It was his only lifeline.

"We shouldn't make any decisions right now," she continued. "I think the wives and I need to have a meeting on our own. Talk over our own objectives and goals. And see how Sterling does or doesn't play a role in that."

It was a perfectly sensible step forward. So why did it make Grant so damn nervous? Oh, right. Because she was suggesting a scenario in which he had zero control.

Miranda cleared her throat. "Fine. I can live with that."

"Me, too," added Astrid. "I'm not rushing back to Norway any time soon."

"Good, then. The three of us will meet tomorrow night. Is my house okay? Seven o'clock?" Tara asked.

"Yes," Miranda agreed while Astrid nodded.

"And in the meantime, Grant, can you present us with an offer so we know what we're working with?" Tara's sights met his and he struggled to figure out whether his previous conclusion that she was on his side was indeed accurate. No wonder she was such a shark in negotiations. She did an excellent job of keeping her cool and remaining above the fray. He wished he didn't find this quality so appealing. It might eventually sink him.

"An offer as in one? Are you three negotiating together?" He hadn't expected the wives would form a coalition.

Tara glanced first at Miranda and then at Astrid. With a nod, they each agreed with her. Then she returned her sights to Grant. "Well, yes. I think so. It only makes sense. No need to hire three lawyers. It's not like I don't work on deals all day long. Or Miranda for that matter."

"I know what I'm doing, too," Astrid said.

"Of course you do." Tara picked up her purse. "I think that's all for now. I'll see you both at my house tomorrow night." Miranda and Astrid both made a break for the door, with Tara bringing up the rear.

"I'd like to ask for one thing." Grant was desperate to end this meeting with some input. "Can I make the offer in person? Maybe kick off your meeting tomorrow?"

Tara smiled wide at him, but it wasn't a warm gesture. "Grant. I see what you're doing. You know very well that it's harder to tell someone no in person."

"I think Johnathon would prefer it that way. I don't want this to become contentious."

"How about a compromise?" she countered. "Email us the offer, Miranda and Astrid and I will meet, then you can come over when we're done and we'll give you our answer in person."

Grant wasn't much for compromises. He'd had to make too many of them when Johnathon was at the helm of Sterling. This was supposed to be his time to take charge and make decisions. Damn Johnathon and this decision he'd made to split majority interest of the company. Why couldn't he have talked to Grant about it? *Eyes on the prize.* He had to deal with the circumstances right in front of his face—three women who held what he desperately wanted. "Yes. Of course."

Miranda and Astrid departed, but Grant had to make one last plea, so he grabbed Tara just outside the door. "Tara. We've known each other for so long. Please don't treat me like I'm the bad guy."

Tara hooked her purse on her arm and looked him right in the eye. "Grant. Please. You have stunning puppy-dog eyes, but you won't get my pity."

For an instant, he was too distracted by her comment about his appearance to think straight. "I'm not asking for that. You and the wives have my entire future in your hands and I'd like to know that I'm not going to get screwed over."

She kissed him on the cheek, leaving him to grapple with the resulting wave of warmth through his body. "You're handsome and rich. No matter what life hands you, I'm guessing you'll be just fine."

Four

Tara hardly slept at all the night of the meeting at Max's office, her head swirling with ideas. She'd gone in unsure of Grant's plan, thinking he might merely be trying to keep the peace. As CEO, he needed the full confidence of a solid core of shareholders. She'd thought he might work on building an alliance. Instead, he was trying to divide and conquer.

Which got Tara thinking about a coalition of her own. An unlikely one, for sure, but one that might free her from the shackles of her current career and let her pivot to something new. One where she could step in at a high level, determine her own destiny and bring her history with Sterling Enterprises full circle. She'd been there on Day One and unfairly spun out before things got good. It was only right that she'd step in after Johnathon's death and make sure the company continued to thrive.

Perhaps this new direction would bring her some of that elusive happiness, exactly what her dad had told her to stop waiting for.

Leaving a late-afternoon home showing, she took the bridge over the bay into Coronado. She always felt more relaxed once she was on the island. It had always been too quiet for Johnathon. He preferred the hustle and bustle of downtown San Diego, which was where he and Astrid had lived together, or the slightly showier homes up on the cliffs in La Jolla, where he'd lived with Miranda. As for Tara, Coronado had the charm of a small town, with very expensive underpinnings. You couldn't buy a piece of property for less than two million and that was for a postage-stamp lot. Her home, a three-bedroom, three-bath beauty several blocks down Ocean Boulevard from the Hotel del Coronado, provided a stunning view of the Pacific while still affording her some privacy. It was the one thing in her life that gave her any peace.

Tonight, there was no telling if serenity and decorum would prevail once Miranda and Astrid were back in the same room. It wasn't difficult to envision a real dustup between those two. They had every reason to not like each other. But in Tara's experience, money did a lot to assuage hurt feelings. The the promise of a big payday might be enough to persuade them both to set aside their differences. Or at least forget about them.

Astrid arrived first, shortly after seven that evening, wearing black from head to toe in the form of a sleek pencil skirt, matching jacket and patent Louboutins. Either Tara was misreading the outfit or Astrid was trying to send the message that she was just as much a grieving widow as Miranda. Tara prayed Miranda wouldn't notice, but it was hard to imagine that she wouldn't pick up on it. Not that Tara had much time to think about it at all—Miranda came walking up the sidewalk less than a minute later.

"Come on in," Tara said, then closed the door behind them. She led them upstairs to the top floor, which was where the kitchen, great room and master suite were located. The ocean views were most stunning up there, on full display through a near-one-eighty degrees of plateglass windows. "Can I offer either of you something to drink? Wine? Sparkling water?" She knew she needed something nonalcoholic on hand for Miranda.

"Water is good for me," Miranda said just as quickly as Tara had thought it.

"I need wine," Astrid said. "I'll call a car if necessary."

Tara poured them each their beverage of choice, and reminded herself that she'd dealt with plenty of prickly situations in her real estate career. She could sell them on her plan. She mostly convinced herself. "Let's get comfortable in the living room so we can talk about Grant's offer." She led them over to the seating area, complete with two large white linen sectionals with a chunky oak coffee table between. Her decor was beach-y, but elegant. Perfect as far as Tara was concerned.

"Can we call it that?" Astrid asked. "He's only offering to buy our shares in small chunks over the next several years. I'm not selling my shares to him. I would rather have my money now."

"You mean the shares of Sterling Enterprises neither of you should own?" Miranda asked.

"Let's back up here for a minute. There's no reason to get upset," Tara started, wanting to keep things civil.

"Upset?" Miranda cut her off. "That doesn't even begin to capture the range of emotions I'm feeling. I shouldn't have to be here right now, having this meeting. I shouldn't have to think about this. I feel betrayed by my dead husband. I feel betrayed by the father of my child." Miranda closed her eyes and pressed her hand to her lower belly.

Oh, no. Tara's sights flew to Astrid's face, anxious to gauge her reaction to the news Tara had been hoping wouldn't come out during this meeting.

Astrid's skin went impossibly pale and ashen. "Child?" she asked, her voice so fragile it was like glass.

Miranda's eyes popped open. It was obvious from her expression that she realized her mistake. She'd just given up the secret she'd wanted to keep from Astrid, at least until she returned to Norway. "Yes." She swallowed hard. "I'm about eight weeks along. It's early days."

Tara sat frozen, bracing for Astrid to explode. Miranda seemed to be doing the same. Neither did so much as blink or dare to utter a single syllable.

But Astrid did something no one ever could have expected. She smiled. "Johnny had a baby on the way?" A tear rolled down her high cheekbone. "He wanted children so badly. So badly."

Tara couldn't believe what she was hearing. Was that happiness in Astrid's voice?

"I'm very pleased for you. Congratulations." The look in Astrid's eyes was unmistakable. She still loved Johnathon.

"Thank you." Miranda blew out a breath. "To be honest, I thought you would be upset. He told me that you'd had trouble conceiving."

Astrid nodded, but she was pursing her lips tightly, as

if she was holding back serious tears. "I can't talk about it. So please, let's just get back to business."

Tara's heart went out to Astrid. She was bearing a terrible burden. "It seems like none of us is particularly pleased with Grant's offer. And I've been thinking about it and there has to be a reason Johnathon did this. Something beyond feeling as though he owed a debt to Astrid and me. Maybe it was his way of trying to bring us together."

Astrid let out a breathy laugh. "One of us didn't know one of the other wives even existed. Why would he want to do that?"

Tara pinched the bridge of her nose and prayed for strength. Apparently going with a more heartfelt approach was not going to work. "Okay, then, let's look at the financial side. Our shares are valuable right now, but they could be worth more later. And it gives us control no one else has."

"We each own seventeen percent. Grant owns twenty. That's not control," Miranda said.

"When our shares are combined, we have Johnathon's majority interest. Fifty-one percent. We could run the company. Together."

"But Grant has been named as CEO. Where does that leave us?" Miranda countered.

"He could still be CEO. It would just be the three of us as a single voting bloc, making decisions about the direction of the company. And filling vacancies. There are senior management positions and spots on the acquisitions team."

"I don't need a job," Miranda said. "My interior design business is booming and I have more than enough money. Johnathon did manage to leave everything else to me."

Tara realized Miranda was making a valid point. "You wouldn't have to take a position at Sterling. The key is voting together. Sticking together."

"I think I would want a job," Astrid offered. "I can't sit around my apartment all day long."

"You've decided to stay in San Diego?" Tara asked.

Astrid shrugged. "If I had a reason, I could stay. At least for a while."

"I'm still not sold on this idea," Miranda said. "Maybe we should let Grant slowly buy us out. It's not like he doesn't deserve it. He's worked plenty hard."

"This isn't about taking anything away from Grant." Tara could feel her frustration growing. She really wanted them to see that this was a fantastic opportunity. "Let's think about what we're leaving for Johnathon's child. Houses and money are great, but wouldn't it be nice to hand off an actual legacy? This was Johnathon's passion and it was immensely important to him. The baby should at least have a chance at that when he or she is grown. If you sell your shares, the baby won't have any piece of the company."

The room fell incredibly quiet. Astrid was staring at Miranda, while Miranda peered down at her belly. She had no baby pooch yet, but it wouldn't be long until it was there. Tara hoped that all of this quiet meant that her plea had been effective. But she also realized how much weight it gave to the situation. There was a baby on the way, and although he or she would always have money, they would never know their dad. All three of them were standing in the midst of tragedy, with Tara trying to get them to look beyond it. See the possibilities.

"What if we have a trial period?" Astrid asked. "I'm not sure I wouldn't prefer to just cash in and move back to Norway, but I can admit that I also don't have much of a life there. I would like a challenge. I know Miranda said she doesn't want a job, but I do. I want some power. I want to be able to make decisions."

That would be one more thing to work out with Grant. Every bit of control to the wives took some away from him. "I think we can make that work. Three months to start and we regroup?"

Miranda looked out the window, pinching her lower lip between her thumb and index finger. "I can do that. But if any of us isn't happy after that time, we sell to Grant, agreed? If we hand over the reins to anyone, it should be him."

Tara wasn't necessarily vested in the idea of fostering loyalty to Grant, but Miranda was right. He was the obvious choice. After the three wives. "I'm fine with that."

"Me, too," Astrid said.

"We'll set up some sort of system where you report to me? So I can stay in the loop?" Miranda asked.

"Sure. I can send you an email or we can talk on the phone or whatever you want."

"Considering the legal ramifications, a letter on company letterhead might be best. Just to protect my own interests."

Okay, then. "Yes. Absolutely."

"And have you thought at all about what projects you want to pursue?"

"I'd like to see Sterling get in the mix with the Seaport Promenade project. It's a chance to work with the city and will be a very high-profile development."

A tiny grin crossed Miranda's face. "You know

Johnathon was interested in pursuing that too but Grant squashed it. I'm not quite sure why."

"Interesting." Tara didn't want to start out by mowing down Grant's opinions of things, but she had a hunch she was right about the Seaport. "Speaking of which, Grant should be here in a bit to hear our answer to his proposal."

Miranda rose from her chair. "If it's all the same to you, I think I'll skip that part. I'm not good at delivering uncomfortable news. This was all your idea anyway."

"I'm not going to stay to tell him, either," Astrid said. "Thanks for the wine. Should I report to the office on Monday morning?"

Tara hadn't stopped to think out this level of logistics. "Let me talk to Grant first. I'll let you know when we need you."

Astrid's eyebrows popped up as she hitched her handbag over her shoulder. "When you need me? I own just as much of the company as you do. So I'd say you need me now."

Tara forced a smile. "Right. I'll figure something out as soon as possible."

Miranda and Astrid made their exit, leaving Tara feeling a bit like she was a lamb who'd been led to slaughter. Yes, this was her idea, but it was going to take all three wives to make it happen and it was clear that for now, this arrangement was tenuous at best. And then there was Grant to worry about. He would be pleased with none of this. It might be time to pour him a very stiff drink.

Grant pulled up in front of Tara's house, happy to have found street parking on the always busy Ocean

Boulevard. He hopped out of his BMW, stuck with the realization that he was walking into the unknown. Tara, Miranda and Astrid could decide to go any number of directions. They could attempt to buy him out. Hell, they could try to unseat him as CEO. He wasn't ready to concede his dream. He'd spent too many years as the number-two person at Sterling, doing the dirty work and cleaning up after Johnathon's messes. Although one could argue that Grant was walking into yet another cleanup job.

He rang the doorbell and Tara quickly answered, wearing a white sweater that fell off her shoulder, revealing her silky-smooth skin, and a pair of jeans that showed off every inch of her lithe frame. He'd known the odds were stacked against him, but her outfit seemed a bit unfair. How was he supposed to concentrate when she looked so damn good? "Come on in," she said, waving him inside. "I have wine upstairs. Or bourbon if you prefer."

"Wine will be just fine." He followed her up the stairs, taking the chance to eye her hips in motion as she took each step. It was a glorious distraction from his worries about business. When they emerged on the top floor, to his great surprise, there was no sign of anyone else. "I thought Miranda and Astrid would still be here."

Tara was standing at the island in her spacious gourmet kitchen, pouring them each a glass of wine. "They left me as proxy." She clinked her glass with his. "Cheers."

He drew a long sip from his glass, her warm gaze connecting with his. She struck him as extremely relaxed right now, comfortable with whatever came next. Her steady demeanor was exactly the reason why she was so successful in real estate. Many of her clients found her presence incredibly calming. Of course, her adversaries thought she had nerves of steel. Grant found that it made his pulse race, but Tara had always had that effect on him. Even after all these years. Once again, he wondered about his loyalty to Johnathon and exactly how long he could stick to it. "So? Do you want to give me the answer? I'm guessing bad news since the other two decided to exit stage left."

"Come on." She took his hand and pulled him from the kitchen to the living room, then led him out to her sprawling balcony, wrapped around the front of the house with an unobstructed view of the beach and ocean beyond. Even with the picturesque setting and a beautiful woman holding on to his hand, Grant braced for the worst. She was being too calm. Too kind. "I don't want you to think of our answer as bad news. I think this could ultimately be a good thing for everyone."

That was all he truly needed to know. She was about to deliver an answer that was less than what he wanted. Still, he'd stick around for the explanation. And the wine. And the company, for that matter. When he wasn't focused on what Tara was about to do to his hopes and dreams, he couldn't deny his intense attraction, the way he wanted to wrap her up in his arms and kiss her. "Just say it, Tara. You're usually far more direct than this."

"Fine. The wives and I want to keep our shares. We want a role in running the company. On a temporary basis to start, and if all goes well, we want to make it permanent."

Grant rested his forearms on the railing, looking out over the vista. The sea breezes blew his hair back from his face. He should have seen this coming. Tara was incredibly driven. She saw opportunity and she took it. "I see."

She inched closer to him and put her hand on his back. For an instant, his eyes drifted shut and he soaked up her touch. He'd had countless thoughts over the years of moments like this, when he could be close to her. It had been his fantasy for so many years that it was nearly hardwired into his brain.

"That's it? You see?" she asked.

"I'm processing." He straightened, and as he'd feared, she let her hand drop. It was for the best, even if it disappointed him. The contact was driving him to distraction. It was too easy to think about his physical desires, when he needed to stay focused on business. "I don't think you three have any idea what you're signing up for. This business is brutal. Absolutely cutthroat."

"You think I don't know that? No, I don't do development now, but I work in a parallel universe. And I was there when you and Johnathon started the company. I know the nuts and bolts for sure. I also saw how hard he worked and how often he got cut down. Astrid and Miranda have witnessed the same. I think you're underestimating us. Plus, Miranda only wants a say in what happens with the company. She doesn't plan on taking an active role."

"Just you and Astrid, then? What is she qualified to do?"

"That, I don't know exactly. But I have to think we can find something for her."

"You know, this isn't a good time. Morale is very low. Everyone was crushed by Johnathon's death. This isn't a great time to bring in the Norwegian supermodel and let her take someone's job."

Tara shook her head. "We won't fire anyone, Grant. We just need to make room. I know there are parts of the company that are short staffed or have vacant positions."

"How exactly do you know that?"

"I have a friend who's an executive recruiter."

Grant took in a deep breath through his nose. There was an open job in project management that might work for Astrid, but that involved working closely with the architects on staff, and Miranda's brother Clay headed up that department. That seemed like a big potential problem. "What about Astrid and Miranda? Can you keep those two in check? They hate each other."

Tara took another sip of her wine. "Well, something sort of miraculous happened tonight. Astrid found out Miranda's pregnant and she didn't freak out. In fact, she congratulated her. I was pleasantly surprised."

"You have *got* to be kidding."

Tara shook her head. "I wouldn't kid about something like that."

So this was really happening. And he couldn't do anything to stop it. "What about you? Where do you fit into this equation?"

"I figured you and I could work together. You can show me the ropes. I can bring my real estate expertise and contacts into it. We could make a blockbuster team."

"Co-CEOs? I don't think so." That was not what he wanted. This was supposed to be his chance to step out of Johnathon's shadow and finally show the world how much he'd been responsible for making Sterling run all these years. It would be too easy to end up in a different Sterling shadow—Tara's.

"So call me an advisor to the CEO. I really don't care about titles."

It was so easy for Tara to set her ego aside. He admired that in her, among other things. "You realize we could have made a different kind of team at one point. Before you let Johnathon get in the way."

Tara knocked her head to the side and a lock of her hair fell across her beautiful face. She slowly swept it back. "I don't know, Grant. We have chemistry. We like to flirt. That's not the basis for a partnership. At least not the kind you're talking about."

"Every relationship starts with chemistry. Plus, you can't deny that you felt something the one time I kissed you."

"You promised we would never talk about that. I was engaged to Johnathon at the time."

Memories of that night flooded his mind. It was the one time he'd thought he might have a chance with her, although he hadn't taken the time to think out the repercussions. Johnathon never would've stood for it. It never could've been a long-term thing. "You'd broken up. You were about to call off the wedding."

Tara drew her lips into a tight and anxious bundle. "But I didn't call it off. I went through with it."

Grant didn't like to think about that day. It still hurt to think about his front-row seat to watching her say those vows to Johnathon. "Yes, you did."

"Look. It was an amazing kiss, but that doesn't mean the world. Plus, you wouldn't last five minutes with me. You're a nice guy. I don't do well with nice men. I tend to chew them up and spit them out and then I feel bad about it."

He'd heard that argument from other women and it made him nuts. He wasn't a nice guy. He merely refused to be a jerk. She could blame his wholesome midwestern upbringing, and a father who treated his mother like a queen. "You think you know me, but you don't."

"Well, it's not a good idea now anyway. We're about to be working together. It's never smart to mix business and pleasure."

If only Tara knew that as far as he was concerned, she was making a case for her to sell him her shares and let him take her to bed. But he didn't see tonight working out that way. "Only on a temporary basis?" He wasn't sure which part of their agreement he was talking about—the work side, or the romantic side, which was admittedly all in his head.

"We'll call it a trial."

"This conversation is a trial."

Tara laughed and it was such a boost to his sense of self, just at the right time, too. He was otherwise feeling a bit beat up. "Why? You're getting what you want. You're CEO of Sterling. And you're going to get to work with me every day, which you know will be fun."

Grant made a silent prayer for strength. He was about to walk into a less than optimal circumstance—finally CEO of the company he'd been running from behind the scenes for years, while working side by side with the woman he'd never stopped wanting. He imagined he would be both incredibly excited to go to work every day and also filled with dread. "Promise? I could use a little fun."

"How about I promise to make it interesting?"

He wasn't happy that she hadn't taken the bait about having fun. He desperately needed that in his life. "I've had my fill of interesting. Let's focus on making it work."

"Don't worry about that. I absolutely will."

Five

The headquarters of Sterling Enterprises took up the top three floors of one of the newest, most exclusive high-rises in downtown San Diego. Johnathon had moved the company two years ago after overseeing the development of the building. Tara hadn't been to these new offices since the night of the grand opening reception, when Johnathon and Miranda were engaged to be married and Tara and Grant were engaged in a different way after a few glasses of champagne—burning through some high-octane flirtation.

Tara had actually considered kissing Grant that night. She'd had a full commentary running through her head as she weighed the pros and cons. *He's so hot. It should be criminal for a man to look that good in a suit. He laughs at my jokes. He notices when my drink needs refilling. And then there are those sweet, puppy-dog eyes of his.* She ultimately decided that it wasn't worth the risk. Johnathon would've gone ballistic, especially if he'd witnessed it, and Tara knew that she would only break Grant's heart. That was what she did, apparently, although not to men like Johnathon. Then it was he who did the breaking. Either way, Grant didn't deserve that. So she'd kept her hands and her lips to herself.

Now she was going to be working with that man who was all kinds of sexy, but all kinds of wrong for her. Luckily, she knew herself well enough to be certain that once she was in the work environment, any stray non-business thoughts would evaporate. She was nothing less than laser focused when it came to any job. Grant would not distract her. She simply wouldn't let him.

Tara was rarely nervous, but she found herself feeling that way as she rode the elevator up to the offices. She'd never started a job near the top of the chain of command. She'd always worked her way from the bottom up. In real estate, it'd taken years to build her business and her reputation. One satisfied client brought many more. One big sale led to a bigger listing. Each day brought another rung on the ladder to reach for. At Sterling, she was about to start near the top, and that created a whole new level of pressure.

When the elevator doors slid open, she was taken aback by the bustle of the office. It was noisy. And busy. The receptionist juggling the ringing phone, the arrival of visitors, parking validations and questions from employees breezing past her desk in a near-continuous stream back and forth. As Grant had promised, he was waiting for her, standing off to one side. He had his cell pressed to his ear. He caught sight of her and raised a finger to suggest he needed a moment. Tara stood and patiently waited until he finished his call. She tried to ignore how good he looked in his charcoal-gray suit. She needed to keep her eye on the prize—figuring out if working at Sterling Enterprises was going to be the key to her finally having the happiness she'd failed to find all these years.

"Reporting for work, Mr. Singleton," Tara quipped as soon as he'd hung up.

"You're late." Grant quirked one eyebrow at her, then waved her down the hall. "Come on. I'll show you your office."

Tara glanced at her phone. "It's five after nine. I couldn't find a parking space."

"Remind me and I'll get you an executive spot in the deck."

"That would be helpful. Thank you." Tara hustled up to walk alongside him. On paper, she might be his subordinate, but she still wanted him to see her as an equal. She and Grant could do great things together, but only as a team. "Is it always this busy first thing in the morning?"

"Yes. It's nonstop."

That was going to take some getting used to. Although she'd had her fair share of tense meetings and phone calls, Tara's office had normally been quiet and serene, by design. She liked calm. She got a lot done in an environment like that.

"Here you go," he said when they arrived at an office. "Will this work?"

Tara surveyed the space. It had a decent view of parts of downtown and the bay, but it was also too masculine. The walls needed a softer color. The furniture would need to be replaced. "I've only been here once, but isn't your office on the opposite end of this floor?"

"Yes."

"Next to Johnathon's, right?"

Grant cleared his throat and looked down at his shoes. "I'm in his office now."

"Oh, of course." It only made sense. He was CEO now. It was time for the company to move ahead. "So why not put me in your old space? We're going to be working together. Wouldn't that be easier?"

"I told you the other night. Morale is low right now. I didn't want too many big changes at one time."

Tara wasn't quite ready to challenge him on the idea of low morale, but the scene she'd walked into when she got off the elevator had seemed nothing short of lively. For now, she wouldn't make waves. "This will work. Long term, I'll want to make some changes."

"Maybe we should get through this three-month trial first." He stuffed his hands into his pockets. Everything in his body language said he was unhappy with her presence. He wandered over to the window and glanced outside, then turned back to her. "I've been meaning to ask, what have you done about your real estate clients?"

"I'm slowly phasing out. No new listings, no new buyers, and selling off what's already on the market. Then I'm done."

"That doesn't sound like a trial, Tara. That sounds permanent."

She set her laptop bag down on the desk and wound around to where he was standing. "The good thing about my business is that it's not hard to put it on pause. And I'd like for this to be permanent. I was not happy when

Johnathon suggested I exit Sterling after the first few months. It didn't feel fair. I hardly got a chance."

"I know. He talked to me about it several times. Wondered if he was being a jerk about it."

"He said he didn't think it was good for our marriage, but I think he was threatened."

Grant looked at her, first scanning her face, but she couldn't help but notice the way he stole a gander at the rest of her, as well. From the glimmer in his eyes, he liked what he saw. "I can see that. You can be intimidating."

So much for thinking that look was one of admiration. Tara disliked being characterized that way. She put herself in front of the world as a confident person because it got her the things she wanted. She never meant to be daunting. "I think he was worried that people would like me more than they liked him. He wanted everyone to worship him, even when he wasn't being nice."

"That's why he loved to make me the bad guy. He needed people to see him as the good one."

That had always been true of Johnathon. He often hid the unlikable parts of himself in an effort to get people to adore him. It was only the people closest to him who saw the real man. "Can I see what you did with Johnathon's office?"

Grant glanced at the Tag Heuer watch Johnathon had given him years ago. "I have a meeting in a few minutes. Why don't you get settled and we can chat later?"

She could see what he was doing and she disliked it greatly. "Grant. My getting settled is going to involve me opening my laptop and you telling me the WiFi password. Don't tuck me away in a corner and expect me to go away. I want to work. Let's talk about a project for me."

"Like?"

Tara already knew from Miranda that what she was about to say would be met with little enthusiasm. It didn't stop her from marching ahead. "The Seaport Promenade. It's a travesty that Sterling isn't in on this bidding process with the city and it isn't too late for us to make it happen."

As expected, Grant met her comment with a distinct scowl. "Not a good idea. It'll end up being nothing but a huge waste of time and resources."

"Well, gee. Tell me how you really feel."

"If you can't deal with my opinions on things, Tara, we're going to have some serious problems. I'm in charge now."

Tara had to wonder if perhaps this was Grant flexing his new muscle. She liked seeing him like this, showing some fight and exerting his control. She stepped closer and picked a fleck of lint from his jacket, then smoothed her hand over his lapel. "Of course you are. You're the boss and I'm here to learn."

Grant cleared his throat, staring down at her hand. "I know you're capable and smart, but there's still a lot you don't know about this side of real estate."

"Okay, then. I'm ready to learn. But if we're going to argue about Seaport Promenade, I think we should do it in your office." She made her way for the door, but cast a look back at him over her shoulder. "It's got to be more comfortable than mine."

One thing Tara had said was now permanently stuck in Grant's mind: *we should do it in your office.* He knew he shouldn't let his brain go there, but it had already happened, and now the rest of his body was having a field day with the idea. Grant felt as though all blood flow had left his brain for regions south. This was not a good start to his work day.

Against his better judgment, he gave in to her suggestion. "Come on. I'll postpone my meeting so we can talk this out."

He and Tara started down the hall to his office. Grant had no idea how he was going to live through this. Being around Tara was already an excruciating exercise in holding back and it had only been fifteen minutes. He'd spent the last decade not getting what he wanted. And now he couldn't have her, either. It would make everything too messy if they became involved, especially for the company.

Sterling was already on unsteady ground. He was truly torn about how best to handle Tara in the scope of the business—give her what she wanted in order to create less friction? Or fight her on it all and ultimately convince her that this trial of hers wasn't going to work? It was a conundrum for sure. He wanted to be with her. He'd wanted her for a decade. And this business idea of hers was ruining any chance of that.

They arrived at his office, on the exact opposite end of the building. He'd purposely put Tara as far away as possible. He hoped that she'd be less of a distraction. Perhaps things could ultimately play out that way, but for today, his strategy had failed. "Here you go." With a flourish of his hand, he welcomed her inside. "It still doesn't feel like mine. I have a feeling my job is going to be like that for a while, too." He didn't want to be vulnerable, but he knew he could be honest with Tara. If he wasn't, she'd probably figure it out anyway.

"But you've wanted this for a long time, right?"

Funny, but he'd always been sure that being in charge would make things better. Now that he was in this role he'd longed for, it wasn't yet feeling like everything he'd waited for. "What I've most wanted is the chance to run things the way I see fit. Johnathon and I butted heads a lot and he always managed to win. That got to be tiresome." It was no exaggeration. Johnathon came out on top with everything.

"So what are *you* wanting to tackle first?" Tara asked. "Anything in particular that you and Johnathon had been fighting over that wasn't going the way you wanted it to?"

"Well, since you put it that way, I have to tell you that my first priority was to put an end to any talk of pursuing the Seaport Promenade project. Johnathon really wanted to put in a bid with the city, but he wasn't the one who had to deal with the red tape."

The Seaport Promenade was a strip of property along the bay which was owned by the city. The current facilities included an aging park, some open space, and a small shopping center set to be knocked down. In its place would eventually be more ecologically friendly buildings, along with amenities to draw families to downtown. It was a big municipal contract, although there were certainly hoops to jump through. No city gave out a job like this without making sure they were getting everything they wanted.

"It's not my habit to agree with Johnathon, but I think it's a smart idea. I think we should go for it. It's such a high-profile project and it would be amazing publicity if we landed the contract."

"Your ex-husband pissed off a lot of people with the city. You have no idea the headache this would be."

"He was your best friend, too, you know. And he's not here to make people mad anymore. Let me try with the city. Let me see if we can throw our hat in the ring."

Grant pinched the bridge of his nose. A terrible headache was brewing. "It's not what we do. We do large private projects. Office buildings. Like this one. Big paydays. The margins are so thin with a government contract. I don't see the point."

Tara gestured to a chair opposite Grant's desk. "May I?"

"Be my guest."

She perched on the very edge of the seat and crossed her legs. He tried to ignore how amazingly sexy they were in her sky-high heels. "Look. You need to know how Sterling is seen in this town."

Grant stepped closer, unsure of where she was going with this. "I know our reputation. Smart. Nimble. Timely."

"You're also known as a bad neighbor. You only go after massive projects, the big kill. Greed and profits at all costs is not a good look."

He could see some people viewing Sterling in that light. It still didn't make it easy to hear. "You keep saying *you*. You need to turn that into a *we*. We're in this together now. Working together, remember?"

"And you put me on the other end of the building. That's not togetherness. You're assuming I'm going to be a pain in your butt. It's fair."

If only Tara knew that the pain she was putting him

through was of a different variety. It was probably time to go with his first idea—give in and take away the friction. "Okay. Fine. We can talk about Seaport Promenade. Why don't you call down to the city today and see where they are with the application process? I've been doing nothing but stalling this whole time, hoping Johnathon would get distracted by something else. For all I know, we've missed several key deadlines."

Just then, there was a knock on the door frame to Grant's office. It was Sandy, Johnathon's assistant. "Mr. Singleton, I'm sorry to bother you, but I don't know what I'm supposed to be doing today."

Grant sighed. He'd told Sandy to take last week off, but he'd forgotten to get back in touch with her about new responsibilities moving forward. Sandy was inexperienced, but she was an excellent employee—a self-starter who always arrived early and stayed late. "Yes, Sandy. I'm sorry. Come on in." Grant gestured for her to have a seat. "I want you to meet Tara Sterling. I'll be working with her over the next several months, keeping our heads above water as we move forward without Mr. Sterling."

Sandy offered her hand to shake Tara's. "I know who you are, Ms. Sterling. I've seen your Realtor ads on the bus benches."

Tara smiled warmly. "Well, I'm moving out of selling and into developing. Hopefully you won't have to look at those ads too much longer."

"I'd love to hear more about what you used to do. I'm interested in all aspects of real estate." Sandy took a seat next to Tara.

All of this was giving Grant an idea. He needed a place to put Sandy and he needed a way to keep Tara preoccupied for at least part of the day. He had work to do and a lot of it. "Sandy, I apologize for springing this on you at the spur of the moment, but how would you feel about working for Ms. Sterling? As her admin? It seems like a logical step. You know the ins and outs of the various projects we're working on right now. And you know everyone in the office and how things run."

"I'd be happy to work for Ms. Sterling. I'd love it, in fact."

That was one less organizational challenge Grant needed to face today. He was thankful for that. "Perfect."

Tara nodded, but seemed wary of having this new person foisted upon her. "Sandy, maybe you and I can brainstorm some changes to my office when you have a minute. If I'm going to be over in no-man's land, I might as well make it look good."

"Sure thing, Ms. Sterling. Whatever you need."

Tara rose from her chair. "Okay, then." She made her way for the door, following Sandy, but she stopped at Grant's side. "On my way to the other end of the building now. I'll call you when I get there. Should probably only take an hour." She cocked an eyebrow at him.

"Tara. It wasn't personal. I made a choice, okay?" Except that it *was* personal. Everything between them would always be that way.

"It feels a bit intentional. I'm not hurt. Just don't want to let you off the hook too easy."

If only she knew that deep down, he wanted to be on her hook. He might already be on it. "Would it make you happier if you had my old office?"

"It would. It would certainly send a better message to the rest of the company regarding my role."

Grant drew in a deep breath through his nose. "Okay.

But let's get maintenance in there to paint first. The walls are scuffed up. It should be nice."

"You get a little wild and crazy a few times in there, Grant?"

"More like tired and frustrated. I might have kicked the wall once or twice, but only out of exasperation."

A crease formed between her eyes as she narrowed her sights on him. "I keep giving you opportunities to flirt with me and you aren't taking the bait. Are you feeling okay?"

I need you to give up this crazy idea of yours. "That's for after work. You know that." He regretted the words the instant they left his mouth. He should have said that he and Tara were done flirting, forever.

"Okay. What are you doing tomorrow night?"

Grant blinked so fast it nearly knocked one of his contact lenses out of his eye. "What?"

"I have an invite to a party hosted by a friend of mine. Another real estate agent. It's on the rooftop of the Sussex Building. It has an amazing view of the ballpark and there's a game going on during the party."

"Why not take Miranda? Or Astrid? They're your closest confidantes these days, aren't they?"

"But they're not as much fun as you are."

Grant found it difficult to swallow. His mouth had gone incredibly dry.

"Just say yes," she continued. "It'll be good for you. Get out. See some people. Maybe squeeze in some flirting?"

He hated the way the heat rose in his cheeks. It was so damn predictable. "I like baseball."

Tara elbowed him in the ribs. "Oh, come on. You like me, too. I know you do."

Six

The Sussex building was only a few blocks from Sterling Enterprises, so Tara and Grant walked over after work. The day had been unremarkable—Grant was always in meetings, which left Tara stumbling around in the dark trying to sort out the process for the Seaport Promenade pitch. Sandy had been an invaluable resource, dealing with the city directly and gathering the needed information.

"How are you feeling about Seaport after your first two days?" Grant asked.

"Good, so far. We need to meet with Clay as soon as Sandy and I are done pulling the basics together. We have six weeks before we need to present. Do you think that's doable?"

Grant opened the door when they reached the address for the party. "It'll be tight, but I think we can make it work."

They presented their security passes and Tara pressed the button for the fifteenth floor. "Hold on a minute. You almost sound enthusiastic for this idea."

They stepped onto the elevator and rode up alone. "I don't have to do the hard work. That's all on you."

"Would you consider being there for the presentation to the city? It might help with our credibility."

Grant looked at the numbers light up as they reached each new floor. "I'll think about it."

Tara decided not to push it, but this seemed like yet another example of Grant creating distance between them. It didn't bode well for her future at Sterling, being an integral part of the team. She was going to have to keep pushing.

They reached the top floor of the building and stepped out into the lavish party space. Tara had been to several wedding receptions and extravagant bashes there, and it was a jaw-dropping location for festivities. Inside the expansive lounge area, partygoers chattered away on chic black leather sofas, enjoyed drinks at high-top tables and nabbed passed appetizers from the waitstaff, all against the backdrop of a stunning city view provided by floor-to-ceiling windows. But the real showstopper was the outdoor area just off the main room, with a glitzy fireplace taking the edge off the nighttime chill in the air, and bar tables for two alongside the balcony's unique glass railing.

The panorama was spectacular—a view of the baseball stadium below, the green field all lit up and the muffled sounds of the game floating up to their high perch. They were surrounded by shorter buildings, and off in the distance, you could see the dark ripples of the bay and the soaring steel structure of the bridge to Coronado.

Tara loved this city, just as Johnathon had, and she hoped that her role at Sterling could prove that point. She was eager to do more than drag Grant begrudgingly along with the idea of pursuing the Seaport Promenade project. She wanted to prove to him that it was worthwhile. It wasn't folly. She had the vision. It might not bring the money rolling in right away, but it was important to be a part of the community and make a contribution that would pay off in the long term.

The party was casual, but still a business affair, and Grant had dressed accordingly, in charcoal trousers and a pale blue dress shirt that really brought out his eyes. It wasn't conjecture to say her date was the best-looking guy at the party. It was a fact. Of course, flirtation aside, this was no date. It was a chance for two colleagues and friends to spend some time together. She wanted Grant and her to be close again. It could only help when it came to work.

After they made small talk with several agents Tara knew, Grant seemed antsy. "Can I get you something to drink?" he asked, gently placing his hand at the small of her back.

It was nice to have the male attention, to have someone take care of her for once. She was usually so busy being independent. "Sure. I'll take a beer. An IPA if they have it."

"It's San Diego. I'm sure they'll have one."

Grant wandered off, and Tara finished up her conversation, realizing just how glad she was to be making a shift in her career. All this talk of house showings and demanding clients was tiresome. She was happy she didn't have to wake up tomorrow morning to that reality. When Grant returned with their beers, Tara wanted the chance to move on to something different. "You'll have to excuse us. Grant and I want to check out the game."

They stepped out onto the balcony and into the slightly cooler night air. "It's an amazing way to see a baseball game, huh?" Tara asked.

Grant shook his head and leaned against the railing. Tara was not so brave. She loved the view, but hated heights, so she stood back from the edge. "We are not at a baseball game. We're at a business function with a sport being played nearby. The players are like ants. You can't follow the ball."

Tara was a bit disappointed. She'd hoped Grant would enjoy this outing and he clearly was not having fun. She'd wanted this to be a time for them to bond. "There's free beer though. Hard to complain about that."

"I'm not complaining. I just find it funny that this group of people thinks we're at a baseball game. This is for someone who doesn't care about the sport, which is fine. But call it what it is."

"A schmoozefest?"

He straightened and pointed his beer bottle at her, a slight smile breaking across his face. "Exactly."

Tara again surveyed the crowd of beautiful people, talking away about their jobs and their successes. No one mentioned their failures at an event like this, or even their struggles. It was all to put on a good face. Tara could see why Grant found it annoyingly empty.

"I recognize the value in seeing and being seen," Grant continued. "But it always feels so phony to me. Johnathon was better at this than I am. I don't enjoy playing the game. I'd much prefer to simply do the work."

"Is that why you don't want to pursue Seaport?" she asked. "Too many politics to play?"

"In part, yes. And the person who played the politics before us left behind a steep uphill climb."

Grant had given Tara even more to think about, but then she got distracted by a glimpse of a man over at the bar. She didn't want to stare, but she couldn't help it. Needing confirmation, she grabbed Grant's arm and popped up onto her tiptoes, whispering into his ear. "Am I crazy or is that Johnathon's brother Andrew over there?" Not wanting to be too obvious, she grasped his other hand so she was facing him. "Right over my shoulder. Ordering a drink."

Grant scoped out the scene, then dropped his sights to Tara. His eyes were intense. Nearly blazing. "What in the hell is he doing in San Diego? He couldn't come to his own brother's funeral two weeks ago, but he could come down here for a party or a baseball game?" Grant rarely had a reaction that heated. Tara couldn't ignore how much more attracted she was to him when he was being this way.

"This is not a baseball game. You were very clear about that."

Grant finished his beer and clunked the bottle down on a nearby table. "This is weird, Tara. And I don't like it."

"Yeah. Me neither." Tara rolled her head to one side and glanced back at Andrew. He looked so much like Johnathon, it was uncanny. Same handsome features, same head of thick brown hair. Tara hadn't laid eyes on Andrew since her own wedding, back when he and Johnathon were still on speaking terms. Soon after, Sterling Enterprises was launched. Johnathon offered Andrew a job, but that inexplicably created a deep rift between the brothers. Johnathon was only trying to help after Andrew's first attempt at his own development firm had failed. The brothers stopped speaking to each other, and Andrew moved to Seattle because of it, starting a second company in a market where he wouldn't have to compete against Johnathon. "Should we go talk to him?"

"And say what? Tell him he's a jerk for not attending his own brother's funeral? I want nothing to do with that guy. At all." Grant turned his head, tracking Andrew across the room.

Tara looked back again. Andrew was winding his way through the crowd, away from them. "Is he leaving?"

"I hope so."

Tara didn't want to let this opportunity go. It wasn't right that Andrew hadn't been at Johnathon's funeral. And she knew Grant felt that way, too. "Come on. We can't let this go. We need to talk to him." She grabbed Grant's hand and led him across the room, weaving past the other guests, some of whom were trying to stop her to talk.

"Every time you lead me somewhere, something bad happens. Case in point, the other night out on your balcony."

"Shush. This has to be done." With one last tug on Grant's hand, they emerged from the crowd and out into the elevator vestibule. Andrew was standing there, checking his phone. "Andrew," she said, clearly.

He looked up, shock coloring his face. "Tara. Grant. This is a surprise."

Before Tara had a chance to respond, Grant dropped her hand and confronted Andrew. "That's bull and you know it. You had to have seen us inside. Is that why you're leaving?"

Andrew fumbled with his phone and slid it into his

back pocket. He seemed nothing short of nervous. Good. Let him be put on the spot. "I didn't see you. And I was only here for a moment. I had a friend who was here, but this isn't really my scene."

"You didn't come to the funeral." Grant took a solid step forward, nearly encroaching on Andrew's personal space. "You told me you would try to make it."

Andrew jabbed the elevator button several times, as if that would make it appear faster. "I was busy. Something came up."

"Okay," Grant said, sounding nothing short of skeptical. "Why come to town now?"

"Business."

"Anything I need to know about? This isn't exactly your corner of the world."

Andrew slid Grant an unkind look. "Just a partnership. I didn't come to town to step on your toes if that's what you think."

"And yet you still couldn't make the funeral."

"Look, it's not like Johnathon would've known I was there. Funerals are for the living and nobody at that funeral cares whether or not I show up."

"I cared. I cared a lot. You weren't there for your brother. It's not right." Grant's voice was resolute. For someone who wanted nothing to do with Andrew, he was having no problem speaking his mind to him.

"It wasn't nice, Andrew," Tara said. "Johnathon was always there for you."

Andrew shook his head. "Not always." The elevator door slid open and he quickly stepped inside.

Grant lunged to hold it open. "Johnathon's wife, Miranda, is pregnant. You're going to be an uncle."

It was Andrew's turn to step in the way of the door and keep it from closing. "Wait. What?"

"It's true," Tara said, wanting to take part in this, although she wasn't entirely sure why Grant would choose to divulge this piece of information. It was still early in Miranda's pregnancy. Did she want everyone to know about it?

Andrew blew out a deep breath. "Well, give her my best."

"Or you could call and tell her yourself, then apologize for missing Johnathon's service," Grant said.

"I'm heading to the airport right now and flying home to Seattle. I'll call her soon."

"Just don't be a jerk, okay? She's been through a lot." Grant stepped back.

Andrew did the same. The elevator doors whooshed shut. And he was gone.

"Wow. That was weird," Tara said.

"It was infuriating—that's what that was." Grant wandered over to a small window and pounded the side of his fist against the frame. She loved seeing this side of him—fiery and passionate. She wished he'd be like this more often. "You know, I had plenty of problems with Johnathon, but he was nothing short of an amazing person. Andrew was his only family on this earth, and he couldn't show up when it mattered? It's pathetic." He turned back to Tara and she could see the fire in his eyes again. She understood what a confluence of emotions Johnathon brought up, and she admired that Grant wasn't afraid to show it. He was being brave in ways she wasn't always able to be.

"I'm sorry that happened. It was my idea to talk to him. I should've just let him leave."

Grant shook his head and reached out for Tara's arm, dragging his fingers down the back of it until he reached her hand. "No. It was a good thing." His voice was quieter now. "I needed to say those things to him and Andrew needed to hear them, even if he didn't know it. You push me, Tara, and that's a good thing."

His statement brought a smile to her face, but it also sent goose bumps racing over the surface of her skin. The idea of her and Grant as a team wasn't hopeless. She knew they could work together well. She just needed to prove it to him. "Does that mean I can push you on the Seaport Promenade?"

A breathy laugh escaped his lips and he raked his hands through his hair. At that moment, Tara fought an intense urge to kiss him, or at the very least, take the chance to run her own fingers into the dark mop atop his head. "It might take a lot of pushing."

"I'm up to the task."

Grant pressed the button to call the elevator back to their floor. "Let's get out of here. I don't need any more free beer or fake conversation."

"What did you have in mind?" Tara was thinking that a drive to her place might be in order. They could open a bottle of wine. She could try to press him some more on the Seaport project.

"Let's walk over to the ballpark, buy some tickets and watch the rest of the game. From actual seats. Not a luxury box."

"It's got to be the fourth inning, at least."

"So? Still plenty of baseball to be played."

"Neither of us is dressed for it." She looked down at her clothes. She was wearing heels, a black skirt and a silver silk blouse. Not exactly the right attire for a sporting event.

The elevator dinged. "Something tells me they'll still take our money."

With a beer in his hand and Tara at his side, Grant was having the most fun he'd had in…well, he couldn't remember a time he'd had more fun. "This was one of my best ideas, ever."

Tara popped some popcorn into her mouth, then licked the salt from her fingers. "We can definitely see a lot better. I'm just not sure it was worth it to drop five hundred bucks on seats right behind home plate when we aren't even going to see the whole game."

Grant reached over and took a handful of popcorn. "You only live once. I'd say it was worth every penny."

She cast a smile at him, which made his entire body warmer. "The view is so much better close up."

You're so much better close up.

He sat back and draped his arm across the back of Tara's seat. He didn't buy this whole notion that he was a nice guy and therefore not right for her. In fact, he thought it was complete bull. He'd proved back at the Sussex that he was capable of being a jerk when needed, and more important, he could tell that she appreciated having nice things done for her.

No, as far as Grant was concerned, the big thing standing between Tara and him was Sterling Enterprises. It was one thing for the founder's ex-wife to show up on staff because she'd inherited a chunk of the company. It was quite another for her to take up with the new CEO. There would be talk, and that would prompt questions about Grant's fitness for his role. He'd worked too hard to let a romance with Tara get in his way.

Still, he was all kinds of tempted. He couldn't take his eyes off her, even when she was distracted by the game and everything going on around them. He was only vaguely aware of the rest of the world. Her beauty demanded his focus, but it was about more than her flawless facade. He knew what was behind the pretty face and kissable lips. Tara was smart as a whip and a total handful. Full of life and surprises.

A chant of voices broke out around them, growing louder and louder. *What are they saying?* One word, over and over again. *Kiss?* Tara looked up. She pointed at the mammoth television monitor nearest them and laughed. Grant followed her line of sight and there they were onscreen, just the two of them. They looked amazing together. Absolutely perfect.

Before he knew what was happening, Tara's mouth was zeroing in on his. "We have to kiss."

"What?"

"We're on the kiss cam." She placed her hand on his cheek and angled his face toward hers.

Finally, Grant's brain clicked in on what was happening and he went for it with all of the enthusiasm of a kid who has just discovered an unguarded cookie jar. His hand shot to her jaw, then his fingertips were curling into the soft skin of her neck. With his other arm he pulled her closer. Their lips met. She was everything he'd remembered from the last time they did this. Ripples of electricity ran through his body as she parted her lips and gently nudged his lower lip with her tongue.

And then it was over. She pulled away from him, but they remained entangled. His arm was still holding her close. His chest heaved as he tried to breathe in her scent as much as humanly possible.

"That was fun," she said, the color rising in her cheeks.

"It was more than that, Tara." *I want you.* He wasn't sure he'd ever wanted anything or anyone as much as he wanted her at that moment. It was more than sexual desire, although that had been so firmly planted in his brain he wasn't sure he'd ever forget it. This was about quenching a thirst. One that had gone unsatisfied since the moment he met her.

She smiled and granted him another peck, this one on the cheek. "You're too handsome for your own good. You know that, right?"

"Thanks. Do you want to get out of here?" The words rushed from his mouth before he had a chance to think about them. That was definitely for the best. There was something magical about this moment and he wasn't about to let it slip between his fingers.

"You don't want to stay for the rest of the game?"

"I don't."

She cast him some side-eye. "Can I show you something first?"

He gathered their drink cups and stood. "Absolutely."

With no time to waste, they scooted past the other fans in their aisle, then up the concrete stadium stairs and out onto the concourse. He took her hand, but he let her lead the way out to the sidewalk. "This way." With the streets closed off to traffic, she didn't need to look for cars as she led him across the boulevard and to the other side.

"Where are we going?"

"The promenade site. I want to show you my idea."

Grant didn't want to encourage Tara. Except that he did. Her enthusiasm was infectious. It was like an electrical jolt to the system and he quite frankly couldn't get enough. "Yeah. Sure. Let's go."

They wound their way between buildings and emerged out by the bay, with the wide promenade extending in either direction along the water. The night air was cooler here, the breeze strong, blowing Tara's hair every which way.

"Picture this," she said, swiping her hands in midair as if she was washing windows. "An open-air food hall, with tons of outdoor seating and space beyond for food trucks. We put in artificial turf for kids to play." She turned to Grant as she forged ahead down the sidewalk. "Soft, of course. We don't want anyone getting hurt, but it is more eco-friendly. Beyond that, we put in a shopping pavilion with more outdoor space for seasonal markets. The city could invite farmers in during spring and summer, and there could be one at Christmas, as well. Or the Fourth of July. We could add a large stage area for performances of all kinds. Music and dance. It would be a real destination. Families, retirees, young people."

"And no high-rises? There's density to consider in downtown. The city is going to want to know that you're giving them the most bang for their buck."

"We're already surrounded by big buildings. I think that with the right architect, you'd have no problem maximizing the square footage. And you put in lots of multipurpose space. You'd have to be smart and innovative about it." She looked off in the distance at what was there right now, the outdated facilities the city was set to soon demolish, and it was as if she could see it all.

"I had no idea you had such a vision for this."

"Does that make you more inclined to want to pursue it? Because I have more ideas. Lots more."

He was tempted to tell her that he might agree to anything she wanted right now. "Wow. Seriously?"

She turned to him, her face lit up with excitement. It was intoxicating and infectious. She was a wonder. "I get it from my dad. He was a contractor, but he'd always wanted to be an architect. He could see things other people couldn't."

This was the first time Tara had ever talked about her family in front of him. Everything Grant knew was secondhand information he'd gotten from Johnathon. "Your mom passed away when you were young, didn't she?"

Tara pressed her lips together firmly, seeming caught off guard. "Johnathon told you that."

"He did. Is it difficult for you to talk about?"

She turned away from him. "It's not my favorite topic if that's what you're asking."

"I'm sorry. I'm just trying to peel back the layers a little bit here. That's all. Your dad clearly meant a lot to you."

Again she turned, this time to face him. The wind had picked up and Tara was leaning right into it. It was like everything she did—facing it all head-on. "He meant everything. He was my rock my entire life. He was the one man in my life who never let me down."

It broke his heart to hear that. He made a silent vow to never be a man who would let her down. "Obviously you don't put Johnathon in that category."

"I loved him, but I didn't love the fact that he basically got bored with me. No one wants to feel like that. I wasn't the shiny new toy anymore. I wasn't Astrid, that's for sure."

He hated hearing Tara talk about herself like that, but she wasn't off base. Johnathon had been pure of heart, but he'd also let the wind carry him in many directions. He always found a way to rationalize his changing allegiances. *Tara's better off without me*, he'd said to Grant when he'd decided it was over with her. All Grant could think at the time was that Johnathon was a damn fool— a fool who covered all his bases, since he was quick to add one warning to his best friend. *I'm begging you. Please don't go there. I've seen the way you look at her. It would kill me if you and Tara ever became a thing.*

And so Grant had abided by Johnathon's wishes. But things were different now. And he was tired of wasting precious time. "I told him he was an idiot when he left you."

"No you did not."

Grant nodded. "I did. Not that it was in my best interest."

"He hated being criticized."

"It had to be said." Did Grant have the nerve to tell Tara the way he'd really felt that day? The way he'd felt before then, when it had been sheer torture to see his best friend married to the woman he'd always wanted? It seemed too heavy a topic for a moment like this, especially now that they were working together. "I told him that only someone stupid would walk away from you. I never would've done that. Not if I'd been the one who was with you."

She smiled and nodded. "You're a loyal guy. Everyone knows that about you."

She wasn't getting the point. This wasn't about him. It was about her. He stepped closer and put his hand at her elbow. "Loyal to a point."

"I don't know if that's true. You can be pushed pretty far."

"Everyone has their breaking point. I think mine actually happened tonight. When we kissed." Their gazes connected and he welcomed the jolt of electricity between them. It didn't seem possible she didn't feel it, too.

She leaned into him and put her hand on his shoulder. "That was nice."

"It was better than nice, Tara. It was amazing." He threaded his fingers through her hair, cupped her jaw and brought her mouth to his. Now that they were away from the crowd and the cameras, the importance of the kiss was magnified. He wanted Tara. He'd wanted her for too long. And this might be his only chance with her.

Which meant that for tonight, he was going to turn his back on his promise to Johnathon. He dared to break free from the kiss. Tara looked up at him, mouth slack and beckoning. If he wasn't afraid of violating a few public-decency laws, he would've made love to her right then and there. But he wanted a bed. And privacy. And time. "I think we need to get out of here. Together. Now."

It felt like a lifetime until she replied. "Let's go get your car."

Seven

Tara had never traveled over the bridge so quickly. Grant zipped through traffic like a man on a mission. For a moment she found herself wondering why. Yes, their attraction had been simmering away for years. Was that it? Too much buildup? Or was there something more?

He parked his BMW out in front of her house and they both did their best to not act as though they were rushing as they hurried to her gate, then through the courtyard beyond, leading to the front door. There was a part of this that made her feel like a teenager—making a choice she knew wasn't smart. Granted, she'd done exactly everything she was supposed to do when she was younger. She never disappointed her dad. Ever.

Tara keyed her way in through the door, but Grant didn't wait, taking her handbag and plopping it on the entry table, then threading both hands against her neck and combing his fingers into her hair. He raised her lips to his and claimed them, his mouth open and wet. Commanding. Taking everything he wanted. Tara gave it all enthusiastically. She'd always suspected Grant would be passionate, but not like this. Not so eager to be in charge.

"Do you want to go upstairs?" she asked breathlessly.

"Not yet." He pinned her against the wall with his body weight and reached for the hem of her skirt. He hitched one side up over her hip. "I want you to come for me, first."

Whatever you want raced through her head, but then she got lightheaded from the intensity of his kiss.

His fingers sped through the buttons of her blouse and he pulled it back, revealing her lacy bra. Grant's eyes were dark in the soft light of the foyer, and Tara felt like she was seeing a different side of him. So sexy. So red-blooded. He pulled down the cup of her bra with no hesitation. The combination of cool air against her skin, and the realization that he was going to touch her there made her nipple tighten, a rush of blood making her breast heavy. She nearly bucked against him. He pinched her already taut skin, scanning her face for a reaction. Raising her chin, she met his gaze, not to be outdone by him, but her mouth dropped open. It felt too good as he plucked at the hard bud. It sent sizzles of electricity down the length of her torso, aimed right between her legs.

He gathered her hands and raised them above her head, pinning them against the wall with one hand while the other slipped down the front of her panties. He pressed against her hard with his torso as his fingers found her center. Her most delicate and sensitive spot. The place where she most yearned for his touch.

He nuzzled his face into her neck and kissed and licked, all while keeping her pinned in place and working her apex in tight circles with his nimble fingers. There was zero question in her mind as to whether Grant knew what he was doing. He was playing her like a fiddle, and she was completely at his mercy.

Tara's eyes drifted open and shut, then open and shut again as the pleasure wound through her. There was too much thrill of the new, too much excitement from the unexpected. This was wrong. So wrong. And that made it feel so right.

"You are so damn sexy," Grant growled into her ear. He bit her neck softly; he licked her skin. His mouth was sheer heaven and part of her really hoped that she'd get to experience it all over her body tonight.

"So are you," she muttered, her thoughts so disjointed it was like her head was in the clouds. "I had no idea you'd be like this."

"Like what? Not nice?"

He moved to the other side of her neck, but he slid his fingers down lower and slipped one inside her. He thrust hard, the heel of his hand hitting her apex, over and over again. *Damn.* She was so close to the peak she could hardly think straight. "Everything you're doing right now is better than nice." *So much better.*

Tara's breaths were so ragged it was as if they were being ripped from her lungs. All the while the pressure was building between her legs and her knees were growing weaker. Grant squeezed her wrists hard, pressing them into the wall as she thrust her hips forward, needing more. Craving. Wanting. Finally the orgasm tore through her and she called out, a cry that was quickly extinguished by the crush of Grant's mouth. He kissed her deeply and with a passion she'd never experienced. It was raw and untamed, nothing but pure want. Their tongues wound together in a languid circle as he slowed the passes with his finger, but didn't relinquish control. She didn't begrudge him any of it. It was the sexiest thing she'd experienced in, well, quite frankly, ever.

She buried her face in his neck as she rode out the final waves of pleasure. She kissed his Adam's apple, which seemed to be bulging from his neck. "I want to make you happy," she said, realizing too late that it might sound like more of a promise than she was willing to keep.

"Good. Because that's just the start."

He let go of her hands and Tara collected herself, tugging down her skirt, but not bothering with buttoning her blouse. It wasn't going to be on long. She kicked off her heels as Grant removed his suit coat, then she took his hand and led him upstairs.

As soon as they were in her room, she began working on his shirt, eager to get rid of it and start exploring his body the way he had hers. The sight of his chest and bare shoulders elicited a groan from deep in her throat. He was broad and firm with a lovely patch of dark hair in the center. He'd been working out and she was going to reap the benefits. She kissed his pecs, her fingers curling into his defined and muscular biceps. He threaded his hands inside her blouse and pushed it from her shoulders, then teased her by tracing his fingers up and down the channel of her back, over the strap of her bra, bypassing the chance to take it off. Tara shifted one hand from his arm to the front of his pants, where his steely erection was waiting for her. She pressed against his length and he groaned his approval. She rubbed up and down, using a delicate pressure, just enough to make him harder.

"What do you want, Grant?"

He reached for her chin and raised it so that they were gazing into each other's eyes. "I want everything you want to give me. Absolutely everything."

It was like she was breathing in his words and they served only to embolden her. She wanted to rock his world. She wanted tonight to be memorable. This had to be a one-time thing. There was too much on the line with their shared business interests for it to be anything more than that. That was the only coherent thought she could muster.

She kissed him one more time to make sure this was what she wanted. The way he pulled her into his arms and dug his fingers into the back of her hair spoke of possessiveness. He was being dominant and she loved every minute of it. This was not a characteristic she expected from Grant, the good-looking guy next door. The heartbreaker with the puppy-dog eyes. And so she went with it, just to see what was next.

Grant was so overwhelmed by the sensory pleasure of having Tara half-naked in his arms that all logical thought was gone. His body and mind had been at war, and his brain had been defeated. This was Tara. The woman he'd wanted for so long. The woman he'd fantasized about hundreds of times. Her beautiful body was at his command right now. She was his for the taking. And there was part of him that was telling his brain to keep track of every unbelievable detail. The curve of her hips under his hand, the creamy skin of her breasts and the sweet sin of her mouth.

He kissed her deeply and then led her over to the bed, where he perched on the very edge. "I want to watch you undress."

A coy smile crossed her lips, which made his erection that much harder. He ached for her so badly it was hard to believe he'd ever be able to walk again. "You naughty boy," she said, pushing on his chest with a playful nudge.

Grant eased back on his elbows, wishing his pants were off. He could hardly stand the strain of his rigid length against his boxer briefs. Still, he relished the view as Tara, still wearing her black lace bra, unzipped her skirt with her back to him. She looked over her shoulder, her bright eyes conveying everything he'd ever wanted in a single glance. She wriggled it past her hips, bending at the waist and giving him a magnificent view of her backside in matching panties. She stepped out of the skirt and reached back to unhook her bra, nudging it from each shoulder as if she was a burlesque dancer accustomed to giving the audience the best possible show. He was dying of anticipation, but it was so worth the wait when she dropped the garment to the floor and turned around to face him. Her breasts were simply magnificent and he couldn't wait to have them in his hands again. To take her nipples between his lips.

She stepped closer and dropped to her knees before him. His heart was about to pound its way through his chest as he watched her delicate fingers unclasp his belt and unzip his trousers. He raised his hips from the bed as she tugged them down, taking his boxer briefs at the same time. That first brush of her fingertips against his length was like a rocket straight to the center of his body. It made him lightheaded. It made him delirious and thankful and hundreds of other things he couldn't begin to put a label on. He did his best to stay grounded in the moment as she took him in her hand and stroked firmly.

If only she knew that every single thing she did only made him want and need her even more. As she rolled her thumb over the tip when she reached the top, he thought he might pass out. If he didn't concentrate and get with the program, he was going to come from only a few passes. He focused on her, on the beauty of her face and on the recollection that he'd waited too long for this to be anything less than perfect.

Still, when she lowered her head and took him into her mouth, his mind and body resumed their battle, and this time, it was a full-body campaign. He could hardly believe this was happening. He eased his head back on the bed and combed his fingers into her hair, trying to wrap his mind around her hot and velvety lips riding his length. Luckily, she knew to take things slowly and carefully. She didn't apply too much pressure, just enough to make him wish that this moment would go on forever. When she loosened the grip of her lips, he was disappointed for only a second. He opened his eyes to watch her removing her panties, then she straddled him on the bed, bracketing his hips with her knees.

She ground her center against his erection, which was an awful lot of physical gratification considering how badly he wanted to be inside her. She was wet and warm against his length and she was clearly enjoying it, as she moaned softly and dropped her head to one shoulder, her beautiful blond hair cascading to the side. It was a vision worth holding on to, but he needed to make love to her the way he needed air and water.

"Do you have a condom?" he asked.

She hopped off the bed so quickly it was as if she had anticipated the question. "I do." Sliding the bedside-table drawer open, she pulled out a foil packet, tore it open and rolled it onto his length. She then stretched out next to him on the bed. He rolled to his side and kissed her, cupping her breast with his hand, relishing the velvety feel of her skin against his. Tara rolled to her back and he followed, positioning himself between her legs. She let her knees drop to the bed and he took another moment to admire her beauty before he drove inside. Her body welcomed him, then gathered around him tightly, wrapping him up in the most mind-blowing heat. He was overwhelmed by the sensations as they began to move together. She was perfect. Exactly as he'd always hoped.

He focused on her breaths as he found the perfect spot to deliver the pressure he knew she'd need. The tension coiled deep in his belly, pulling tighter and tighter until he was worried he couldn't take it much longer. But Tara was showing her own signs of approaching that blissful moment when you come undone and still want more. She dug her heels into the backs of his thighs, meeting his every thrust with a forceful rock of her hips. A few more thrusts and she fell apart, tossing her head back on the bed and thrashing from side to side. Grant sucked in a deep breath as he felt the dam break and wave after wave of intense pleasure rolled through him. He closed his eyes and let every serious thought of friendship and foes, and love and loyalty float away. He knew that they would return, but for now, everything was perfect.

Eight

Tara didn't like the idea of regret over sleeping with Grant. But in the light of day, as the early-morning sun streamed in through her bedroom window, casting him in a golden glow, she was torn. Last night had been incredible, and it had been too long since she'd had a man in her bed. But her choice of man might not have been the best. She hadn't been looking at the long-term ramifications last night. She'd only been looking at how hot Grant was, and reacting to the pure power of his kiss.

But she couldn't afford for her position with Sterling to be compromised, not when she was just getting started. A woman couldn't start work at the company her dead ex-husband had founded, sleep with the CEO and expect her colleagues to hold her in high esteem. It simply wasn't how things worked in the real world.

"Last night was amazing." She didn't want to lay it

on too thick, but Grant had earned the accolade. Tara smoothed her hand over his sculpted shoulder and kissed his collarbone, allowing her lips to linger a few extra heartbeats. Now that they'd had sex, it was impossible to be around him and not touch him. She was going to have to find a remedy to that.

"What time is it?" He had one eye open and the other closed. His voice was groggy and sleepy. So sexy.

"A little before seven. I wasn't sure what time you wanted to get up. You must want to get back to your place to get dressed for work."

Grant groaned and rolled to his side, draping his arm across her waist and then pulling her closer. "Let's call in sick. No one will care if we aren't there."

"You're the boss. Everyone will care."

He drew in a deep breath and blew it out, seeming duly exasperated. "I suppose you're right. Still doesn't make it any better."

Tara was about to agree with him when the doorbell rang. For a moment, she and Grant looked at each other in confusion, and then it dawned on her. "It's probably Britney next door. She's always complaining that my sprinklers are watering the sidewalk. Her dog doesn't like it. He has very sensitive paws." She threw back the covers and grabbed her silk robe from the chair opposite the bed. She loved seeing her clothes and Grant's mingling on the floor, a distinct trail leading from her bedroom door to the bed. "I'll be right back."

"Don't be long." Grant swished his hand across the spot on the bed where she'd just been. "I'd like a replay of last night before I go."

"Which part? There's no way there's time for all of it."

"So we start and see how far we get."

Tara smiled, but a wave of goose bumps raced across the surface of her skin. Grant had always been sexy and fun, but she hadn't banked on how different he would be in bed. She never, ever would have guessed that there was a growling alpha beneath that quiet exterior. The doorbell rang again and she rushed down the stairs. "I'll be there in a minute." Tara arrived in the foyer and plucked last night's heels from the floor, chucking them into the front closet. She flipped the dead bolt for the front door, amazed she'd had the presence of mind to lock it. Grant had been all consuming and he'd wasted no time getting things started.

She opened the door and her mouth fell open. *Astrid.*

"Good morning, Tara," Astrid said, snoopily peering inside.

Tara left the door open only a sliver. "Astrid. What are you doing here?"

"I thought I'd drop by and say hello."

This was all kinds of strange. It was seven in the morning and Astrid lived downtown. Why had she decided to turn up at Tara's door on a lark? "I'm about to get ready for work, so now's not a good time. I'm sorry. Maybe we could grab lunch sometime soon?"

"I haven't heard from you about my position at Sterling. I've been waiting and there's been nothing."

Dammit. No, Tara hadn't pushed Grant on the question of where Astrid would fit within the company structure. "I'm sorry. It's been a crazy week. Just trying to get settled and everything."

"That's great for you, but I own just as much of the company as you do, and I feel like I'm being left behind. If we're going to do this, I need to be included.

Right now, I'm just sitting in my apartment all day long. It isn't fair."

These were all valid points. Tara had promised Astrid a role and she'd done nothing about it. She needed to get her act together or this was all going to fall apart. Astrid could do anything she wanted with her share of the company...like sell it to someone who had no interest in keeping Grant and Tara in their positions. "I'm genuinely sorry. I'll talk to Grant and we'll get something worked out."

"He's upstairs, isn't he?"

The air was knocked right out of Tara's lungs. She wanted to construct a cover for what was going on, especially since it was never going to happen again, but she couldn't lie. She didn't have it in her. She opened the door a little wider. "How did you know?"

"I was at the game last night. I couldn't sit in my apartment for another night. The kiss cam? You two really went for it. It was almost like this has been going on for some time." Astrid pressed her camera-ready lips together, playing coy.

"It hasn't. At all."

Astrid shrugged, but it was apparent she didn't believe Tara's answer. "Well, whatever. I followed my hunch and drove over this morning. As soon as I saw Grant's car in front of your house, I knew I was right."

Tara's neighbor Britney with the sensitive dog was standing out on the sidewalk, watching Tara's exchange with Astrid. Just what Tara didn't need—more people talking. Tara had to take away the show. "Do you want to come in?" she asked Astrid.

"I thought you'd never ask." Astrid stepped across the threshold.

Tara closed the door behind her, struggling to come to terms with this turn of events. She was always so careful about things like discretion, but she hadn't ever had someone as shrewd as Astrid watching her. There was no question now that things with Grant could not continue. They could not be sleeping together while he was in charge at Sterling and she was carving out her niche. It was stupid of her to think for even a moment that it might work. She'd let her desire for him overshadow everything that was truly important—her new career, her rightful place at Sterling and her chance to finally stop waiting to be happy. Work made her happy. Not men. That had been proven time and again in her life. Aside from any of that, she'd promised Miranda and Astrid that she would make this work for *all* of them. She'd been entirely too focused on herself.

Tara led Astrid into the kitchen and made her a quick cappuccino with the professional machine she'd had installed when renovating the kitchen. "Do you want to go sit out on the balcony? It's a beautiful morning. I'll only be a minute."

"Tell Grant I say hi," Astrid quipped before sliding the glass door open and letting in a rush of sea air.

You'll probably get to tell him yourself. "I'll be right back."

Tara took her time walking to her bedroom, carefully composing her thoughts. She didn't want to hurt Grant's feelings, but Astrid's arrival was her wake-up call. She'd made promises to her and Miranda, and she had a duty to perform at Sterling. Being involved with Grant stood in direct opposition to that. Drawing in a deep breath for confidence, she opened the door and slipped inside, discovering that Grant was getting dressed.

"I forgot that I have a meeting at the office at nine. I really do need to get home and grab a shower." He shook out his shirt and threaded his arms through the sleeves.

"We have a problem."

"I wanted to spend more time with you, too, but I can't blow off this meeting."

"That's not what I mean. Astrid is here. She was at the game last night. She saw the kiss. There's no telling who else saw it." She didn't want to be so annoyed by something as silly as a kiss cam, but she was. If it hadn't happened, if they hadn't gone to the game at all, they wouldn't be in this situation. Then again, something told her that she and Grant might have found another excuse to fall into bed. Their attraction was that incendiary.

"I didn't even think about that." Grant furrowed his brow. "This is not good."

She nodded. "No kidding. What are we going to say if someone calls us on it?"

"Honestly? I have no idea. I mean, it was a pretty hot kiss."

Incredibly hot. Just thinking about it sent a shudder through Tara. But she didn't have time for that. Not now. "We have to tell people it meant nothing." Tara gestured to the bed, where the sheets were rumpled and the comforter twisted and piled. "Just like we have to tell each other that this meant nothing. There's too much on the line."

Grant cast a look at the site of their tryst. "I agree. It was impulsive. We obviously weren't thinking straight."

Apparently Tara had hoped for at least a little resistance from Grant. Why else was she feeling so utterly disappointed by his agreement that they'd made a mistake? "I don't think you can say that about everything last night. I got you to agree to move forward with the Seaport project. We were both thinking straight when that conversation happened."

Grant buttoned his shirt, shaking his head. "That's all that really matters, isn't it?"

"What's that supposed to mean?" She greatly disliked his tone.

"It means that you took me out and flirted with me all night, then you kissed me at the baseball game. Now that it's the next day, I'm starting to think that the whole night was a campaign to butter me up. To get what you want out of me."

"Do you honestly think that?"

"We were both caught up in the moment. I got wrapped up in your vision and you got wrapped up in me saying yes to your ideas. It might not have been the best time to decide to sleep together." He stuffed the tails of his shirt into his pants and buckled his belt.

Something in Tara wanted to challenge Grant, but he wasn't wrong. She *had* been swept away by him taking her seriously. It was so validating. "In the meantime, what do we do about Astrid? I can't lie and tell her nothing happened." Tara sat on the bed, her mind scrambling for a way to deal with Astrid.

"She's not stupid. You know that."

"Of course."

"We need to convince her to keep this to herself. She owns a sizable piece of Sterling and this could damage the company. Therefore, she needs to keep it quiet. Which I mean, is the only fair thing, anyway. We're consenting adults—it was a one-time thing. Time for all of us to move on."

A one-time thing. Tara had thought that at one point

last night, but that was before they'd arrived back at her house and he'd pinned her hands against the wall in the foyer. Just like the moment out on the promenade, that made her see him differently. She'd even gone to sleep with nothing more than thoughts of wanting more from him. But maybe she'd been delirious from orgasms. "So we'll go talk to her now?"

Grant shook his head and pulled on his socks, then stuffed his feet into his shoes. "I think this is all on you. You three are the ones who made the decision to band together. I don't want it to be seen as me interfering if I say something to her. But I do want you to make it clear to her that she needs to stay quiet."

The only trouble was that Astrid had a mind of her own. There was no telling what she might do or say if it benefitted her in any way. "It'll make my job a lot easier if I can tell her when and where she should report to work. She's mad that an entire week has gone by and she's been sitting in her apartment with nothing to do."

"Tell her I'll call her this afternoon. She can start on Monday." Grant glanced in the mirror and straightened his shirt. Tara was taken aback by the change in his demeanor. A switch had been flipped. He was no longer sweet, fun and sexy Grant, nor was he the take-charge man she'd slept with. He was all business and all too ready to distance himself from her. About to leave, he held out his hand. "Thanks for a nice night, Tara."

"A handshake? Seriously?"

He cocked an eyebrow at her, which felt like he was telling her she was an idiot for asking. "We're back to being colleagues and nothing else. It's probably for the best."

"It's just us in this room. You can at least give me a hug."

"Honestly, I think a hug will make this more difficult."

Tara choked back a sigh and shook Grant's hand. "Got it, boss. I'll see you in a little bit." She leaned against the doorway as he strode down the hall and escaped into the stairwell. The sound of the front door closing a minute later confirmed that he was gone.

Tara wasn't sure what she was feeling right now. Regret came to mind, but as for what she wished she hadn't set in motion, she wasn't sure. Had this idea to bring the wives together and shoehorn themselves into Sterling been a stupid idea? Or was Grant the poor choice? She didn't want to slap that label on either of her decisions, but she knew that she couldn't have it both ways. She couldn't have this powerful new job *and* Grant. And since she knew that her compatibility with Grant in bed was zero predictor of anything beyond sex, she needed to get back on track. She needed to get back into Astrid's good graces.

After throwing on a pair of yoga pants and a light sweater, Tara grabbed a cup of coffee and went out to the balcony. Astrid was reading something on her phone, but she quickly tucked it inside her purse.

"Sorry about that," Tara said.

"I saw Grant leave. I decided to be discreet and not yell goodbye."

"Thanks." Tara curled up in the chair next to Astrid. "Last night was a mistake. And it won't happen again. I told Grant as much. I think he and I had some issues to work out. Stuff from before Johnathon and I were together. But it's all over now. I don't want you to worry about it. I'm also hoping we can count on your discretion."

Astrid sipped her coffee, staring ahead at the ocean. "Sure. As long as I get the right job within the company."

There was no mistaking the implied threat. "Of course. Grant said he'd call you this afternoon and you can start on Monday. It looks like we're moving ahead with the Seaport Promenade project, so hopefully you can be involved with that. We can work together on it."

Astrid smiled, which made Tara feel slightly better, although she still wasn't sure she could trust her completely. "Sounds good. I'll look forward to hearing from Grant."

"Everything else okay?" Tara asked.

"For the most part, yes. I spoke to Miranda yesterday."

"You did?" Tara wished she didn't sound so flabbergasted, but she was.

"I called to see how she's doing."

"That was nice of you." Honestly, it was astounding of her.

"I don't want things to be so strained between us." Astrid tucked herself farther back in the chair. "I'm sure this sounds crazy, but it feels like she's one of the only connections I have to Johnny. I'm having such a hard time coming to terms with his death."

They were each struggling in their own way. "That makes a lot of sense. She was certainly more connected than most of us when he died."

"And she was there when he passed. I can't explain it, but I feel tied to her. Also, I'm trying to tamp down my envy over the baby. I told myself that if Miranda and I became close, maybe it would help me be more purely happy about it." She took a sip of her coffee. "I also talked to my therapist over the phone earlier this week. She helped me through some of this."

Maybe I need to talk to a therapist, too. Tara admired Astrid's willingness to be kind to Miranda. It had to be difficult for her. But it also confounded Tara a bit. Between the pregnancy and the revelation that Johnathon had not told Astrid he'd married a third time, Tara had only envisioned those two having problems. And she couldn't help but think about the unstable nature of a group of three people sharing the same interest. Alliances would naturally form, and if the one between Miranda and Astrid became especially strong, that would leave Tara out in the cold.

"Is that crazy?" Astrid asked. "Telling myself that getting close to Miranda will make me less jealous?"

It was then that Tara heard the utter heartbreak in Astrid's voice. It was clear as the morning air, and just as strong as the sun. The loss she felt over her inability to conceive with Johnathon was still front and center. It might follow her for the rest of her life. It was only natural that she'd seek some way to come to terms with it. It was certainly a healthier approach than living in denial, or worse, allowing herself to be angry.

Tara set aside her coffee cup and leaned forward in her chair, reaching for Astrid's hand. "I don't think it's crazy. I think it's admirable. I think it's very big of you to set aside your own hurt and support Miranda right now. Frankly, I need to do more to reach out to her and see if she needs anything."

"I'm sure she'd like to hear from you."

Tara let go of her hold on Astrid and sat back. "Maybe the three of us could have dinner one night. That could be fun." She could hardly believe what was coming out of her mouth—the idea of the three of them seeing each other in a social setting of their own planning would have been entirely implausible a few weeks ago.

"I like that idea. Plus, it'll give me something to do."

"I'll get going on that. I've just been so distracted this week."

"By Grant?"

Tara shook her head. She'd made a huge mistake by letting the heat between Grant and her get in the way of the goals she had with Sterling and the promises she'd made to the other wives. In many ways, her conversation with Astrid only confirmed how far she'd strayed off the path and how she needed to get back on it quickly. "No. I swear that won't happen again. I'm focused on we three wives getting the most out of our stake in Sterling. That's all I care about right now."

"Good. Because I'm ready to get to work. First thing Monday morning."

Nine

Grant drove a little too fast getting home. He didn't care about rules or limitations or, apparently, traffic laws right now. Frustration was grinding away inside his head, filtering down into his body and getting entirely too comfortable. How could last night with Tara go so spectacularly only to have everything fall apart this morning? Damn Astrid and her amateur sleuthing. Damn that stupid kiss cam.

And there in the back of his head was the real thing that was bothering him—why did everything he touched seem to go just ever-so-slightly off the rails? Was this a sign of what was to come now that he was at the helm of Sterling? Because Johnathon never had a problem running the company and he'd certainly never seemed to have a problem with women, especially Tara. Yes, their marriage had ended, but he'd been the one to cut it off.

He had three years of wedded bliss with her and a good year before that. Grant would've gladly taken that time with her. He would've taken a fraction of it.

Grant pulled into one of three garage bays at his home in La Jolla, perched up on a cliff overlooking the Pacific. He turned off the ignition, drew in a deep, cleansing breath and knew he had to find a way to win out over his own inner struggle. His heart and body had been greedy last night. Tara was right there, breathtaking and bold, everything he'd ever wanted in a woman, and everything that wasn't his to have. And so he'd gone there. He'd stomped on loyalty. He'd slept with the woman who had once been his best friend's wife, the woman who he also had to run Sterling Enterprises with. It was as stupid a choice as he could have made. He had to own that.

He strode into the house, his big empty showplace. It was modern and minimalist, and situated in one of the most enviable settings in the world, windswept but pristine, with the untamed cobalt ocean at its feet. It was everything he could ever want in a home. Except that it was also a multimillion-dollar testament to his unwanted bachelorhood. He didn't want to be the sole inhabitant. He'd never wanted it that way. Hope had always been in the back of his head, or perhaps in the center of his heart. He'd always thought he'd meet the right woman, get married and have children. He'd even envisioned little ones riding tricycles or kicking a ball through these expansive halls, across the wood floors that cost a fortune, quite possibly ruining them, and Grant not caring at all. Sure, it was traditional and not terribly original, but it was his true desire. Coming from a loving family and having four siblings might make for dull cocktail-party conversation, but he'd always been thankful for it.

In this high-stakes, big-money world he lived in, those roots kept him grounded.

In his bedroom, he took off his clothes, forcing himself to throw them in the hamper destined to go to the cleaners. His shirt held the faintest traces of Tara's beguiling scent. It was going to be hard enough to breathe it in at work. He didn't need to torture himself with it.

He climbed into the shower, lathering up his chest and attempting to scrub away the remnants of last night. The hot spray wasn't doing nearly enough to help him shake off the effects of Tara. He was twice torn, between what was and what should have been—the business he'd helped build was now at his command, but if that fateful moment hadn't happened on the golf course, Johnathon would've been here to lead the way instead. He never would have had last night with Tara. He didn't want to regret it, but how could part of him not? He couldn't ignore the feeling that he had betrayed his best friend by taking Tara to bed. It didn't matter that Johnathon wasn't here anymore. He wouldn't have liked it if he was. And Grant truly wished his best friend was still alive. For all of Johnathon's faults, Grant still missed him. He missed talking to him every day, reining him in at his more erratic moments and marveling at his brilliant ones. He missed having a true partner in this business that was all consuming. The two of them had been through so much together. It was impossible to turn his back on the memories.

He had to hustle to get back to the office before nine. As he strolled out of the elevator and into the reception area, his stomach sank. The full staff wasn't in yet, but it was still entirely too quiet. There was an unmistakable air in the office. There were whispers and glances. The office grapevine was just as aware of Astrid's findings as he'd feared—they all knew about the kiss cam. They knew about the very real heat between Tara and him.

Roz the office receptionist was unpacking her bag. "Good morning, Mr. Singleton." She eyed him with suspicion as he walked past.

"Morning," he replied, doing his best to act as though nothing was going on. Still, a walk down the hall told him that his wariness was warranted. People knew about the kiss and they were talking about it. It was now his job to squash that as quickly as possible. That started with keeping Tara in the office on the opposite end of the building. He needed as little proximity as they could get away with. It was too dangerous. He knew how tempted he was by her.

He sat at his desk and his assistant checked in with him a few minutes later. If she knew what was going on, she didn't let on, and that was a relief. Perhaps the rumors could die quickly. Unfortunately, Tara showed up in his doorway several minutes later, looking like a dream in a sleek red dress that showed off her curves and her legs. It was appropriate for the office, but it was still as sexy as anything Grant had ever seen. He truly wished he could go for five minutes without being tested.

She knocked on the door frame. "Do you have a minute? We need to talk."

"Sure." His body immediately responded to her presence. It felt like every hair on his head was standing straight up. Everything below his waist went tight.

Tara took a step inside and went to close the door.

"Leave it open," he blurted, bolting out of his seat.

Tara cast him a questioning look. "What's up?"

"Everyone knows," he whispered.

"I realize that. Precisely why I'd like to close the door. So we can have some privacy."

A deep grumble left his throat. He hated playing these games, especially at work. It was not the way he liked to do things. He was supposed to be the guy with nothing to hide. "No. Leave it open. If there's anything we can't discuss with the door open, we shouldn't be talking about it at all. At least not here."

"Fine." Tara marched to one of the armchairs opposite his desk and sat. "There are three things we need to talk about. Astrid, the Seaport Promenade and my office move."

She wasn't making this any easier on him. "I think we make Astrid the project coordinator for the Seaport. You can oversee her work," Grant said.

"Do you really think she'll go for that? She owns just as much of the company as I do."

"And you have experience in this realm. She does not. She'll learn a lot by doing this, and quite frankly, I think it'll help her decide if this is something she really wants to do long term. I'm not convinced she's cut out for this."

Tara pursed her lips, but nodded in agreement. "Okay. You'll call her and let her know?"

"Yes." He only hoped Astrid wouldn't give him crap about what happened last night. "As for the project itself, it should be obvious that I'm committed to us submitting a proposal and bid to the city. I'd like to assign Clay Morgan as lead architect. He has background in designing public spaces, he's incredibly smart and well suited to working within the constraints the city sets. I think he'd be perfect."

"Interesting."

"What?" Grant disliked Tara's leading tone. He was

doing his best to make this work, when really all he wanted to do was shut the door and get her to take off that red dress.

"It feels a little bit like you're setting up Astrid for failure. She and Miranda are still working on their differences, but you saw the way they talked to each other in the lawyer's meeting. I could see them returning to that dynamic at any time. Miranda and her brother are extremely close. Do you not see a potential problem there?"

"And do you want to give Astrid a job or not?"

Tara leaned back in her chair and surveyed the view through his doorway, presumably looking to see if anyone might overhear what she was about to say. "We have to. Not only because of her shares of the company, but because it might be the only way we can keep her from talking."

"I think we need to be able to keep tabs on her, too. We can't simply hand her something and let her run with it. She's an unknown quantity right now."

"That's fair."

"I realize this isn't ideal, but I'm doing my best, okay?" Grant felt a headache starting to brew, right in the center of his forehead. His shoulders were tightening. Not a great way to start a Friday, especially when he knew that he had a long, frustratingly lonely weekend ahead of him.

"I know you are. I'm sorry. I'm sorry everything got so messy."

"Yeah, well, so am I. You were right about what you said earlier this morning. It was a mistake." Those last four words had barely left his mouth, and he couldn't help but want to take them back. They were the right thing to say, but damn it all if they didn't feel wrong.

He'd dreamed for so many years of being with Tara. He hated that the memory of their one night together was now tainted by everything that had happened since then.

"Right. Of course. Not to be repeated."

"Exactly." That was that then—the beginning and end of Grant and Tara had transpired in fewer than twenty-four hours.

"If we're back to focusing on work, I have to ask about next steps with Seaport."

Grant shuffled some papers on his desk, desperate to hide his wounded pride. "Run with it and keep me apprised. You have your team—Astrid, Clay and Sandy. It's your project to bring together."

Tara shifted in her seat and recrossed her legs. His stupid eyes were drawn to them the way a horse is drawn to cool water. Those beautiful stretches of her skin had been wrapped around him last night. And he couldn't have that happen again. "That's it then?" she asked.

He was trying so hard to keep it together right now. He did want to close the door to his office. He wanted to take her into his arms and kiss her exactly like he'd been brave enough to do last night. "That's it. Green light from me. Go ahead and prove me wrong."

"Okay. I will." She got up from her seat and stepped closer to his desk. "One more thing before I go. What about my office? We can't work together closely when I'm so far away."

Distance would help him keep his head straight. It would help him focus on big-picture projects at Sterling and let Tara do her thing. He hoped they could peacefully coexist. They had to. Or he had to find a way to raise the capital to buy her, Miranda and Astrid out of their chunk of the company. At this point, he was going to have to offer them far more than the shares were worth, a reality he found especially grating. The value was something he'd created. He didn't want to have to pay for it. "Considering what happened last night, and the fact that Astrid knows about it, as well as most of the office, I think it's in our best interest to keep you where you are."

She folded her arms across her chest, which only served to frame her bustline in a too-pleasing way. "I don't want this to be a long-term answer."

"We can re-evaluate in a month. The office chatter will only get worse if you move into the office next to mine. I also think that for the time being, we should keep our talks to email as much as possible. Avoid being seen together." He dared to look her in the eye, wanting to underscore his seriousness. Too bad he hated having to say it. "That's my decision, okay?"

"Hmm. Exercising some authority?"

"As a matter of fact, I am. I still know what's best for the company."

Tara knocked her knuckle on Grant's desk. "I guess you're right. It doesn't mean I like it."

Sandy appeared at Grant's door. He was happy for the interruption. "Ms. Sterling, the other Ms. Sterling is on the phone for you. Astrid."

Grant had to laugh at that, although he did it under his breath. There were far too many Ms. Sterlings in his orbit right now. And for the moment, one of them—Tara—needed to circle as far away from him as possible.

The weekend came and went with little rest, as Tara spent most of it deep in thought over everything that had happened since Johnathon's death. And in some instances, everything that came before it. She'd even scrounged around in a storage closet and found an old photo album from the time when she'd been married to Johnathon. Many of the pictures were from the lavish vacations they took, all of which were made with Grant and his girlfriend at the time, which was never the same. They rented a sprawling villa in Tuscany one autumn, where they drank wine for days, toured art museums and spent hours sunning themselves by the pool. There was the chalet perched atop a mountain in Switzerland, a getaway filled with endless ski runs and nights devoted to conversation in front of the fire.

Quite possibly the most memorable trip was to Costa Rica. Grant had hunted down a two-bedroom, two-bath treehouse tucked up into the rainforest canopy. That had been a grand adventure. They went on zip-line tours, swam in natural pools under waterfalls and sat on the porch for hours, sipping rum and watching the antics of the howler monkeys and macaws. Tara realized that she and Grant had taken most of the pictures from these vacations, which meant she was stuck trying to remember the names of these random women he'd brought along as his companions. She couldn't recall a single one. When Grant and Johnathon were in the frame together, their genuine connection was always there. They had been like brothers, which was such a gift for Johnathon—he and his own brother had always had a contentious relationship.

Tara had to wonder if that was part of what had made Grant so eager to step away from her the other morning. Setting aside the obvious conflict of their working relationship, and what had been the immediate threat of Astrid telling everyone she knew that Grant and Tara had slept together, perhaps it was Grant's history with Johnathon that made him second-guess what they'd done. Grant was in a far different situation than Tara—his allegiance to Johnathon had gone right up until the moment he'd died. Much of Tara's went away when he filed for divorce. It wasn't the same. And perhaps she needed to give Grant some credit for not wanting to violate the trust that had come with his brotherly bond with Johnathon. Things like that didn't simply dissolve when someone passed away.

As she drove to work on Monday morning, it occurred to her that there might be something else going on here—perhaps she had underestimated Grant. Not only in the bedroom, but in the sphere of work. He'd shown himself as nothing less than a formidable man. He was not to be messed with. He'd also made it obvious that his allegiance was to Sterling Enterprises above all else. As to how much that was wrapped up in his friendship with Johnathon, she didn't know. But still, the fact that he'd taken Tara to bed wasn't about to slow him down with staking his claim on Sterling. And now she was in the position of having to stay away from him, when the reality was that he'd done nothing less than pique her interest by making love to her.

But sex would solve nothing. *Stay on your path, Tara. Get back to work.*

When she arrived at the office, she found Astrid in reception, looking absolutely stunning in a gray wool pencil skirt and black turtleneck. On anyone else, it would've looked a little too prim for the modern workplace. On Astrid, it was jaw-dropping.

"You ready to get to work?" Tara asked.

"Absolutely."

Tara guided Astrid through the maze of halls, passing her office, so she could lead Astrid to the one she'd be occupying. "This will be where you'll be working for the time being. Everything's in a state of flux right now, so I don't think this is where you'll end up permanently. I know it's maybe not quite as nice as you might have wanted." Tara braced for commentary on the small and spartan nature of the space. Astrid was accustomed to luxury and the finest of everything.

"This will work fine. I don't need a fancy office. I just need a place to sit and a desk. The window is nice." Astrid offered a quick smile, seeming satisfied.

Tara admired Astrid's willingness to go with the flow. She hadn't expected it, at all. Johnathon had always painted Astrid as being incredibly high-maintenance, the sort of woman who needed constant attention and adulation. That hadn't been Tara's experience thus far. Astrid certainly had a flair for high drama—showing up at the first meeting of the wives dressed as Widow of the Year, and then again turning up at Tara's house and busting her on her tryst with Grant. But as for being needy, Astrid seemed nothing less than self-sufficient.

"You'll be working on the Seaport Promenade project with me," Tara said. "Since you're just getting started in the world of development, Grant thought it best for us to work together so I and a few other key people in the office can show you the ropes."

Astrid nodded eagerly and tucked her long blond hair behind her ear. "Yes, of course. I'm ready to learn."

Yet again, Tara was pleasantly surprised. Astrid might have owned seventeen percent of the company, but she sure wasn't acting as though she was entitled to anything other than an opportunity. "Great. Let's go chat with Clay Morgan, the lead architect on the project. I can explain everything to you on our way down to his office."

Astrid reached for Tara's arm, her face now painted with concern. "He's Miranda's brother, isn't he?"

"He is. But you and Miranda have started to iron things out, haven't you?"

Astrid nodded. "Yes. But I'm still not sure she likes me."

Tara patted Astrid on the arm, wanting to reassure her. "She's been through a lot. We've all been through a lot. All the more reason for us to have that dinner together. Does Friday still work for you?"

"It does. I wouldn't miss it."

"Great."

The two women strode down the hall to the suite where the architects' offices were. She loved this part of the Sterling operation. It made her think of her dad, and his dreams. He would've been excited to see so many talented people hard at work. He'd always hoped to find himself in a place exactly like this, but he'd never reached that goal. All the more reason for Tara to keep striving for more in this new phase of her professional life. She wasn't waiting to be happy. She was making her dad proud by going for it.

Tara reached Clay's door, which was wide open. Inside, Clay was hard at work at his drafting table. In the background, classical music played, but at a volume so low that it was hardly audible. Tara had met Clay a few times, and if she had to stick him with a label, it would have been *intense*. His hair was very dark, nearly black, just like Miranda's. It was longish on top, and he was always threading his fingers through it, flopping it from one side to the other. His blue eyes were so dark that they sometimes looked like midnight. He was tall and broad, but quiet and reserved. There always seemed to be quite a lot going on under the surface.

Tara hated to interrupt him, especially when he was so hard at work, but she had to make this introduction. She rapped on his door quietly. He looked up at her with those stormy eyes, but he seemed to quickly see past Tara to Astrid. Tara was accustomed to this response from men when she was with Astrid. The woman had graced hundreds of magazines and the runway for a reason—she was breathtakingly beautiful.

"Clay. Hi," Tara started. "I wanted to introduce you to Astrid Sterling. She's going to be project manager on the Seaport project. You and Grant talked about it, right?"

He took a quick survey of his workspace, which was littered with pencils and large sheets of drafting paper. "Yeah. Sure. I'm sorry. I would've cleaned up if I'd known you were coming."

Astrid walked past Tara and helped him with the pencils. "It's okay. I'm good at straightening up."

Clay was a proverbial deer in the headlights, not saying a thing and frozen in place. Men did all sorts of strange things in Astrid's presence. "Please. Don't." He stopped Astrid by clapping his hand down on hers. He'd apparently snapped back to attention.

Astrid shook off the rebuff, but her cheeks were red with embarrassment. "I'm so sorry."

"It's okay. I just like to have my office a certain way."

Tara was eager to diffuse the sudden tension in the air. "So, Clay, as you know, Grant wants you as lead architect on the project. Astrid will be learning along the way and managing the day-to-day. I'll be dealing with the city, with help from my assistant, Sandy."

Clay picked up one of the pencils from his desk and rattled it back and forth between his fingers. "I've already done my own research on the specs. We're behind the eight ball. The first plans are due in five weeks. If we don't pass the initial phase, we're out of the running. And my workload is already considerable, so this is going to be a big challenge."

Tara decided that getting Clay on her side was of paramount importance. Grant would think she couldn't handle things if Clay went complaining to him about the timeline or the project in general. "You have a daughter, right?"

Clay's eyes narrowed. "I do. She's five."

"One of my prime objectives in our version of the project is to make it more kid friendly. There's not enough for families downtown. I think your knowledge based on that alone is crucial."

"There are other dads in the department."

"But none who are doing it all on their own as a single dad. I'm guessing you bring a specific set of ideas to the equation. Plus, Grant swears up and down that you're the top architect in the firm. I want the best for this project."

Clay pursed his lips, the pencil still wagging in his hand. "Okay. We need to have a planning meeting as soon as possible. A site visit. I'd like to hear some ideas outside of my own. It's important to have more than one perspective."

"That's perfect because I have lots of ideas. Grant really seemed to like them." Just thinking about presenting her ideas to Grant was making her sad about the other night. They'd both been so caught up in the moment, feeding off each other's enthusiasm. It had felt only natural that they'd ended up in bed together, and in the moment, it had been so right. She and Grant fit together like two puzzle pieces. But that was not to be. She had to stay focused on what was ahead of her.

"Okay. Sounds good," Clay said.

Tara breathed a sigh of relief. "Fantastic. I'll have Sandy bring you the official specs this afternoon. Perhaps we can meet first thing tomorrow morning?"

"That works," Clay said.

"Is this your daughter in the picture?" Astrid asked, picking up a frame from the credenza.

"It is. She was a flower girl when my sister and Johnathon got married."

Astrid admired the photograph and Tara stole a glance over her shoulder. Clay was standing next to bride Miranda with his arm around her. Clay's daughter was in a pretty pink dress with a basket of flowers. It made Tara's heart ache to think about how happy everyone was in that photograph, but it also made her equally sad to think about what Astrid must be thinking while looking at it. She hadn't been told that Johnathon had remarried. This was a piece of history she'd only recently learned of.

"When was the wedding?"

"Late May last year. Memorial Day weekend. They were barely married for a year. It's so sad," Clay answered.

"Was it a short engagement?" Astrid asked.

Tara found the question odd. Why would Astrid want to know these details? "A few months, I guess," Tara answered.

"Sounds right to me," Clay added.

Astrid tapped her finger against the frame, then

promptly put the photograph down and made for the door. "Thanks, Clay," she said, hardly looking at him before she disappeared into the hall.

"Is she okay?" Clay asked.

Tara didn't know the answer to that question, but she had a good idea. "I'm sure she's fine. Thanks for letting us steal some of your time today."

"Yeah. Of course."

Tara rushed out into the hall. She expected that she'd have to chase after Astrid, but she was just outside the door, leaning against the wall with her face buried in her hands.

"Come on," Tara said, urging her ahead with a gentle tug of her arm. "Let's you and I get some privacy." She and Astrid filed into the ladies' room. "Was it the photo from Johnathon's wedding to Miranda?"

"Yes." Astrid's voice was soft and unsteady.

"I'm sorry you had to see that, but maybe it's better that it finally happened. You and Miranda are becoming friends. It was only a matter of time before she invited you over one night."

Astrid braced her hands on the bathroom counter, staring into the mirror and shaking her head. She wasn't tearful, but the color was definitely gone from her face. "I can't believe it."

"Believe what?"

Astrid looked Tara right in the eye via her reflection. "Johnathon cheated on Miranda."

"Wait. What? How do you know?"

Astrid turned around and crossed her arms over her chest, leaning back against the vanity. "I know because he cheated on her with me."

Ten

Tara cursed her ex-husband for days. Nearly an entire work week, to be exact. *Damn you, Johnathon.* How could he have done that? Sleep with one ex-wife weeks before marrying the next one? It was unconscionable. It was also a little crazy that Tara had such a burning desire to find out why he'd done it. *Leave it alone*, she kept telling herself. But she couldn't.

Tara had a vested interest in keeping this secret buried, even if it killed her to play a part in Johnathon's misdeeds. If Miranda found out and blew up over it, the wives' majority interest in the company would be compromised. There was no telling what either Astrid or Miranda would do in that situation, but Tara could imagine some terrible scenarios. They might feel pitted against each other and sell to one of the other shareholders, leaving Tara with very few options. If they sold to Grant, it would be game over. Tara would lose her chance to run the company. Miranda and Astrid might even band together against Tara. Crazier things had happened.

The wives needed to be a unified front, but beneath the surface, things were beginning to splinter. First there was the pregnancy and now, the infidelity. Beyond that, Tara was responsible for some of the uneven ground they were walking on. It had been foolish to sleep with Grant. It had been shortsighted to allow herself to get caught up in the moment and give in to those carnal desires, and her own deep-seated curiosity about what it might be like to sleep with him. She couldn't beat herself up about it though. She refused to do that. He rocked her world a week ago. On some level, it had been worth it.

For now, her most pressing problem was that Astrid would not stop asking Tara if she thought Grant knew about the infidelity. It bothered Astrid greatly, and she'd been unable to get a meeting with him. His schedule was ridiculously full. Tara kept putting Astrid off, but she couldn't do it forever. And it benefitted her to ask the question before Astrid had the chance to do it herself. If Astrid unleashed her anger on Grant in the office, Clay might find out about it and that would all lead back to Miranda. It was a risk to ask Grant, but she needed to do it. Luckily, she not only had access to his calendar, but she'd befriended his assistant.

She showed up at his office just as he was getting off a call. "Do you have a minute?" she asked.

"Sure," he answered, typing away at his keyboard.

Tara closed the door behind her. She couldn't let anyone hear their discussion. The rumor mill would gobble up this delicious morsel of gossip and it would spread like wildfire.

"Tara. We talked about this. About the door," he said.

"I know. But we need privacy." That one word—
privacy—and the accompanying knowledge that they
were now alone did a number on her. It made her face
and chest flush with heat. It made her legs feel rubbery.
Being in his presence heightened the memory of his
touch. It boiled it down to a potent serum that streamed
through her body. What would have happened if she and
Grant hadn't had their hands forced the morning after?
Would he have wanted more? Would she have agreed?
She knew she would have. It would have been impossible to turn him down.

"The whole office will talk about it," he said.

"Let them talk. We have bigger fish to fry." Tara
went to the window and looked out over the city sky-
line, her mind running too many disparate pieces of information at one time. Astrid. Johnathon. Miranda. It
was such a mess. And it was time to crack it open. "You
knew, didn't you?"

Grant sat back in his chair and crossed his legs. He'd
removed his suit jacket at some point during the day,
and rolled up the sleeves of his shirt. God, he had sexy
forearms. Strong and long, with the perfect amount of
dark hair. "Sorry. You're going to have to be a little more
specific than that."

"Johnathon and Astrid. The real reason he never told
Astrid about marrying Miranda."

Grant cleared his throat and averted his gaze. That
told her all she needed to know, but she still wanted to
hear it.

"Tell me," she said.

"I didn't find out about it until after the fact. I swear

that if I had known ahead of time, I would have tried to talk him out of it."

"What happened?"

"I guess he just never had the nerve to tell Astrid when he met Miranda and they got involved. He couldn't bring himself to break her heart. He and Astrid still had a very on-again, off-again relationship after the divorce. She went back to Norway and he went there several times trying to reconcile."

This was news to Tara, and it hurt to hear it. Johnathon had no problem moving on after shuttling her out of his life. Astrid was on his arm in what felt like the blink of an eye. "I had no idea."

"It was heartbreaking, really. They both wanted children so badly, but they'd never been able to conceive. Years of trying and waiting every month and never having any luck took its toll on the marriage, but I think they still loved each other deeply."

Tara knew it had been rough for them, but she hadn't been privy to the details. "What about after he and Miranda got engaged? That wasn't enough to keep him away from Astrid?"

"Apparently not. I thought he was flying to London to meet with a potential partner on a project. He didn't tell me he was stopping off in Norway on the way there."

"From what Astrid said, it was only weeks before the wedding. What prompted it?"

Grant shrugged. "You know what he was like. He sometimes simply let the wind carry him in one direction, even when he knew he should probably go the other way."

Tara did know that firsthand. She'd felt like that had been the case when Johnathon jettisoned her from Sterling and pushed her into real estate. It all happened so suddenly. One day she was working at their fledgling operation and the next, he was insisting she do something else and get her real estate license.

Grant pinched his nose and shook his head. "It's hard for me to know what was going through Johnathon's head at that point. All I know is that he went to Norway and he and Astrid slept together."

"He told you when he got back?"

"Actually, no. But he put some items from Norway on his expense report and he was out of the office when the folks in accounting asked me about it. Norway wasn't on his company itinerary, so they were checking to see if it was right."

"Did you confront him?"

"I did, and you can imagine how that went. There was no confronting Johnathon. He never wanted to own up to anything that made him look bad. He never wanted to appear human. He wanted everyone to love him unconditionally."

"And it worked for the most part."

"It did. He just made everyone else deal with his mistakes."

Tara knew that, too. When Johnathon had asked her to set aside her aspirations with Sterling, he'd told several people that it had been her choice to do so. That couldn't have been further from the truth, but Tara believed in a unified front when it came to marriage, and so she'd smiled and nodded and said that being a real estate agent had always been her dream. When it wasn't true.

"I don't really know what to do about this," she said, turning back to Grant. As she shifted, the sun steamed in through the window over her shoulder, first blinding her, then as her eyes adjusted, lighting him in a soft glow. It harkened back to their morning together and waking up next to him. It had been so lovely. He made her feel desired. Wanted. She hadn't felt that way in forever. Good God, she really wanted to kiss him again, to have his lips on the sensitive skin of her neck and feel his commanding hands all over her body. She really wanted to find out if their night together had been a fluke.

"You realize you're asking the wrong person, right?" he asked. "I have every reason imaginable to stir up trouble between Astrid and Miranda. To divide your interests and hopefully convince one of you to sell."

"So why not create problems? You could have told either one of them about it and really driven the wedge between them. The opportunity was there from the moment Max told you he'd split Miranda's shares of the company between us." She didn't want to give him any ideas, but surely this had occurred to him.

"I could never do that. You should know that about me."

Tara drew in a deep breath. How did he manage to stay on the right side of everything? "I know, Grant. I know you're a good guy."

He shook his head and rose up out of his chair. "If it makes me a good guy because I want to win fair and square, then so be it. I guess I'm a good guy. Just please stop saying it like it's a bad thing. I realize that's not what you're attracted to. I guess you'd rather be with the sort of man who cheats on his new wife with his former one."

Ouch. "That's not what I'm attracted to."

"Then prove it to me."

Tara struggled to find a response. What was he saying? "With you?" The idea was all wrong. So why did it have to send such a tide of electricity through her body?

He shrugged and his eyes narrowed. "I don't know, Tara. You tell me."

Grant had nearly told her yes—prove it with him. Hell, he'd nearly come clean with a confession, but he wasn't ready. Something inside him was telling him to stay back. It was already hard enough to admit to himself that he'd been carrying a torch for Tara this whole time, even when she was married to his best friend. It would make him look weak and he didn't want Tara to see him that way. Yes, he'd been standing in Johnathon's shadow for years, but he'd been the backbone of the company and in many ways, he'd been that for Johnathon, too. It was just that nobody wanted to see it. The specter of Johnathon Sterling was too much for people to see past.

"No. I'm really not a good guy. At least not the way you're trying to put it." He stepped closer to her, scanning her face while memories of their night together gathered in his mind like storm clouds threatening torrential rain. He'd thought perhaps that last week might quench his desire for her, but it hadn't. Quite the opposite. She'd awoken something in him, a primal part of his psyche that wasn't willing to lose. Not anymore. He wanted what he wanted and he wasn't about to apologize for it.

"I really think this is a problem you need to rectify on your own, Grant."

She wasn't wrong. But he hoped she'd help him work it out. "I want you too much, Tara, and it's impacting my job. You're too beautiful. Too sexy. Too desirable. That's my real problem."

A crease formed between her eyes as doubt spread across her face. "Oh, please. I'm supposed to believe that you're so taken with me that you aren't still laser focused on the prize? You've always wanted to be at the helm of Sterling, and you're threatened by my presence. I don't think you can blame our battle of wills on attraction. No matter what you might have said to Johnathon over the years about being okay with playing second fiddle to him, I think you've always wanted Sterling first and foremost."

"You're not wrong. I have always wanted to be in charge. I was content in my role, but now that I've had a taste of the control it gives me, I'm not willing to pass up this opportunity." What he really wanted to say was that now that he'd had a taste of Tara, he wasn't willing to let her go. But she could turn on him so quickly, and there was more at stake than hurt feelings.

"Then we're at an impasse," she said. "I have a chance to fulfill my own dreams and I'm not willing to just shrug that off or walk away from it. No way. Not now. Not when I've got Astrid and Miranda and her baby counting on me to make the most of this."

"What happens if there's a rift between Astrid and Miranda? The truth has a way of coming out. Then where will you be, Tara? I know you're worried about them trusting you, but do you really, truly trust them?" It might sound like he was trying to sow discontent between the wives, but he wanted her to face the reality. Astrid and Miranda could turn on her at any point. And depending on which way they chose to go, whether they sold their shares to someone else or each other, it could all mean that control of Sterling would go into the wrong hands. It was a very real possibility. The sort of reality that kept Grant up at night.

"I have to trust that they'll keep up their end of the bargain. I have three months to prove that I can make this work, and we're barely two weeks in. Part of that is the Seaport project. If I can make that a success, I think I'll prove to them what I'm capable of."

Grant sighed as the weight of the situation he was in came crashing down around him once again. Any time he tried to shrug it off, it came roaring back. He wanted control, but so did Tara. He wanted Sterling to be successful, and Tara was on the same page, but in a markedly different way. And then there was this crazy side of himself that was rooting for Tara to realize her dreams, as well. Johnathon had held her back when he could, and it hadn't been fair. Grant cared about her too much for his own good.

"Where does this leave us?" Grant asked.

"The same place we were before I walked into your office. For now, we're on opposite sides of the same table. I want to run Sterling someday. I have to prove my worth to the wives and I need to prove myself to the staff. That means staying out of your bed."

"Technically, we were in *your* bed that night."

"You know what I mean."

"And is that what you really want, Tara? If you were being truly honest with yourself, and there were no repercussions, would you be saying that to me? To stay out of your bed?" He held his breath as he waited for the answer. If she was about to say yes, it would crush his most fragile dream, the one he had no business holding on to. But he wanted a dose of reality. It might help him see a way through this.

"I don't even know what you're asking, Grant. I don't do well with hypotheticals."

"That's not true. The woman who stood down at the waterfront and painted a picture for me with nothing more than her words and her passion is one-hundred-percent capable of seeing the possibilities."

"Are you asking me a question about business? Or us?"

Grant swallowed hard. He hadn't expected to meet this challenge today, to have to double down on what he wanted in his heart. But he had to say it, be done with it and let the dust settle. "I'm asking about us. The other night was spectacular and you know it. We have always had a connection. Don't tell me that years of flirting were for nothing. That there was nothing behind it. I don't believe that."

Tara waved him off and turned back to the window. "Well, of course I'm attracted to you, Grant. But do you really think that I will just throw away a professional opportunity so we can have a fling? I'm not playing a short game here—I'm playing a long one."

"What makes you think it would only be short-term?"

"Two reasons. First off, you have never been able to make a relationship last for more than a month. Second, Sterling isn't going anywhere and we both want the same thing, which there is only one of."

If only Tara knew that the real reason he'd never been able to make a relationship work was because he compared all women to her. It was a stupid, foolish thing to do, and he'd fought it many times, but it always came down to that. Tara had a way of worming her way back into his head. "What if we shared the leadership of Sterling?" He could hardly believe what he was suggesting.

Johnathon would never have thought such a thing was a good idea, and Grant wasn't sure he thought it was smart, either. Still, he was looking for some fissure in the wall Tara had put up between them. There had to be a way in, a chink in her impenetrable armor.

She shook her head with such conviction that he braced for her answer. "No way. I want to win or lose, and really I just want to win. I should have had a role in this company all along. Johnathon should've kept me here. You know it, and I believe he knew it, too. There's no other reason for him to have written me into the will. I don't believe for a minute that he did it simply because he loved me like he loved Astrid and Miranda. I was a pit stop for him, and I paid a price for it. I got pushed off into a career I didn't want, and I got sidelined from the direction I wanted to take, which was to follow in my dad's footsteps. I have the chops, Grant. I know I do."

"I know. I know." He felt himself backing down, and he was tired of pushing himself into a corner. He had to accept that Tara's primary focus right now was on business. He was going to have to let her move forward with her plan. As long as she had the other wives on her side, they could call all the shots they wanted to. Hell, they could ouster him as CEO if they so chose. He couldn't play fast and loose with his role in the company. He had to learn his lesson. "So I guess I have my answer."

"I'd like to hear you say it just so I know we're on the same page," Tara said.

"We're fighting for control of Sterling Enterprises by seeing who can make the best leader. And that means that in the meantime, I'm staying out of your bed."

Eleven

Tara had offered to host dinner for Miranda and Astrid at her house, but Miranda had insisted they do it at her place. Balancing the pregnancy and her job had left her exhausted, and it was easier if she didn't have to go anywhere. Neither Tara nor Astrid had any reason to dispute her.

Tara pulled up to what had once been Miranda and Johnathon's home, now solely belonging to his widow. Situated in La Jolla, overlooking the water, this was close to Grant's home, which was a mile or two south. Grant and Johnathon had always been thick as thieves, and they'd liked being in close proximity. When Johnathon lived with Tara in Coronado, the two had always complained it was too far.

The house was truly magnificent, an absolute showcase of Spanish architecture, with white stucco, black-leaded windows and a red clay roof topping the six different levels of the home. The tropical seaside landscape was lit up dramatically, as was the house, adorned with wrought iron carriage lamps. Tara had seen the property once, but that was before Johnathon and Miranda had bought it. She'd shown it to a couple five years ago, when the asking price was six million. Tara estimated that it had to be worth at least twelve by now. That was quite a nest egg for Miranda, on top of the millions Johnathon had left to her.

Financially, Miranda would do just fine. Emotionally, Tara didn't know, but she was sure she was about to find out how Miranda was faring.

Tara waited in her car in the driveway until Astrid arrived. She wanted the chance to speak to her for a moment before they went inside. Luckily, it was only a five-minute wait until Astrid zipped up in her little silver Porsche—a rental to keep her mobile while she was living in the city.

"You look absolutely gorgeous," Tara said, offering a hug.

"Thank you. You, too," Astrid replied. Tara felt as though it was more of an obligatory reply than anything.

"Before we go inside, I just wanted to say that I don't think it's a good idea to bring up what you told me the other day at work."

Astrid regarded Tara with utter horror. "What do you take me for, Tara? A complete idiot? I would never do that."

Tara was taken aback. Astrid had been asserting herself in ways she hadn't expected. "I didn't mean any offense. I just wanted to be sure we could keep the peace. And I mean, what's done is done. Johnathon is gone. There's no one to answer for that particular misstep."

"I'm well aware that I can't yell and scream at him for that and neither can Miranda. I will have to carry that secret to my grave." She started off for the front door.

Tara followed, utterly relieved. "You're being remarkably calm about this."

Astrid checked her face in a compact mirror, then jabbed at the doorbell. "Vodka helps."

Tara smiled to herself, wondering why she'd bothered to worry about strife between the wives. They could find a way to make their peculiar partnership work. She felt certain of it. Well, reasonably sure. Money and business had a way of making everything more complicated.

Miranda answered and it was immediately apparent that she was not well. There was no glow of pregnancy. She had dark circles under her eyes and appeared pale and gaunt. Her normally gorgeous black hair was up in a messy bun, and she was wearing what appeared to be workout attire—gray yoga pants and a stretchy blue top. Tara was about to ask if they'd come at the wrong time, but Miranda put a quick end to that.

"Come on in." Miranda waved them both in to the two-story foyer, which had a sweeping staircase with an ornate scrolled railing and a spectacular wrought iron chandelier overhead. "I'm sorry I look like hell. Morning sickness is a misnomer. I'm having it all day long."

Astrid was quick to be at her side. "Do you need to sit down? Can I bring you anything?"

Tara found Astrid's attentiveness both sweet and odd. Perhaps Astrid was overcompensating. "Yes. Please. Let us know if we can do something. And we definitely don't have to eat. I can only imagine that the thought of being around food right now isn't particularly fun."

Miranda led them down a short hall and they emerged

in the soaring great room, this space with a three-story-high ceiling and ringed with two levels of balconies. On the far side was a wall of windows overlooking the pool and beautifully landscaped yard, and up a half level was a gourmet kitchen, complete with eight-burner stove and Sub-Zero fridge. The house was even more of a show-place now than it had been the time Tara had seen it. Miranda had put her expert interior design touches on it, and she'd chosen very well, with sophisticated white sofas and splashes of color from throw pillows and modern art on the wall. Tara could only imagine what a nightmare it was going to be to babyproof this house, but that was a discussion for another day.

"My personal chef prepared dinner. I'm going to attempt to eat, but no promises." Miranda walked over to the bar. "Can I get either of you a drink?"

Tara was quick to assume bartender duties. "I can do this. It hardly seems fair that the woman who can't drink would have to make them. Astrid, what can I get you?"

"Vodka and soda, please," Astrid replied. Of course, she of zero body fat would choose the least caloric drink imaginable.

"Coming right up. And for you, Miranda?"

"Ginger ale, please. They should be in the fridge down below."

Tara quickly assembled the necessary supplies and delivered everyone's drinks. Astrid and Miranda had situated themselves at opposite ends of one sofa, leaving Tara to occupy the chair nearest Miranda. "So, I guess we should get the business part of our dinner meeting out of the way."

"Yes. I want to know what's going on. How's everyone in the office doing? I only get reports from Clay and he's not really up on office gossip," Miranda said.

"Generally, I think things are going really well. Everyone seems to be handling Johnathon's death as well as can be expected." Tara realized that the real reason morale at Sterling was good was all due to Grant's influence. She was the new person who'd interjected herself into this equation. Maybe her timing hadn't been the best, but she wasn't going to apologize for pursuing what had once been her dream and was now her dream again.

"I started this week," Astrid added. "I'm working with your brother, actually."

"Oh, interesting," Miranda said. "He didn't mention it."

There was a distinct stiffening of Astrid's posture as she took a healthy slug of her drink. Tara knew that Astrid wanted desperately to be taken seriously. All Tara could do to help with that was to put her in a position to prove herself. After that, it was all up to her.

"Yes. They're working on the Seaport Promenade project with the city. I think it will be a real boon if we can land it."

Miranda smiled quietly, seeming wistful as she took a sip of her ginger ale. "Johnathon really wanted to do that project. Grant fought him on it. Hard."

"I heard about that, but I think it's all worked out. We're moving forward with your brother as lead architect." Tara didn't want to mention that Grant's reasoning for staying out of it was because Johnathon had ruffled a lot of feathers with the city over the years. Miranda likely already knew about it, and if she didn't, Tara didn't want to disparage Johnathon. Miranda was carrying his baby, after all.

"Do you think there's a place for Johnathon's name in the project? There's going to be a park, isn't there? A place for children to play? Perhaps it could be the Johnathon Sterling Memorial Park. Or is there a fountain?"

Tara hadn't considered this idea at all. "There will be both, but I don't think we have any say in what they name anything. That's pretty much up to the city."

"Well, I think they should name something after him. Johnathon built half of the new buildings downtown. He's attracted businesses here. And he was a fixture of the community."

Tara looked to Astrid for help, but Astrid didn't say a peep. "I'll ask. That's really all I can promise right now." Tara hoped that was a diplomatic enough answer.

A timer in the kitchen began to beep. "That's dinner," Miranda said, slowly getting up from the sofa.

"Let me help." Tara followed her up to the open kitchen, which overlooked the great room. "What can I do?"

"I'm pregnant. I'm not an invalid." Miranda pulled a large sheet pan from the oven with parchment packets of something wonderful-smelling. She pulled three dinner plates from the cabinet and began piercing the paper bundles with a paring knife. "There's a salad in the fridge, if you can get that for me."

Astrid had joined them and was first to jump into action, leaving Tara to feel as though she was in the way. She brought over a large white ceramic bowl with elaborate relief work along the edges depicting fruit and vines. Everything Miranda chose was beautiful, and Tara silently told herself that she might need to up her game when it came to home decor.

The three of them went out to the patio by the pool, settling at a round scrolled iron table. Miranda's housekeeper had already set the table for them with exquisite silvery linens and water glasses. The meal was delicious—roasted red snapper with citrus and a touch of coconut milk, along with basmati rice. Miranda only picked at it, keeping her ginger ale close. The three shared polite conversation, but Tara couldn't ignore that it wasn't a natural thing for the three of them to be together. They'd all married the same man. They'd all had a very intimate relationship, good and bad, with Johnathon. They were as unlikely a trio of allies as could be.

It brought everything into focus. Not in theory, but in reality. Their arrangement was tenuous and Tara had better not count on any of this working out. Astrid's secret could come out and alienate Miranda forever. Astrid could decide that no one at Sterling would ever take her seriously and she could bail. And as for Tara, well, she was trying very hard at something she desperately wanted to be good at, but she wasn't quite there. Her decade in real estate might not have been her most loved, but at least she knew what she was doing, all the time, and she was exceptionally good at it. That just wasn't the case when it came to development.

Still, Tara had to cling to hope that things would somehow work out for all three of them. Johnathon had brought them together for a reason, and despite his many faults, he was a very good judge of character. There had to be a common thread between them, one that went beyond their love for the same man. Tara was eager to find it. It would make their pact that much more solid. The first thing that came to mind for them to bond over was the baby.

"Miranda, have you started working on the nursery?"

Tara set her dinner napkin across her plate. She wouldn't have brought this up in front of Astrid if she didn't think she could handle it. After all, it had been Astrid who'd reached out to Miranda. It was Astrid who'd wanted to forge a friendship.

"Are you kidding? I started picking stuff out the minute I found out I was pregnant. I just had it painted this week, but it's a work in progress."

"May we see it?" Astrid asked. Tara took that as confirmation that she could manage seeing the baby's room.

The three took their plates inside and left them on the kitchen counter, then Miranda led them to the central hall and up the stairs to the third floor. When they arrived at the landing, Tara remembered that this was the floor with the master bedroom, and it was to the right. Miranda led them to the left. Inside was a generous and quiet space, with butter-yellow walls and creamy-white carpet.

"I haven't picked out a crib yet. I don't want to jinx myself." Miranda's hands went to her belly. "It's still so early."

Tara put her arm around Miranda's shoulders and gave her a squeeze. "There's no rush. You have plenty of time. It's a beautiful start though. I'm sure this room will be amazing when it's all done."

Astrid, who had yet to say a word or give any sign as to what she was feeling, wandered to the far side of the room, where a black-and-white photograph in a lovely white wood frame sat atop a small bookcase. She picked up the picture and looked at it, rubbing her thumb along the edge of the frame. When she looked up at Miranda and Tara, there were tears in her eyes. "Is this Johnny? When he was a boy?"

Miranda nodded and walked over to join Astrid. "It is. His brother Andrew sent it to me a few days ago. He was in town a week or so ago and came by the house."

Tara could hardly believe that Andrew had actually followed through and reached out to Miranda. And he'd visited her. That was a surprise. "Grant and I ran into him at a party."

"He told me," Miranda said. "I was glad that you and Grant asked him to contact me. This baby won't have a lot of family. Johnathon's parents are gone and so are mine. I have my brother and that's it. I hated that Andrew and Johnathon were at odds. And I think he already feels plenty bad about not having gone to the funeral."

"That was a big mistake on his part," Tara said.

"Yeah. I told him as much. I think the picture of Johnathon was his way of trying to say he was sorry."

"It's a beautiful gesture," Astrid said, still teary-eyed. "The baby can look at this and see what their dad looked like as a child."

The full weight of the situation seemed to settle over them, like a heavy blanket, muffling all sound and much of the joy. Johnathon was gone, and yet his child was on the way. The baby would be their one true link to the man who had meant so much to all of them. They all had to do their best to take care of Miranda as she went through this difficult time, and they would all need to be there when the baby was born, so that he or she could know the full circle of people who had been close to their father.

Astrid gently put down the photo. "I need to go. I have a headache. I'm so sorry." She kissed Miranda on the cheek, then Tara. "Thank you so much for a wonderful night. We should do this more often."

"That would be nice," Miranda said. "Can I show you out?"

"I can find my way. But thank you." Just like that, Astrid disappeared through the door.

"Do you think she's okay?" Miranda asked. "I hope that seeing the nursery didn't bother her."

"I think she's still processing Johnathon's death. Like all of us."

"So true." Miranda stepped over to the bookcase and adjusted the picture.

"Did Andrew say anything else while he was here?" Tara asked.

Miranda turned back and drew in a deep breath, seeming even more tired now than she had when they'd arrived. "He's a very conflicted man. I'm sure you know a lot about it, but he and Johnathon had a very rocky childhood and they didn't come out of it with a good relationship."

"Hard times bring some people together, but it can also tear them apart," Tara offered.

"Exactly," Miranda continued. "So, I don't know. He seemed to be going through the full range of emotions while he was here. He's definitely still harboring a lot of anger toward his brother. He said something about a botched deal. Which seems crazy to me. To my knowledge, Johnathon and Andrew were not working together on anything."

Tara was in the dark on that one. "I'm sorry you had to be on the receiving end of that."

"Yeah. I eventually just asked him to leave. I think that's why he sent the photo. I think he realized he'd gone a bit off the rails." Miranda paused for a moment and looked down at her feet. "Andrew and Johnathon are very alike. They both have the same temper. You must have experienced that at least once."

"Absolutely." Tara realized she might have been too quick to join in, but it was nice to be able to talk to someone who fully appreciated what it had been like to be married to a force of nature like Johnathon. He'd been someone who felt things very intensely and expressed them as such.

"Although, to Johnathon's credit, the temper didn't appear very often. Most of the time, he was as loving as could be."

That hadn't quite been Tara's experience, but perhaps Johnathon had gotten better at being a husband the third time around. With Astrid gone, it felt as though it was Tara's time to leave, as well. "I should get out of your hair. I'm sure you'd love to get some sleep."

She nodded. "I would. Problem is that it's impossible to sleep in a house this big when you're here by yourself. It's almost too quiet. And I can't take a sleeping pill because of the baby."

Tara felt bad. This couldn't be great circumstances for dealing with her spouse's death. "Well, hopefully having dinner guests did something to wear you out a little."

Miranda flashed a smile. In that moment, Tara saw exactly what Johnathon must have loved about her—a warmth that radiated when she chose to share it. "I'll walk you downstairs."

"Sounds great." When they reached the front door, Tara turned to say her goodbye. "Thank you for tonight. And thank you for putting your trust in me. I hope that I can make our shares of Sterling even more valuable."

Miranda opened the door and leaned against the edge

of it. "I just need you to prove to me that this is a worth-while venture."

"You mean a successful run at the Seaport Prom-enade?"

"I mean actually landing it. I know how the culture at Sterling works and if you fail at the outset, nobody will respect you. That's just the world Johnathon estab-lished. Win or go home."

Tara swallowed hard. She was starting to feel the pressure from all sides. "I'll do my best."

"And please. Talk to the city about naming something. I'd really love to see Johnathon's name memorialized for the entire city to see."

Once again, she found herself saying that she'd do her best.

Tara climbed into her car, but couldn't bring herself to start the engine. She stared off into space, thinking about everyone's competing wants and how she played a role in it. The whole process was so tiring. She slowly lowered her head until she could rest her forehead on the steering wheel. Why did she feel like she was hold-ing the whole world together by a string? Maybe be-cause she was.

Twelve

Win or go home. That was Tara's new mantra, and it had been for three weeks, ever since Miranda gave her a reality check about working at Sterling. It didn't matter that Tara had been at the company at the very beginning. It didn't matter that she personally had a stake. It only mattered that she produced results. She would get only one shot at making the Seaport project happen.

And so Tara had been working her butt off, and she was starting to see some payoff. Seaport was coming together in ways she'd never imagined. Yes, she'd had a vision, but Clay's experience, training and keen eye had brought in elements she never could've come up with on her own. Tara loved being around him and watching him work. He showed flashes of brilliance on a daily basis, which was helping them make up for the condensed timeline they had. The first presentations to the city would take place in a week and Clay's talent was the main reason they would be fully prepared.

Astrid had been quick to learn along the way and to soak up all the information she could. She had a knack for the small details, and for making sure everything ran smoothly, but Tara had witnessed tension between her and Clay. He'd try to be all business, but Tara saw the way he looked at her in unguarded moments—it was powerful. Frankly, it was a little hot. He'd then be detached and stern with Astrid, as if he was trying to create distance. For Astrid's part, she seemed oblivious to it, but at this point in her life, Tara figured that male attention must be something Astrid expected, rather than something that took her by surprise. Oddly enough, Tara found herself wanting to play matchmaker. After all, they were both physically stunning, divorced and unattached. Tara could see them together, even when she knew it was the stupidest idea ever. The Seaport project was too important, and romance always made things unnecessarily complicated. She'd learned that with Johnathon. And every day with Grant seemed to be another lesson in just how much business and pleasure did not mix.

It'd been three weeks since their big talk, the one where they'd decided they had to keep things professional and couldn't give in to their attraction. Since then, each day had been a new test. Tara found it nearly impossible to talk to him. He was still kind to her, but their rapport had gone cold. Gone was the flirting. There was no playful banter, none of the inside jokes, the sexy moments of eye contact or the occasional touch of his hand on her arm. Everything fun between them had evaporated into thin air and she would've been lying if she said there wasn't a part of her that desperately wanted it back.

Tara could've made peace with the all-business version of their relationship a little easier if Grant didn't continue to be so damn enticing. He'd let his five o'clock shadow fill in a bit. It wasn't quite a full-blown beard, but it did something to make Tara weak. It made the line of his jaw stronger and the dark hair really brought out his eyes. Leave it to Grant to find a way to make himself even more handsome. It wasn't fair.

It might not be so hard to deal with if she didn't have the memories of their one night together emblazoned in her memory. She found herself sitting in meetings with him, not concentrating on the important work of the Seaport project, and instead fixating on what his facial hair might feel like brushing against her cheek. Her lips. Any other part of her body he felt inclined to kiss. His presence made her squirm in her seat and be keenly aware of how one flash of his deep brown eyes was like an arrow into her chest. It was not an ideal way to get through the workday. She was spending a fair amount of time searching for air-conditioning vents to stand in front of. Grant had her running that hot.

Yes, she'd been the one to insist that they return to their previous platonic relationship. It was necessary for her to stay focused on business, the one place where she could finally build herself some true happiness and fulfillment. But it was feeling less and less possible. The workday was not enjoyable, even when they were making progress. It was pure stress, all because Grant did nothing to soften the hard edges. She never should have slept with him. She never should have let him get that close to her. She always did better when she kept men at arm's length. It was the up close and personal that always did her in.

Sandy rapped on Tara's office door. "Unless there's something else you need, I'm going to head out for the weekend," she said. It was Friday and Sandy was headed to Palm Springs for a getaway with her boyfriend.

"Can you bring me the Seaport binder? I'd like to go over it one more time before I head out."

Pure concern crossed Sandy's face. "I've been over every detail at least fifty times, Ms. Sterling. Clay will have the final renderings ready on Monday. I'll pull together the presentation on Tuesday, you and Clay can rehearse it on Wednesday and Thursday, and you'll be ready to go next Friday."

Tara appreciated that Sandy was an excellent assistant, and it was her job to take care of the minute details that Tara shouldn't have to worry about. It still didn't make her any less worried about the things that might go wrong. That had been the advantage of working on her own for all those years as a real estate agent. She got to watch over every point herself. "I just want to give it one more look while we still have time to make changes."

"Sure. Of course." Sandy returned several minutes later with the binder, which she placed on Tara's desk. "Oh, and I just forwarded that status report on the other project sites you asked me to research."

Tara had given Sandy a list of parcels of land available for purchase in and around the county and asked her to compile information like listing price, acreage, site limitations and advantages. "Already?"

Sandy smiled. "I figured you wanted it as soon as possible."

Tara pulled up the email on her laptop, eager to see

what Sandy had come up with. Tara wanted Grant to know that the Seaport project wasn't the end and beginning of her aspirations at Sterling. "I do. Thank you for getting to that so quickly. You're amazing."

"Just doing my job."

"Well, thank you. Have a great weekend."

"You too, Ms. Sterling."

Sandy left and Tara got to work, reading over the report and making notes to herself of which sites had the biggest upside, in order to narrow her choices. She wanted to go to Grant with the best possible project, one that would bowl him over and hopefully convince him that she had what it took to be great at her job. She glanced at the clock on her computer when she was finished. It was already nearly six. She got up out of her seat to stretch, knowing it was time for her to call it a day and head home. She should be out on her balcony right now, gazing at the ocean and drinking a glass of wine. The only trouble was there wasn't anything or anyone waiting for her at home. Just like there hadn't been in so long.

"One more thing," she muttered to herself, plopping back down in her seat and opening up the binder for the Seaport project. She carefully scanned the pages of their draft proposal, getting more excited about presenting it to the city next week. Yes, she was biased, but she was proud of the work they'd done. It was innovative and smart. Surely it would be a slam dunk for them to pass this first round and move on to the finals where the sizable field of developers would be whittled down to three. Then they would take feedback from the city, make revisions and submit a final plan.

She was just about to close the binder when something caught her eye—a detail so essential it would have been impossible to miss—the orientation of the buildings on the site. It could be windy down by the water, and the city had been specific with what they wanted.

Tara could've sworn that the original spec information had said they wanted buildings facing to the northwest. But this said southwest. She flipped back and forth, between the pages from the city and the small-scale renderings Clay had done—all of which faced the northwest, the wrong direction.

Tara shot up out of her seat, grabbed her phone and marched down the hall. She'd worried that something could go wrong with this project at any moment. She just hadn't expected it would be now. Six fifteen in the evening on a Friday, with only a week until presentation day. The office was eerily quiet. Almost everyone had gone home. She wound her way around to Clay's office, hoping this was all a mistake. Maybe the drawings in the binder were old. Except that didn't make sense at all. Everything had always been to the northwest. Her original concept had been that way. Was this all her fault?

She knocked on Clay's door, but there was no answer. She rattled the doorknob and it was locked. Her heart was pounding, her pulse racing so fast it made it hard to think. But she had to do exactly that. *Sandy.* She pulled up her assistant's number, but it only rang once before going to voice mail. "Dammit." Tara looked to her right and then to her left. The light was still on in Grant's office. He was her only hope.

She drew in a deep breath and steeled herself for his reaction. She had wanted so badly for this project to go perfectly. She had wanted Grant to see her as fully capable, not just the woman who'd had a sizable chunk of a company land in her lap. This would have been an easier conversation a month ago, when she and Grant were still enjoying the warmth of their friendship. But everything had gone cold, all because of sex.

Tara barged into Grant's office like a tornado in heels. "We have a problem."

Yes, we do. Grant nearly uttered the words out loud, but he knew better. He was having little luck getting used to the idea of them being nothing more than colleagues. It had been three weeks of that exercise, and Grant felt as though he was experiencing the slowest, most painful death possible. It killed him to be around her. It killed him to keep her at a distance, but that was what was required. "I was just about to head home. Maybe we can talk about this on Monday?" He shuffled papers on his desk so that he wouldn't have to look at her. He'd damn near perfected the art of avoiding the vision of her. In meetings where she was present, he'd stare at documents, and when she dropped by his office, he typically resorted to directing his attention to his computer. Anything to avoid looking at what he couldn't have.

Tara dropped a large binder on his desk with a thud. Grant jumped. He couldn't help it. It wasn't like her to be so forceful. The cover of the folder said Seaport Promenade. "Grant. I'm serious. We have a crisis. And I need you to look at me. We need to talk. Now."

He begrudgingly did as she asked, his sights traveling from her hands and up her toned arms, to her sculpted shoulders, graceful neck and ultimately to that face. The one he had no answer for. He didn't know why looking at her made him feel so powerless, but it did. Her lips were ridiculously kissable right now, even when the corners were turned down with an expression that spoke of nothing but being unhappy. "Yeah. Okay. You have my full and undivided attention." *Even if it kills me.*

"I made a mistake with the Seaport project. A big one."

"So fix it. You still have a week. This stuff happens all the time. It's always a fire drill when you're at the finish line."

She shook her head slowly from side to side, as if she could tell him how deeply serious this was by sending wafts of her perfume his way. If only she knew how distracting it was. "You don't understand. I misread the site orientation. Our entire plan needs a ninety-degree turn."

Grant then realized why she was so deadly serious. This was indeed a major gaffe. "You can't do that. You'll have to rethink the entire project." His mind went to elevations and utilities. The placement of exterior doors and the flow of people. "There's no way there's enough time to get it done. Clay's gone for the weekend and I can't call him in. He took his daughter up to Anaheim to do the theme parks for her birthday. I promised I wouldn't even send him a text." Maybe this was for the best. If Grant couldn't have Tara, he might as well keep control of Sterling. Astrid and Miranda would likely recant their support of Tara's idea when they found out about her error and that it might cost them the project.

Tara slumped into one of the chairs in front of his desk. "I messed up. Big time." There was a small quiver in her voice, one that was rarely there. In fact, Grant hadn't heard it since the day of Johnathon's accident.

"I don't understand what happened."

"I don't either. I swear I went over the city's requirements a million times. So did Sandy. There must have been a miscommunication along the line somewhere."

Grant didn't want to tell Tara that he'd warned her that working with the city could be a very big pain, even when her problem was solid evidence of that very fact. "Maybe this wasn't meant to be, Tara. I'm sorry."

"I can't just give up. I've put so much work into this. So has Astrid. And Clay. We have to at least try to save it."

"Sometimes we put a lot of effort into something and it doesn't work out." This was an apt description of his situation with Tara. He'd tried to let her know that he wanted more, but at every turn, she was trying to push him away.

"Don't treat me like a first grader. This isn't a school project. This is millions of dollars. This is me proving my worth." Again, her voice wobbled, but this time the falter was much more dramatic. She got up out of the chair, seeking the refuge of the window, where she could turn away from him. Where she could hide. Again.

"Hey. It's okay to be upset. I won't hold it against you if you cry."

"I am *not* going to cry." There was a determined sob hiding behind the word *not*.

"You don't have to be so tough all the time. It's okay to allow yourself a human moment, even when we're talking about work."

"You don't understand." She sniffled. "This is me basically proving Johnathon's theory about why I shouldn't be here. He was convinced I would make a big mistake and it would be impossible for him to reprimand me because of our marriage. Now you're being soft on me because of our friendship. Well, what's left of it."

"Don't say that." Grant got up from his seat and approached her slowly. This was so much like their meeting a few weeks ago, it felt like a déjà vu. Once again, she was doing everything to keep him at arm's length, even when there was some small part of her that was willing to admit that she needed him and his help. "What can I do?"

Tara shot him a look over her shoulder, then turned her sights to the floor as she began pacing. "You know you don't want to do anything. You were against this project from the very beginning. You're probably happy it's turned out this way. It's a prime example of you being the person who should be in charge and me being the person who's running to try to catch up with you."

Yes, it was absolutely against his best business interests to help Tara. If he was smart, he'd leave her to deal with her own mess and he'd quietly claim victory. But he didn't have it in him. There was this voice in the back of his head that knew two things—he could not be like Johnathon and push her aside, and he could not ignore the feelings he had for her, even when he'd lied and said he was fine with them being nothing more than colleagues. "Don't talk about yourself that way. None of that is true. Even though you have a lot of experience in this world, you're still learning. It's okay to make mistakes."

She shot him a pitiful look that stopped him dead in his tracks. This blunder might take down tough-as-nails Tara. "This is the dumbest mistake ever. Only an idiot would make it."

It didn't make sense that someone as thorough as Tara would make a flub like this, but perhaps she'd let her enthusiasm get the best of her. "I've made far worse."

"Name one."

Carrying a torch for her came to mind, but once again, he kept his thoughts to himself. "Look. Do you want my help or not? Because if you don't, I'm going home for the weekend." He walked back behind his desk and powered down his computer. Silence seemed to swell in the confined space of his office. He could easily imagine her saying no. She likely already regretted that she'd allowed herself such a moment of weakness.

"No. I do want your help." She took a step toward his desk. "If you truly want to help me, that is. I would understand if you just let me deal with this on my own."

He drew in a deep breath through his nose and mustered the courage to look at her. The sun through the window was showing off every inch of her delicious curves in silhouette. It made his hands twitch to think about touching her. He wanted to do it so badly. "Your mistake is Sterling's mistake. And the reality is that a lot of our competitors are in this hunt. They all know we're in it, so saving face is a worthwhile investment. We can't show up at the presentation with the wrong orientation. We'll look incompetent, and I certainly don't want that."

"If you're trying to cheer me up, it isn't working."

He laughed quietly. "I'm saying that I do have a reason to help you. And more than anything, I don't want to see you fail." There was only one solution to this and it was staring him in the face. He was duly torn by what he saw as a logical answer—part of him wanted to have so much time with her. And another part of him knew how much it hurt when she tore herself away. "With Clay out of town, you and I are the only ones who can fix this. Which means we're going to have to work all weekend."

"How can we possibly do it without an architect?"

"I don't do renderings and site plans anymore, but I

am still licensed. We can at least come up with a workable plan to bring to Clay on Monday morning. We'll just have to hope that he can pull it off by next Friday."

"You'd do that for me?"

In an instant, he wanted to say. "I'd do it for the firm. As I said, I don't want us to look bad in front of our competitors. I'd rather squash them like a bug."

"This means so much to me. Truly. It means the world that you'd want to help. How do you want to do this? Should we set up a space in one of the conference rooms?"

Grant then saw that this might be a glimmer of what he thought he might not get again—one more chance with Tara. "No. We'll work at my house. All weekend." He was pleased with the fact that he'd come out with it with so much confidence. That wasn't what he was feeling, at all. Still, he knew that this might be his final opportunity with her. He stood a much greater chance of showing her that they could work together in more ways than one while they were at his place. And he was far more likely to finally come clean with the things he'd been hiding for a decade if he'd at least had a glass of wine or two.

"The two of us? Alone? Are you sure that's a good idea?"

"It was different a month ago. The office atmosphere was still shaky after Johnathon's death. I think we've all started to come to terms with it."

"Okay then." She nodded eagerly as she took the binder from his desk. "I'll run home and change before I come over."

"And pack a bag, Tara. I have a feeling you're going to want to stay over."

Thirteen

Despite having designs on Tara, Grant refused to be obvious in setting the stage for romance. He couldn't handle any more rejection from her. No, if he was going to have the chance to kiss her again, and perhaps take her to bed, he needed it to happen of its own accord. He might give it a nudge here or there, but it would ultimately be something that happened between them because they both wanted it wholeheartedly. No more reservations. No more second-guessing whether it was a good idea.

He knew what a dangerous line he was walking. Tara and the other wives still held all of the cards when it came to Sterling. If they wanted him out, they could make it happen. But here he had a chance to play a role in the Seaport proposal. At worst, he could make the case that he'd done everything to save Tara's pet proj-

ect. That had to earn him at least a few brownie points
with the wives.

Grant had set up a work area at the table in his infor-
mal dining area next to the kitchen. He opened one of the
sliding glass doors to let in the ocean breeze. This was
one of the most spectacular views on his property—tall
frameless windows showed off the windblown landscape
of his backyard—palm trees and a seemingly endless
stretch of bright green grass, which dropped off to the
Pacific below.

He'd stood out near the edge of that cliff many times
and thought about Tara, across the bay in Coronado. He'd
done it when he had women with him. He'd done it when
he had women in his bed, waiting for him to return. Perhaps it was just that Tara had always felt like unfinished
business. They had an unbelievable connection, and for
so long, Johnathon had been in the way. Now that was
no longer true, and he really didn't want the business of
Sterling Enterprises to be the roadblock anymore. If he
and Tara were not meant to be, he could accept that, but
only if it was because she couldn't return his feelings.
He was tired of letting other factors stand between him
and a glimmer of happiness.

Tara arrived a little after eight o'clock, looking absolutely breathtaking in a pair of jeans and a turquoise
top that clung to every curve. It was a nice and casual
counterpoint to her usual businesslike demeanor. "I'm
freaking out," she said, breezing past him.

He closed the door and followed her through the foyer,
down the central corridor to the back of the house where
the kitchen and great room were. "Don't panic. All we
can do is try."

"I appreciate that, but I'm still panicked. Miranda and Astrid are going to wonder what in the world I'm doing."

"That's between you three." Once again, he wasn't about to let anyone else stand between Tara and him. "For now, I think that saving yourself and your pet project is the right call. Plus, Clay has sunk a ton of hours into this already. We can't let all of that go to waste."

She sighed and shook her head. "Do you have any wine?"

Grant was so relieved he hadn't had to offer. "Of course."

Tara took a seat at the kitchen island while he pulled out a bottle from the fridge. "White okay?"

"Yes. Red gives me a headache sometimes."

"We don't want that."

"Not tonight, that's for sure." She smoothed her hand over the white marble countertops, looking all over the room. "I forgot how incredible your house is. I haven't been here in so long. Eight years, maybe?"

"Sounds about right. I don't think you've been here since you and Johnathon got divorced." He offered her a glass. "I'd like to propose a toast. To fixing mistakes."

She smiled and clinked her glass with his. "It's really sweet of you to do this."

"Please don't start with the nice-guy routine." He rounded the kitchen island so he could stand next to her.

"Oh, I won't. The guy who wants to squash the competition like a bug is definitely not a good guy."

He and Tara sat at the table and got right to work. She went over the site limitations, the city's requirements and the plan as it was. She and Clay had made quite a lot of changes since Grant had last been in the loop several weeks ago. Even though she was in a trouble spot with the deadline looming, once she started talking her way through it, he could see exactly how capable she was of doing this job. Hell, she could run Sterling if she truly wanted to do that. It made Grant sad to think that might end up being the case, and he would fight for his rightful place at the company, but if he had to lose to someone, Tara would be a hell of a victor.

After an hour or so of discussion of possible changes, Grant took out a large pad of drafting paper and began working on a rough sketch of the new layout. It would ultimately take far more detail than what he was able to create here. For now, he and Tara were concerned with the flow of pedestrians and bicycle traffic, along with ample handicapped accessibility. There were noise issues to think about with the live music venue they were proposing, and then there were the aesthetics—the way it would look from both the water and the city sides of the project. In truth, it was a mountain of work, and Grant was truly burned out by one in the morning.

"I don't know if I can work anymore tonight," he said, leaning back in his chair and stretching his arms high above his head.

Tara finished off her glass of wine. "Do you think this is feasible?" She tapped the stack of sketches he'd done so far. They were incredibly rough and would take some explaining to Clay, but they were a solid start.

"I do. I mean, you and I need to figure out the elevations since some of the structures have had to be moved out of the previous order. But we have tomorrow. And Sunday."

It was Tara's turn to sit back in her chair and stretch, showing off the lithe lines of her beautiful body. Everything in Grant's body went tight. Even under the strain of sheer exhaustion, he wanted her.

"You and I make a good team. I'm sorry that this project had to be so adversarial," she said.

Grant shrugged and sat forward, drawing a circle with his finger on the pad of paper before him. He wanted so badly to touch her. To kiss her. To take her to bed. "I'm the one who should be saying I'm sorry. I knew from the night of the baseball game that you had an incredible vision. And I should've stayed fully on board with that. I should've backed you up, rather than letting you sink or swim."

"You were protecting your position within Sterling. As the person carving out her own spot in that company, I have to admire that."

She was being gracious and Grant was exceptionally tired of the obstacles they'd faced. He really wanted to strip it all away until there was nothing left but the two of them. "It's not more important than our friendship."

"Do you mean that? Because there are times when I doubted that."

"Our friendship? When?"

"The last few weeks. You were so cold to me in the office. I felt like I'd been demoted or something. It was so clear that you'd drawn the battle lines and saw our relationship as combative."

He shook his head and sat back farther in his chair, stuffing his hands into his pockets. "I only felt that way because we went from sharing the most amazing night ever to you being too worried about what Astrid and Miranda might think."

"You were equally worried about office gossip."

"And that died back pretty quickly. Which means my attitude toward you at work did its job."

"I still didn't like it."

Grant swallowed back the emotion of the moment. "I didn't like it either. I hated every minute of it. I don't like being cool to you, Tara."

Tara bit down on her lower lip like she was fighting a smile. "Our night together was pretty amazing, wasn't it?"

"The absolute best." He answered a little too quickly, but it was exactly the way he felt. "And I'm not exaggerating."

"But the business is standing between us."

"Only if we let it."

She eyed him with suspicion, scanning his face like she was looking for clues. Did she not trust him? Was she truly more loyal to the wives than she was to him? Or would it all come down to being nothing more than business? "You don't really mean that," she said.

Grant pushed aside the papers and stood. He easily took the two short strides to Tara's side, but it felt as though he was crossing a dividing line. He placed his hand on her upper arm and walked behind her, not letting go as he used his other hand to pull her hair back from her shoulder. All the while, ocean breezes streamed in through the open slider door, heightening every sense— touch, smell and sight. He lowered his head and spoke into her ear. "I've never been more serious about anything in my entire life."

With his breath hot against the nape of her neck, Grant was taking charge again. And Tara was completely powerless against it. She wanted him just as much as she'd wanted him before. Possibly more. The last several weeks of fighting back her attraction to him had been pure hell. He'd been cold to her and she wanted him warm again. She wanted his white-hot body against hers.

She turned her head to make eye contact, to be sure that he wanted what she did, but he countered not with his gaze, but with his mouth on hers and his hand at her nape. He pulled her head back to deepen the kiss, their tongues quickly finding the satisfying dance they'd discovered mere weeks ago. Tara's entire body flooded with heat and desire. Craving. Unlike before, this wasn't about curiosity, this was about another taste of this man she couldn't get out of her system.

She stood to be closer to him and he walked her back to the kitchen island, pressing her backside against the counter. She grabbed him by the waist and tugged him closer, wanting him to flatten her right then and there. He was hard already; she could feel it through his jeans, and it made anticipation bubble up inside her.

Tara lifted one butt cheek and eased herself up onto the countertop, wrapping her legs around Grant and muscling him close. His erection rubbed right against her center, and even through several layers of denim, it made her so hot. He kissed her deeply, their noses bumping into each other, and she placed her hands on either side of his face, rubbing her thumbs against the thicker texture of his facial hair. It was somewhere between silky and scratchy, and she loved the contrast in sensations. It so perfectly mirrored her inner conflict about making love with him again. She knew she shouldn't, that sex would only make things more complicated, but she also knew that she was tired of waiting for happiness, and if this was the only blip of it she got for the foreseeable future, she'd better grab it while she could.

She pulled at the lightweight sweater Grant wore, tugging it up over his head. She spread her hands across his chest, kissing his warm skin. His muscles seemed to twitch beneath her touch, and she loved having that effect on him. "You are too sexy, Grant. Working with you while staying away from you is impossible." That was an issue she was going to have to resolve, but not now. Not when she had a one-way ticket to his bedroom and they had an entire weekend stretching out before them. Astrid wouldn't find her here. Not this time. They could be all alone.

Grant growled into her ear. "You have no idea how much I love hearing that."

Before she could respond, he'd lifted her off the kitchen island and was walking her to the back of the house. Tara was a tall woman—she'd never been whisked off to bed like this, and she loved the way it made her feel so desired. She spent so much of her day trying to be tough and formidable. It was wonderful to feel as though she was at someone else's mercy.

When they arrived at Grant's bedroom, he didn't bother with the light, but instead laid her down on the bed and put all of his body weight on hers. The kiss they fell into had no limits—she could have kissed him forever and she would have made time for more. She didn't want it to end. She also wanted him to know that she was his equal partner in this endeavor, so she rolled to her side, taking him with her. He eased to his back and she straddled his hips, grinding her center against him as she sat up, crossed her arms at the waist and lifted her top up over her head. She wanted Grant's hands all over her, but he instead folded his arms back behind his head.

"Don't you want to take my bra off?" she asked.

"I like watching you do it," he answered playfully.

"Fair enough." He'd made the first move. He deserved to have his way at least a little bit. She reached behind her and unhooked the garment, then teased one strap from her shoulder, then the other, before she flung it aside. His hands found her breasts, and molded around them, teasing her nipples and causing her breath to hitch. His touch was pure magic, his hands warm and purely focused on her pleasure. It felt so good that she gasped, and she dropped her head back, letting her hair cascade down her naked shoulders. Grant took his chance to unbutton and unzip her jeans and Tara realized just how impatient she was for the main event. She wanted Grant naked and she wanted the same for herself.

She hopped off the bed and quickly shucked her jeans, while Grant followed her lead, climbing off the mattress and leaving his pants on the floor. He pulled back the silky duvet and picked her up again, this time sweeping her legs up with his arm. He planted a knee on the bed and placed her gently against the cool sheets. She swished her hand against the smooth fabric, but arched her back. The need for him to be touching her and weighing her down again was too much.

He reached into his bedside drawer and pulled out a condom, which he rolled on himself. She waited in anticipation as he climbed into bed and kissed her again, but this time there was something about it that truly made her breath catch. It was so intense it felt like he was sending a message. Perhaps he was trying to say he was sorry for the cold shoulder all of these weeks. Sorry for the many arguments they'd had.

He put his arms around her and urged her on top of him. Tara eagerly accepted the challenge, rising up onto her knees, and then taking his length in her hand. She guided him inside and sank down against his body, soaking up every blissful second of the way he filled her so perfectly. They began to move together and he took his time with the rotation of his hips, hitting her center in just the right spot, already pushing her close to the edge. She struggled to stay in the moment and not let her mind wander. The pure ecstasy made it a difficult proposition. He felt too good inside her, and she slipped into a daydream about what it would be like to actually be with a man who was her match. Was Grant that man? Could they work past all that stood between them?

She struggled for her breaths as the pressure began to build. She kissed him and caught just how shallow his own breath had become. It was clear that they were both close, and she was torn between wanting to cross the goal line and wanting it to last forever. This right now was perfect. As messy as everything around them could be, being in bed with Grant at this moment was where she belonged. No question about that. The orgasm barreled into her from out of nowhere, shattering the tension between them. Grant followed almost immediately and they were both calling out, a chorus of pleasured and breathless words.

She collapsed at his side and spread her hand across his chest as he wrapped his arm around her. He smoothed her hair back, and kissed the top of her head. Over and over again. Each kiss came with a tiny tug, bringing her closer to him. Contentment blanketed her body just as his body heat poured into her. She couldn't remember feeling like this with a man before. Not with anyone who'd come before him. She and Grant were equals. They were friends. And they would always have a connection. Now deeper than the one they'd had before.

Fourteen

Tara slept over for two nights. There wasn't much sleeping going on, but that was better than fine with Grant. He wanted this to go on forever—Tara in his bed, giving him untold pleasures and welcoming his touch. They'd quickly reached the point where he could simply walk up to her, take her in his arms and kiss her. He didn't want to call it a fantasy brought to life. It was more like a dream, and it felt like that, seeing her walk around his home in bare feet, watching her wrap her hair up in a towel after a shower, bearing witness to the moment when she woke up in his bed. She was what this house had been missing. She was the missing puzzle piece in his life.

He had to find a way to tell her before she had the chance to go home. It was Sunday morning and they'd already made love twice and had breakfast. They'd long since finished as much of the Seaport proposal as they could without Clay's help. It was only a matter of time before she'd be gone, they'd return to their previous arrangement at Sterling and he'd be in the hot seat. If she was successful with the Seaport pitch, he might lose his hold on the company. He was essentially standing in her way, and he already knew that her relationship with Astrid and Miranda had grown stronger.

But there was another way out of this, at least as far as Grant saw it. They could run the company together, as a true partnership, in the office and out. Could Tara ever see them that way or had this been just another instance of him being lucky enough to get her into bed? Would she ever want to share that lead role at work? Or would strong and determined Tara, the woman dead set on winning at all costs, simply decide that Grant didn't measure up? Would she ultimately reach the conclusion that she was too much for him?

"This weekend has been amazing." Grant put the last plate from breakfast in the dishwasher.

Tara was seated at the kitchen island, still hugging her mug of coffee in her hands. She turned her sights to the backyard and the Pacific. The palm trees rustled in the wind, the sun casting short shadows on the grass. He studied her profile, and it was hard not to see her through the lens of everything she'd been through. She'd had so much loss in her life, and still she kept forging ahead. She was a survivor and that was not only what he adored in her, but it was the quality he feared most. Could she ever need him the way he needed her?

"It really was." She took a sip of her coffee and turned to look at him. "Thank you so much for saving my butt with the Seaport project. It remains to be seen whether or not Clay and I can actually pull this off, but I couldn't have put us in that position without your help. So thank you."

Grant walked around to her side of the island and stood next to her. "I think we make a great team." He believed that in every sense, and he wanted to tell her as much. *I love you. I have always loved you.* The words were swimming around in his head, but he couldn't begin to imagine he would ever have the perfect chance to utter them, to say them in a way that wouldn't scare her off and send her running.

"About that. I know you've been against this project from the beginning, but would you consider coming with me to the presentation on Friday? We could use a heavy hitter like you."

Grant wanted to be supportive, but he also wanted to give Tara the chance to shine. He hadn't been in on this project from the ground floor and plenty of people in the office knew he had reservations about it. If he was going to convince her that they should run Sterling together, she would need her own win to show the staff that she was there because she'd earned it. He didn't want to put her in the position Johnathon had all those years ago, of being marginalized because she happened to be romantically entangled with the CEO.

"I don't think you need my help. I really don't."

Tara frowned and peered up at him with those big blue eyes that somehow seemed to reflect the whole world. "After all of the work we did? You don't want to take credit? I thought you wanted to step out from behind the shadow of Johnathon. I thought it was time for you to put your career first."

"Maybe I'm tired of doing that. Maybe I want you to have your own win, Tara."

"Or maybe you're trying to save your own hide because you don't truly believe in this project."

He had to be honest. "I'm still not sold on Seaport. I'm sorry. I wish I was. But I am sold on you and your vision. If anyone can make this work, it's you."

Tara shook her head and got up from her seat, the barstool leg scraping against the floor. "I was worried about this. You don't want to put your name on this project. You don't want to put your stamp of approval on it."

He reached for her, over what felt like a monumental difference. "I told you. I want you to have your own win."

She scanned his face as if she was looking for answers or perhaps some hint that he wasn't being truthful. He wasn't sure what he had to do to convince her. "I know you, Grant. You'll always put your career first. That's why you never got married. That's why you could never settle on one woman."

He almost wanted to laugh at that. The assumption she'd made was remarkably off base. "That's not the reason."

"Johnathon always said you were the perfect partner because you were married to your work."

Grant didn't want to get angry with the dead. He'd already done plenty of that as far as Johnathon was concerned. But he greatly disliked that his best friend had painted him in that light. It couldn't have been further from the truth. "I worked hard. That much is true. But that was because I believed in the vision of the company and I enjoyed the challenges I had set out before me. But it's not the reason I never got married."

She smirked and cocked an eyebrow at him. "Right. Too many fish in the sea."

He shook his head. "No. I never settled down because I couldn't have the perfect woman."

"You mean you couldn't *find* the perfect woman. That's a myth, by the way. There is no perfect person."

But there was. At least for him.

"Look, Tara. This weekend has shown me a lot. You and I work well together in every sense. But I have feelings for you. Strong feelings." That was as far out on the ledge as he could go. He was still gun-shy. Her rejection stung that badly.

Tara swallowed hard. "How am I supposed to believe that when just last week you were being truly unkind to me? How am I supposed to believe that when you won't stand by my side and make the presentation with me?"

"You have to believe it because it's true. I know that you said you only want to see me as a colleague, but I need you to at least try to see me as more than that. And if you don't, I think we're at an impasse. I can't work with you and feel the way I feel about you. I couldn't do it when Sterling was first getting started and I can't do it now." As soon as he'd said the words, he realized that he'd finally let the cat out of the bag.

"What did you say?" There was already an edge of betrayal in her voice, like she knew what was coming.

"I don't want to dredge up the past. I want to talk about the here and now. About us. About everything that happened this weekend. It has meant something to me. I think I'm falling in love with you." The words had been tumbling around in his head for so long that it was liberating to finally say them. It was also scary as hell.

"No. Don't muddy the waters by saying that to me. I

want you to tell me what you were talking about when you said that you couldn't work with me when Sterling was first getting started."

It was time to finally come clean, even when he knew this might be the point of no return. She might never forgive him for what he was about to say. "When Johnathon told me his concerns about having you work at the company, I sided with him. I told him that it was better if you went."

Tara's jaw tightened and her eyes blazed with a hurt he'd never seen. "Excuse me? You bought into that whole idea that we couldn't work together because we were married?" She shook her head and crossed her arms, as if she needed to protect herself from him. "I can't believe you backed him up on that. It was the stupidest excuse ever."

He sucked in a deep breath to steel himself, hoping against hope that he could make a plausible argument for why what he'd done before was wrong, but he was prepared to make amends now. "That wasn't the argument he made, Tara. He may have told you that, but that wasn't what he said to me."

Tara's eyes were wide and pleading. "Then what did he say?"

"He called you a distraction."

"We were married. I was nothing of the sort. If I was, he wouldn't have left me."

Once again, Grant was tempted to curse Johnathon. She wasn't wrong. As soon as she'd been out of the company, Johnathon's eyes began to wander. He knew that had hurt her, but those weren't his wounds to heal. He had to focus on the things he'd done and the reasons for his actions. "You were a distraction for *me*. He saw the way I looked at you. He knew that I never got past that first night when we met. I tried, Tara, but it was impossible. I think it would have been different if you hadn't ended up with Johnathon."

"So this was all about you two trying to outdo each other? He had to win and you just couldn't stand the fact that he had?"

He reached for her, but she pulled away. It felt as though his heart was being torn from his chest as he once again relived the history he had with Johnathon and Tara. All of the nights when they'd gone out, all of the dinners at each other's houses. The vacations, where he'd drag along whatever woman he was seeing at the time, but really only wanted Tara. He felt such shame over that, but it was the truth. Grant had to watch his best friend be with the woman he wanted and there was nothing he could do about it. "No. It was about seeing how amazing you were, and experiencing our connection, but not being able to act on it. It drove me crazy."

"I have to go." She stalked down the hall back to the bedroom.

Grant thought for a moment about just letting her go, but he knew that it would be forever. And he couldn't live with that. He was so tired of living with regret. So he followed her. When he arrived in his room, she was stuffing her clothes into her overnight bag. "Can we please talk about this? I feel like this has gone sideways."

"I need space to think, Grant." She planted one hand on her hip and the other at her forehead. She stared off into space, her eyes darting from side to side. "I find it very hard to believe that you were carrying a torch for me all these years, Grant. You had no problem distracting yourself, and it's not like you didn't have plenty of opportunity after Johnathon ended our marriage."

"But…" he started.

She turned on him. "No. I think this is about you and Johnathon. He thought of me as a prize to snatch away from you, and you never forgave him for it. I think you felt that same way about Sterling, and then he went and died, but he screwed you over when he gave the wives the shares of the company. So now you have a new thing you can't forgive him for and that's made you decide that I'm the thing to be won."

He reached for her arm and her vision flew to his hand. It made him drop his grip. "Do you want to know what I think? I think you're afraid to let anyone in. Johnathon destroyed you when he left you and you never recovered. And then you lost your dad, so you built up this wall and convinced yourself that the best way to never lose again was to never get involved. To never get close to anyone again. I just want you to let down your guard and let me in. That's all I want."

She pressed her lips together tightly, fighting back tears. "You think you have me figured out, Grant, but you don't. I let plenty of people in. I'm just choosy when I do it. And I don't think I can choose you."

"Why?"

"We have too many competing wants. It's what destroyed my marriage with Johnathon and it would only destroy us."

"Are you saying you don't have feelings for me, too? Because if that's the case, I swear I'll never bring it up again."

"I think my problem is I have too many feelings for you right now, Grant. And not all of them are good ones."

Fifteen

Tara arrived at work on the day of the big presentation with a headache the size of San Diego County. She'd been working like crazy all week, but so had Clay and Astrid. The three of them were all going the extra mile to make this happen, which was a bigger workload than expected. Sandy had called in sick every day this week. Apparently she'd picked up a bug of some sort in Palm Springs.

There had been many times when Tara had considered soliciting Grant's help, but he'd been keeping his distance. She felt bad about the argument they'd had at his house, and she wanted to apologize for her role in it, but she had to get through the presentation. It was a huge hurdle, one she'd been staring down for weeks, and deep down, she knew that the outcome would determine her course from here out. If it went well, she'd try to stay at Sterling, and hope to find a working arrangement with Grant. If it went badly, she'd leave. It was the only logical answer. She'd sell off her shares to Grant or possibly just give them to him. He'd more than earned them.

As for the personal side of their relationship, that was an entirely different conversation. She was still wrapping her head around the things he'd said on Sunday, especially the part about her unwillingness to let people get close to her. She couldn't help it—distance had become her default. It made things easier. It made it possible to survive. There'd been so much hurt and loss in her life, but she'd always found a way to forge ahead. She couldn't allow herself to be wounded. But perhaps her persistence had been her downfall. She hadn't taken the time to slow down and see what was around her. Perhaps it was a case of trying to be a moving target—it made her harder to hit.

As for what this realization meant for the question of love, she wasn't sure. She cared about Grant deeply. She was closer to him than any person she knew. He'd become her best friend, and at times, her biggest champion. But they'd spent so much time in opposition to each other that it was hard to figure out what the good times had meant. Were they an aberration? A break from the contention around the office? Or had he truly fallen for her? Did he really want more? She knew she wanted more, but she also needed more—a guarantee of some sort. A sign that if she let Grant in, that he'd stay. That if he truly loved her, he'd love her forever. She couldn't take another loss, and losing her friendship with Grant would be a crushing blow.

Astrid knocked on Tara's office door, then waved a

piece of paper in the air. "I don't think Sandy was sick all week."

"Why do you say that?"

"Read this." Astrid set the fax on Tara's desk. It was a resignation letter, with no explanation from Sandy, other than the fact that she was quitting. It was such a shame—she'd been an integral part of the team.

"Did I do something wrong?" If this was an omen of how things were going to go today, Tara was wondering if it might be time to throw in the towel.

Astrid shook her head. "I doubt it. She probably took a job somewhere else."

"Maybe." None of this sat well with Tara, but she needed to focus on the task ahead. Then she could begin the process of finding her way with Grant. "Let's finish getting packed up, grab Clay and head over."

It took about a half hour to load the model and presentation boards into a Sterling Enterprises van. The three rode over with Clay driving, to a large meeting space the city had rented in one of the hotels near the Seaport location. There was a bustle of activity when they arrived. It was hard not to ogle the models from the other firms that would be presenting. It was hard not to feel intimidated by the whole thing. There were a lot of heavy hitters filing inside, people who Tara had read about or Johnathon had pointed out at social functions. Many were CEO or president of their company. It only underscored Grant's lack of confidence in the project. He hadn't changed his mind about joining her today. If he had, he would have said something.

They went inside and set up their materials as instructed, then waited for their turn to make their case. The competing firms were not allowed in the room as one team was presenting, which left Tara to pace in the hall.

"Please stop," Astrid said with a hand on Tara's arm. "It will be fine."

Clay cast a doubtful look at them both. "You don't know that. It might not be fine."

Astrid returned his unpleasant expression. "Don't be so negative. All we can do is try."

Tara stopped her pacing, but that left her to lean against the wall and tap her foot. Damn, she wished Grant was here. She wished he believed in the things she did. She wished they could find a way, together.

A few minutes later, the Sterling team was called into the room. As Tara crossed the threshold and saw the long table of representatives from the city waiting to be dazzled, she had absolutely every reason to be intimidated. This was it. Do or die.

"Ladies and gentlemen, my name is Tara Sterling and I'm here to represent Sterling Enterprises. We're very excited for the opportunity to present our plan for the Seaport Promenade."

Miraculously, it all clicked into place—she and Clay made an amazing team, playing off each other, and explaining the vision that Tara had originally had, fixed by Grant after Tara had made her big mistake, and finally brought to life by Clay's brilliance. When they were done and exited the room, Astrid and the normally subdued Clay were both ecstatic.

"Okay. I was wrong. That went well," Clay said.

"I told you." Astrid swatted his arm. "Now we wait for the city's answer on Monday."

Tara had to force her smile. It *had* gone incredibly well. But it felt empty. It wasn't the same without Grant here. It didn't feel like the win she was supposed to get. Not even close. It felt like it meant nothing, all because Grant hadn't been there to witness it. The thought made her incredibly sad, but it also made her realize that the biggest mistake she'd made wasn't on the plans for the Seaport site. It had been in letting work, once again, determine her course. She should have worked everything out with Grant first—the personal stuff—and she'd waited an entire week. Once again, she'd let distance be her buffer.

"Let's head back," Tara said. "I want to give Grant a full report." Her heart began to race. It was time to put it all on the line, but for him. Damn it all if he couldn't give her assurances about love. If she didn't let him in, everything in her life was going to feel as empty as it did right now.

They were on their way to the parking deck when Tara's phone rang. She pulled it out of her purse and saw that it was the main Sterling office number. Normally Grant would call her from his cell, but maybe he'd instead picked up the extension on his desk. "Grant? I'm so glad you called. We have to talk. Right away."

"Ms. Sterling, it's Roz in reception. There's been an accident. It's Mr. Singleton."

Tara's head spun. Her vision went blurry. *No no no no.* This was not happening. She felt queasy. "What happened? Where is he? Please tell me he's alive."

"Yes, he's alive. He was hit by a car."

"Hit by a car?" Her heart plummeted to her stomach.

"He's at the hospital downtown," Roz continued. "If you're still at the presentation, it's only five blocks."

"I'm on my way." Tara hung up and chucked her

phone into her bag. "Grant's in the hospital. And I've got to go right now."

"The hospital? What happened?" Astrid seemed just as horrified as Tara was feeling.

"There's no time to explain," Tara blurted.

"I'll drive you." Clay rattled the keys to the van.

"I'll get there faster if I run."

"In heels?" Astrid asked.

"Yes. In heels."

"Should we come with you?" Clay asked.

"Just drive over and meet me there." Tara took off before either of them could argue with her any more. It didn't take long before she realized her shoes were only slowing her down. She took them off and ran in bare feet down the city sidewalks, bobbing between people and trying to see as her eyes clouded with threatening tears.

"If you die, Grant Singleton, I will never, ever forgive you," she said to herself while anxiously waiting for the signal to change at a crosswalk. She darted across as soon as the cars had passed, all the while imagining a life without Grant. It was unthinkable. If she thought she felt empty from doing a presentation without him, what would the rest of her life be like? Her hopes for Sterling would mean nothing without him there. She'd never be able to return without thinking of him, but his absence would haunt her in a way that Johnathon's never had. She and Grant had shared so much in that office. They'd put each other through the wringer. And yet, he was the only person's approval she wanted. He was the one she wanted to share her triumphs with, as well as her failures.

Oh God. He told me he was falling in love with me

and I left. Tara couldn't believe she'd done that to him. She hoped against hope that he would be okay when she got to the hospital. He had to be okay, and if he wasn't, she had to hope that he'd be there long enough for her to tell him everything. All of this emotion swelling up inside her had to go somewhere. She couldn't let him go without telling him everything.

As she ran up to the emergency room entrance, the flashbacks started. Johnathon. Her dad. Even her mom. So many people she loved, all gone. She couldn't handle it if it happened again. She simply couldn't go on. Especially if she lost Grant.

She rushed over to the nurses' station. "Grant Singleton?" She could barely get the words out before tears started to stream down her face. This wasn't like her at all. She usually kept it together, especially in a crisis.

The nurse hit a few keys on the computer. "And you are?"

"The woman who loves him and ran in bare feet five blocks to be here for him."

The nurse's mouth pulled into a wide smile. "You need to put those shoes back on before you walk around in the hospital."

"Yeah. Okay." Tara worked her feet back into her shoes. They hurt like hell, but she didn't care.

"He's in room 18. Down the hall, first right, then a left."

Tara was already on her way, but she couldn't sprint here like she had out on the street. Her heart was still pounding and dammit if those tears would not stop. They were running down her cheeks and mascara was staining her blouse. When she got to eighteen, it was one of those big rooms with sliding glass doors. A doctor and several nurses were huddled around him. Tara burst through the door.

"Grant. I'm here. I'm here." She caught sight of his face—the one she loved so much, and something squeezed her heart so tight she could barely stand up. He had bruises and scrapes. One of his amazing eyes was taped shut.

"Tara," he managed, his voice raspy. He even had a tiny smile on his face. Was he delirious?

She pushed one of the nurses out of the way. "I'm sorry. But I have to talk to him." She grabbed his hand and kissed his knuckles, holding them to her lips and drinking in his smell. "You can't die on me. I won't let you."

One of the nurses laughed, which seemed horribly rude.

But then an even bigger smile spread across Grant's lips. "I'm not going to die."

The doctor leaned in. "He's not going to die. He has a concussion and a few broken ribs. That taxi hit him good."

He's not going to die. He's not going to leave me. Tara gasped for air and the tears flowed like a faucet.

"You're crying," Grant said.

"Of course I'm crying." She leaned down and kissed his temple what felt like one hundred times.

"You don't like to cry. You hate it. You never do it."

That was the old Tara he was talking about. Hopefully, she wouldn't return. "I love you. I love you so much and I was an idiot for not seeing it all along."

He managed one more smile, his poor battered face lighting up. "I love you, too, darling."

Oh, thank God. Finally, some relief. She wiped away the tears from her eyes. "You're the best thing in my entire world. I'm resigning from Sterling. I will give you my shares. You can just have them."

"Tara. What about the other wives?"

That seemed to catch the attention of the nurses. They all stopped what they were doing and looked at Tara and Grant.

"It's a long story," Tara said. "I'll tell you when I'm done here." She returned her attention to Grant. "I care about them both, and I hate the idea of breaking promises, but I'll do it. All I want is you."

"Please don't resign. We need you. I need you. You can't leave." Grant pushed back to sit up straighter in bed, but it was clear he was in a lot of pain. Still, he did it. Tara perched on the edge of the bed so she could be closer to him. "Johnathon cut you out of the company in part because he couldn't work with his wife. But I'm not Johnathon."

Tara looked at him as her mind struggled to catch up with his words. "What are you saying?"

"Where's the nurse? She has my clothes."

"Your clothes?" Tara asked.

"They're right here," the nurse answered, handing over a clear plastic bag. Grant's ultraexpensive suit was crammed in there.

He struggled to open it, so Tara helped. "What could possibly be so important that you need to get it out of there?"

"Hold on one minute." He pulled out his suit coat and rummaged around until he found the pocket. He fished a small black box out of it.

Tara's hand flew to her mouth. "No."

"This is not the way I wanted to do this. I was on my way to your presentation when I ducked into the street. The cab came out of nowhere. I wanted to be there for you. I wanted to surprise you."

She pointed at the box. "You were going to give me that afterward?"

"It was so clear on Sunday that you needed convincing. I thought this might help." He popped the box open. Inside was a glimmering diamond solitaire on a slender platinum band. "This isn't the way I planned this. At all. But I'm tired of waiting. Will you marry me?"

Don't wait to be happy. Her dad's words rang through her head like church bells. "Yes, Grant. God, yes. Of course I will." She lowered her head and placed a careful kiss on his lips. She didn't want to hurt him. Not now. Not ever.

He surprised her by gripping her arm and he pulled her closer, then kissed her with such passion that it made her dizzy. When he pulled back, Tara rested her forehead against his.

"That kiss hurt, but it was totally worth it," Grant said.

Grant stayed in the hospital for three days, which as far as he was concerned was three days too long. He still couldn't believe his big plan to propose to Tara had been ruined in that way, although he had to admit that it paralleled their entire history—rocky, but ultimately solid. She made him so happy by saying yes. It was the sweetest word he'd ever heard, and he'd been waiting an awfully long time to hear it.

Tara brought him back to his house, where he would work from bed for a week until he could return to the office. He wasn't eager to get back to business; he was more eager to feel well enough to make love to Tara and take full advantage of their new status as engaged couple.

"Hey there. How's my handsome patient?" Tara padded into his bedroom with an armful of stuff—a bottle of water, an orange and his laptop. "I figured you would probably want to check email. The whole world has been so worried about you."

Grant took the computer from her and set it aside on the bed. Tara placed the other things on the bedside table. He scooted over and patted the mattress. "Come. Sit. I want to talk."

She delivered a sly grin. "You sure that's all you want to do?"

"I'm working up to that. For now, yes, a conversation."

Tara planted herself on the edge of the bed and pulled up one leg, intently focused on his face. "Okay. Go."

He laughed and took her hand, bringing her fingers to his lips. "You need to stay at Sterling. I know you said you aren't sure about that part, but if you want to stay, you should. We need you. I need you."

"We haven't heard back from the city yet. They're supposed to announce who made it to the next round today. I keep checking my phone for an answer."

She was missing the point. "I don't care about the city. I mean, I do, because I want this for you, but long term, it doesn't matter. You were always meant to be a driving force at the company and it's my job to make that happen. To restore things to the way they were supposed to be."

"We'd have to figure out how that's going to work. What my real responsibilities would be."

"I think we should be co-CEOs. Run the company together. As equals."

True shock crossed her face. "Oh wow. Do you really think that will work? Won't that ruin your dream of running the ship?"

"Tara. Darling. You are the love of my life. *You* are my dream. Everything with Sterling is gravy. Seriously."

Tara drew in a deep breath, nodding, seeming to process everything he'd said. "I'd get to have the office next to yours?"

"That goes without saying. Whatever you want. You can start picking out furniture as soon as possible."

"And you won't get sick of me? Being with me at work all day and then having to see me at night, too?"

A deep and hearty laugh left his throat. "You have got to be kidding. That sounds amazing."

She smiled and leaned closer, then kissed him softly on the lips. "I love you, Grant Singleton."

"I love you, too." It felt so good to be able to say that. To let the words flow freely from his lips. It felt like he'd waited a lifetime to do that.

Tara's phone beeped with a text. She pulled it out of her pants pocket, then her eyes eagerly scanned it. Her hand flew to her mouth. "It's from Astrid. We made it to the second round." Tara turned her phone around to show him the message.

The happiness he felt for her was so pure, he could hardly stand it. He'd been opposed to the project and now it seemed like the greatest thing in the whole world.

Well, maybe after having Tara in his life for real. "That's amazing. I knew you would do it. I knew it."

Tara tapped out an answer. "Astrid will be excited to be working with Clay some more. I think there might be a love connection going on there."

"Oh, geez. I think one office romance is plenty to think about."

"You know…" Tara set down her phone. "We wouldn't even need to get approval from the other shareholders for you and I to be co-CEOs. Between you, me, Astrid and Miranda, that's seventy-one percent. That's more than enough to pass a vote."

"You sure you can keep the other wives in line?"

She nodded, seeming certain of herself. "Astrid is on board, for sure. She's really come into her own in the last few weeks. And Miranda will be ecstatic that we've passed the first hurdle with the Seaport project." Tara gnawed on her finger. "I still need to talk to the city about naming the park after Johnathon. She wants me to work on that."

Grant shook his head and curled his finger to invite Tara closer. "Come here." He didn't want to talk any more about Johnathon or Astrid or Miranda. He didn't want to talk about work. He wanted to enjoy this moment with his future wife. She pressed another soft kiss against his lips.

"We shouldn't start anything, Grant. You're still recovering."

The hell with that. He wrapped his arms around her and pulled her close, then rolled her onto her back. He hovered above her, his ribs aching, but not caring at all about the pain. She was everything he'd ever wanted. And it was time to start their lives together, for real.

Her eyes were wide, her hair splayed across the bed. "Grant. You're injured. What's gotten into you?"

"I love you, Tara. That's what's gotten into me." He lowered his head and whispered in her ear, "And I can't wait to turn you from a Sterling into a Singleton."

* * * * *

COMING SOON!

We really hope you enjoyed reading this book. If you're looking for more romance, be sure to head to the shops when new books are available on

Thursday 3rd September

LET'S TALK
Romance

For exclusive extracts, competitions
and special offers, find us online:

 facebook.com/millsandboon

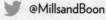 @MillsandBoon

@MillsandBoonUK

Get in touch on 01413 063232

For all the latest titles coming soon, visit
millsandboon.co.uk/nextmonth

MILLS & BOON

THE HEART OF ROMANCE

A ROMANCE FOR EVERY KIND OF READER

MODERN

Prepare to be swept off your feet by sophisticated, sexy and seductive heroes, in some of the world's most glamourous and romantic locations, where power and passion collide.
8 stories per month.

HISTORICAL

Escape with historical heroes from time gone by. Whether your passion is for wicked Regency Rakes, muscled Vikings or rugged Highlanders, awaken the romance of the past.
6 stories per month.

MEDICAL

Set your pulse racing with dedicated, delectable doctors in the high-pressure world of medicine, where emotions run high and passion, comfort and love are the best medicine.
6 stories per month.

True Love

Celebrate true love with tender stories of heartfelt romance, from the rush of falling in love to the joy a new baby can bring, and a focus on the emotional heart of a relationship.
8 stories per month.

Desire

Indulge in secrets and scandal, intense drama and plenty of sizzling hot action with powerful and passionate heroes who have it all: wealth, status, good looks…everything but the right woman.
6 stories per month.

HEROES

Experience all the excitement of a gripping thriller, with an intense romance at its heart. Resourceful, true-to-life women and strong, fearless men face danger and desire - a killer combination!
8 stories per month.

DARE

Sensual love stories featuring smart, sassy heroines you'd want as a best friend, and compelling intense heroes who are worthy of them.
4 stories per month.

To see which titles are coming soon, please visit

millsandboon.co.uk/nextmonth

JOIN US ON SOCIAL MEDIA!

Stay up to date with our latest releases, author
news and gossip, special offers and discounts, and
all the behind-the-scenes action
from Mills & Boon...

 millsandboon

 millsandboonuk

 millsandboon

might just be true love...

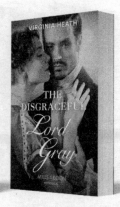